RUN 3
LONG ROAD HOME

RICH RESTUCCI

SEVERED PRESS
HOBART TASMANIA

RUN 3

Copyright © 2018 Rich Restucci

WWW.SEVEREDPRESS.COM

ISBN: 978-1-925711-77-6

Death is not the greatest loss in life. The greatest loss is what dies inside us while we live.

-Norman Cousins

POST STREET, SAN FRANCISCO

Run. Sooner or later, he would have to run. They knew he was here someplace and there was no hiding from the dead. At least not for any length of time. Ducked down on his haunches behind an abandoned Toyota Prius, he peered into a bakery window to catch a reflection of the street behind him. There were many of them. Lots. Maybe he could skirt them and juke through, but one misstep, one successful grab and he was dead. Even if he made it past them, they would give a slow and plodding chase. They would never tire. They would never cease coming. No. No, he needed to be furtive. Sneak past them and gain altitude. Climb one of the dozens of fire escape ladders that had been left down by him and other survivors in San Francisco and get to a roof to wait them out.

He might not be able to hide, but if he could get up high, eventually something else; a rat, a bird, or one of the trucks driven by the human threat would grab their attention and he could climb down and get back to his family.

Leaving in the early morning, he had kissed his wife and thirteen-year-old daughter good-bye. They were perilously low on supplies and there was an untouched convenience store near the ruins of Crocker Plaza. The Plaza was thick with the things, but a diversion would bring them out, giving him enough time to get inside the store, loot it, lock it with his padlock, and make a hasty retreat.

He had descended the ladder affixed to the wall of his fortified apartment building, leaving the second-floor refuge they called home. He made his way down the alley quietly, as sound was the primary method which these things used to hunt. The passage had been clear, he and his wife having blocked it at its open-end months before to prevent access. He got down on his stomach, examining the perpendicular street on the opposite side of the cargo van which was the alleyway's obstacle. The tires of the vehicle had long since been slashed, so nothing could crawl under it. Two feet shuffled across his narrow field of vision from left to right. One was adorned with a sneaker with a red swish on it, an emblem of a forgotten time. The other was barefoot, with two toes missing.

He checked his watch a bit later and tentatively stood, leaning forward to peek through the windows of the van on three sides. Clear.

Climbing over the metal rampart, he put both feet cautiously on the far side of the vehicle. Real fear began to edge its way into his already frightened psyche. Not being scared would be folly, as everything in this cursed city wanted him dead. Fear stalled him for a moment, but it was fear which also got him moving. A static position meant doom.

He reached his vantage point, down the street from the store, without incident. Plenty of the things were roaming around, but they hadn't seen him. After a lengthy recon of the area around the store, he moved off to start his distraction. Two streets over, he removed a battery-operated alarm clock and two AA batteries from his pack. In short order, he was moving off back the way he had come, the clock set to explode into life fifteen minutes hence. He wondered briefly if the sound of an alarm clock in the morning was as annoying to them as it had been to him in a previous life.

Once again on his belly, he was trying to survey the inside of the shop when he heard the intense buzzing noise begin down the road. *Wah! Wah! Wah!* He smiled sadly, wishing the alarm meant he needed to shower and get to work. Part of that statement was true and he noticed that those in the street in front of him began to lumber off toward the sounds of his clock. It was time to get to work. The noise of the timepiece was preternaturally loud in the eerie quiet of the dead city.

When the area was clear, he removed a homemade tool from his pack: a pair of bolt cutters with a crowbar duct-taped to one of the handles. The tape mostly obscured the neon green of the crowbar and he had to ponder where he had come across this oddly colored tool. He dashed across the street to the shop, put his hand between his forehead and the protective steel mesh, and peered through the smoky door window. He rapped his knuckles against the steel shutter and waited an entire minute, glancing in all directions, before using the bolt cutters to cut the padlock. The sound of the mesh sliding to the left was akin to the decibel level of a rock concert in his fear-clouded mind. He quickly used the crowbar to snap the door open. Stepping inside, he panned his flashlight around what he could see of the inside of the store. There were no revealing signs of the dead; bloodstains, drag marks, shelves, or stands knocked over. The store looked as untouched as he had surmised. He slid the tube steel of his own padlock through the ring on the door, but didn't click it home. This would give him valuable seconds should something attempt to gain access through this entrance.

He was efficient in padding his duffle full of sundries. He even got two packages of cookies for the girls. Just a few minutes later, he was peering back out the door window at the street. It was still clear and he could just barely hear the alarm he had tied to a street sign. He thought there must be a hundred of the things on top of the noise by now. In a half hour, the street would be clogged for half a mile in both directions. Opening the door, he stuck his head out then stepped onto the sidewalk. He closed the door, shut the shutter, and locked it with his lock.

He once more raced across the empty street, glancing both ways to make sure there was nothing stumbling toward him. There was, undoubtedly drawn to the sound of the clock, but they were far enough away that he would have no trouble escaping them. He made it all the way across the street before a scream from his left rent the air. Icy tendrils of terror shot down his spine. He knew what that terrible sound was. It was the shriek of a Runner. A former human, infected with whatever this plague was, but condemned to live instead of receiving blissful death. This thing was every bit as dangerous as a horde of undead. Where the dead were slow and shambling, this creature was agile and super-fast, all claws and teeth. Its scream also told every undead and infected Runner in the vicinity that something uninfected was on the menu. The upside of the living infected was that you could kill it. It was subject to the same laws of nature that would kill a human being. Stab it, shoot it, bash it on the head, and it will die. It would be back up in minutes though, as one of its shambling cousins. The downside was that this creature was equally as fast or faster than the average person. In addition, with its incredibly high tolerance to pain, it would never tire. It would sprint until its infected heart burst.

He ran. Sprinting down the street, he dodged past a grasping hand that snaked out of a vehicle window. He heard the slapping of shod feet on the asphalt behind him and knew the swift creature was almost on him. Spinning, he brought the bolt cutter-crowbar assembly around in a wide sweep. He missed and was hit by 120 pounds of infected demon. It was a tackle that would have made a footballer proud, man and former man tumbling down and leaving skin behind on the road. The creature wound up atop him and immediately began to slash with its nails. He pushed the bolt cutters straight up, catching the Runner below the jaw, stunning it. Scrambling away from the thing's grasp, he brought the heavy tool up for a killing blow when the thing whipped its head up and glared at him with bloody eyes. It was a teenage girl. It reminded him of his own child and the plague-ridden creature used that instant of indecision to leap at him. He crushed her skull with a sideswipe of the apparatus, killing her instantly. She wouldn't rise and for that, he was at least partially grateful.

He was not grateful for the chorus of moans that echoed from down the road. He turned slowly to look at the source. Dozens of the shamblers were plodding toward him. He moved down the street at a good clip, rounding the corner and almost slamming into a post box. Dropping behind a small car, he avoided the gaze of the twenty or so things that were still here, but moving toward the sound of the alarm clock. The ones behind him trudged into the street, seeing their brothers, but not him. He had but moments to make a decision that would either unite him with his family or result in his brief but agonizing death. Either way, he couldn't stay here.

He would have to run.

SUTTER STREET, SAN FRANCISCO

San Francisco seemed to waken as the din of an alarm clock echoed through the empty streets. Figures staggered out of every conceivable crevice, ambling toward the ruckus, but the clamor ceased after a few minutes. The figures didn't seem to care and most of them continued their shuffle in the direction the sound last came from. A man had ducked quietly into a doorway when he heard the clock, knowing that the empty roads would soon fill.

The shop he had entered was not as empty as he had initially assumed, a lone character traipsing within. He tried to speak to it, but it no longer possessed the capacity to understand him.

"I just… I don't think…darn it. You're just not getting me. He was a bunny, is all. A *bunny*. I mean, no matter how you dress him up or if he flies a plane or outwits Fudd, or sings a song, he's still a bunny. Bunnies are cute. Kids love bunnies. I mean, the original was a mouse, but he was all old and stuff. Like from the forties or something. Outdated. Bugs was new and sarcastic and didn't have that stupid high-pitched laugh that the mouse had. The stuff that rabbit came out with!"

The thing reached for him again, but stopped when he ceased talking and tried to meander off.

The man put a hand on its shoulder and spun it to face him. It almost went over, but staggered and stood erect. Well, as erect as it could with one foot missing.

"Oh, am I boring you? Would you rather discuss making lemonade out of lemons? The ramifications of the undead on the stock market?"

A scream of pain and terror ripped through the day. It was the sound of someone caught by something and it was close. The man briefly wondered if he could help, but he had heard that scream before. It meant death. The screaming rose to a high pitch, then abruptly ceased, the only sound remaining; a brief echo throughout the abandoned city streets.

The creature looked past him, searching for the source of the sound and again tried to lurch away.

"Rude."

The man looked at the creature as it shuffled by him. The thing moved slower than the others because of its missing appendage. The nub of bone protruding from the bottom of its right leg made a scraping sound as it moved across the black and white floor of the abandoned pizza joint the two were in. Having only one foot, the thing had a pronounced starboard list.

A wicked smile crossed the face of the young man, then he began to chuckle. "Eileen!" he shouted, "I'm gonna call you Eileen!" Proud of himself, the man beamed and nodded. He stuck his hand out. "Eileen, my name is Billy."

The dead woman turned again and came at him with her gray arms reaching. He sighed and let her pass by, moving deeper into the small restaurant. Others had heard him shout and were pawing at the smashed front window, lacerating their arms. Dark fluids rained from the cuts and ran down the shards of broken plate glass as they climbed through.

Billy removed a bolo machete from a sheath on his hip. He gripped the worn polypropylene handle with one hand, the other balled into a fist inside a canvas work glove with brass knuckles wired to it. He had a revolver on each hip as well and a pistol-grip pump shotgun slung on his back.

The door to the shop had a broken lock and a few creatures staggered through the open portal, searching for the source of the sound. They had just entered a restaurant looking for a bite to eat, which a year ago would have been the model of normalcy. Now, the scenario had a more sinister implication. The bites would be taken from a living human being if the creatures had their way of things, although said food was becoming scarce.

Billy didn't tense even slightly as seven more former humans entered the building. He swung his weapon in a vicious sideways arc, taking the top of the head off of the gray-skinned debutante that tried to walk by him. He dispatched five others in a likewise manner, but the last was wearing a motorcycle helmet, complete with face plate. The man rolled his eyes. "Now how are you going to bite anybody with that on? Duh." He rolled his left sleeve up, careful not to get any of the infected fluids which coated his machete on him. "Go for it there, genius, take a nibble." He thrust his bare arm out, but the dead biker shuffled past him like all the others.

"Son of a..." The young man shook his head. "Let me help you with that." He snagged the dead man by its tattered shirt, the fabric giving slightly as the thing tried to continue on its way. The living man pulled the helmet off the dead one, scalp, skin, and an ear coming with it.

Scrunching up his face, Billy looked disgusted. "Ick." He swung the machete overhand and it went neck-deep through the cranium of the dead man. He put his boot on the back of the thing and pushed, extricating his weapon. The re-killed biker fell forward. "Eight hundred eighty-eight."

Turning, he noticed the crippled creature staring at him. "Eileen! Tell me, kiddo, when there's a swarm of you dead folks, vying to get some vittles, do you always lose the race by a foot?" He looked dejected, putting his palms up. "Nothing? Really? Okay, Eileen, whatever. Be that way." He decapitated her with the blade, her head rolling next to his boot.

Getting down on his haunches, he looked into her dead, red eyes. She looked back.

"Pelé style," he said, standing. He kicked the head into the base of the large pizza oven. The eyes rolled back into the skull. "Eight hundred eighty-nine." He wiped his weapon on Eileen's filthy jeans.

The man strode from the pizza shop with a can of Diet Dr. Pepper and a Slim Jim. He put the can on the ground, the beef treat in his mouth, bent over, and righted an overturned bench. He sat on the bench and began to people watch.

He snapped a bite off the Slim Jim and pointed at a dead man in a blue smock. "Walmart." He pointed at another, this one hand in handcuffs. "Criminal." A third man in a tattered leather vest staggered by. "Hell's Angel," he continued. "Fireman, postal worker, butcher, executive…" He shook his head sadly and stood up, drawing the machete. Leaving his Dr. Pepper on the bench, he strode forward and used the weapon to destroy another of the nameless, dressed in pink. "Pre-schooler." He wiped his right eye and sat back down. "Eight ninety."

Younger than Sam, he thought. *I wonder how she's doing. Should I have stayed? No, that would have been awful, especially for her. They probably would have locked me up, or killed me. I couldn't let her see that. Did they tell her who I was? I hope not.*

Sam was his friend. He hadn't met her until the plague had arrived, but he still thought of her as a little sister. She was safe on Alcatraz with her dad and some good people he had met. A little girl was easier for him to associate with than the adults of both the collapsed society and the new one springing up around him.

Billy often stared at the island in the middle of San Francisco Bay with nostalgia, longing to go talk to Sam. He thought of sneaking over to see her, but if he got caught, it would go badly for him. He sent her messages through the people he had gotten out of the city, both verbal and written. His immunity to whatever made the dead want to eat people allowed him certain liberties and he had decided to be the good guy. In the time since he fled from Alcatraz, he had personally gotten more than sixty people on boats to go toward the island refuge. All of whom were more than willing to transport a little toy he had found here and there, or a written message.

Billy had also noticed a huge, black cylinder floating off to the north of the island. Originally, he thought it was an alien spaceship, which could be the cause of the plague, but then he realized it was a submarine. A big one. Not that he would know the difference between a big one and a small one, but it looked pretty big to him

He had dispatched more than eight hundred of the things that stumbled around looking for human flesh. Not a monumental achievement considering the population of San Francisco, but he was sure nobody had taken out more of them than he had. Especially using primarily melee weapons. He was industrious and the things he used to take the creatures out varied from day to day, although his weapon of choice was the machete. Thin, strong, and deadly, the blade would easily go through even the most stubborn of craniums. He had used it on one live person too, a really bad person.

Nineteen living humans had also been killed by this man in his post-plague wanderings. While certainly not a saint, he had never killed anyone that didn't need killing... He looked up into the face (well, most of the face) of another of the creatures. This one had stopped and thrown a shadow over him as he sat there pondering. The thing looked atrocious and it stank. A filthy, matted beard with bits of stuff attached here and there, protruded from the creature's face, which was mostly obscured by the whiskers. A red baseball cap adorned the thing's head, but was barely on because it had so much hair. The cap rested on the hair instead of the skull. The thing pointed at the beef treat. He held it out and the creature took it from him, biting off a sizable portion and then handing it back. It sat down on the bench next to him.

"Hi," it said.

"Hi yourself."

"Got anything more than a Slim Jim? I'm starved."

"There's a whole pizza joint right there," Billy jerked a thumb over his right shoulder, "full of snack stuff and there were some jars too. Probably pickles and stuff like that. They might still be good."

"I like pickles."

"Who doesn't?"

"Them." The new person pointed at the things staggering around.

He nodded in affirmation. "Where's your shopping cart?"

"Next street over. The wheel squeaks and they get in my way when they come to see what it is."

"Ah. Have you thought about using WD-40?"

"Whazzat? A Reggae band?"

"No," Billy offered, "it stops stuff from squeaking... How can you not know what WD-40 is?"

"I do, it was a joke. I'm gonna go on a pickle raid, you want?"

"I'll wait here. Stay frosty; there's some of them inside."

"Mmm hmm. They won't touch me any more than they will you."

"Yeah," the man agreed, "today we're undesirable, who knows what will happen tomorrow?"

The other man stood up, turning around to face the restaurant. He stopped. "Uh?"

The seated man turned around as well. The entire street full of dead people had stopped to look at them. A hundred or so red eyes staring.

"Oh," he stammered and the things all moved toward the two living men.

They ran.

The bearded man panted heavily as he and his young compatriot stopped to rest. "What...what was that...about?"

"Dunno," the younger man breathed, touching the slight scar on his jaw, "but they sure looked hungry."

The two had run a block or so, leaving the pursuing crowd behind. The odd thing was that there were dozens of dead people shuffling quite close to them and none seemed to want to eat the living duo.

"Was it 'cause we were talking?"

"Excellent incentive for us to shut up then, yeah?"

"Yeah okay."

"Let's get inside, shall we?" Billy whispered.

"I got a penthouse suite at the Hilton downtown."

"That's like, five miles from here!"

"Didn't say it was close, more like a mile though..."

The men's poor attempt at shutting up was cut off by a backup alarm from a nearby vehicle. It had come from somewhere to the north, in the direction of the water. They looked at each other then at the creatures in the street, who were already lurching and staggering toward the sound.

"My dear Lester, I believe someone is about to get eaten."

"Yeah, well it ain't gonna be me. Come on by if you get the chance, I got tons of Doritos." With that, Billy's friend Lester strode toward a shopping cart and began pushing it away. Several creatures paused in their trek toward the backup alarm to stare at the squeaking wheel and two began to follow the ex-homeless man, but the others continued on toward the louder sound.

BENEATH VANTEL CORPORATE LAB

Rick was exhausted. He stared at the battleship-gray wall in the cool room as he lay on his side in his bunk. He thought about his daughter, who was probably as far away from him as possible in the continental United States. A former San Francisco detective, he had left his little girl on Alcatraz. The island bastion sat in close proximity to several cities which had been claimed by monstrosities; millions of rotting corpses which refused to stay dead and felt a burning need to consume the living. He doubted his decision to leave his child. He doubted it every day. Rick had crossed an entire nation full of the insatiable dead and worse to find his ex-wife and bring her to an underground facility in Massachusetts. His former spouse and her group of scientists held the key to a vaccine that would either keep the dead dead, or stop the living from contracting the infection that would ultimately kill them and have them reanimate as something inhuman.

An operative by the name of Brooks had trapped Rick and his group in the subterranean complex using a bomb and the living dead. The bomb hadn't gone off yet, but it was sitting at the bottom of an elevator shaft just outside the sealed steel door to the compound. Any move to open the doors or disarm the explosive could set it off. Rick's people were currently in search of a secondary means of egress from the facility.

Rick's plan was to leave this fortified bunker in just a few days to go back to Sam, his daughter. The odds were stacked against him that he would make it back to the west coast from the east, but he had successfully traversed the breadth of the nation once. His job was done and he needed to return to his little girl. He hoped he wouldn't have to go alone, but he knew many of his group would remain to support those working in the lab, and he couldn't stay much longer.

The former detective rolled over and stared at the bunk across from him. It held a lone occupant, small and sleeping, the olive-drab army blanket pulled up to its blonde curls.

Blonde curls. Nobody had hair like that in this entire facility. He reached for his sidearm, a Sig Sauer P226, which he had left on the footlocker he had placed next to his bed. Both the footlocker and the weapon were missing. He made a quick check under his pillow but came up empty.

Rick dared a glance back toward the other cot and noticed it was now empty. The previous occupant was standing and staring at him. It was rotten and he couldn't believe he hadn't smelled it until now. Blood-red eyes ripped into his soul as he recognized the thing in front of him.

It pointed at his face. "You did this to me!" it screamed. "You left me, Daddy!" Blood poured out of the creature's mouth as it staggered on unsteady feet the few steps between them. "I hate you!" It fell on him and he felt it crawling up his blanket. Panic began to set in and he tried to fight it off, but it had his arms pinned under the sheets and it was incredibly strong.

"Gonna make you like me, Daddy! Like me!" Its fetid maw hovered above him, dripping fluids on his face. It bared its broken teeth in a rictus of horror as it leaned in. "Kiss me, Daddy..."

Rick blinked his eyes a few times, Sam's last word *Daddy* echoing through his newly woken mind. It was the same dream he had almost every day. Subtle differences defined each dream, but the gist of it was always his dead little girl casting blame then attacking. The dreams were horrible, but he was used to them by now. He stared at the gray wall, willing himself to get up.

He sighed and looked at his watch. Almost 0600. Rick thought of getting back to Sam, but he also thought about what the crazy CIA bastard Brooks had insisted prior to making his escape: *There's no way out of that bunker for thirty-five years.* The evil son of a bitch had also declared he was going to attack Alcatraz out of spite. Rick had no doubt he would do it either. He had to return to The Rock, he had to. At the very least, he had to warn Captain McInerney about what was coming so they could plan.

McInerney, captain of the USS *Florida*, a nuke sub, had sent a team of SEALs with Rick and his friends on this rescue and relocation mission. They had suffered losses along the way to both the dead and an enclave of survivors calling themselves The Triumvirate. Three men; Bourne, Brooks, and Recht, had pulled a few thousand people together and were holding their own in Nebraska, sending out radio messages and search parties to bring people to safety. They met Bourne, an army colonel, who defected from the Triumvirate, joining forces with Rick's group in an attempt to secure a vaccine for the plague. The remaining two leaders of the Triumvirate didn't like the defection and chased their former partner halfway across the country. Bourne, a good man and a good leader, had been killed by one of Brooks' associates in the main facility sixty or so feet above the shelter where Rick lay on his bunk.

Rick looked at his watch again, 0603. Time flies when you're having fun. He sat up, thinking about the firefight they had been in a few days ago. Brooks and his government stooges, wanting to kill Bourne and secure the vaccine for themselves, had attacked the facility. The fire teams had failed and had been killed or pushed back by Rick's group. Brooks had sent several dozen of the dead down into the bunker via elevator and another battle took place. Some of the group had been injured, but none seriously. None had been bitten, although the battle had eventually gone hand-to-hand.

One of those hands belonged to a computer guy that had been trapped alone in the underground Vantel facility's server security room. He had turned out to be an important asset. Bob, like Brooks and another acquaintance of Rick's, Billy, could stand next to the dead without being attacked. The scientists at Vantel had theories on how this was possible, but hadn't tested anything yet.

Anna looked at Bob's injured hand and figured it probably needed to be glued or stitched. Androwski said it would have to wait, as they needed to lock the place down properly. They welded the steel doors to the common room closed from three of the modules, giving them access to the labs, PX, which held the kitchens and supply warehouse and the final module, the living quarters. They swept the place for a solid day, covering each room, (especially bathrooms) three times, but Androwski wasn't satisfied. They had dealt with four more undead inside the perimeter, but that still left several unaccounted for. In addition, a living person had crawled into a vent and had never come out. The assumption was that the person had died and was still crawling around, unseen. Standing orders from Androwski were that no one went anywhere alone (especially not to the bathroom) and everyone was to be armed at all times. Brenda had balked at having to carry a weapon, but the SEAL shut her up with a glare. One thing was true: the place was huge.

The PX weapons lockers had been stocked with six M16s, two M1014 tactical shotguns, and six M9 tactical pistols. Two G36C carbines were also discovered. Several thousand rounds of .223 ammunition were available for the M16s and G36Cs. There were two crates of twelve gauge shells in both buckshot and slug rounds for the shotguns, and the pistols would have plenty of ammo with six dozen boxes of 9mm. The big find was two thousand rounds of NATO 5.56mm ammunition, (same as.223) which would work with the HK416s and Rick's M4, all chambered for those rounds. Basically, they found a shit load of ammo for all their weapons.

Someone had tried to jimmy the formidable locks on the lockers to no avail and Dr. Crisp assured everyone that it hadn't been him. This concerned Androwski, as they hadn't found anyone alive other than Crisp in any of the modules.

On day three, after Bob's heroic sojourn to shut the blast doors, it was decided that a recon team would need to go down into the power station and check things out. Rick, Androwski, Stenner, and Wilcox would go, while Anna, Dallas, and Seyfert would remain behind as protection for the scientists while they worked.

Anna looked across the top of her hand. "Go fish." Stenner picked a card off of the table. "So can they smell or not?"

"Not," said Linda, who was making coffee in a small kitchenette in one of the living quarters. "They don't breathe, so they can't smell."

"So then how did they know that Bob was there if they couldn't read his brainwaves? I mean, he did cut his hand and was bleeding everywhere. Are you sure they can't smell without breathing?"

Linda sat down. "At this point, no. I mean, they're dead for Christ's sake, they shouldn't be doing anything."

Anna moved her cards around in her hand. "That's true. Bob, how you doing over there?" she called.

He raised his bandaged hand from his position on a cot and gave a thumbs up. "A-OK."

Stenner leaned forward. "How is he really?"

"Well, his hand is pretty infected. I cleaned it out and gave him some antibiotics from the pharmacy, but I wasn't able to treat him for an entire day and a half. We didn't have the meds until the PX was cleared."

"How do you know he isn't *infected* infected?"

Anna shook her head. "Because he'd be dead already. Nobody lives a full day, you know that, and we're on day three."

"Right, but didn't one of your buddies die from a normal infection and then turn?"

"Yeah. Martinez. He was a good guy."

"So…"

"So what?" She raised her eyebrows but didn't look away from her cards. "You want to shoot him now just in case? Hey, Bob! Stenner thinks we should blow you away in case you're infected."

"Couldja get me a drink first?" he asked to anyone. "I would rather a bullet enter my noggin without me being so thirsty." Bob rolled over.

Stenner smiled. "Guy has balls of steel, I'll give him that. Still, we should keep an eye on him. Any threes?"

"I just asked you for threes!"

"I picked it up just now. Keep an eye on him, yeah?"

"Way ahead of you, Army. Linda, so back to the blood, why do you think they went after him when he was bloody if they couldn't smell it?"

"The creature's reaction might not have had anything to do with the blood. It *is* coincidental that they attacked only when he was bleeding though. Best I can see it, they don't possess any superior abilities to us other than the ability to read brainwaves and that's still just a theory."

Dallas, Rick, and Androwski walked in just then. "Stenner, it's time."

"Roger that, sir." He tossed his cards on the table and Anna immediately grabbed them and looked at them. She put them down quickly. Stenner picked up his weapon and began checking the slide action and extra magazines.

Dallas sat down and picked up Stenner's cards. "Me n' Jersey's gonna sit this'n out. Get some much needed R n R." He rubbed his calf.

Stenner pulled his combat knife from its sheath on his left breast, checked it, and re-sheathed it. "Where's Seyfert?"

"Watchin' the lab rats do their thing." The Texan looked at Linda. "Sorry, ma'am."

She laughed. "Lab rats. I like it. I guess I should be getting back too." She stood up.

"We'll walk you back," Androwski told her. "We need to speak with Crisp anyway. Bob, how big is this power plant?"

Bob rolled over. "Mmmm?"

"The geothermal plant, how big?"

"Dunno, I never did anything down there. Crisp will know where the schematics are."

Androwski stretched and rubbed his shoulder. "Let's rock and roll then."

Dr. Crisp didn't know where the blueprints were, but he had been down to the power plant on several occasions. He drew the recon team a crude schematic and the place didn't look huge, but it would still take some time to clear it. Androwski wanted to make sure that if anyone were alive down there, that they were friendly and hopefully could operate the plant's systems, keeping the lights on indefinitely.

Three sets of concrete stairwells brought the team from the back of the PX module down to a fire door. 6332 was printed in yellow block numbers on the green door. The door was not locked.

"Weapons check," the SEAL demanded. "Suppressors on." Everyone double-checked their gear again and Rick put his hand on the door handle as three battle rifles trained on the entry. Androwski nodded and Rick pulled the door wide. It was bright in the hallway and nothing came at them.

"Stay frosty. Constant-zero and stick together."

Wilcox had opted for one of the M1014 shotguns and he went first with Androwski, the men moving two by two, Rick and Stenner to the rear.

The hallway was approximately fifteen meters long. Eight doors, all closed, lined the hall equidistant from each other. A ninth door, open, ended the corridor. The hum of equipment could be heard through the ninth door.

Wilcox threw his closed fist in the air and everyone hunkered down, weapons pointing in all directions. Androwski looked at the young private and the kid simply pointed toward the floor. A single drop of blood stood out in stark contrast to the dark industrial-gray paint. Androwski nodded and moved to the first door on the left. It was locked. As was the second. And the third. The fourth was open and led into an empty office with large filing cabinets and a chart cabinet as well. The office, approximately four meters by four meters, also held a desk and a computer monitor. Pictures of a heavyset woman and two equally heavyset boys were in some frames on the desk. Rick closed the door as the team moved further down the hall.

The rest of the closed doors were locked as well.

Although the fluorescent bulbs on the corridor ceiling threw plenty of light, it was dark inside the final, open door. The night vision goggles that the team had been issued when the mission began had died weeks ago from battery loss and Androwski cursed the proprietary batteries that they used. They were only available through military channels and such channels no longer existed. The SEAL flipped on his tac light and the others followed suit. They moved forward as a cohesive unit, lights pointed toward the floor.

The hum got louder as they approached and Wilcox raised his shotgun. Androwski moved quickly and shone his light into the darkened portal. Nothing stumbled or came at them shrieking. Androwski let out a loud whistle and the team waited. Again, nothing came. The SEAL made some gestures with his right hand and Wilcox nodded. He pointed to Stenner and into the room and to Rick, then back down the corridor behind them. Stenner and Rick both nodded, Stenner going to one knee five meters in front of the door, Rick next to him, standing but aiming back the way they had come.

Androwski and Wilcox each moved to one side of the open door. The SEAL held up three fingers and the Army kid nodded once more, curtly. Androwski bobbed his head once, twice, and on the third time, both men entered the room quickly, each turning toward the direction he was facing. No gunfire erupted and a few seconds later, a light switched on in the room. Wilcox moved in front of the now-illuminated doorway and waved the other two in.

When he got inside the door, Rick couldn't believe his eyes. The room looked like the bridge of a ship. Controls, dials, lights, handles, and screens, all arranged in an outward bow shape, greeted them. Six large rectangular windows at the top of the bow looked into a small natural cave below. Doors to the left and right side of the large room led to catwalks with stairs leading down. Rick looked out the windows and saw three five-meter-long, five-meter-wide turbines on the ground perhaps ten meters below. Each turbine had two large pipes extending into the ground, one on each side. Thick cables ran from each turbine to a series of gray panels fastened to the walls above and to the sides. The walls looked like the surface of a golf ball but as if you were inside it looking out.

"Epcot," Wilcox thought aloud as he closed the door behind them. "It looks like the inside of that big ball thingie at the Epcot Center in Disney World."

Rick pointed through the glass. "LT, look down there."

At the base of the concrete floor, perhaps sixty feet past the farthest turbine, a ladder ascended up past the catwalks into the darkness.

"How far up do you think that goes?"

Androwski thought for a moment. "We've got to be past the edge of the kitchen module down here; otherwise, the power plant would be in the middle of the kitchen. These geothermal plants must have some kind of exhaust, right? Maybe that's a maintenance ladder for the exhaust tube."

"Which means it's a way out," Stenner proclaimed.

"Not necessarily, but we have to check anyway. I'm having a hard time believing that if this is a nuke bunker, they would want a tube that leads to the surface. Radiation could get down here through that tube."

"Not if they have filters," Wilcox chimed. They all looked at him. "Well, how is everybody gonna breathe down here if everything is locked down? There must be some way of getting filtered air down here right? I mean, doesn't that make sense?"

The other three men began to nod. "It does," agreed Rick.

"Stenner, Wilcox, get back to that open office and look for blueprints, specifically maintenance tunnels, piping, and wiring diagrams for this entire plant."

"Roger that, sir," responded Stenner. "Let's do it, kid."

Wilcox pouted. "I'm twenty for Christ's sake, when do I stop being the kid?"

Stenner opened the door to the corridor with a smile. "When we find somebody—" The door came crashing backward as a dead man pushed through it and grabbed Stenner by the wrist and tac-webbing. Before Stenner, the SEAL, or Rick could react, the thing had an inch of steel blade sticking out of the top of its cranium. Wilcox had pulled his combat knife and thrust it up under the creature's chin with a backward stab, perforating the brain and skull. The thing stood stock-still and Stenner pushed it away. It slumped to the floor, never having made a sound. Wilcox checked the corridor then put a booted foot on the zombie's head and ripped out his knife. He raised his eyebrows as he looked at Stenner smugly. "Am I still the kid?"

"My hand to God," Stenner announced, raising his hand, "he was like a friggin' ninja."

"Kid's afraid o' his own shadow and you're tellin' me he smoked one of 'em up close? With a knife? Huh. Willy the kid." Dallas chuckled and shifted his huge frame in the chair he dwarfed, rearranging cards in his hand.

"I shit you not. You got any fives?"

The Texan looked at his hand, then over the cards at Stenner. "Go fish. So we gots us a way out then huh?"

"Looks that way. We checked out the maps n' shit and they're telling us that the ladder leads to a series of small rooms with more ladders and it goes all the way to the surface, to a hatch or door. The top of it looks to come out in some small concrete outbuilding or something."

Bob sat up on his cot and flexed his hand. "That's the best news I've heard all day."

"Back from the dead," Dallas joked and immediately regretted it. "I mean...well, you know what I mean."

Bob smiled. "Don't sweat it, big guy." He flexed his hand again. "Feels better. Anna really knows her stuff."

"Damn skippy," agreed the young woman as she strode into the room with a glass of water and some pills. "Take these and call me in the morning." She handed him the antibiotics and the water then sat down next to Dallas. "So what now?"

"Now I ask for sixes." He looked at Stenner eyebrows raised. "Got any?"

Stenner made a face and passed the Texan two cards.

"No, you dumb redneck, what do we all do now?"

Dallas was stumped. "Huh?"

"We got across the country, got the geeks, and got them here. Now what?"

"Dunno. Ask Andy."

"The scientists aren't done with their work," Bob said, undoing the strap that held him to the cot. "Thanks for this by the way."

"Dint want ya surprisin' me if'n ya decided t' die."

"Good thinking." He stood. "I'm staying here regardless. I've got no place else to go. We have food and guns and they can't get in. Here's as good a place as any and besides, I can keep the rigs running."

"Rigs?"

"Yeah, I'm an IT guy, remember?"

Dallas looked confused. "Eye Tee?"

"Yeah, I'm the dude who makes the computer thingies work. They need me here."

"True, but they don't need *us*," Anna countered. "Deal me in. Dallas, are we staying or going?"

"Whatever Rick says, but I don' see him stayin'. He's got Sam t' think about."

It was Bob's turn to look confused. "Who's Sam?"

"Rick's kid. She's back on Alcatraz with Rick's dad and a buncha other folks."

Stenner dealt three hands and picked up his cards, shuffling them. "That's crazy. It was luck. Pure, blind luck, that we got this far and I only came halfway with you guys. You're signing up to be a banquet if you try to go back."

Rick, Androwski, and a limping Seyfert came in the room just then. "Who's having a banquet?" demanded the injured SEAL. "Is there steak?"

"Dammit, Jersey, shut it with the meat talk, I'm droolin' now! Stenner was tellin' us we's gonna die if we try t' get back home."

"Shit, Hillbilly, we're probably going to die here. And you're all assuming we can get out of this bunker in the first place. We need to recon that ladder and where it goes before we make any decisions."

Rick looked at Seyfert. "I'm not dying here. I've got responsibilities back in California. However worried I am about Sam and my dad, I haven't forgotten how much they must be worried about me." Rick looked at Androwski. "You're mission commander now, Trent, so what you say goes…for military personnel. I've taken orders and bled just like everyone else. Please don't give me an order I can't follow."

Androwski shook his head. "I won't. I never for one second believed we would make it here alive. We did. If we made it here, we can make it back. Well, you can."

Everyone was looking at Androwski now. "I'm staying and I need at least two more soldiers to stay with me." He looked at his SEAL buddy. "Seyfert is wounded, so he should stay, but he's also the best trained and would be an excellent asset on your journey back to Alcatraz. Also, we need to report back to the commander that we were successful in getting the scientists here and that they are working. Rick, I trust you and your group with my life and that means something coming from a guy like me. That having been said, Commander McInerney will want to hear the intel, including intel on the Triumvirate and this spook guy from a sailor, preferably one he knows. I think Seyfert should heal for another week and then go with you back to Alcatraz."

Stenner sighed. "So I'm staying here with you and Wilcox?"

"We need to plan, but yeah, I think Rick's group and Seyfert will go back and the rest of us will stay here. I'll prepare a brief that Seyfert can take with him and all of you will memorize it, in case he doesn't make it."

"Thanks for the vote of confidence, LT."

"John, look at yourself. You're full of holes."

"Yeah, but none of them came from a Lima and I'm still kicking." He stuck his foot out and winced. "Mostly."

Androwski smiled. "I would like to keep Anna here too, but I wouldn't think for a moment she doesn't want to get back to Nebraska, then California."

"Everybody wants me," Anna assured him and flipped her ponytail with her head. "I'm so popular."

"You're a damn fine medic. You've kept us alive."

She harrumphed. "I was training to be an EMT when the plague sprouted, but honestly, I'd never seen any wounds like you guys have had until you got them. I did one ride-along on an ambulance and then the dead rose. This is all learn-on-the-fly stuff. Oh and sorry, but I'm going back, too."

"There's a plane," Bob blurted out. "At least there's supposed to be one."

Androwski blinked. "A plane?"

"Yeah, it's supposed to be a big one."

Rick turned toward him "Wait…what?"

"When they pulled out all the big mucky-mucks, the soldiers were all talking about how they didn't have time to get to the secondary airfield. They pulled all the big money folks out of here on helicopters that were supposed to go to a primary airfield and the soldiers were bitching about how the planes there were all small, but the one at the other field was a big one. Major Mello was talking about getting to it if we had to and said it would carry everyone here. He just didn't know where to go once on the plane and thought we would all be safe in the bunker."

"What plane? Where is it?" demanded Rick.

"No idea. I bet I know someone who does though."

MONTGOMERY STREET, SAN FRANCISCO

"Jesus, how could you have been so stupid!"

"I didn't hear you saying jack shit about truck alarms!"

"You're the goddamned mechanic!"

"Shut it both of you, we already have company." A third man pointed down the street with his battle rifle. "I don't want a swarm of them on us before we finish. Dave, you stay with me."

A woman and a kid of about fifteen jumped out of the pickup truck. "Sure, Tony." The three others ran toward a convenience store with an intact front window. The door was locked, but one of the men produced a crowbar and they were inside, with flashlights on the ends of their weapons shining.

They weren't being as quiet in their search as Tony would have liked them to be, but the backup alarm had already given them away. "Two behind," warned the boy and he raised a suppressed pistol.

Tony held his hand up. "Save ammo." He passed the boy a red fire axe from the back of the truck and he picked an aluminum baseball bat for himself. "Just like we practiced."

The boy nodded and they moved toward the undead. They split up, using hand gestures, each grabbing the focus of the dead eyes of a different creature. The humans separated the things, backing off when they were close. Tony slugged his with the bat. He wrung his hands together afterward. "Stings every time with these damn metal bats." The creature did not get up. The other, smaller dead man was stalking Dave, who stuck his axe out like a pole arm, thumping the creature in the chest and forcing it back a few steps. It faltered only slightly, however, and then began its relentless pursuit of the meal in front of it. Tony bashed its skull in from behind.

"Done and done." He looked down the street. "Oh shit."

Dave turned around, his eyes grew wide, and he ran to the store. "Now, guys! Take what you've got and we go now!"

Tony smiled and got in the driver's side of the truck. "Who the hell has a backup alarm on an F250?" He shook his head.

The three looters ran from the store, carrying various boxes and bags, all of which they unceremoniously tossed in the back of the truck. One man ran back and closed the door, marking it with blue spray paint. He got in and Tony threw the truck in drive. One of the men leaned to the side to look out the front window at the oncoming horde. "Holy shit, I knew we should have brought some soldiers."

"We're all soldiers now," the woman replied.

Tony smiled again. "Amen, Abbey, amen. Buckle up." He did a three-point turn, the alarm sounding very loud. The noise seemed to catalyze the zombies and they upped their gait. There were hundreds now and they were coming from several directions.

One of the men in the back began loading a revolver in his lap. "Friggin' things come out of the woodwork when a mouse farts."

"Then don't fart," Tony bandied. His statement was punctuated by a thud against Dave's door, fists beating hard and fast against the window.

Dave screamed and moved as far left as his seatbelt would allow. "Runner!"

The glass spider-webbed before Tony could pull away. The infected latched onto the truck and began pulling itself into the rear. It began to scream as it fought to get in, a hideous clamor that raked spectral fingernails down Dave's spine. The thing gained access to the bed and launched itself at the rear glass.

"Abbey, deal with him."

Tony jammed on the brakes and the infected man slammed into the rear of the cab, stunning him. It was the impetus Abbey needed to pop open the rear sliding window and aim her pistol at the prone form. The creature stood and Abbey fired one round, hitting it in the throat. It grasped the wound and gurgled and Tony picked that moment to floor the gas pedal, throwing the infected from the rear of the truck onto the street.

Abbey closed the slider. "Shit, I missed his noggin."

"At least he won't be fast anymore," Tony remarked. He looked forward and slowed the truck. "Jesus."

"Oh man, we are in some shit now," breathed Dave.

"You said it, kid." The street was thick with undead, plodding their way toward the truck from the north. Dozens were coming from the other cardinal directions as well, pulling themselves from smashed store fronts, alleys, under and inside crashed cars, from collapsed barricades, and broken front doors.

An industrious zombie had taken Tony's second of indecision to latch itself onto the large exterior mirror of the truck and it pressed its face to the window in an attempt to bite the driver. Vile fluids smeared across the glass.

A streak in blue jeans and a red T-shirt leapt from the side and Dave had time to yell that another Runner was close when the red-shirted man drew a machete and ended the hitchhiker's misery with a blow to the side of its head. The newcomer spun and decapitated two more things and punched a third in the face, dropping it to the ground. He spun around and faced the driver, who lowered the window for a moment.

The newcomer had a yellow smiley face with a bullet hole in the head on his shirt. "Howdy!"

Recognition slammed into Tony like a runaway train. "Billy!"

"None other than! Do you want to hang out here, or should we take that left at Albuquerque?"

"Get in the truck!"

"Always the bossy one," Billy harrumphed as, like the infected before him, he leapt into the bed of the F250.

The rear window slid aside again and Abbey looked at him through the open portal. "Nice to see you, kid."

"Abbey! Hi! Let's get out of here before you get eaten. Is that Dave up front? Hey, Dave! You made it to Alcatraz! Tony, the dead folks are thin if we move west up the 101. Lotta hills and they have trouble standing still on the hills."

"Got it!" Tony banged a right and they thudded through a few zombies before they were clear. The going was slow, as the devastation from months of the plague and city neglect had taken its toll on the roads. Their average speed was about fifteen miles per hour, which ironically, was faster than when the city had been full of vehicles. Many of those vehicles were now abandoned or crashed into poles or buildings and Tony skirted them with practiced ease.

Billy stuck his head in the open window. "Hang a right up here on Fillmore, yeah, that's it. Annnndddd, here we are! The Woodrow Wilson Elementary School."

Tony blinked. "What? Here? Are you kidding?"

"Nope, let's disembark, shall we? Got maybe ten minutes before they begin showing up. I'll help you carry your stuff." Billy got out of the truck and grabbed a box of food. "Uh, speed is of the essence people." He began walking away from the school. There were no dead in sight.

The six scroungers got out of the truck and each grabbed a box or a bag and followed Billy.

"Uh, Billy, the school is behind us," Dave told him.

"Um, yeah, I know."

They followed him for another fifty yards or so and he moved into a wide ditch between the north and southbound lanes of Fillmore Street. A black Cadillac Escalade was in the ditch. He opened the door. "Follow me!" The Escalade hid a culvert under the road and Billy moved through the SUV, opening the door on the other side, his friends following. "Close the door behind you there, killer."

They walked down the culvert for fifteen feet when a six-foot grate made of heavy iron suddenly blocked their path and Billy put his box down. He reached into his pocket and brought out a small set of keys, thumbing through them until he found the one he was looking for. Unlocking the grate, he motioned for the others to move beyond and they did. It was dark.

"Do not panic, friends. It's only a few feet more and we shall be bathed in light." Tony got to thinking it was taking a damn long time from the grate to wherever they were going when Billy snapped a green chemlight, shook it, and held it up. A heavy steel door that looked like it should be in a prison stood in front of them. Billy brought out his keys again and found a big one. He unlocked the door and stepped through into candlelight. "Home sweet home."

They were in a boiler room. A dirty, dingy, dank, boiler room. There was a welcome mat on the floor by a set of stairs and a single red rose in a vase on a table next to the mat. On an easel next to the mat, drawn in chalk, was a simple sign which read: *Except Zombies!* A green stick figure with its arms forward had a red chalk circle around it with a line through it.

Billy stepped on the mat. "Please wipe your feet." He walked up the short flight of stairs and knocked on another metal door, *Shave and a haircut.*

"Who is it?" demanded a small voice from the other side.

Billy turned around, obviously embarrassed. "That's not how it's supposed to go." He turned back to the door. "Richie, that's not what you're supposed to say."

"Oh, yeah. What's the password?"

"Ahem; *I am not a zombie.*"

The door made a rattling sound. "It won't open, Billy."

"Turn the key the other way, Richie."

"Oh, yeah."

The door rattled again and then opened three inches, everyone looked down into the scared blue eyes of a small boy. "Who's them?" the boy asked.

"Friends, Richie. They needed help and will help us back."

"K." The boy opened the door and the group filed in.

"Shut the door and lock it back up, kiddo, we're going to go talk in the office."

"Can I come, too?"

Billy got down to eye level with the kid. "Of course! You're the best guard in the whole world. I can't leave you down here while we talk about important stuff."

The child looked relieved and smiled a semi-toothless smile. He picked up a small backpack and a spear made from an ice pick duct-taped to what looked like a wrought iron curtain rod. Billy ruffled his hair and the boy smiled again.

The group walked down the hall, the only light coming from skylights in the ceiling. Lockers and other items told the newcomers that they were in a school. All the doors but one were closed and they took a right at the open door, going up a flight of stairs. The stairs were wide and windows were on each landing, but the glass had been covered with various types of cloth.

"To keep the lights in," Richie told them.

The second floor of the school held the offices, and Billy took everyone into the principal's office; where seven other kids, none older than ten, sat playing with various small toys or coloring on paper. They looked up simultaneously as Billy came in and they jumped up and ran to him, all grabbing and hugging him. They didn't make a sound.

When the hugging stopped, the kids looked at the adults. A girl of nine or ten walked forward and stuck her hand out to Abbey. "My name is Jenny," she whispered.

"Abbey. How old are you?"

"Nine and three quarters. My birthday is in October and I'll be double digits."

Abbey looked around. "Billy, where did these kids come from?"

"Shhhh!" Several small fingers pressed against mouths as the kids tried to silence the adult.

"We try to stay quiet," Billy offered in a low voice. "You never know who's listening."

BENEATH VANTEL CORPORATE LAB

"Brenda, Linda, look at this please, Arnold, you too," Ravi added. He was looking at a computer monitor. Crisp and the ladies looked up from their respective monitors then approached the Indian man. "The code, do you see this?" He pointed to a string of commands on the screen. "The PLC rootkit has been...altered."

All four of them were looking at the screen. "Yes! Yes, the SCADA payload is like nothing I've seen!" cried Brenda. "This isn't our work; it has been modified."

"What's PLC and SCADA?" asked Wilcox as he munched on a bag of pretzels. "And *payload* sounds kinda dangerous."

"PLC is programmable logic controller," Ravi explained, not re-directing his gaze. "It is a computer program that will access and control mechanical devices. It is almost a computer within a computer and can suffice as automation for mechanical processes. Thank you."

Wilcox blinked.

Brenda sighed. "It makes machines do stuff."

Wilcox crunched his pretzels. "Why didn't he just say that then? What's SCADA?"

This time, Ravi did look up. "Supervisory control and data acquisition. An ICS...uh...industrial control system to monitor and control computer processes. Usually for large-scale factories or industrial complexes."

"Okay, that makes sense."

"Thank you. This PLC is years ahead of where we were and we are the top minds in this field, or so I thought." Ravi looked hard at Crisp. "Arnold, what is this?"

"You must understand that Stuxnet and its successors were dangerous. Crippling, in fact. Several deaths and the possible loss of a nuclear submarine were attributed to these monster programs. The CIA was infected for Christ's sake! We tried to alter the PLC such that it could be run via a wireless network. If it could access and control a mechanical system, why not a biological one? We tried for a year, but we were unable to get a working prototype of a biological virus that could use human brainwaves as a transmitter and receiver. The technology already existed, as evidenced by several key systems that had been infected with Abaddon. Human test subjects were examined and their brainwaves were...not normal. This was almost a year ago."

Wilcox stopped his crunching. "So you let it out, huh, Doc?"

"No! We were never able to get it to work! Major Mello and his military contacts were beginning to get…threatening. They told us to go in a different direction and some men showed up with a new type of crystal-based computer system that I had never seen before. None of the staff were allowed to even see it, except me. It was beautiful and gave off no heat. I've never seen the like. I don't think anyone has. They took some Rama files and left. A week later, the first newscasts of plague victims began to surface."

Wilcox crumpled his empty bag of pretzels, tossing it in a small wastebasket. "Rama is the name of your anti-virus, yeah?"

Crisp nodded. "Yes."

"The timeframe is fairly coincidental, is it not?" Ravi demanded.

"What's coincidental?" Androwski asked as he and the others strode into the lab.

Wilcox gave him the rundown with the scientist's help.

The SEAL shook his head. "Can you fix it?"

The scientists looked at him dumbfounded, "Fix what?" asked Linda.

"The plague. Can you fix that friggin' computer virus," Androwski pointed at the screen, "so that if we get bitten, we won't turn?"

"In time, maybe," Brenda considered, "but this is new and exciting stuff. We've not seen this type of programming before."

"Fine. Do what you have to do. Just so you know, if the ladder we found leads to an egress point, our little team is splitting up. Rick's group is heading back to Alcatraz with Seyfert as escort."

Brenda looked at Rick. "You're leaving? You're leaving now?"

"Brenda, Sam is back there. Of course I'm leaving. I've come to ask you if…if you'll come with me."

"No," she replied instantly. "I'm needed here. I love my daughter, Rick, you know that, but if I can help end this, or at least slow it down, it would be selfish to leave."

Rick shook his head. "I understand. Make sure you write something I can take back to Sam."

With that, Rick left. Dallas quickly followed. "Hey, pard, ya know ya ain't supposed to go nowheres alone!"

Woodrow Wilson Elementary School, San Francisco

Billy wiped soup from his mouth with a monogrammed napkin. "I picked up three of them in a candy store. I was the only living adult they had seen in a few days and they were pigging out on gummy bears. Zombies had found them and were starting to bang on the window. The other kids I brought here as I found them." A small boy got up from the circle they were in, walked over to Billy, gave him a high-five, and sat back down. "I brought in one other adult, but he…he turned out to be not so nice."

Jenny did not look up from her soup, but nodded slowly in agreement.

"Any other adults I've sent to Alcatraz. Most of them I get to a boat and send them off. Some of them don't make it, some of them do."

Dave looked at Jenny. "He got me to the island." He winked at her and she smiled.

One of the other kids looked up from his bowl. "We want to go to the Alc-traz too."

Billy looked at his kids. "That's why I brought these people, Dennis. They're going to get you guys out of the city."

Tony looked at Abbey. "Uh, Billy…"

Billy held up his hand. "My price for saving your lives, feeding you, and bringing you into the sanctum."

Dave stood up and moved to Billy. He stuck his hand out for a shake. "Done."

"Dave, how are we…?"

Dave pointed at Tony. "Done!" Tony put his palms up in surrender.

The boy who had gotten up before walked over to Dave and high-fived him.

The kids were all asleep on the third floor of the school. Billy had somehow appropriated bunk beds and constructed them for the kids to sleep in. Each child had their own bed, most with colored pictures or stuffed toys hanging on it. All of the windows in the classroom were painted black and had heavy drapes covering them. Billy had screwed large, ornate iron curtain rods into the concrete with concrete screws to hang the drapes from.

The adults had moved into the class next door, where eight desks sat in a small semi-circle in front of a huge green chalkboard. The board had several simple addition problems chalked on it, along with a dozen spelling words. They sat in a small circle around a battery-operated lantern.

Abbey started to cry. "All the kids that didn't make it..."

Billy wiped his eyes too. "I put them down first if there's a group of zombies. I can't stand the thought of one of those things wearing a kid suit."

Tony looked around at everything. "Billy, are you teaching the kids?"

Billy perked up. "Yeah! I figured my kids needed some semblance of normalcy, so we learn some stuff each day. There's a ton of books here."

"Your kids?"

"Yeah, mine. I found them, they're mine. And I'm theirs, at least until you get them to Rick and Pittsburgh," he looked wistful, "and Sam."

"What you've done here is amazing," said a guy Billy didn't know. He squinted at the man.

"Oh man, sorry, Billy, this is Derek, Tony, and Steve."

"Charmed," Billy quipped in his best Bugs Bunny voice.

"How did you do all of this?" Derek asked, looking around.

"Had to. The kids needed the stuff. I needed to help the kids. I wasn't going to let them sleep on the floor. Not when there's an IKEA store on the next street over." He tipped Derek a wink and Derek smiled back. "I found that Caddy we climbed through; it was full of gas. Had a dead woman in it. Well, sort of dead. I got rid of her and used it to bring the beds and curtain rods and drapes and the dresser in there. It was easy. Whenever the zombies come for the car, I turn it off and open the windows. They come over to it and then shuffle off after a minute or so."

"Where did you get the food?"

"It's everywhere. You just need to know where to look." He screwed his face up a little in thought. "Pickings *are* getting slimmer out there though. Kinda funny when you think of it. There were zillions of people here a couple months ago, all wanting food...well, I guess *that's* still true...but now that all the living people are dead people, you would think there'd be tons of food just laying around. All the outlying little mom and pop stores have been cleaned out, but the inner city is loaded with packaged stuff. Unfortunately, anybody going on a food run has to go deeper into the city and they usually come out stumbling. There are just too many zombies downtown. I'm lucky, I guess."

Steve looked up. "How so?"

"Zombies don't like me," Billy pinched up his face again, "or maybe they like me too much. I must admit, I haven't figured that one out yet," he ended to himself. He looked up at Tony suddenly. "How's Ali?"

"She's good. She and Sam have hit it off huge. Actually, she's hit it off with everybody, especially the kids. They love her."

"Lotta kids then?"

"Twenty-two kids under the age of sixteen, including me," Dave whispered.

Billy nodded and looked at the door to the next classroom over. "Good. Going to get a few more, too."

Steve finished his Diet Sprite and wiped his mouth with his sleeve. "What did you mean zombies don't like you?"

"Wow. Nobody has been forthcoming about my super-power?"

Steve gave him a blank look.

"Well, sir, I can..." Billy went stock still. "Everybody quiet. Douse the light and follow me to the window." Derek picked up the light and switched it off, everyone following Billy across the darkened classroom. He went to a specific drape and moved it to the side. He pulled on a room-darkening shade and brought it slowly up then a set of mini blinds. They looked out across a field toward the street, approximately two hundred yards away. Two vehicles, large, probably trucks, were moving slowly down the road, headlights piercing the evening. "They're getting closer."

"Who are they?"

"Bad guys. They call themselves The New Society."

Tony chuckled slightly. "Gangs? Lots of gangs in San Francisco? Did they used to be gay waiters?"

Billy didn't look away from the trucks. "They're from L.A. There's about two hundred of them and they aren't nice. Don't know if they were waiters. They pick up everyone they can. Some they let live, some they don't." He looked at Abbey. "Bad luck if you're a girl too." Billy shifted his gaze to the left. "Uh oh. Abbey, could you please go sit with the kids? Get them down below the windows against the walls. I think this is going to get loud."

"What is it?"

He pointed to the left and out of the gloom, a throng of undead were stumbling their way toward the sound of the trucks. Hundreds were crossing the street, moving through the playground on the corner. The moans were just becoming perceptible.

"Billy!" one of the kids whisper-yelled.

"Abbey, go, please. The kids know what to do."

Abbey moved from the room and started getting the kids out of bed, each one waking up instantly and performing a pre-assigned task. A few got food and water out of the IKEA pantry, others went about securing the door with an iron bar set in the floor. The two biggest kids began moving mattresses, pillows, and blankets from the beds to the floor. All had been done with military precision and in total silence.

The trucks stopped in front of a boarded-up house and living men descended upon it. Searchlights from the trucks snapped on and began to survey the area. Gunshots began to break the eerie silence of the abandoned city.

Billy turned to face the group. "We should probably get away from the windows." He dropped the blinds, pulled the shade, and let the drape fall back in place. The adults moved back to the room with the kids, who looked scared. Billy sat on a mattress and the kids all came to him, getting as close as they could. He put his arms around as many as possible. "What do we do when we see them?"

"Stay quiet, stay low," the children responded together in a whisper.

"And if they find us?"

The response from the kids was immediate, "They won't."

Billy looked at the rest of the adults. "Welcome back to San Francisco."

The gunfire increased from sporadic to sustained. For a solid five minutes, several different weapon sounds were heard, from auto fire, to heavy machine guns, to explosions that were undoubtedly grenades. All at once, the shots subsided and the trucks moved away. They tactically withdrew several minutes before the dead reached them, but it was still close.

Dawn came with the kids and Billy sleeping on the mattresses. The other adults stayed awake in fear of the horde that was now traipsing around their sanctuary. Their host woke with a yawn and extricated himself from the tangle of children. He looked at Tony and smiled. "No sleep at all, huh?"

"Are you kidding? Did you see the size of that swarm?"

Billy stood and stretched, the kids rolling over or scrunching together, but not waking. "I sure did. Not the biggest that's passed through these here parts, but it was large. I'll give the kids another hour then it's up and at 'em! In the meantime, you folks and I are going to talk about getting my new family out of here." He looked at the window. "It's becoming unsafe."

Tony folded his arms and leaned against the wall. "So, what's your plan, chief? How do we get the kids to the boat? And don't say we go through the sewers, cuz that ain't happenin'."

"No way! I'm all kinds of done with the sewers. Stinks down there."

Abbey and Tony both nodded in agreement.

"But I do have a doozy of a plan. A doozy." He smiled a wicked smile.

"So?"

"We're going to rob a bank."

BENEATH VANTEL CORPORATE LAB

Androwski and Stenner performed recon on the ladder the morning after Crisp's computer revelation. As indicated on the schematic, it led into a series of concrete vents, which, after they cut the locks on several grates and a steel door, led to the surface. A small smokestack, hidden in the trees toward the far end of the facility vented white steam exhaust from the geothermal plant a hundred feet below. Stenner waited inside the base of the stack behind an exit door, as his SEAL partner climbed the ladder all the way to the top. He was up there for a solid ten minutes with his binoculars before he came back down.

"Well, it definitely leads to the surface. Actually about forty feet above it."

"So why do you look like your dog just died?"

"Because the place is crawling with Limas."

"Shit."

"Yeah." Androwski wiped his forearm across his brow. "Hot in here. Let's get back with the intel."

Androwski and Stenner returned to one of the small rooms to discuss the plan with everyone.

Seyfert had found a bag of chips. "So it's up a hundred feet of ladders, then we fight off a horde of infected, get to the cars, then to the airfield, and figure out if we can fly a plane that nobody here is rated on. Easy peasy."

Androwski shook his head in the negative. "From what I could see, the vehicles have all been destroyed by heavy weapons fire. Vehicles will need to be appropriated off-site."

"Keeps gettin' better n' better."

Crisp had been interrogated on where the aircraft that Bob spoke of was located. Dr. Crisp had given Bob the stink-eye when they all came barging in on him, but had reluctantly given up the information. The plane was at a defunct Air Force base on Cape Cod, approximately forty-five miles away.

"But I don't have keys or access codes for the plane," Crisp added.

Seyfert crushed his potato chip bag and threw it in a wastebasket. "You let me worry about that." He turned to Androwski. "LT, before we go out that stack, I would like to do a little recon of my own."

"Of course, but give it a couple of days. Heal your leg."

"So it's me, Rick, Dallas, and Anna." Seyfert looked at Anna. "How are we going to stop to get Chris?"

"We find a runway," she answered. "Wasn't there an airfield near the garage? Didn't you guys get that little helicopter there?"

"That was a civilian airfield. The runway was a mile at best," Seyfert appeared thoughtful, "but the area is flat. I mean, it's Nebraska. Shockingly, we will have to see when we get there."

"Before this takes place, we have a more immediate problem."

Everyone looked at Androwski.

"We need to take care of the Limas in the common room. I can hear them banging on the door at the end of the corridor."

Indeed, muffled thumps were heard by all. The hermetic steel and fiberglass door would withstand the repeated beatings by the undead, but all things considered, the creatures were only fifteen meters away.

Wilcox cleared his throat. "We can see the common room through the monitors in the security room, right? Let's bang on the lab security door and make some noise. Get them all in that corridor then we run out a different module door and shoot them as they come out of the corridor." He looked at Seyfert. "Easy peasy."

"Yeah, except we welded the other doors closed."

"Still got the welder. It's just tac-welded. Cut it."

The SEALs looked at each other. "That isn't bad," concluded Seyfert.

"No, let's work out the details and see if it's feasible."

Wilcox, Androwski, and Rick stood behind the welded door to the living quarters. Wilcox had just cut through the welds they had made prior and some creatures must have noticed or heard because they were now pounding on the other side of the door. Androwski radioed to Seyfert and he and Dallas began thumping on their door and yelling like crazy.

"How we looking, Stenner?"

Stenner peered into the security monitor, Bob sitting next to him, looking at his pistol with some awe. "Pretty good, LT. They're moving away from your door and heading toward the hillbilly."

Dallas yelled in his baritone voice, "Heard that!"

"How many do you count, Stenner?"

"I came up with thirty-six and thirty-three after two counts. I can see the common room, but not the corridor between it and the lab."

"Now's as good a time as any. Triple-check your weapons."

When the weapons check was complete, Androwski used his fingers to count down from three. He threw the door open when the countdown expired and the three men looked on a scene from Hell. The common room looked like an abattoir. Contaminated blood covered nearly every surface. Dozens of bodies littered the floor, including the unfortunates that had been lined up by the group a few days ago, when Brooks had sealed them down here.

The parade of new walking dead had traipsed their rotting carcasses throughout the entire area, depositing portions of themselves on everything. Fluids and pieces of discolored flesh and clothing were here and there. Wilcox gagged at the stench.

The gagging was more than the things needed to alert them and they began to plod from the short lab corridor back into the common room in search of the noise. The living men opened fire slowly, methodically dropping the dead with headshots. They destroyed eleven infected before Androwski commanded that they withdraw back into the corridor to repeat the procedure. It took three hours, but they destroyed all of the undead in the common room. The three men checked every nook and cranny, including the bathrooms, but nothing lurked in the shadows. When the search was over, Androwski told Wilcox to re-weld the door they had opened. "But we would lose this area," the kid argued.

"We've already lost it. There's no way to de-con this place and where are we going to dispose of the bodies? Nobody's coming back in here without full MOPP or a hazmat suit. Seal it up. We can figure out how to prevent the stink later, but I think the doors will keep it out. If for some crazy reason we do need to get back in here, we can just cut the welds again."

Wilcox pulled his mask down and fired up the welder.

Seyfert threw himself onto a couch in the room that the non-scientists were about to play cards in and began rubbing his leg. "Well, you weren't lying. There's a shitload of Limas. I'm thinking well over two hundred. The cars are screwed too and the LAV..." He looked down. "Stark..."

"I know. It was quick though, better than what's probably going to happen to the rest of us."

"Right. Anyway, the critters seem to be focused on the main structure, but there are dozens just wandering aimlessly." Seyfert stood. He grabbed the deck of cards and stacked them in the center of the table then moved a can of Coke to one side and put other single cards here and there. He produced a pen and began pointing. "This," he indicated the deck of cards, "is the main structure. These cards are outbuildings and wrecked vehicles. The soda can is the stack I was looking out of. There's a door at the base of the stack, here. We go at night, just after the sun goes down so we have plenty of time. We'll need to get to the boundary fence, probably here," he pointed the pen to what would be north of the stack, "in the woods. The main issue is we won't be able to see very well and our NVGs are shit out of batteries."

Bob perked up. "What kind do they take?"

"Mine take one double A," Rick offered, "but everybody else's takes some weird military battery."

"Ours take the mil-specs, but they are attached to a helmet mount." It was Seyfert's turn to perk up. "But my IR optic takes some weird watch-type battery. Bob, tell me you have batteries!"

"Dude, I was a boy scout. Only problem is they're up a floor. But did you try the PX? I bet they have a nice selection."

Androwski was staring at the makeshift 3D map. "Wilcox, take Bob and go find us some batteries. Seyfert, continue with the brief."

"Roger that. So, we're here at the northern fence. I don't see anybody ever having control of the exterior again, so rather than climb, we cut it and move on. If we can find a vehicle, that's great, but if not, we hole up someplace when the sun comes up, then we get back to the coast, grab a boat, and head south to Cape Cod. LT, the map?"

Androwski handed his buddy a map of Massachusetts, which he promptly unfolded and refolded so Cape Cod was visible. "We sail south to the Cape Cod Canal and then west and then a little south to this spot here in… West Falmouth. Then we hoof it to the base. It's under ten miles from the coast."

"Ten miles of probable Hell," Bob lamented as he stood to go with Wilcox.

"Agreed, but what choice do we have?"

Dallas sighed. "I'm just thinkin' out loud here, but what if we get to the airport and there ain't no plane?"

"Then we find some bicycles and pedal back to Alcatraz, Hillbilly. *You've* got point."

"Ha-ha."

"You leave in four days, if Seyfert's leg is okay," Androwski told them. "Get your weapons ready and stock up on ammo and food. Pack light."

Four days went by quickly and on the morning of the day they were going to leave, by all accounts a Saturday, Rick pulled Androwski aside. "There's one thing we didn't discuss, LT."

"What's that?"

"Communications. How are we going to talk to you once we get home?"

"I was thinking about that yesterday. Let's talk to Bob and Crisp and see if they have any equipment. I can't believe a fallout shelter for big-wigs would have no comms."

They found Crisp with the rest of the scientists in the lab. "We have hand-held ham radios, but they won't work now. There is some ancient ham radio equipment behind the PX."

"And you didn't think this was important information to tell us because…?"

"Because all the relays will be down. If you can get the system working, you might be able to contact folks to a few hundred miles. I don't know the range, but I know it's limited. We have a system that uses the internet and one that uses a satellite, but the internet is down and no one is controlling the satellites from the ground now. Even if the satellite is operational, it has to be in orbit above us to make use of it."

"Unless you use the shortwave," Ravi interjected. "Shortwave could travel across a vast distance."

Crisp turned to Ravi. "Ravindra, do you have a ham license?"

"Yes, Arnold. I was not always a computer geek. Well, actually, I have always been a computer geek, but when I was young, my grandfather was a policeman in India. He had a shortwave radio and we used to speak to people all over the world. I found this amazing and took up the hobby for myself. I took a brief test and received my radio license perhaps ten years ago when I first came to the United States. Although it has been a very long while, I could look at your system. Thank you."

"Would we be able to speak to McInerney?"

Androwski rubbed the back of his neck. "I don't know, Rick. Of course we'll try. Ravi, can you escape for a little while and check the radio? This is critical."

"I believe it would be fun. Thank you for the opportunity."

Ravi, Androwski, and Rick made their way to the PX. Rick grabbed a jar of half sour pickles from a nearby shelf and offered one to each man, both of whom accepted. They were munching their prizes when they reached a spare room at the back of the PX. The radio equipment was on a shelf with various other old machines.

"Ah, this is an old one. It has tubes!" The tall Indian man moved forward to get a better look. Androwski asked for another pickle and turned to Rick. Behind Rick, off to the side near another shelf was a dark gray piece of metal. It was out of place, leaning against the shelving. Androwski cocked his head and moved to it. He stared at it for a second before realizing it was a vent to a heating duct. He looked up and saw a gaping hole in the duct work above his head.

The alarm that went off in the SEAL's head occurred simultaneously with a short scream from Ravi. He had reached into the shelving to appropriate the radio. When he moved it, a hand snaked through the gap and grabbed him, pulling him forward. The grip was like steel and it wouldn't let go. Ravi struggled, but refused to release the equipment. Before either Rick or Androwski could do anything, the tall shelf pitched forward and came down on their friend. A dead man came with it and it continued to pull on Ravi, who was now pinned under the shelf.

The creature was leaning in to bite at Ravi's exposed wrist when Rick shot it. Its head snapped to the side and then it fell forward, adding to the weight of the shelf on the unfortunate man. Rick and the SEAL pulled the dead thing off the shelf and then the shelf off of the living man.

"Thank you," Ravi rasped and passed out.

THE EMBARCADERO, SAN FRANCISCO

"I have not seen such wanton aggression before," uttered a modest man of indeterminate age. "My old doctor would have been overcome with delight to analyze you." The man removed his wire glasses and pinched his nose. He looked tired. Several men stood or were seated in a warehouse office, watching what transpired.

"It is hardly wanton," a taller man replied. "I understand your trepidations, Father, but sometimes corporal punishment is necessary to instill respect in the troops. If not, anarchy would reign and then where would we be?" The man drove a fist into the ribs of a figure hanging from the ceiling. The trussed man gave a whimper. "This fool questioned my lineage, doubted you. I would think that at the very least you would desire the respect you deserve."

"Yes, of course. Yet we linger here when there is work to be done. The members of our little group already know who's in charge. Let me ask you this: What do they fear most?"

"I was hoping it was me."

"Perhaps, but think a moment. Members of rival gangs, people picked up on the street, all creeds and colors. All of them here and listening to you. All of them *getting along*. Not one fight since this started. That is astounding. Pure magic. I would think that one thing would scare them even more than your wrath."

"And what is that?"

The smaller man put his glasses back on. "Banishment."

The restrained man looked blankly at his captors through one eye, the other swollen shut from repeated beatings. The taller of the two rolled his eyes. "It means we throw you out."

A look of fear and horror took over the captive's face. "No! You can't do that, Doc, please!"

"What would you have me do? I can't have disloyalty. I won't." The speaker looked sad and angry at the same time.

"I'm loyal! I swear! It was just a joke! I wouldn't have said it if I knew you were there!"

"My father is white. I am black. This is funny to you?" The man turned and looked at the others in the room. He pointed at one of them. "Is it funny to you?" He pointed at another. "Or you?" Both men vehemently nodded in the negative. He looked at a man leaning against the wall, cleaning his fingernails with a knife. "Masta G, do you take comedic pleasure in the fact that my father is a white man?"

"No."

"So then it isn't funny." He turned to the trussed man. "It would seem that only you think it's funny."

The captive opened his mouth as if to say something, but thought better of it and kept quiet.

"Banishment. Excellent. Our new punishment for disloyalty. Pee Wee, if you would be kind enough to enforce our new policy? Remove this dolt from my sight."

An ebony giant stepped forward, grasping the tied man by the wrists. He lifted him up slightly, releasing the captive from a jury-rigged hook. Cords in his massive arms rippling, the colossal gang-banger threw the unfortunate victim over his shoulder then moved away down a set of metal stairs. Footsteps echoed through the warehouse loft as did the pleadings of the doomed man.

The smaller man nodded. "Fine work, Doc Murda."

"Thank you. Now if we could begin discussing the items at hand. The destruction of the submarine currently anchored off of Alcatraz and the group of survivors currently in the city that keeps outwitting my soldiers at every turn. "

Masta G stepped forward, putting his hands on the table and pointing to a map. "That's where I saw them. They must have just finished loading up when we got there and we would have had them if not for the crowd of infected that fell on us at that exact time. It was the same blond, scar-faced prick that I've seen a bunch of times."

The smaller man perked up and walked forward, seemingly more interested.

Doc Murda looked at his captain, Masta G. "And you're going to stick to your story?"

"Yeah. Son of a bitch had a bunch of kids with him. They were like little ninjas, the maggot-bags never even got close to 'em. They went straight for us."

"So my troops are being outfoxed by children." It was a statement, not a question.

The small man spoke up. "No. They are being outwitted by a sociopath who has some kind of immunity to the dead." Everyone looked at him, and he looked at Masta G. "This man, he has a wide scar here," he drew a line down the right side of his jaw, "and he's about your height?"

"That's the dude, yeah."

"His name is William, although he calls himself Billy. He was a resident of Morningside when I was there. Level four. Quite dangerous. He has children with him, you say?"

Masta G nodded.

"Interesting."

"Cyrus," asked G, "what did you mean when you said he was immune?"

"The dead don't seem to want to consume him. I'm unsure as to why." Cyrus looked at Doc Murda. "He could be valuable."

"Agreed. Send the word out. This man is not to be killed. I want him alive. Triple rations and a full day in the brothel to whoever brings him in."

"Unhurt," added Cyrus.

"Indeed, unhurt. Now the sub. I'm open to ideas on how we get our substantial amount of explosives close enough to damage it."

The men moved toward the map on the table and planning began.

BENEATH VANTEL CORPORATE LAB

The radio hadn't been damaged. Ravi had held onto it and protected it even though the thing on the other side of the shelving was trying to eat him. It had been a miracle that nothing had been broken, either on the radio or on the man when the shelf went over. One of the metal cross members had opened a serious gash on the man's head and Anna had cleaned and stitched it while he remained unconscious.

When Anna had completed her sewing and they left Ravi to sleep it off, (strapped to his bunk with ratcheting tie-downs), Anna asked where the thing in the PX had come from. The only thing anyone could think of was that whoever had climbed into the ductwork in the men's bathroom weeks ago must have been infected and died in the ducts. The unfortunate man must have turned and then began searching for a way out. Seyfert acquired schematics of the ducts and they figured out that there were ways into the facility that hadn't been thought of, but most of them were too small for a human, alive or dead, to fit through. The only ones large enough to accommodate a lurking undead were contained inside the bunker. The tubes leading to the outside were less than a foot in diameter and they all led to interior filtration systems. The inner workings, however, led from the safety of the welded bunker to the common room filled with fifty decomposing bodies. A plan would have to be put in place in order to either block up the vents, or dispose of the corpses. No ductwork led from the upper facility into the bunker, although there were power conduits that did so. All the bunker venting came directly from outside and all were filtered.

They set up the radio in the security room. A hookup to a radio tower on the surface existed in an antechamber. The installation of the radio would have taken significantly less time had Ravi been there, but he was still out cold. Seyfert and Wilcox worked on the unit for a few hours and they were finally able to transmit.

Androwski pressed the silver pedal on the old microphone. "Rock, this is Wanderer One. Come in, over? I say again, Rock, this is Wanderer One. Do you read, over?"

"*Wanderer One, this is Rock, we read you. Rock Actual inbound to this position. ETA three mikes, over. SITREP?*"

"Holy shit," breathed Seyfert. The two SEALs looked at each other, broad smiles appearing on both faces.

"Get Crisp and Poole. The captain will want to speak with them." Androwski put a hand on Seyfert's arm as he stood. "Get Rick, too."

"Rock, Wanderer. Have reached mission objective with most parties necessary. Parties currently working on special project in secure location. Have critical information on other players for Actual. Over."

"*Wanderer, Rock. Relay information now. Code is Panacea. Over.*"

"Wanderer copies all. Elements of U.S. military and government in Nebraska have formed a cooperative. They have multiple resources, including aircraft and dozens of personnel. Also several thousand civilians on site. Group calls itself the Triumvirate, repeat Triumvirate. Group is covertly hostile."

Androwski related what he could about the Triumvirate and also the fact that there was a massive swarm of undead on the move from east to west. Commander McInerney, captain of the USS *Florida* and Androwski's commanding officer, arrived with detective Captain Michael Meara of the San Francisco police department some minutes later.

"*Wanderer, this is Actual. Good to hear your voice, son.*" Androwski smiled, instantly recognizing the man on the other end of the radio.

"Good to be heard, sir. I've just briefed Rock on our mission."

"*I see the notes. Tell me about the Triumvirate.*"

"We began hearing them on the radio calling for people to come to Lincoln, Nebraska when we reached the mid-west. Then we encountered a heavily armed checkpoint. We met one of the founding members of the Triumvirate, Col. Bourne, who defected from that group and came with us all the way to Massachusetts. Sir, they knew about our mission. We were the second group contacted and briefed by Dr. Poole and her associates, not the first."

"*Where is the colonel now?*"

"Dead, sir. He was killed by a Triumvirate spy that we took with us to this location from MIT. The spy was definitely Alphabet trained."

"*Wanderer, there are several personnel who wish to know how many of your original team are mission capable.*"

"There were casualties, sir. Rick's group is present and accounted for, minus two. We left Chris, the nerd, in Nebraska to assist with another group. Nerd's whereabouts unknown as of now. Sniper Martinez was KIA."

There was a slight pause as the information was assimilated. "*And the tac-team?*"

"Four casualties. Seyfert and I are vertical, but Seyfert is damaged. Not bitten," he added quickly. "Wanderer has also absorbed several capable elements."

"*Actual copies all.*"

BROADWAY, SAN FRANCISCO

"Uhhh. No."

Billy looked at Steve. "What?"

Steve held his hand above his eyes to block the bright sun and get a better look. "No goddamn way am I going down there." He pointed into the dark, gaping maw of an underground parking garage beneath the American Securities Bank and Trust building. An abandoned military Humvee stood partially burned with its doors open. Bullet casings littered the asphalt and there were brown stains inside the vehicle. A rusty M4 rifle lay on the ground near the vehicle. "I choose to live."

"Well, you won't. You'll end up in the stomachs of a bunch of zombies, or worse, like him." Billy pointed at a dead soldier in digital camouflage staggering out of the darkness toward them. "Excuse me." He strode toward the thing and stopped a few feet in front of it. The thing shuffled toward him and he pulled his machete. It reached for him and stopped, leaning, with hungry eyes, to the side to look at the small group of people. It tried to move past Billy, but he shifted positions to block it.

Steve raised his eyebrows. "Da fuck?"

The thing moved past Billy and he ended the soldier's misery with his machete, wiped the blade on the corpse's stained clothes, and moved back to the group. "We don't have tons of time. Any noise at all in this dead city and they're on you in a couple of minutes at most. Stay here and you're all dead. At least down there, we get prizes." Billy pointed into the garage.

The plan had been made earlier that morning. They would drive to the American Securities building and pilfer two armored trucks. The trucks Billy had seen in the basement garage when he had to hide from some of the New Society. They were heavy and as the name said, armored. Zombie-proof. The only problem was the abandoned Hummer. It was parked crossways across the entrance ramp. Armored itself, the F250 might be able to move it, but not far enough and certainly not quickly. The decibel level of moving the vehicle would be high and then the group could get overwhelmed by a crowd of slavering cannibals while in the process.

The armored trucks were twelve thousand pounds of diesel-powered currency transporters. They could push the busted military car out of the way without the crew ever having to leave the safety of the vehicle. The glass and tires were bullet resistant, as were the undercarriage and all five other sides. The doors were three-inch-thick steel and the diesel fuel in each one would still be good. They were the perfect vehicles for an excursion through hostile territory and they didn't need to go far.

The problem was where they were located. The group was filled with apprehension as they stared into the foreboding darkness. There were two gates that normally would have blocked the entrance to the underground garage, but they were wide open and from the looks of them, had been for some time.

Tony said what everyone else was thinking, "There could be a hundred of them in there."

"Going to be a thousand up here in twenty minutes," Billy promised. "The bank trucks will make it through a crowd. It's probably already too late to get out safely with your Ford anyway. Look."

He pointed down the road and they could see a small crowd shuffling in their direction.

Tony looked at the sky. "He's right. We're committed now. We're here. We get those trucks or we're dead." He snapped his flashlight on and moved down the ramp toward the garage. The rest of the group followed.

"Hang on there, Anthony, let me go first. Give me ten seconds then follow."

Billy, machete in hand, strolled down the ramp like it was any normal summer day. He disappeared into the gloom and the cluster of friends followed soon after. Billy didn't use a light, so he couldn't be seen, but the rest of the group all switched lights on. Everyone was terrified. "Keep quiet and check those corners," Abbey told them. Two corpses, one headless, were on the concrete in front of them, another further up. The lights cut into the darkness and evidence of violence was everywhere. Broken car windows, bullet brass, most of a human skeleton, brown stains.

"Stay in the center of the lane," whispered Tony. "Don't go near the cars or the support columns." A dead man in the rags of a blue uniform staggered out from behind one of the columns Tony had wanted to avoid. It saw them and began immediately coming toward them. "Get in tight together!" The creature moaned loudly, the sound echoing throughout the structure. A chorus of other moans followed, filling the survivors with the most common dread on the planet.

Tony moved forward and the uniformed thing hissed at him. The living human used his bat and thumped the dead one on the head. It collapsed and Tony shook out his hand. "Every time."

Scraping and shuffling were coming from all directions.

"Get in tight! Make a circle and don't shoot unless we're getting overrun! Push 'em back and cave their friggin' roofs in!"

Dave hefted his fire axe and Tony his bat. Abbey and Derek also had bats, but they were wooden. Steve checked the action on his AR15, preferring to wield that as opposed to the tonfa baton at his hip. Tony unsheathed a katana and pointed it toward two white vans. "Here they come."

Moaning turned to hissing and growling as three of the dead came from between the vans and noticed their prey. They surged forward on rotten legs, stumbling faster in anticipation of a meal to come. Tony moved forward and met them, slashing with his sword. The top of the head of a woman in blue scrubs landed on the windshield of one of the vans. Before she hit the ground, Tony had impaled another creature through the eye. He yanked the blade out and spun to meet the third creature, but Dave beat him to it and crushed its skull with his axe.

"Dave, stay with me," Tony chastised. "Tony, don't stray out too far. Where the hell is Billy?"

Sliding footsteps from the rear alerted them to more of the things. They were coming up a ramp from deeper in the garage and as their heads cleared the concrete dividers, they growled and sped up slightly as their counterparts had. The sunlight that filtered in through the open garage walls illuminated many.

Steve swallowed hard. "Holy shit, I knew this was a bad idea."

Something crawled out from under a Honda Civic and moved toward them. Three former humans staggered toward them from behind a yellow SUV. Two came from the shadows to the left, more materialized from the right.

Dave put his axe on the ground and Tony looked at him with incredulity. Dave smiled. "Not giving up just yet." He pulled something from his back pocket, attaching it to his arm. Dave immediately pulled back on something, aimed, and let go. The front teeth of a dead businessman shattered and he stumbled back. Tony turned to look at Dave, but not before he saw the businessman's crimson iris explode, the creature dropping to the ground. Tony stared at Dave. "Wrist rocket. My brother gave it to me for my birthday." He drew the rubber tubes back again and let go, the steel ball smashing into the nose of a dead woman closing from the gloom. She didn't fall, but kept on coming with a small hole in her face.

Steve's voice was on the edge of panic and he raised his rifle. "Jesus Christ! There's a hundred of them and we're fighting them off with sling-shots! We're gonna die!"

"Not today!" Billy strode from the shadows as the zombies had, but he was behind them. "Nine oh one! Nine oh two! Three! Four! Gonna make a grand today!" Each number he spoke ended with a destroyed creature.

The main body of the small horde had rounded the corner of the ramp and begun to soldier on toward their breakfast. "This-a-way," Billy shouted as he decapitated a dead woman. "I got them all cleared out this way, follow me!" He turned and ran back into the darkness the way he had come.

Tony slashed once more and they all ran after Billy, lights bobbing with the dead in pursuit. They arrived at a guard station next to an elevator with the number 1 on the wall in large, yellow block print. Three white trucks with American Securities printed on the side in red, white, and blue letters sat parked in a row, noses out. Bloody handprints and smears covered the first truck and bullet casings were on the ground near the driver's side. A thump caused Abbey to whip around and look at the cab. A dead man in a blue uniform tried to get at the survivors through the bullet-resistant glass.

Billy tried to reassure his friends. "The other two trucks are empty, I looked. The keys are in the guard house. That's empty too."

Tony and Derek ran into the small room; the door, also covered in blood marks, had been pushed in from the outside. The room was not totally empty as Billy had indicated. What was left of yet another man in a blue uniform was slumped in a chair. A hole in his head and a Glock nineteen pistol on the floor near him indicated he didn't wait for the things that had trapped him to get in. His co-worker in the armored vehicle had apparently held out for help until he starved or died of a bite. Tony would never know as he had no intentions of opening the door to the vehicle.

Derek grabbed two sets of keys with 8081 and 8082 on each respective yellow tag. He tossed one set to Tony and they moved back to the trucks. Each man checking the cab of his vehicle, they both moved to the back doors. The cries and moans of the dead grew louder as Tony called for everyone to get behind the trucks. "Alright, if there's any dead ones in the back, shoot them fast and get them out!" He put the key in the lock on the back door and turned it. The door was much heavier than he had thought it would be as he yanked it open. The rear of the vehicle was devoid of anything alive or dead.

Derek did the same with his door and everyone shone their lights into the back as he pulled the heavy steel open. Six tall locked bags sat between the panels in the back of this vehicle.

"Dave, Abbey, Billy with me; you three in the other truck. Screw the back, everybody up front!" They closed and locked the doors and each person ran to get in the cab of their assigned vehicle. It was a squeeze, but four fit in one cab and three fit comfortably on the bench seat of the other truck. Tony jammed his foot on the clutch and put the key in the ignition. The truck started on the first turn. The other truck started up immediately as well. The growing horde of dead began to appear out of the shadows, all wanting the living people just beyond reach.

Tony released his emergency brake, let his foot slowly off the clutch, and the truck began to move forward. They hit the first wave of dead, thumping sounding on all sides of the vehicle before Tony realized the other truck wasn't with them. The horn sounded on the other truck and the headlights flashed. "Jesus, really?" Tony demanded and jammed on the brakes. He threw the shift in reverse and backed up to the other armored car. "What the hell are you doing?" he screamed at Derek. Derek made unintelligible hand signals and then Billy moved Dave off his lap on to Abbey's and rolled his window down.

"So, um, can we go now?"

Derek rolled his window partly down as well. "The damn thing won't move! I'm giving it gas but it's like the wheels are locked!"

Tony yelled across the other three in his cab, "Release the fuckin' emergency brake, you goddamn idiot!" The three men in Derek's truck began frantically looking around and Tony rolled his eyes. "The stick next to the driver! Left side!"

Derek stretched down and suddenly truck 8082 lurched forward, straight into the group of dead that had just reached them. Several creatures flew backward, but more were there to take their place. Fifty or so creatures were crowding the trucks, hammering on the sides. Billy rolled up his window, but Derek just tried to push his way through the crowd. One of the things grabbed the large chrome side mirror and pulled itself up, slapping its dead hand on Derek's partially open window. The man let out a short scream and rolled his window up, but not before the dead man got his fingers inside. Derek closed the window on the creature's hand, its four fingers on the inside of the truck. Although uncoordinated and slow, the creature possessed a sturdy tenacity and hung on to the window and the mirror as it tried to bite through the bullet-resistant glass.

Truck 8082 began to plod forward, with 8081 behind. "This is not how I pictured this in my head when we were planning it," fretted Billy. "We should be in front so I can get us back to the school."

The two armored vehicles moved up the ramp toward daylight with fists thumping on the sides. Several undead moved into the paths of the vehicles only to go down, crushed beneath the weighty tires.

Suddenly, the front truck slammed on the brakes, only to have it lurch forward again almost immediately. The truck did this a few times in rapid succession. Tony squinted at the back of 8082. "What the hell is he doin'?"

Billy pointed. "Betcha he's trying to shake his hitchhiker." The dead man was still clinging to the mirror of the first truck.

"Dave, call those dumbasses!" Tony pointed to a CB radio attached to the dash. Dave grabbed the mic and keyed it. "Hey, what are you guys doing up there? Hello?" He looked back at Tony helplessly.

The first truck sped out of the garage at approximately thirty miles per hour, headed toward the abandoned Hummer. Tony slowed down considerably and looked on, incredulous. "What…what is he doin'?"

Billy raised his eyebrows. "Ramming speed?"

The truck hit the military vehicle with the sound of rending metal. The Hummer spun off to the side, impacting the wall of the garage ramp with exploding glass. The American Securities vehicle lurched to the right and sideswiped the other side of the concrete ramp wall, but Derek must have regained control and they kept moving. Tony followed and as truck 8081 crested the ramp, a phantom hand clamped down on Tony's testicles. The street in front of them was wall to wall dead people, all heading toward the trucks.

Tony stopped, but Derek opted to drive through the mob. Abbey put a hand to her mouth. "They'll never make it."

"Neither will we if we sit here," Billy told them and pointed south. "Turn here and go that way."

Dave looked at Tony. "But what about—?"

Tony slammed his hands into the steering wheel. "Damn it, I don't know! Follow the friggin' plan is all he had to do!" The truck in front of them mowed down dozens of infected, but it was slowing by the moment, the sheer numbers of undead impeding the progress of the truck.

"They were scared is all," Abbey lamented softly.

Tony turned left and drove south. "So am I."

VANTEL PARKING LOT, MARSHFIELD, MASSACHUSETTS

Five shadowy figures slunk between forgotten vehicles under the starry New England sky, a sliver of shimmering moon the only illumination. Clouds moved across the moon, their voluminous masses confiscating what little light there was. On the near side of the parking lot, the SUVs and vans glinted with the intermittent light from that same moon shining off their bumpers and mirrors. One hundred or so meters away, the vehicles were charred and skeletal, the result of previous sustained firepower from an attack helicopter.

Dozens of different forms shuffled and stumbled in and out of the destroyed vehicles, their single-minded search driving them on.

"Jesus, there must be five hundred of them."

"Quiet, Wilcox," Seyfert admonished. "We see them." The SEAL rubbed his wounded leg and shook his head. He wanted to look at his map, but didn't relish the thought of turning his light on to do so. The moonlight was not enough to suffice.

Rick peered through the dusty window of a blue Honda Civic. He was none too keen to be so close to a horde of infected with no walls between them. He ducked back down and looked up at the smokestack. He shivered involuntarily. The dead still creeped him out.

Seyfert decided it was time to move and he whispered as much to his friends. He, Dallas, Rick, Anna, and Wilcox were making their escape to Cape Cod to find a plane they didn't know would be there or not. Hope was on full blast.

The group moved as silently as possible to the south, away from the horde of rot. When confronted with a seven-foot chain-link fence topped with razor wire, the SEAL produced a pair of cutters. The group fanned out behind him, covering his back while he went to work. The first snip of the fence sounded like a gunshot and all of the survivors cringed. Undeterred, Seyfert kept clipping, moving up with each cut.

A growl alerted them to an incoming roamer and Wilcox put it down with a stab to the creature's forehead. Two more came from around the far side of the smokestack and Wilcox and Dallas took them out quietly. A piercing scream rent the night, the thudding footsteps of a sprinting infected giving it away to the team. It came into view, but they were ready. Rick double-tapped the thing as it dashed toward them. He had used a suppressed M9, but the sound had been louder than they would have liked. Whether it was the noise of the weapon or the call of the Runner, the rest of the undead pack threaded among the ruined vehicles toward the living humans, drawn by the sound.

"Hurry up, Jersey, they're almost on us."

"Thank you for that," the SEAL told Dallas as he continued to cut. "That helps me. I need to make the hole extra big for your pasta-slurping ass anyway."

Anna smiled despite the imminent danger and nodded to Dallas. "You do like the spaghetti, Big Man."

Rick looked back over his shoulder. "Thirty seconds and we're dead."

"Done!" Seyfert pulled the fence off to one side and crawled through. "Come on!" he whispered loudly, holding the fence for the others. When Wilcox came through last, the Army kid and the SEAL produced a few wide cable ties and zipped the fence closed. The vanguard of the horde was still some distance off.

Dallas smirked. "Now, how long do ya think that'll hold—"

Seyfert rounded on him. "One second is enough! Anything to slow them down."

The team moved off as a group toward the woods.

The dead reached the fence and they began to shake it. Their cries and moans got louder as they saw their prey disappear into the trees.

Rick checked his watch. "The road is to the north, which is behind us, so we need to circle around. We need to go left."

Seyfert seemed to be looking in all directions at once. "Yeah, I'm working on it." He checked his own watch, the dials illuminating when he pushed a button on the housing. A hissing infected crashed through the brush on his left, hitting him. They both went down and Dallas gave the thing a kick in the head. The Texan kicked the creature again to finish it. The SEAL was up quickly with a nod of thanks and the group moved off left at a brisk pace, Seyfert brushing himself off.

Footsteps crunching on the corpses of dead leaves, rustling bushes, and moans all around the humans dissuaded any notions that the tackler had been the only infected in the forest. Things moved close to the group just out of sight on the right side.

The frightening sounds of undead in the vicinity spurred the living group on. The creatures began to materialize out of the darkness, searching for a meal. One such thing stumbled into the path in front of Anna and grabbed her. She gave a surprised shriek, but was able to get the long barrel of her suppressed M9 under the thing's chin and destroy it before it could bite her. The noises the infected made got exponentially louder with the shriek and the shot. Now the plague-ridden monsters understood in which direction their food was. Seyfert's pistol sounded, then Rick's. A nauseating crunch meant Dallas had dispatched an infected with his rebar.

"This shit is beginning to get thick," whispered Seyfert into his mic. "We need to pick up the pace." The SEAL began to move quickly, the others straining to keep up. He looked back to make sure they were close and tumbled down a small hill into a wet area. He stood and flicked his hands to get rid of whatever was on him. It was too dark to see what he had fallen into, but the trickle of a small creek meant it was just water. There were suddenly many splashes coming from relatively close by.

A half-dozen rotten dead crested a small hillock on the right and descended on the group. There were dozens following behind them and now two moved toward them from the front. Seyfert and Rick both fired at the same time, Rick missing his target. The thing stumbled on a root and Seyfert shot it in the back of the head. The group continued forward at close to a run, the infected on their heels. They broke through the trees in a moment of confusion.

Dallas was breathing hard when the team broke through the trees, climbed a small embankment, and spilled out onto the asphalt of a road. A huge mob crashed through the brush behind them.

"I'ma need...t' take...a breather soon," the Texan heaved.

Wilcox pointed back at the woods. "You stop to breathe and you'll stop breathing!" The first of the undead had broken through the tree line and were stalking toward the tired survivors. Across the street were more woods, the darkness between the trees both menacing and welcoming at the same time. A screech ripped through the night and the team knew they would have a sprinter to deal with shortly.

"Down the road half a mile then into the woods on the other side," Seyfert said as he pulled on the much larger man's arm. "Move, Hillbilly!"

They ran.

Scores of the dead followed. The piercing cries and wailing moans trailed after them as well. Infected began to pour from the woods on the right side of the road in front of them. Dallas stopped to fire into the crowd with his shotgun, but Wilcox grabbed him. "Are you nuts? Keep moving!" The kid pulled the significantly larger man forward by his shirt and got the big man moving again.

A jackknifed tractor-trailer sat abandoned across the small rural road, half a dozen cars rested forgotten with their doors open on the nearside. The band of friends wove between the vehicles, looking for a way around the truck without entering the woods just yet. Dallas put his hand on one of the smaller cars and leaned over a bit, gulping the cool air in giant drags, his weariness apparent. An emaciated hand darted out of the open window of the Hyundai Elantra he was resting against and latched onto the hip pocket of his BDU's. He backed up quickly, but the creature was still belted into the vehicle, preventing him from escape.

"Nope!" he grunted a bit loudly and brought his forearm down across the wrist of the dead thing. He pulled for a moment and the thing was dragged almost halfway out of the car window. He twisted and the dry, rotten arm came off at the elbow. The creature began its dry rasp as Dallas pried the desiccated fingers off him with disgust.

"You can have it back," he told it and flung the arm back in the window.

Seyfert rubbed his injured leg again. "Under the trailer and keep running!"

Rick put his hand on the SEAL's shoulder and advised calmly, "This isn't going to work. You're broken and he's almost done." Seyfert spun and looked at Dallas, the big guy sweating and breathing heavily.

"Thinkin' I shoulda stayed back in the basement." It started to rain and Dallas looked up. He blinked as the drops hit his face. "Are you...kiddin' me?"

The SEAL frantically searched for an egress. A Runner's howl came from in front of them someplace and two more answered from the woods behind them.

"Up! Up on the truck. They can't see us and they'll walk past!"

"What if they don't?" asked Anna.

"Then we're fucked! Get up!" They climbed the front of the huge vehicle and the skies opened up. Each of them hopped across the gap to the top of the trailer and got as flat as possible on their stomachs, except Wilcox, who chose to lie on his back.

The horrible noises the dead made preceded the arrival of the horde by mere moments. The team on the roof heard and felt thuds against the side of the tuck's body as dozens of infected bumped into the vehicle. Scratching sounds down the side of the aluminum made Anna's skin crawl and she silently shuddered. She looked left and saw Rick shuddering as well.

Rain continued to pelt the survivors during the exodus of the dead. Seyfert moved to the edge of the truck and peered over the side. Hundreds of the things plodded along the road, weaving in and out of the abandoned vehicles in the darkness. A flash of lightning showed the SEAL that the creatures were moving through of the woods as well. At least one of them was of the faster variety, dashing past its shambling cousins, pushing them out of the way in the search for something uninfected to eviscerate. The thing, or one like it, screamed in the distance, with several more screams echoing from other directions.

Anna looked at Wilcox. Through the darkness, she could barely see that the kid was on his back with his hands covering his ears. She decided to follow suit. She covered her own ears and the sounds the dead made were diminished. The rasps and moans were terrifying, especially now that she had no hardened concrete and steel walls around her. Stealth would be her only salvation. She tried to make herself as small as possible and think about something else.

It was still raining, albeit significantly less, when dawn peeked through the trees over the eastern horizon. Infected stragglers, intent on following their brothers in search of a meal, still meandered past the vehicle crash scene. Wilcox gave a substantial snore and Rick elbowed him in the ribs hard.

"Shut up, dumbass!" the former policeman whispered. Chastised, Wilcox nodded vigorously.

Anna wondered how the soldier was able to sleep through a passing horde of insatiable living dead, while it was raining, and he was on the roof of an abandoned eighteen-wheeler.

A lone figure stalked the center of the street moving away from them when Seyfert whispered it was time to go. The SEAL looked over one side of the truck while Rick and Wilcox checked the other.

"We need a boat," announced Rick. "A boat would keep most of the things off of us until we got to the Cape. Then we make landing and find the airfield."

Seyfert nodded and rubbed his leg. He sat up. "Not a bad idea. How far to the coast?"

"Maybe two miles? Three?" Rick shrugged. "But that's not the important question, is it?"

Wilcox stretched and glanced at Seyfert. "What's the important question?"

Anna gave the young soldier a smack on the back of his head. "Duh. Will there be a boat? Can we figure out how to start it and drive it? Will we get eaten on the way?" She thumbed at a rebuked Wilcox and gave an exaggerated eye-roll. "This kid."

"That was three questions," he said, rubbing his neck.

"Whatever we do, we might wanna do it now," Dallas drawled. He pointed back behind them. Two figures stumbled out of the trees and headed for the compound, following the track the survivors had just taken, in reverse. Another shuffled into view as well, trailing those in front of it.

Seyfert stood and the rest of the group got up as well. The SEAL climbed down between the front of the trailer and the cab, checking under and between things as he did so. When the group was all on the ground, they moved off at a brisk pace to the east.

It was easy to tell that a horde of infected had just been on the road. Bits of filthy cloth, a stained running shoe, and an eyeball were indicators, as were the muddy footprints which moved off into the woods. More cloth and nasty bits of the creatures themselves draped from the thorns and bushes where the throng of dead had entered the forest.

Seyfert made a quick gesture, pointing down the street to the east. The group moved forward through the morning.

HIGH ABOVE BROADWAY, SAN FRANCISCO

Masta G gripped the polycarbonate housing of a pair of Steiner Marine binoculars. The power of the binoculars was such that he could easily make out individuals in the throng of infected that had swarmed the armored truck. There had to be at least a few thousand creatures, all clamoring for a taste of what was in the vehicle. The road was thick with the undead. From the broken pastry shop windows to the west, to the office building across the street, there wasn't a square inch of real estate not covered with the moving mass of dead people. For a quarter-mile in both directions, the dead were all fighting each other to get to the tasty morsels which undoubtedly resided in the box in the center of the mass of them.

The truck had stopped in the worst possible place. Whether the driver stopped it, or the sheer mass of bodies, or the tires slipping on fluids, the truck was doomed. The driver tried several times to rock the vehicle back and forth, but it wouldn't budge. Masta G passed the binocs to Cyrus, who was standing next to him on the twelfth floor of a burned-out skyscraper. "They didn't make it. Look at the wheels; they're full of dead freaks."

Cyrus put the glasses to his eyes. "Indeed. It would seem those unfortunates in the truck didn't study physics, or they would have known that their vehicle couldn't possibly pass through so many bodies. It matters not, however, as we need to speak with those inside. Options?"

"Options? Our options are to get gone before that group of freaks figures out we're here. That truck may as well be on the moon."

"That is but a single option, David. It is imperative we speak with the surviving humans in that truck. They can lead us to William."

Cyrus continued looking at the mired vehicle, but Masta G had turned to look at the two thugs behind him keeping watch on the office corridor. One looked away quickly, but the other just shrugged. Masta G sighed and whispered to Cyrus, "Doc wants you to call me Masta G instead of David in front of the New Society."

Cyrus looked surprised as he lowered the binoculars and looked at his escort. "Of course, Masta G, my humble apologies. Do you have any ideas on how to get the people out of there?" He nodded toward the truck without removing his gaze from the gangster.

G stuck his hand out and Cyrus returned the binoculars to him. He gazed at the truck, the swarm and up the street in both directions then shook his head slowly. "No. Anyone going down there ain't coming back. Live bait would work, but the moment that swarm moves away, the truck will drive off and then we're back to square one. We need to incapacitate the truck before we lure the freaks away, or block the street somehow. Problem is, that's an *armored* truck. It's made specifically to repel thieves. We have a couple of rocket launchers, but they could kill the poor bastards inside, or worse, blow a hole in the truck and let the freaks in."

Masta G heard growling behind him and then a suppressed shot. He turned to look at the two guards and one of them nodded and held up one finger.

"It appears that we have some time to decide what to do, Masta G. That vehicle isn't going anywhere." Cyrus sat at a desk and moved a phone out of the way. He pulled a paper bag from his small pack and placed it on the table, removing two peanut butter and jelly sandwiches. He handed one to an incredulous Masta G, who accepted it. Cyrus stood and strode to the two guards, passing them the bag with two more sandwiches. The guards looked at each other for a moment, shrugged, and leaned their rifles against the door frame. Cyrus smiled as he walked back to the desk and sat down. Masta G just stared at him as he unfolded the wax paper to get at his sandwich. Cyrus was about to take a bite when he noticed the banger staring. "I make a mean PB&J, I assure you…"

Masta G rolled a wheeled office chair over and sat next to Cyrus, unfolding his own wax paper. "I still got nothin'."

He took a bite, as did Cyrus. "It will come to you, Dav…ah… Masta G. It always does." The men finished their sandwiches and each opened a bottle of water. G took a long pull and stood up, taking the binoculars. Cyrus smiled and wiped his mouth with a napkin.

The banger peered up and down the street, high and low. He was moving the binoculars back to the left when he jerked them up and seemed to focus on something. He smiled and turned to Cyrus. His smile got wider, his eyebrows raised, and he began to nod. "Done and done."

He motioned for Cyrus to join him at the window and pointed high above the city. Masta G handed over the glasses. "Up there, second building over, on the roof."

Cyrus focused on what G had pointed to. "Yes. Yes, that just might work."

THE WOODROW WILSON SCHOOL, SAN FRANCISCO

Truck 8081 pulled up in front of the Woodrow Wilson School. A lone infected woman came toward them walking down the center of the street. A discussion between the living people egged on the dead one and she sped up when she saw them exit the vehicle.

"We can't just leave them there!"

"I know, Abbey, but what do you want me to do? Do you wanna walk into that swarm and knock on the door?"

"We'll figure something out," Dave coaxed and grabbed Tony's bat. He strode up to the approaching zombie and caved her skull in with two whacks.

"Dave, you gotta stay with me! Don't go—"

"I'm tired of being a kid. Being a kid is going to get me killed. Or you, or her." He pointed to Abbey. "I can kill them just as good as you can." He wiped the bat with a rag which he discarded on the street and tossed the bat to Tony, who deftly caught it with one hand.

Billy was smiling and looking at Dave. "Let's not dilly-dally. They'll be here in a few minutes and I want them gone before we leave in the morning."

The foursome made their way to the culvert and into the building. Richie was on guard duty again and he admitted them, turning the key the right way the first time, "Are we goin' to Alc-traz today?"

"Tomorrow, kiddo, as long as there aren't any dead people near the truck."

"Where's the other guys?" Richie looked at his feet. "*They* got them, huh." It wasn't a question.

Abbey looked at the small boy. "Not yet, but they're trapped in a truck, and we need to go back for them."

"Billy'll get 'em! He saves everybody."

They reached the floor where the rest of the kids were and sat down. A little girl was making place settings on a teacher's desk for everybody to eat. Abbey was amazed at the resilience of the kids, who had undoubtedly endured horrors no child ever should. She looked at Dave and thought he looked much older than fourteen. She shifted her gaze toward their host. "So how do we get our friends, Billy?"

"You got me. I have no idea. I guess I could go down there with my machete and go head hunting," he winked at one of the kids and the kid smiled, "but there were thousands of deads down there. It would take a week and my swinging arm would get tired. I'm up for ideas."

"Is there any way we could kill them all at once?"

"I can't come up with anything. Dave, you got any ideas?"

Dave thanked the little girl for the bottle of water she handed him. "Yup. What about a garbage truck?"

"You been talking to Dallas? What *about* a garbage truck?"

"Well, if we could get the armored trucks, why couldn't we get a couple of garbage trucks? We weld mesh or something over the windows then drive right into the deaders. Use the garbage scoop to lift them up and drop them into the back of the truck. Then squish them with the compactor-thingie. When the truck is full, just spit them out the back."

Billy had his feet up on a desk, leaning back with his hands clasped behind his head. He was wearing a huge smile. He looked at Tony. "I love this kid. Great idea, but I don't know where any garbage trucks are…well, that isn't exactly true, I know where there's one."

Abbey thought for a moment. "There's a bunch of garbage trucks at the transfer station down by the docks."

"Do they have welding equipment and metal bars and power, too?" demanded Tony. "We just don't have the time for this type of operation. Not to mention that by now there's another couple thousand cannibals trying to get at the guys in the truck. The noise the deaders are making would attract more deaders. Place is prolly full to burstin' by now with pus sacks."

"So how do we get them?"

Tony looked at his shoes. "Bait."

***

Tony, Billy, Abbey, and Dave were on the ninth floor of the Sessions building downtown. They stared down at the large white 8082 painted on the top of an armored truck in the center of a sea of living dead three blocks away. Tony passed a pair of binoculars to Billy, who scanned the area. The dead stretched for about a quarter-mile in either direction, pressed up against the store fronts, packed in like sardines. More were coming from the east and west, their slow stagger indicative of what they truly were.

Tony swallowed. "Never seen a swarm that big before."

"Me neither," agreed Billy nodding, "and I get around."

Tony looked at him. "Look, I know you ain't playin' with a full deck, but are you sure about this? I don't think you're comin' back from that." He pointed at the street.

"They haven't bitten me yet."

"Yeah, but what if one of them accidentally scratches you, or they have something sharp on them and you get cut? There's a million ways they could infect you. Actually, with you using your machete, it's a miracle you haven't been infected already. Spray, I mean."

"Yeah. Ew. Well, I haven't yet. And I seem to remember somebody, I think it was you when we were in the sewers, who said that I wouldn't be coming back." Billy looked at them and scowled. "I'll be back," he threatened, using his best Arnold Schwarzenegger impression.

Nobody smiled.

"Tough week. Nobody going to try to talk me out of this, huh?"

"Damn whack job, I just tried! Don't you think that...?" Tony stopped talking as a relatively loud diesel engine noise could be heard over the din of the moans and wails of the dead.

Billy raised the binoculars again. "Um...you guys are seeing this right?"

"Yes."

"Dave, you see a flat thing coming from the sky, right?"

"Yes."

"Good man. Thought it might just be me."

The flat thing moved slowly toward the truck. It impacted the top right corner and spun away a little. It raised in the air, moved slightly, and came back down to rest on top of the vehicle. A few seconds later, the cable holding the flat thing sprang taut and the truck began to rise very slowly. The undead howls seemed to grow in intensity as their canned food moved out of reach. Several infected hung on, not wanting to be denied their meal. The truck rose higher and higher into the sky, the dead on the ground reaching for it as it climbed. Two of the mobile corpses let go and impacted their brethren below with crippling thuds. The others continued to hang on.

Billy peered up above the giant magnet to the roof of the building down the street. "Huh. Big crane. Who would have thought?"

"Can I see?" Abbey tapped Billy on the shoulder and he passed her the binoculars. "Oh."

"What is it?" demanded Tony harshly. "What do you see through those?"

"I see a guy looking back at me through another pair of these." She lowered the glasses and looked at Tony. "His are bigger."

Billy snatched the binocs back, once again looking at the roof. "Where? I don't... Oh. Oh, this might not be so good."

"Why? What is it?"

"Cyrus."

Dave moved forward and asked for the glasses. "Who's Cyrus?" he asked as he put the glasses to his eyes.

57

"Cyrus is a sociopath. Actually, *I'm* a sociopath, my doctor said *he* is a psychopath. I guess there's a difference. Anyway, he's really, *really* smart. And he likes to kill people. Seems he's working with the perfect group too, because the guy standing with him is part of the New Society and they kill lots of people. He's been chasing me for weeks."

"Why is he chasing you?" demanded Tony and Dave at the same time.

Abbey looked at Billy a little differently. "And what doctor are you talking about?"

Billy looked at them sternly. "We need to get the kids out of the city now. Right now."

"Billy," began Abbey, "we need to get our friends back. I'm sure if we just talked to those guys, they would be willing to bargain or something. Like a ransom."

"Your friends are dead. They just don't know it yet and I guess you don't either. Those people are going to kill them, or torture and kill them. You can't help them." Billy pointed down the street and shook his head. "That's *Cyrus*."

"But why would he...?"

"Because that's what he does!" Billy had shouted, ruining their noise discipline, and he looked embarrassed. "Now we really need to go, we can talk on the way."

Dave began packing up, but Tony and Abbey were resolute. Tony folded his arms. "Billy, we have to try to reason with them to get our friends back."

"Knock your socks off. Go wade through that," he pointed at the swarm, "to get to him," he pointed at Cyrus, "and reason your butt off. All you'll have is no socks, no butt, and no friends. Dave, you with me?"

Dave had his backpack already shouldered. "Yup."

Tony was incredulous. "Dave..."

"They were my friends, too," the boy began, "but I also know those gang bangers. I don't know this Cyrus guy, but if he's with the gang, Steve, Derek, and Tony are gone." Dave looked at his shoes. "They knew the risks just like we did when we came out here. If I could save them, I would. The gang will make them tell where Billy's hideout is and then the kids will get caught up in whatever stuff is going on. Maybe Tony can ninja his way out." He looked at Billy. "I'm ready." He stuck his hand out to Tony. "The keys to the truck."

Tony looked at Abbey and back at Dave then he sighed. "I'll drive."

HIGH ABOVE BROADWAY, SAN FRANCISCO

The tires of truck 8082 came to rest on the newly constructed roof of what had been intended to be an office building in downtown San Francisco. The wheels of the vehicle groaned in protest as the short flight they had taken had somehow relieved them of their duties, if only for a moment, and now they were back at work.

Steve looked at Derek and Tony. "Did that just happen?"

Derek blinked hard. "Jesus! I think I shit myself. Let's get out of here before..." Derek had placed his hand on the passenger door handle, but Tony yelled at him, "Don't touch that fucking door!" Derek ripped his hand away from the door as if it had burned his fingers, staring at Tony.

"Why?"

"Because we don't know who brought us up here."

"Who gives a fuck? It's better than where we were!"

A single shot rang out and the men in the truck cringed. A moment later, a young man stepped up on the side-step of the truck and knocked on the window. "Hey, don't worry, we just shot a hitchhiker you brought up with you. Open up and we'll get you out of here to someplace safe."

Derek reached for the handle again. "I will cut your fucking hand off," Tony growled. The handle again appeared to be a thousand degrees as Derek yanked his hand away. He rolled the bulletproof window down slightly. "Who are you?"

The man looked incredulous. "I'm the guy who just saved your ass. Come on, we don't have much time."

"My friend in here doesn't trust new people," Derek told him. "We might want to have you back up a little before we get out."

"Seriously? I just brought you out of Hell with a giant fuckin' magnet and you're cryin' about it?" The man shrugged. "Sure, okay, I'll back up." He stepped off the truck and slung his carbine, putting his hands up in placation.

"Good enough for me," Derek said and opened the passenger side door. He stepped out, brandishing his rifle, and Tony slammed the door closed behind him. Tony shook his head. "Idiot."

Several other men, all armed, walked up to Derek and began clapping him on the shoulder and shaking his hand. "C'mon, man, we really gotta go!" one man shouted at Tony through the glass.

"Steve, start the truck."

Steve did and the men, including Derek, backed up slightly. They stood there for thirty seconds in a standoff before one of the men spoke,

"Alright, fuck this." He put his shotgun up to Derek's head and another man removed his weapons. Derek raised his hands.

"You got ten seconds to get your asses out of the truck or I fuck up the paint job with your buddy's brains."

Inside the truck, Steve swallowed hard. "Tony, they're gonna—"

"Yeah, Steve. Dumbass should've stayed in here with us."

The man with the shotgun counted down from ten. When he reached one, he put the weapon to his shoulder and yelled, but didn't pull the trigger. Frustrated, he passed his gun to one of the other men and pulled a knife. "Fine, assholes. Hold him." The others held Derek and the man grabbed his hand. He put his knife to Derek's pinky finger and shaved off most of the flesh on the inside of it. To Derek's credit, he didn't scream; he just ground his teeth and shut his eyes. The man then drew the knife across Derek's forearm. Blood welled up and began to drop to the roof in crimson splashes.

"I can do this all day, motherfuckers!" He jabbed the point of the blade into Derek's right thigh.

Derek went absolutely ape-shit and broke free of his attackers. He punched one and grabbed another, biting the man in the face. He spit out a large chunk of cheek and the man dropped his weapon and began screaming. "Holy shit, how did he turn? We didn't kill him yet!" The men began to back away with their rifles aimed at Derek.

Derek pulled a small pistol hidden in his waistband, aiming it at the men. "I didn't turn, you sick fucks, I just..." A shot rang out and Derek spun around, dropping to the ground, clutching his shoulder. Two more men, one an obvious gangbanger, the other a shorter man with glasses, strode forward from behind the crane. The gangbanger had shot Derek and he kicked the pistol away from him. The banger looked at his gang. "Fuckin' morons. How many times I gotta tell you? Pat them the fuck down!" He walked back to the gang and spoke to one of the men who climbed the crane. A moment later, the truck's wheels groaned again as they left the roof. The truck spun out into space, twenty-two stories in the air above a swarm of several thousand hungry undead. The armored vehicle spun such that the windshield faced the building.

"Last chance, motherfuckers," said the tough guy who had shot Derek.

Steve frantically put his hand on the windshield and started to scream.

Tony flipped the man off and the man shook his head. He glanced at the crane operator and drew his finger across his throat. The man in the crane pushed a lever forward and the electro-magnet shut off.

The truck plummeted approximately two hundred and forty feet, back into the unwavering arms of the swarm. Masta G watched as 8082 popped like a grape underfoot upon impact. Infected under the truck were put out of their misery. The creatures that were on the outside edge of the newly formed crater in the street were thrown back as far as was possible into the thick crowd. They got back up quickly and fought for position at the truck. Masta G turned around when he saw the corpses crawling into the destroyed vehicle. He rolled his eyes and looked at his troops. "Didja pat him down?"

The men looked sideways at each other. Masta G sighed. "Next time, I'ma shoot a bitch. Motherfuckers is too poor to pay attention." He strode toward Derek. "You got any guns or knives on you? It will go better for you if you tell me the truth."

Derek sat up clutching his shoulder. "No. These dickweeds took my bat and you have my guns."

G got on his haunches and looked at his captive eye to eye. "You have no idea what I gotta deal with, bro. Just answer some questions and we'll let you live."

Derek laughed at him. "Cut the shit, pal. We both know what happens. I'll tell you what you want to know then you'll man up and shoot me in the head."

"I wish I had some guys like you, I really do. You got stones. Dumb as shit for getting out of the truck, but you got big ones."

"Yeah, well, I'm alive, they ain't."

Masta G nodded in affirmation then pointed the gun at Derek's groin. "Where's Billy?"

FELL STREET, SAN FRANCISCO

Armored truck 8081 was a mile away from the Woodrow Wilson School, traveling slowly. Sporadic infected lurched toward the truck as it drove by, but none came from houses or alleys. It seemed their attention was elsewhere.

Abbey stared at Billy for a moment. He had his hand out the open bulletproof window, his palm flat, and riding the air currents of the moving vehicle.

"So...what did you mean by *your doctor said you were a sociopath*?"

"Wow, really? I guess you didn't know that I'm certifiable." Billy scrunched his face up in thought. "I don't really know what that means, but I was in the booby hatch for six years, so you can imagine the things they said to me."

Abbey looked at him funny. "Booby hatch?"

Billy stopped riding the currents and turned toward Abbey. "Yeah, booby hatch. You know, loony-bin? Nut house? Whack shack?"

She stared at him blankly.

"Wow. Okay, funny farm, rubber room, cuckoo's nest?"

Abbey blinked. "You mean an insane asylum?"

Incredulous, Billy shook his head slowly. "Isn't that what I just said?"

Dave got into the conversation. "You mean you were locked up?"

Billy nodded. "Yeah. They had the best cherries jubilee at Morningside."

Tony kept his eyes on the road, but had to join the conversation too. "You were at *Morningside*?"

"What are you, a gaggle of parrots or something? Yeah. Morningside. I lived there for almost six years."

"Why were you there?" demanded Abbey.

"And they called me crazy... I. Lived. There."

"But why did they make you live there?"

"Didn't Rick or that other cop tell you guys?"

Tony cut in, "Abbey, Morningside is a sanitarium for the criminally insane."

Billy put a finger on his nose. "Waarrrp! You got it! Give that man a cigar! That's me, criminally insane. Except for the whole criminal part. I didn't do it."

"Do what?"

"What they stuck me in there for."

"Which was..."

Billy looked at the three of them, one at a time. "Rick really didn't tell you? Huh. Thought the other cop would have blabbed for sure. He knew me; I saw it the second he looked at me." Billy sighed. "I was wrongly incarcerated for killing a dentist. But I didn't do it," he added hastily, "I mean, I was going to do it, but someone beat me to it. Besides, I would have been quick and clean, whoever got there first was…messy."

"Wait. Wait a minute," demanded Tony. "The dentist in Presidio Heights, about five years ago?"

"Six!"

"Jesus, that was you?"

"Does nobody ever listen? No, it was *not* me. It was someone else. They chopped him up into little pieces, but they knew how to do it so he would live through most of it. Like I said, it was messy."

They pulled up in front of the school and filed out of the truck toward the Cadillac in the ditch. When they were in the basement, Tony put a hand on Billy's shoulder and turned him around. "Billy, what exactly happened between you and the dentist?"

"He was a nasty pedophile. He hurt kids, but no one could prove it. The cops wouldn't even listen to her. She told me what he did and I went to the cops, but they said he couldn't have done such terrible things and told me to leave. Two days later, she went missing."

"Who? Who went missing?"

"My sister." Billy folded his arms and sighed. "He took her. He took her after she told me what he did to her. I went to his house to get her back and when I got inside, he was upstairs all dead and stuff. Her bracelet was on his zillion dollar nightstand, so I took it. The cops caught me leaving his driveway because I set off an alarm when I broke in. Now what do you think they believed, that I didn't do it, or that I not only shaved this guy's parts off, but I disappeared my sister, too? Yeah, I had her bracelet and she was gone, so I got stuck with that bit of fun, as well."

Dave looked mad. "But you didn't kill the guy?"

"I didn't."

"And they locked you up anyway."

"Yeah, but only for six years. I got out when the end of the world happened. It was a prisoner transfer and I escaped when the transferrers got eaten. Now that you're all caught up, let's get the kids. We're leaving now."

Billy and Dave walked up the cement stairs and Billy knocked and recited the secret password. Richie let them in, Tony and Abbey hanging back a little.

"I knew that guy was crazy as a shit-house rat."

"Yeah, Tony, but he's saved so many people. Especially the kids. I honestly believe he would die for them."

"Me too. I also believe he would kill for them."

63

"Is that such a bad thing?"

Tony harrumphed. "Depends on who he's killing, I guess."

The group reached the classroom the kids were in. True to form, they all ran to Billy and hugged him. "Okay, guys, listen up: we're getting the duck out of Fodge. I dunno what that means other than that we are leaving. We're finally going to Alcatraz, where there are soldiers and teachers and other kids to play with. You'll be safe there. Who's in?"

Every child immediately put their hand up.

"Good. Richie, you get the duffel bags. Dennis, you and Jenny start packing all the food into the three big green duffels that Richie brings. Everybody else, get all the favorite toys and put them in the toy sack. We're leaving in fifteen minutes." The kids all ran off smiling.

***

Dave, Tony, and Billy each had a huge, olive drab army-surplus duffel bag filled to the brim with food and drinks over their shoulder. Abbey had the toy sack and each kid carried a stuffed animal. Billy opened the basement door and all the kids, except Richie, got apprehensive. "There's nothing to be afraid of yet," Billy told them. "If we see any of the bad people, you can be afraid, but nobody yells, right?" They all nodded. "Everybody hold hands and don't let go. We have to go back through the tunnel and into a truck that's parked on the road."

Dennis looked into the basement. "I don't like the tunnel." A few of the kids nodded in agreement.

Whether they liked the tunnel or not, they all followed Billy and Dave through the basement, with Abbey and Tony in the rear. Billy cracked nine green chem-lights and hung one on each kid's neck with the enclosed lanyard. He gave one to Tony and kept one for himself. "That's all I got, sorry," he told Dave.

They moved as a group through the dark tunnel toward the Cadillac. No sounds were made as the survivors climbed through the SUV and emerged into the warm, starry evening. Richie pulled on Billy's pants and pointed toward the other side of the culvert. A lone creature was standing approximately twenty meters away, with its back to the group. Dave started toward it, hefting his bat, but Billy put a hand on his arm and stopped him. Tony emerged from the Escalade last and they all climbed up the culvert hill and onto the street, making their way quickly to the armored truck.

The back doors squeaked loudly when Billy opened them. He and the other adults placed the duffels and toy sack into the back and then helped the kids in as well. The infected man from the culvert was staggering across the road toward them moaning and Dave looked at Billy with his eyes raised in question. "Knock your socks off, Dave…uh, or better yet, his head off." Dave strode to the creature, who immediately picked up its pace and growled. The teenager let go with a terrific swing and the bat impacted the creature's cranium with a crunch. It fell forward and Dave had to sidestep or it would have hit him on the way down. Dave turned to walk back, but the thing grabbed his pant leg. Dave fell forward, scraping his hands on the street. The monster wasted no time and pulled the struggling boy to its rotten maw.

Dave kicked frantically, but the infected man was twice his size and pulled him ever closer. It bit down on the youth's boot. Fear got the better of him and he started yelling. Billy and Abbey were already on their way, but the zombie had decided that boot leather wasn't very appealing and it began to crawl up the pinned kid for a choicer morsel. Dave fought desperately as the thing got on top of him and he just barely held the creature's face away from his with both hands, when it latched onto his shirt and began to pull again. It snapped at him and bit through its tongue, the black flap of flesh hitting the teen in the cheek as it fell to the ground.

A shot rang out and the creature went limp, falling on the hapless kid. Dave was still fighting the re-killed zombie when Billy reached them and pulled the dead thing off him. Dave got up quickly and started to cry a little, but stopped immediately. He wiped his eyes and face as Billy looked him over.

"You're alright! C'mon, that shot will draw them all to us!"

As if on cue, moans and cries broke the silence of the night and the things came from everywhere. The three men reached the truck and Billy and Dave jumped in the back. Tony hopped behind the wheel and Abbey climbed into the passenger side as Billy shut and locked the back doors. Abbey looked out the windows while Tony started the vehicle. "Jesus, where did they all come from?"

"They must have followed the sound of the truck but couldn't figure out where the noise was coming from when we stopped."

The vehicle lurched forward, but not before headlights came around the corner behind them. A cargo van and a tow truck sped after truck 8081, gunfire erupting from the van. Bullets plinked harmlessly against the side of the armored vehicle, but it was loud inside and some of the kids began to cry. "Don't worry, guys, nobody can get us in here! Look," Billy reached into a bag and pulled out two handfuls of twenty dollar bills, "we're rich!" He threw the money in the air and many little hands reached for it as it floated down.

In the cab, Tony pointed to undead who lurched into their path as they drove. The vehicle's headlights cut twin beams of illumination in front of them, the light marred by grotesque figures coming from all directions. The first thump gave Abbey the willies, but the feeling went away quickly as the thumps increased in occurrence. More plinks from the back caused Tony to smile.

"What the hell could possibly be funny?" demanded Abbey.

"We're in an armored car. Unless they got a rocket launcher, they can shoot all day and all they'll do is waste ammo."

"Yeah, but they also bring more of *them* with every shot!" She pointed at the growing crowd of dead beginning to fill the street in front of them. A small group lurched straight at 8081 from the middle of the road and Tony ran them down, their broken bodies flying away or going under the wheels. The dead that weren't run down made feeble attempts to grab the truck. Infected began to get thick as they came from seemingly everywhere and nowhere at the same time.

Just as there was a break in the ever massing dead, 8081's headlights illuminated two SFPD Crown Victoria police cruisers nose to nose across the street a scant hundred feet away. The cars had probably been there since the onset of the plague in San Francisco, as the tires were flat and the windows were broken out. Dozens of partial skeletons decorated the road and Tony was indiscriminate as to which ones he ran over. A large caliber bullet shattered the driver's side mirror, prompting him to stomp on the accelerator. "Tell them to hang on to something!"

Abbey slid a small partition aside and shouted to Billy, Dave, and the kids, telling them what was about to happen. Tony locked his elbows and prepared for impact, yelling nothing. Abbey grasped the Jesus Christ handle in a death grip immediately prior to the crash. With a rending of sheet metal, the truck slammed into the front fenders of both police cars, spinning the noses forward. Armored vehicle 8081 suffered little damage, but the fronts of the police cars exploded into dozens of pieces of broken metal and plastic, littering the road behind them. The tow truck didn't escape the shrapnel and the right front tire of the vehicle exploded, sending it careening into a parked stretch limousine. Three men vacated the tow truck quickly and were picked up by the van behind them.

Tony stopped the truck for a moment to look in his broken rear view mirror. "What the hell are you doing?" shouted Abbey. "Let's go!"

"I told you, unless they have a rocket launcher or a big friggin magnet, we're okay." Tony looked into the sky to check for flying electromagnets; Abbey did the same. "Looks like we're gonna be fine, kiddo. It will take them a few minutes to clear the debris and we'll be gone by then."

A loud WHOOOOSSSHH moved past them quickly and a car in front and to the left exploded, rocking 8081 on its axles. Abbey switched her gaze over to gape at Tony, who floored the accelerator. "What the hell was that now?"

"A fuckin' rocket launcher!"

The armored vehicle sped away toward the docks. Another rocket screamed past them slamming into a store front. The building's façade collapsed, spilling a modest chunk of the structure directly in front of the truck and Tony had no time to avoid it. He hit the concrete and steel, moving at twenty miles per hour, the truck climbing up on the debris. Tony shook his head and tried to drive away, but the vehicle was stuck. "Shit, get 'em out! This ride's over!"

Tony and Abbey fled the truck, running around to the back. They pounded on the doors and shouted for Billy and Dave to get the kids and get out. The doors flew open, Billy and Dave handing kids and bags to Abbey and Tony. Headlights two hundred feet behind them were approaching slowly.

"They're coming," Abbey pointed. "We should move through the buildings and use them as cover!"

"Bad plan, Abbey," Billy said, "unless you want to be a smorgasbord for the dead folks who are in there. Rules have changed. The safest place is usually the middle of the road, not crouched stealthily next to a door or dumpster. No grabsies. If we get surrounded, *then* we get inside."

Tony took quick stock of his surroundings. "We're two blocks from the boat! We can make it if we go now!" A dead man lurched into his path and he dispatched it with a single-handed swing of his aluminum bat. He wrung out his left hand afterward.

Billy pointed. "Keep the kids between us and we run! Stick to the center of the street and let me deal with anything that gets in our way."

Brakes squealed behind them as the van came to a halt. The sound of the side door sliding open let the group of survivors know that the bad guys couldn't be far behind. They moved away quickly, their pursuers as relentless as the dead.

Tony and Billy destroyed several creatures before they simultaneously realized there was no way to elude both the dead and the gangsters chasing them. Billy came to a stop and the kids were grateful as they were all panting heavily. Some dead were on the way, but this section of the city was devoid of swarms for some reason. Abbey picked up a small girl. "We can't outrun them."

"No, we can't." Billy pulled his shotgun and walked to the back of the group. "Tony, you know where the boat is, right?"

"Yeah, it's right down there," he pointed down toward the piers, "a couple hundred yards is all."

"Get the kids and get back. I'll slow them down."

"Billy," Richie asked, his eyes beginning to well up, "what?"

Billy got down on one knee. "Richie, I need you to help get everybody on the boat. Everybody needs you now. You help, okay?"

Richie nodded, clearly crying. "Everybody listen," Billy said, standing. "You all have to go with Richie and Dave and get on the boat." Gunshots came from around the corner, the New Society engaging some stray zombies. All the kids were crying now and the little girl Abbey was holding buried her face in Abbey's neck.

"I'll come visit you guys, I promise!"

Billy ran back the way they had come. Dave started after him but Richie grabbed his arm. "No. Billy said t'get ever'body to the boat." He had stopped crying and wiped his nose on his T-shirt sleeve. He started walking in the wrong direction and that got everybody moving. Tony grabbed him and they moved northeast.

Billy stood in the shadows of the broken door to Vera's Pizza and Sandwiches. Six thugs were hurriedly arguing over which way their prey had gone and although he couldn't hear them, Billy saw one of them point in the right direction. He knew that the shotgun might get a few, but not before they got him, so he slung it. Noise in the pizza shop behind him made him turn around and he was face to face with a dead man in a UPS uniform. Billy nodded to it while stepping aside and it strode into the street after the miscreants, dismissing him completely. The dead were getting thicker and the reprobates were getting scared as they came toward the shop from the left, directly to the rear of Tony and the kids. One of the men shot the UPS creature and it crumpled. Billy shook his head and waited.

"Musta gone this way," one of the men said in a harsh whisper. Billy thought the whisper was ridiculous after the gunfire and smiled to himself, pulling a round object from his vest. When the last man, who was perilously close to the smashed-in door and windows, slunk past, Billy waited five seconds and stepped out into the street.

He yanked on the pin and tossed the M67 fragmentation grenade as close to the center of the slinking pack of men as he could. The throw was almost fifty feet and Billy swelled with pride. Not knowing how large the explosion would be, he high-tailed it back into the pizza parlor and dove behind the counter. The men reacted to the sound of the impact of the metal ball on the street, but had no idea what to expect.

Billy was amazed at how loud the explosion was. It shook the walls of the building he was in and dust rained from the dropped ceiling. Every piece of glass in the vicinity shattered from the overpressure.

When the 6.5 ounces of composition B exploded, dozens of steel fragments shot out at almost twelve hundred feet per second. Some of the men were killed instantly, but others were just thrown aside, soon to realize they were missing important bits of themselves.

Then the screaming began and Billy stood and peeked out the door. "Ewww. Several birds with that stone."

Forms staggered and lurched in the direction of the screaming men. Billy didn't wait around for what would happen next. He wanted to see how many men had actually been killed by the grenade but with all the parts and goo, he couldn't really tell.

He moved through the back of the store and out into an alley. He followed the alley and came out into a street on the other corner of the block, where he slipped into a small diner to rest a minute.

He sat down at a small table inside the diner and leaned back, letting out a long breath.

The unmistakable sound of a striking match and the subsequent flare of light two booths over made him reach for the machete he had just put down.

"Uh-uh. Now ain't that just like a crazy man? Brings a knife to a gun fight," said someone Billy didn't know. The man had a military rifle. The rifle was pointing at Billy. Another man was sitting in the booth and two more were standing, both with weapons ready. Billy hadn't seen any of them when he had entered the store.

"That's him, right, G? We got him?"

The man smoking a cigarette looked across to the other, seated man. The bespectacled man leaned forward slightly. "Hello, William."

Billy sighed and slumped in his chair. "Hi, Cyrus." He looked at the ceiling. "I knew I should have taken that left turn at Albuquerque."

***

The motor on the small boat reverberated loudly across San Francisco Bay as Tony piloted the overloaded craft toward sanctuary. The entire time he was getting the kids in the boat, he expected to feel a bullet enter his back, but it never came. Billy must have done his job and stopped or delayed the bastards long enough for Tony's group and the kids to make their escape.

Dave and Richie were talking, but other than some sniffles and quiet crying from the other kids, nobody else said anything.

"He'll come, right? He promised."

Dave ruffled Richie's hair as he had seen Billy do. "He will. Have you ever known Billy to lie?"

Richie smiled a little. "No. Hear that, guys?" he asked the other kids. "Billy will come visit."

Dennis looked up from his sniffles. "But what if them bad guys get him?"

Richie's smile evaporated, but Dave was quick. "Then we'll go get him just like we got you guys."

"And we can all live on Alc-traz?"

"Yup."

"Can we get a dog?" asked Dennis.

Every kid looked up at that and Dave had no idea how to respond. Abbey saved him. "Well, we don't have a dog yet, but we have a cat!"

"A hero-cat," Tony added quickly.

"What's a hero cat?"

Tony looked at the mix of well-armed military and police waiting to greet them on the south dock and sighed with relief. "You'll have to get that story from Sam. She's one of the kids on the island. Pickles, the hero-cat, came in with her."

As the boat pulled up to the dock, Tony glanced behind him towards the corpse of San Francisco. He hoped Billy made it. He didn't want to go looking for him in that damn dead city.

UNKNOWN ROAD, MASSACHUSETTS

Rick and his group moved cautiously down the side of a misty New England road. The asphalt cut through the trees with no end in sight, not that the survivors could see anything. The rain had given way to a dense fog, the soupy air trapped by the woods. On both sides of them, the thick forest was barely evident, the outermost branches of needles the only discernable features of the pines. Visibility was nil.

They had been skulking after the horde which had passed them by a few hours prior. The thought process was that the horde would move in one direction unless stimulus drove it in another. The throng of infected traveled in the same track the living needed to go. Wilcox was on point and he held up a hand for the group to stop, but no one could see him through the fog until they were on him. The kid pointed out something through the thick opaque air. It was unmoving and about four feet tall. The soldier looked back at Seyfert who nodded in the affirmative. Wilcox snuck up behind the thing as the group moved forward in unison, weapons aimed in every direction.

Wilcox brought his M4 up to smash the skull of the thing in front of him. He stopped and harrumphed quietly. The thing was a mailbox on a post.

Seyfert shook his head. "We need to tighten up our formation," he whispered. "We stay within five feet of Wilcox."

"Wait," whispered Anna. "Doesn't that mean there's a house up there?" She pointed to the mailbox and a break in the road which could only be a driveway.

"Yeah, it does," Rick nodded, agreeing. "They might have some stuff too and I'm not too keen about walking through this damn fog."

Seyfert sighed. "I don't like it either. Hillbilly, what do you say to a sit-down?"

Dallas, normally a talker, said only two words, "I'm in."

Shifting their direction, the group followed the lane off the main road. The sun had climbed higher, but still wasn't strong enough to burn off the fog. They were mostly blind as they slunk toward the far end of the driveway.

Without warning, an ornate, fifteen-foot wrought-iron gate loomed in front of them. An equally high brick wall topped with a white ledge disappeared into the murk in both directions. The gate was closed, but no chain kept it locked. Wilcox pushed on it, but it wouldn't budge.

"Up and over?" the kid asked Seyfert.

"Unless you want to dig a tunnel."

Wilcox put his pack on the ground in front of him. He pulled out an entrenching tool and glanced at Seyfert, the kid's eyebrows pumping up and down a few times.

"Yeah, I was kidding," Seyfert told him.

Wilcox reached into his pack again and pulled out a length of black, knotted nylon cord. He attached the line to the folding shovel, threw the shovel over the gate, and hooked it to one of the metal pieces on the first try. The soldier climbed up the rope and made it look easy. He dropped to the other side, brushed his hands together, and smirked.

"Whenever you old-timers are ready, I can—"

Seyfert pointed behind Wilcox and whisper-yelled, "Your six!"

Wilcox spun around to face several dead which materialized out of the fog quickly. He evaded the first groping claws, bringing his M4 to bear. Before he could fire, the dead swarmed him and he went down. To his credit, the kid didn't panic. He kicked and fought, the dead trying to get bites in whenever they could and he evading them by twisting or punching. He heard suppressed shots from the other side of the gate and noticed more of the things were coming from the mist.

His struggles were mostly silent but he could hear Anna yelling, "I can't get a shot! I can't get a shot!"

Pain exploded in his shoulder and he knew that he was doomed. He would be damned if he would let the things tear him to pieces though, so he continued to fight. He rolled left, out from under three of the things as they reached for him. One got a firm grip on his pant leg and he kicked for all he was worth, breaking the facial bones of the young boy who had latched onto him. Wilcox slithered across the driveway, leaving a bit of his forearm behind. Seyfert and Rick dropped the last few and Wilcox stood, holding his shoulder. He glanced at the bodies around him, then at the group on the other side of the gate. He pulled his left hand from his right shoulder. He hissed in pain and his hand came away bloody.

"Might as well just go," he sighed, hanging his head. "Think I'll stay here for a while."

Anna was incredulous. "Horse-shit! Let me see it!"

Wilcox trudged to the gate and stuck his shoulder through the bars. Anna ripped his T-shirt and looked at the wound. It was her turn to sigh.

"I'm sorry, kid." She reached through the bars with her hand and caressed his face. He looked at her and smiled then she gave him a delicate slap on the forehead. "Idiot. Nothing bit you, you were shot. Grazed, more like."

His head shot up and stared at her, then struggled to look at his wound.

"Holy shit! Holy shit, I'm not gonna die!"

"You will if you don't keep yer voice down," Dallas whispered harshly.

Wilcox brought his head up slowly, narrowing his eyes. "So I'm being attacked by the dead and one of you assholes shot me?" He shook his head in disbelief as both Rick and Seyfert stared at him with blank faces and then pointed at each other.

The walk up the driveway was uninterrupted by the dead or anything else. The fog remained, so the group stayed on their toes. Soon enough a small, circular fountain emerged from the mist, followed by a garage attached kitty-corner to a giant house with a stone front. The three doors to the garage were down and the great oak front door was closed. Steel shutters covered the front windows on the first floor. Only the bottom of the second-floor windows was visible through the dense fog.

"Wow," Wilcox and Dallas whispered at the same time, no doubt marveling at the size of the home.

Anna glanced at Seyfert. "Should we knock?"

"No. We do an entire perimeter check to make sure no doors are open or windows broken. There were some dead already in here, so we have to assume the wall is down someplace. That means there could be a hundred of them in here and we just can't see them through the fog."

"I'll take Dallas and Anna," Wilcox whispered. "You take Rick. Circle around the house and meet back here?"

The SEAL shook his head. "Negative. We stick together and protect our zones."

They moved in a tight formation down the right side of the garages. Two of the rear garage windows were broken, but one was too high to reach. The other had half-inch bars set into the stone. The group came upon a patio and Wilcox nosed his weapon behind a stone fireplace grill and checked over a low wall. Human bones littered the far side of the patio, as did two rotten corpses. A dozen tables, some tipped over and others with complete table settings and formerly white tablecloths, stretched into the fog. A white arbor with dead, dry flowers attached to it was knocked over on its side. Dallas picked up a bottle of whiskey from the stainless steel bar top, opened it, and took a pull.

"Miss that," he said and put the bottle back.

The rear of the house was covered in gore spatter, reddish brown handprints marking everything. The steel shutters had held though and were still intact.

A lone undead shuffled out of the fog, issuing a horrible wheezing sound. The middle-aged woman was missing all of the right side of her face and throat, her right arm nothing but a nub of humerus bone. Dallas swung his rebar and with a crunch, the thing's misery ceased.

More bloody handprints and other evidence of a failed siege were evident. Overturned patio furniture, a broken wicker table, an arbor column off its foundation, and a few more truly dead people, all with head trauma.

It took twenty minutes to circle the mini-mansion. When the group was staring at the front door again, Wilcox climbed the four circular stone steps and stood in front of it, looking up.

"Why not?" he asked and tried the knob. He shrugged when it wouldn't open.

Seyfert put his hand on the Texan and the big man jumped a little. "Dallas, do you think you can climb up there if I can hook a rope?" Seyfert pointed to the covering over the entryway.

"Yeah. You think we can get in up there?"

"I don't know, but we aren't splitting up again. We all go or none of us do."

Wilcox rubbed his shoulder. "I'll go first." He tossed the shovel attached to the rope up onto the top of the façade, once again catching it on something on the first try. He put his hands on the rope to begin his climb, but Rick stopped him

"How about you let me take point this time, kiddo?" Without waiting for an answer, Rick scaled the knotted line and disappeared over the top of the circular stone carriage porch.

"Clear," he told the rest of the group. "Wilcox, come on up."

"Holy shit," Seyfert exclaimed when they crawled through the broken arched window of the foyer. He looked up at a massive chandelier, the centerpiece of a marble entrance hall with two winding stairways leading to the upper floors.

Anna's eyes wandered over the art and statuary. "Must have been really shitty to live in all this squalor. Poor family must have had the misfortune to have been rock stars or something."

"Dibs on the master bedroom," Wilcox blurted.

Seyfert was still taking in the splendor of the foyer. He looked at Wilcox and shook his head in the negative. "We stay together, all in one room."

"I have to pee," Anna groused. "Can we clear this place, so I can take care of business?"

The steel shutters, which covered the windows on the bottom floor, kept most of the lower rooms in shadow. The group moved as a tactical unit and checked a massive family room with two pinball tables, a pool table, and two huge televisions.

They moved into a beautiful kitchen with green granite countertops. All the appliances were stainless steel. Wilcox opened one of the cabinets and jumped back with a small shout. A mouse skittered away across the tile and disappeared through the door to the family room.

Dallas stared at Wilcox, nodding. "Mmm hmm."

The young soldier shuddered. "I hate mice."

The door to the garage was locked from the house side, but the door to what was probably the basement was secured from the other side.

"I bet they have a Lamborghini or something in there," Wilcox dreamed as he put his hand on the knob to the garage door. "We could get to the coast in—" He pulled the door open and rotting hands grabbed him. They pulled him to them, while at the same time they surged out of the three-car garage. Dozens of dead lurched through the open door, biting and tearing. Wilcox started to scream as they bit into him, arterial spray from his neck splashing the white kitchen wall.

Seyfert fired into the group, Dallas following suit with his shotgun. The big Texan tried to get to his friend, but Rick grabbed his arm. "No! He's gone! Fall back now!"

The four friends ran back to the foyer and to the front door. Seyfert unlocked the ornate brass entry furnishing and yanked the door open. Staggering figures filled the front driveway and yard area. Several of the dead things were already coming up the steps to the front door. The SEAL slammed the heavy oak door closed, securing the lock.

"Behind!" Anna shouted when she saw the first of the dead from the garage come through the kitchen entryway into the hall. It was a young boy in a suit, his throat cut from ear to ear. Two more adult undead staggered into view, both also with their throats slit. Red eyes locked on the survivors and the things coursed forward.

"Come on!" Seyfert yelled and the group followed him up the winding staircase on the left.

A body in a red-stained wedding dress sat slumped on the floor at the top of the stairs. The corpse had a framed photograph clutched to its chest and a small chrome revolver rested on the floor next to it.

"Dallas, Anna," Seyfert said calmly, "clear one of the rooms behind us. Find one with an exit window!" The SEAL and Rick aimed their weapons at the undead who had begun to trudge up the long marble staircase. Seyfert dropped to a firing position and squeezed his trigger. Rick followed suit with single shots, choosing targets. The dead kept coming around the corner from the kitchen and thuds from the front door announced the arrival of the exterior contingent.

Dallas came back huffing. "I got better than a window! I got a door to a third floor. We checked, it's clear." Seyfert fired twice more and got off his knee.

They began to move past Dallas, but he stood his ground. "One sec." He grabbed a large stone statue of a horse, jockeyed it into position, and toppled it down the stairs. It broke when it made impact with the steps and chunks of stone rained down on the approaching infected in a mini avalanche. Many of them went down with broken bones, and several of the ones in front fell backward into their brothers.

Anna stood in front of the door to the third floor, waving them on. Stairs ascended a skinny hallway into brightness, Seyfert vaulting two at a time with his injured leg as he climbed them. Dallas shut the door behind him, but it had no lock. Rick, Seyfert, and Anna cleared the three upstairs bedrooms together, while Dallas covered the entry at the bottom of the stairs they had just come through.

Rick noticed a pull-string in the ceiling and quickly yanked a foldaway set of stairs down with a series of creaks.

Dallas backed into the short hallway and looked left at the extended stairs. He looked up and shook his head. "Not my first rodeo with this type o' thing, Hoss."

Rick nodded. The sounds of the infected searching for them on the floor below rattled Dallas a bit. "I really don't wanna go up there. Didn't end so good last time."

"Consider the alternative," Rick whispered.

"So we came from a basement surrounded by them things to an attic surrounded by them things? Our fortunes ain't improved much."

"Wilcox..." Anna began, "he was there and then he was just...gone."

Seyfert sighed. "We didn't clear the area properly. He never should have opened that door like that."

"A year and a half ago, it was okay to just open a door!" she snapped and immediately regretted it.

"Your doors and mine were very different, even then."

She nodded. Rick moved to one of the third-floor bedroom windows. He could just barely see through the fog. Dozens of infected were moving against the house, searching for a way in.

DIVISADERO STREET, SAN FRANCISCO

"William, I must know. How is it that you can move through the dead with impunity?"

Billy looked confused. "What?"

Cyrus sighed and stubbed out his cigarette on the glass-topped diner table. "I asked you how—"

Billy stopped him. "No, I know what you said, I just don't know what impunity means."

Both members of the New Society who were standing looked at each other. One shrugged. The other began to disarm Billy and check through his pack.

"Ah, it means without punishment." Cyrus could see that Billy still didn't understand. "You are able to walk through throngs of the dead without them eating you. I want to know how."

"Oh! Oh, that's easy; I'm nuts." Billy passed his shotgun to one of the men.

It was Cyrus' turn to look confused. "I don't understand."

"It's okay, not everybody gets me right off." Billy furrowed his brow in thought. "But... but I thought you did. I mean, we were in the same level of the booby hatch." The thugs again looked at each other, this time with concern. Billy started talking to himself, muttering under his breath.

"Ali could do it too, but not when she was on her meds. I wonder if Lester is taking meds? Nah, he can't be, they don't want to chow on him either. And the Slim Jims! They all wanted to eat both of us then, but we got away and maybe it was the Slim Jims? Nah, that's just crazy. But I'm crazy, so maybe two crazies make a right? I dunno I'll have to—"

"William," interrupted Cyrus.

"—think about it some more and Martin had ideas so maybe they know what's going on, but if Ali—"

"William," Cyrus said a bit louder.

"—can do it too, maybe Lester and me and her should get together and—"

Cyrus had had enough and slammed his palm on the green table. "BILLY!"

Billy jumped a bit and looked at Cyrus, his eyes wide. He blinked a few times. Cyrus looked him in the eye, his gaze captivating. "How do you do it? How is it that you can stroll through the dead without them attacking you?"

Billy shrugged. "No idea. I was kind of hoping you would be able to tell me.

I thought it was because I'm crazy," Billy changed the tone of his voice a bit, "but you are *waaaay* more crazy than I am, so I was thinking the zombies would bake you cookies or something."

Cyrus began to say something, but Billy put his index finger up, his focus elsewhere. It looked like he was listening for something. A wicked smile creased the young man's face and he slowly turned his gaze to Masta G and Cyrus.

The cacophony of hisses, moans, and rasping hacks that accompany a vast legion of the undead now flooded the diner. Everybody looked nervous, but Billy laced his fingers together and put his hands behind his head. He threw one foot up on the diner table.

"*Run*," he said in a menacing whisper as the terrifying noises reached a crescendo. The smile on Billy's face grew even wider. He cupped his hands together in front of his face and yelled, "Yoo-hoo! Dead people! Come and get it!"

"He *is* crazy!" one of the men breathed.

They were all peering through the diner window at the first of the dead as they shuffled into view across the street. The creatures must have been drawn by the recent sounds of vehicles and weapons fire. They were searching in all directions.

The men were momentarily stunned by the approaching dead and got as low and small as they could. Billy removed his leg from the table, grabbed his pack, and bowled over the two guards as he ran for the door. He burst out into the street and yelled to the crowd of infected.

From inside the diner, Masta G stubbed his cigarette out. "You," he said and pointed at one of the guards, "go get him."

The man was incredulous and thumbed to the door. "Out there?"

"Better hurry," added Cyrus. "Don't kill him."

The man swallowed hard, spun on his heel, and sprinted from the diner. Billy saw him and ran off to the right. The man followed, and the horde followed him.

Cyrus sighed. "This is irksome. He continues to avoid capture."

"Looked to me like he really didn't know how he does it," Masta G whispered. The three men watched as a Runner fought its way through the throng, desperate to get to the men who had run away.

Billy rounded a corner and realized he was back on Fell Street. One of the shop fronts had crumbled into the road and the building was on fire from the rocket attack. Several dead milled about and turned to face him when he came into view. The thug chasing him put his rifle to his shoulder and destroyed three of the things.

"You better fuck'n stop, asshole!"

"Or what? You gonna shoot me? Pretty sure Cyrus wants me alive!"

"How about I put a hole in your leg then? Think the smell of blood will be okay to the dead ones?"

Billy hadn't thought of that, so he put his hands up and stopped running. The Runner came screaming around the end of the building and the guy shot it in the chest. He ran over to Billy and poked him with the barrel of his weapon. "Move."

"Uh, you sure?" Billy pointed back the way they had come.

The vanguard of the horde were now streaming onto Fell Street.

The man's eyes grew wide. "Shit! This way!"

He forced Billy to run down the street, but each way he tried to go, a swarm of dead blocked that direction. The things began to come from under cars, out of open doors, and from down the street. The men were forced into an alley, but it was a dead end, the far side a solid brick wall, four stories high. The man pushed Billy down next to a dumpster and pointed his rifle at his head.

"You tell me! You tell me right now how you do it, or I'll take my chances with Cyrus and blow your damn head off!"

Billy blinked and the man looked down the alley. A wall of rot had entered and was on the way.

"Tell me!" the man almost screamed and poked Billy in the head with the rifle.

"Ow! Okay, okay!" Billy rubbed his head, unzipped his pack and reached in, rummaging around. He came out with a bottle of something and opened it. He poured a bit of the thick solution into his hand, rubbed it with his other hand, and then applied it to his face.

"That's it? That's all you have to do?"

"Yup and they won't touch you. I've been doing it for months."

The man glanced back down the alley and inhaled an involuntary sharp breath. He slung his rifle over his shoulder and grabbed the bottle, immediately dumping half the contents onto his hands, then rubbing his hands all over himself.

"Don't forget your head," Billy said and pointed to the man's hair.

The desperate man applied more of the solution to his face and head and sniffed. "It smells like…"

"It is. That's all I've ever used. It works."

"You sure?" The man was breathing fast and terrified. The dead were twenty feet away and getting loud.

Billy nodded and made a diagonal slicing gesture with his right hand. "Totally sure. I'm still alive and by now you know I can walk through them, right? Got to stop talking though," he added, "or they might figure you out."

His rifle aimed at the oncoming tide, the man was about to begin firing.

Billy shook his head. "Don't shoot or they'll know!"

Billy's captor nodded furiously. The younger man leaned against the dumpster and began picking his thumbnail with his index nail. The dead walked right past Billy and headed for the other man, who backed up. He retreated until there was nowhere else to go, a solid wall behind him. The wave of infection never stopped and Billy rolled his eyes as the man started screaming. The things tore him apart as he stood against the wall, the press of the crowd such that he never hit the ground and was devoured standing up.

It didn't take long, as there were many creatures. What did take a while was Billy's escape from the alley. The dead in the rear pressed forward even when the meal was done, trapping their brothers, sisters, and Billy. When the infected which were denied a feeding realized that they had missed out and there was no more food in sight, they and the rest of the horde moved off back down the alley as slowly as they had come. The last of the dead to move on, an older man in a filthy undershirt and nothing else, glanced briefly at Billy with its crimson eyes as it passed him. Billy nodded to it.

The living man moved to what was left of his pursuer. Stains on the littered ground, torn and bloody clothes, scattered bones, and a skull were all that remained.

Billy made a face. "Ew, nasty." He shook his head in disgust. "Ugh."

He stared at the man's military rifle. The entire weapon was covered in gore. He reached down to pick it up by the sling and it dripped with fluids when he lifted it.

"Seriously?"

He brought his yellow backpack around in front of him and dug into it. He was able to wash off most of the infected fluids with two bottles of water and wipe the weapon down with a sock. The sling had been permeated by the rank blood though and he discarded it. There were two extra magazines in the dead man's pack, a knife on his belt, and assorted other sundries that needed appropriation.

Billy put the weapon to his shoulder and looked down the sight. By the light of the moon, he checked for a safety. It had been disengaged the entire time and the dead man had never fired. Billy smiled and found the magazine ejector lever. He figured out the charging handle as well and drew it back a bit, nodding. He had never used a military rifle before.

"Just one," he said and fired off a round down the alley. "Oooooh! This is nice."

Immediately, he realized his mistake. He knew that the lane would fill back up with the dead in a moment because of the gunfire and he would have to wait to get out again.

Taking a step toward the mouth of the alley, he kicked the empty bottle he had given the thug. Billy pouted. He would be without barbeque sauce for his next meal. He loved that sauce on everything, especially potato chips, and it was becoming harder to find. He hoped the dead had enjoyed it.

UNKNOWN RESIDENCE, MASSACHUSETTS

Anna's legs were crossed as she sat on an overturned bucket in an attic in Massachusetts. "I have to pee."

"You're sitting on a bucket," Seyfert told her. "Turn it over and pee."

She made a face and was about to retort when a crash from the floor below them interrupted her.

"So they're upstairs now," the Texan drawled. "If I was gonna pick between bein' trapped here an' bein' trapped with tons of food an' big walls, I'd pick—"

Rick smiled. "We know, Hillbilly. You may have mentioned this before."

"I can't see how many there are through the fog," Seyfert squinted through the attic dormer window, "but it looks like they're thinning out back. Might be that now is the best time to go."

The SEAL surveyed his surroundings one more time. This attic was gigantic, spanning the length of the house and the garage. It looked like there had been construction happening prior to the onset of the plague, as a stack of plywood and two-by-fours sat unused in a corner. Several power tools and some extension cords lay forgotten where they had been last used. A few wall frames had been installed and some electrical cable had been threaded, but that was it.

There were stored items in the attic as well, but nothing the group could use. Furniture covered in canvas tarps. A large oval mirror in a wooden frame. A dozen steamer trunks and a few banker's boxes, all containing clothes or personal items.

Rick searched the trunks again while Dallas and Seyfert moved to the far end of the long room.

Seyfert and Dallas returned a few minutes later to find Rick inspecting a leather jacket.

"Red ain't your color, Hoss."

"We either have a big problem, or a possible solution to our current issue," Seyfert told Rick. Rick looked at the SEAL expectantly and Seyfert continued. "There's a stairwell that leads into the garage at the far end of the attic. There's a flimsy door at the bottom of the stairs. If they figure that out, we're dead. We might be able to use that set of stairs to go through the garage and out the back though."

"Wilcox died because of that garage," Anna said, moving quietly up next to the men.

"Wilcox died because we didn't properly recon the house. My fault as much as his." The SEAL shook his head. "Think of what's in front of us, not what's behind. We need to get out of here and that stairwell is our only option other than out one of the dormer windows, but then it's a thirty-foot drop to the backyard."

"Dunno about big drops with our legs there, Pard. Mine hurts now, how's yours?"

"It's fine," Seyfert answered, rubbing his leg. "We should go now." The SEAL moved to the dormer windows and opened all three of them. "Just in case."

Rick finished adding loose rounds to a magazine. He ejected his other magazine and replaced it with the full one, pulling back the charging handle to charge a round. He added six more rounds to the partially expended magazine.

"Ready," he said with a nod.

"Doing this quietly would be preferable," Seyfert told his three teammates, "but I would expect we will have to fire on them. Check your targets and your zones."

The quartet moved down the plywood floor toward the stairwell. They could hear the sounds of multiple threats on the second floor below them. The noises the dead made were loud.

The humans reached the stairwell and started down. When they reached the bottom, Seyfert turned to them.

"If I slam the door, that means there're too many and we have to fall back," he whispered. "This door won't hold long, so go right out the windows and we'll find a way down." He raised his eyebrows. "Ready?"

Everyone nodded and Seyfert cracked the door, using the sight on his sidearm to track targets. The garage was vast, capable of holding several vehicles, but he only one housed was unusable. A luxury sedan sat in the third bay, all the windows broken out with the vehicle positively drenched in mostly dried infected fluids. Shelves of skiing and rock climbing equipment sat toward the back of the structure.

The SEAL opened the door a bit more with his foot and checked behind it. He held up two fingers and drew his knife. He moved down the two steps to the concrete floor. The last step creaked, but neither the young dead boy, nor the middle-aged dead man turned to look at him. Dallas, Rick, and Anna filed out behind Seyfert, Dallas with his piece of rebar. Seyfert moved left and stood behind the boy, nodding to Dallas. They struck their targets simultaneously, Seyfert utilizing a sideways temple strike and the big Texan using his strength to bring the rebar overhand through the softened skull all the way to the trachea. Both men kicked their victims forward to extricate their weapons.

Anna covered Rick as he moved to the open door between the garage and the house. He hurriedly shut it, but not before the living heard the hungry cries of the dead grow in intensity.

"Yeah, so, they saw me," Rick told his friends.

Seyfert studied the garage doors. Each of the three had an electric door opener. He reached up and yanked on a red line attached to one of the opener boxes and a chain released with a thud. Moving to the large, wide door, he got down on his belly a few feet back on the concrete of the garage floor. The first thumps from dead hands landed on the entry between them and the dead inside the house.

"Rick, cover Dallas with me. Dallas, lift the door up a foot, and we'll check to see if it's clear. If it isn't, slam it back down fast."

Dallas nodded and put his hand on the ornate garage door handle as Rick got down next to Seyfert.

"Go!" Seyfert told Dallas.

The door came up quickly for one so large and both Rick and the SEAL said, "Clear!"

Dallas threw the heavy wooden door all the way open and the four friends rushed out into the fog. They could hear the terrifying noises of the dead around them, but still couldn't see through the fog.

"Stay close!" the SEAL whispered. "Within sight of each other at all times!"

Seyfert's whisper didn't go unnoticed and something lunged at him from the fog. It latched on to his tactical vest and he spun with it and took it to the ground. He held its mouth at bay and struggled to get it off him before Rick got the former human off of his friend with a vicious kick. A second kick and a stomp to the back of its neck destroyed the thing, but not before several others materialized out of the fog beside the team.

Two of the things grabbed at Anna, but she nimbly side-stepped away…and into the waiting claws of a third. She used the butt of her rifle to break its jaw, while Dallas brought his rebar around in a sideways arc, nearly decapitating it. Rick was covering Seyfert while the SEAL got up, but was assaulted by a dead woman in half of a disgusting floral dress. He kicked her knee and she stumbled backward into the two that had gone for Anna and Dallas. More of the creatures emerged from the murk and Seyfert realized they were surrounded.

"Go live!" he said and fired his suppressed pistol into the face of a dead thing in a blue smock. "Break after me!"

Rick shot a mailman through the right eye, then hurried behind Seyfert, Anna and Dallas on their heels. The four of them created a diamond-shaped pattern with Dallas in the rear. They were beginning to fire more rapidly as the targets came at them out of the fog. Anna's suppressor hissed noisily as she destroyed a shambler and her next shot was significantly louder. Her suppressor was almost spent.

"Switching to my rifle," she told her friends and brought the weapon up from its sling. She aimed the M4 battle rifle to her right as the group progressed.

Seyfert stopped moving forward and glanced to his left, then right. "Got a stone wall in front of me, moving right. Stay tight."

The group moved down the wall in close formation, destroying anything that came at them. Anna tripped on something and the something reached up and grabbed her. She fell over it onto the ground and it began to crawl up her to get a bite in. With no legs and one arm, it was easy to push off, but its remaining hand would not let go. Another thing stumbled out of the mist and fell on the ground to feast. She had no choice but to fire her rifle and the unsuppressed shot was incredibly loud.

The noises of the dead grew in intensity, although they were hard to pinpoint through the fog. The horrifying sounds echoed through the mist and against the long stone wall. A dead woman appeared to the right and another, then a dead boy. Anna smashed the first thing in the face with the butt of her rifle, driving her back. Dallas did the same and lashed out with a kick that snapped the dead kid's leg at the knee sending the former boy sprawling. More of the things emerged and Seyfert decided to pick up speed. Two more steps and he fired twice, dropping one creature and scoring a non-killing headshot on the second. Its head snapped to the side, but it didn't even fall over and came on with one less eye.

Seyfert tried to holster his sidearm, but the suppressor caught on the holster and he fumbled and dropped it. He made to reach for it, but a rotten, growling thing plowed into him, sending him into the high wall. He smacked his head and the thing caught him by the tactical vest, biting into his shoulder. The creature only got the tac webbing and tried to move in for a better bite as the SEAL fought it off. He gave it an elbow under the chin and then one to the nose, smearing the appendage off of the rotten thing's face. A gaping black hole was left where the cartilage had been.

Rick shot it in the side of the head with his pistol and the group picked up speed. They began a slow, deliberate jog, and suddenly Seyfert found a section of the wall that had come down.

"Through here!"

The rest of his group followed him through the collapsed and broken stones, the dead hot on their heels. Two of the things stumbled on the large chunks of stone, impeding the progress of the others.

"Into the woods, stay together!"

The group followed Seyfert's command and moved quickly into the neighboring forest. The surreal landscape was beautiful but terrifying, as it held a legion of plague-ridden, vicious undead. The thick fog covered everything in a blanket of opaque coolness, with only the bases of the trees visible. Oaks, maples, and huge pines loomed before them, disappearing into the murk above as if the canopy had been stolen by some enormous entity.

A growling dead women came from the left side, and Dallas smashed her with the butt of his weapon. Each of the group took small but deliberate strides in an attempt to remain in contact with the others. They moved quickly, but in a moment, Seyfert heard a scuffle and he spun to see what was happening. Dallas and Rick were behind him, but Anna was nowhere to be seen.

Noises to the right alerted the men and they sped off in that direction to find Anna going hand to hand with two infected. She lashed out with her right boot, the left knee of the dead man bending backward with a snap. The thing went down, but not before its brother grabbed Anna and moved in to eat her face. She brought her elbow up, catching the thing under the jaw. Even from ten feet away, Rick heard the thing's teeth shatter. Not even stunned, it came at her with renewed vigor, but Seyfert was there and ended it using a downward stab with his blade. The other creature was attempting to stand and Anna moved to finish it, but Seyfert grabbed her and mouthed *Let's go!* She nodded and the four of them moved deeper into the trees.

They were nearly out of breath and sore from running when they could no longer hear the horrifying sounds of pursuit. For the first time, the sun was visible as its own object in the sky as opposed to it just lighting up the fog.

"East," Seyfert said as he stopped and put his hands on his knees. He pointed to the sun. "We need to move east." He shook his head. "Holy shit, I'm getting soft. All this easy living in an underground bunker and I didn't work out enough." He spit.

"Well, you did get shot in the leg," Anna quipped.

"Seems like that was a year ago." The SEAL stood upright, panning his eyes in all directions. "I think we lost them, or at least the majority of them."

"Yeah," Dallas started, "they's way back behind us, an' I think—"

Something exploded from the thickets on the right. It impacted Seyfert, bowling him over and knocking him to the ground. The group was prepared to fight, but the creature kept going, a brown streak through the haze. It had been a large deer, but its passage had been so fast that it hadn't been possible to tell if it had been male or female.

The SEAL issued a slight groan and lay still. He was on his side and his friends rushed to him, Dallas reaching to turn him over.

"Wait!" Anna hissed. She knelt down next to him and felt his neck, then moved her hands down his ribs. The SEAL gave another involuntary groan but remained motionless. Anna put her pack down next to a semiconscious Seyfert, rummaged through it, and came out with her medic bag. She produced some bandages and antiseptic, applying the cream liberally to a bandage and dabbing Seyfert's bloody face. He was cut above his right eye and his lip and nose were bleeding. She continued to work on the Navy man as Dallas and Rick surveyed the area.

The fog was lifting, but visibility was still only fifty feet or so.

"That deer musta been runnin' from sumthin'."

"Agreed, Hillbilly, but our SEAL looks to be questionable for the remainder of the game. Carrying him is going to be a bitch."

"Nobody's fuck'n carrying me." Seyfert tried to sit up, but Anna stopped him with a hand on his chest.

"Hang on there, soldier. You probably have a concussion." She flashed a light into his eyes, one at a time. "Is your neck okay?"

Seyfert moved his head and spat some blood onto the ground. "Yeah. Yeah, I'm good."

"Bullshit. You just got absolutely *bundled* by that deer. Let me check you out for a sec and then we can move on."

A lone infected stumbled out of the fog, but it didn't see the group and moved laterally away from them.

"We don't have a sec." Seyfert gently removed Anna's hand from his chest and sat up. "Fuck." He touched the back of his hand to his nose and it came away bloody.

"Here, shove this up there and pinch." Anna handed him a small piece of gauze.

He dabbed his nose then put the gauze up his left nostril. He tried to stand, but a sharp pain in his side stopped him. He uttered an involuntary hiss and Anna looked at him, raising her eyebrows.

"I said I'm good." He reached up a hand and she helped him up. He rubbed his side.

"Bruised for sure, but I don't think those ribs are broken. Should be a fun walk to the coast."

A brief fracas in the lessening mist behind the SEAL and the medic caused them both to spin around. Rick was using the butt of his rifle to finish off a single infected which he had already put on the ground.

"You done screwing around?" he demanded of Seyfert with a smile.

The SEAL shook his head. "No respect."

ALCATRAZ, SAN FRANCISCO

Detective Captain Mike Meara, formerly of the San Francisco Police department, studied the six people sitting around the ancient metal table with him. Tony and Abbey, who had just returned from a run to the mainland to procure supplies sat to his left, as did Mr. Martingale, another survivor. Captain McInerney, captain of the USS *Florida* and the ranking military officer in the region, sat next to Meara on the right, as did Ali, one of the survivors that had come to Alcatraz in the early days. Meara glanced out the window of the Model Industries building at San Francisco Bay, wishing he could say what needed to be said without causing dissension. He filled his lungs with the salt air from a broken window then released it, returning his gaze to the folks at the table. His eyes roamed over them and settled on the wiry, auburn-haired girl, Ali. She would be the source of his troubles, but they wouldn't end with her. Several of the survivors in this large room would also balk at what he had to say.

"He's a murderer," Meara began and was immediately met with rebuke.

"Seriously?" demanded the red-head. "How many people has he brought or gotten safely to this island? Twenty? Fifty?"

One of the two people who was not seated stepped forward, lifting one piece of paper on a clipboard and looking briefly at what was underneath. "Thirty-eight at last count."

Everyone glared at him and he stepped back. "Sorry."

"Thank you, Weathers," the red-haired girl said with a slight smile. "Thirty-eight," she continued. "Thirty-eight people that he not only didn't kill, but risked his own life to save. Most of them are kids."

Tony, a former PG&E worker and a hell of a brave man, was another of the people Meara knew would take issue with Meara's incoming directive. Tony raised his hand. "He saved us, too. He tried to save all of us, but he couldn't." Tony sighed. "Ali is right," he added, smiling at her across the table. "Billy is not a threat."

"He's a *murderer*," Mike added with emphasis.

Ali, whose personality was as fiery as her ginger locks, was enraged. "So am I if you count those dead bastards! So are you!" She pointed her finger at Meara. "Are you going to tell me you haven't killed a human being before? Especially since the end of the world?"

"I shot and killed one man in the line of duty twenty years ago. I think about it every damn day. I doubt Billy even knows how many people he's killed. I doubt he has the capacity to care."

Ali put her hands on the table. "Yeah, but—"

The police captain held up his hand, forestalling her. "It doesn't matter if he doesn't mean to kill, or if he's sick and needs help. He'll kill someone here and that person will turn and kill someone else." Mike shook his head. "He can't stay on this island."

Abbey, a dark-haired athletic woman, piped up. "He said he didn't do it." She had said it almost under her breath.

"What?" asked McInerney, captain of the *Florida*, a nuclear attack submarine anchored to the north of Alcatraz.

Abbey spoke a bit louder, "He said he didn't kill the dentist. The dentist murdered his sister and Billy went to the dentist's house to confront him, but the guy was already butchered."

"Oh, well that changes *everything*," Martingale, one of the civilian survivors, said sarcastically. He leaned back in his chair, folding his arms. "If a convicted killer says he didn't do it, it *must* be true."

Neither Meara nor McInerney wanted this man at the meeting, but he had been appointed the civilian liaison to all things military or concerning Alcatraz.

Ali glared at him. "Shut up, asshole. If we want any shit out of you, we'll squeeze your head."

Meara sighed again, tasting the salt air once more. "Okay, that's enough. I'm very sorry, but I just don't trust Billy. You can't guarantee me that he won't hurt anybody here and until you can, I can't allow him on Alcatraz."

A young sailor hurried into the room, moving to McInerney, and whispering something to him.

"Confirmed?" asked the captain.

"Aye, sir. We can see them with binoculars. They're only about three thousand feet southeast of us."

"Thank you, Warren." The man backed up a few steps and put his hands behind his back, at parade rest. "Ladies, gentlemen," McInerney began, "we have some folks in need of assistance. There are some families on the Pampanito that are in trouble."

Tony looked confused. "What's a Pampanito?"

"It's a decommissioned World War Two submarine docked next to Fisherman's Wharf. There are some people living on it and they're under siege by the dead. They've been breached and there are several dead inside the sub."

Martingale harrumphed. "I hope you're not asking any of our civilians to—"

"We'll handle it," interrupted McInerney. "It's a military situation."

"I'll come," Tony said, raising his hand and looking meekly at Martingale. "I can help." Martingale glared back.

McInerney stood. "Thank you, Tony, but one of our fire teams will take care of it. I'm sorry, folks, but I need to step away to coordinate. Please continue without me and Weathers will take notes." The captain strode briskly from the room.

Ali also stood. "I can see where this is going and you don't need me. I'll go do something productive." She stormed away in a different direction than the captain had. Pushing open a broken door, she took a set of metal stairs downward and disappeared from sight.

Meara sighed. He had sighed a lot in the past year or so. He looked at the other man standing at parade rest and nodded toward the now empty chair where McInerney had sat. "Mr. Pitt?"

The older, powerfully built man took a seat next to Meara, giving a curt nod. "Thank you." He hiked his chair in a bit and put his elbows on the table. "I appreciate you all coming to this meeting. The reason I asked you here is simple: Mr. Martingale, you are our liaison between the crew of the *Florida* and the civilians here. Tony and Abbey, you two are our lead scroungers, and Captain Meara is our civilian leader." Pitt put his elbows on the table and looked at each person in turn.

"We need to think about securing another location as a larger, more fortified base. I was thinking about Catalina Island eventually. We considered Angel Island and we're going to set up an outpost on the main Farallon Island, but Catalina is the best option."

Martingale smiled and raised his eyebrows, looking at Pitt, who did not smile. The grin slowly lost its power and faded, Martingale blinked.

"You're serious?"

"Yes," Pitt told him.

"Catalina Island, off of LA? That's like, four hundred miles from here. You know that, right?"

"Yes."

"Forgetting about the monumental task of moving us all there, what if it's already claimed by other survivors? What if the dead have it?"

Pitt shrugged. "All questions I've considered. If the dead have it, we clear it. If there are other survivors, then we integrate."

"What if they don't want to integrate?"

"We have a United States attack submarine and three professional fire teams—"

"You mean we take it from them?" interrupted Martingale. "That makes us no better than the gang members that came up from LA!"

Pitt, not used to being interrupted, took a breath. "My suggestion was that we show them how we can help them, not force them into anything. Did we force you to do anything or kill any of you when we came here?"

Martingale shook his head. "I'm still voting no."

"Shocker there," Abbey said a bit too loud.

"There won't be a vote," Pitt told them. "We will scout the area and after we're sure it isn't compromised, we will take anyone who wants to go. If you want to stay here, you are more than welcome. You can shore up the fortifications and go find food, because you won't be able to grow it here in two years; the soil is bad and getting worse. In addition, as I have previously stated, the structures here are old and in disrepair. Eventually, someone will get hurt. There are two towns on Catalina, with an area of roughly seventy-five square miles and a pre-plague population of less than five thousand. It's a lot to clear, but we need the space."

"I'm in," Tony said.

"Me too," agreed Abbey.

CORNER OF BATTERY AND PACIFIC, SAN FRANCISCO

"Well, somebody's in a heap of trouble," Billy said as he watched a large group of dead try to smash their way through the metal grated windows of a Starbucks. A loud scream rent the air and Billy jumped a bit, looking in all directions. He finally locked his gaze on the thing that was sprinting at him from further down Pacific Avenue. The creature was young, perhaps in her early teens, wearing jeans, yellow sneakers, and a disgusting tank top. She might have been cute before the plague had turned her into a carrier, but now she was horrifying. Half her hair was in a blonde ponytail, the other half had slipped out and was crusted to her face with sweat and blood. Feverish, shaking and coated in gore, this thing had killed recently and was looking to continue her streak by adding Billy to her list of victims.

Billy sighed, aimed down the sight at his target's chest, and squeezed the trigger on his new weapon.

Nothing happened.

"Uhh…" He pulled the trigger again with the same outcome.

He had time for one more forced "UHHH!" and the thing was on him, slashing with its nails and trying to punch and bite anywhere it could reach. He stretched his right hand for his back sheath to bring his machete around and remembered just a half-second too late that he had left both it and his shotgun sitting on the green diner table with Cyrus and his friends.

The infected girl weighed in at a whopping ninety-five pounds or so, but she was determined to steal Billy's life away and she punched and kicked him repeatedly as he tried to fight her off. The thing reared its right hand back to rake its claws across Billy's face, but he shot his left foot out, his sneaker impacting the creature's right thigh. She stumbled a bit and he thumped her in the face with the butt of his rifle. He heard and saw the bones in her face break and she stumbled back, bleeding.

"Oh!" Billy blurted and reversed the rifle. He flicked off the safety and aimed at her again. He squeezed the trigger just once, rewarded with the exceptionally earsplitting sound of the rifle bark. The disease-ridden thing grabbed its shoulder as it pitched back, landing on its side, gasping. Then it did something Billy hadn't seen before: it started crying.

The girl held her ruined face in her hands as she bawled. Blood streamed from between her fingers, running down her arms and splashing her jeans. Her shoulder wound also bled freely and Billy was horrified. He took a step forward then two back when she looked up at him.

Billy had been told by some other survivors that these creatures were totally devoid of emotion, but looking at this thing, he knew that was not true. There was a deep sadness on her face, most of which was lost behind a rictus of infinite hatred. Blood flowed from her broken nose as she tried to stand. She put her hand down on the street to push herself up, but slipped and fell back on her side. She screamed as Runners do and Billy shot her in the face.

"What the heck was—?" he began before he realized the dead were on him. They walked past him and glared at the dead girl. Each of the rotting things glanced at Billy as they moved back to the coffee shop and began to smack on the steel grate once more.

"Well, that sure was interesting." Billy followed them to the store, stooping down to grab an abandoned tire iron on the way. "Fudge-sickles," he said when he saw what was coming down the street. Many undead were on the way, attracted by the shots he had fired.

"Got to do this in a jiffy!" He leaned his new rifle against the brick of the coffee shop's exterior and began to destroy the undead with the angled piece of steel. "Ow," he grumbled after crushing the fourth skull. On the sixth, his hands stung from the impact.

"OW!"

The remaining dead turned to look at him and he destroyed two more before he wrung his hands out. "Really hurts, you know?" he asked a dead man. Again, the thing stared at him for a moment then went back to pushing its friends to get at the steel-grated windows.

Billy cursed himself a fool, chucked the tire iron away, and pulled the knife he had appropriated from his pursuer earlier. Several of the undead twisted and craned their necks to check out the sound of the metal hitting the pavement and Billy used that time to jab his knife into the eye socket of the nearest infected. It dropped and he moved on.

"Excuse me." He stabbed another.

"Pardon?" Another.

He repeated this a few times, the knife skidding off of a couple skulls, but eventually, he had destroyed the group of infected in front of the Starbucks.

The other dead had arrived and they were coming toward him. Billy began to shout.

"Hey! Hey over here, dummies!" He grabbed the rifle, waved his arms, and ran down Battery Street a bit, stooping to retrieve the gore-covered tire iron one more time. "Down here!" He ran down the road a bit more and banged the metal on a blue post box. Maybe two hundred dead were in the area, all of which streamed toward him. When they were close, he walked instead of ran around the corner of a building. They followed him and he threw the tire iron through the side window of a Mazda Miata. Billy was hoping for an alarm, but he didn't get one. The smashing window was enough for the dead to swarm the car. They flooded past him and began to search the car, the ones in the back jostling for a nonexistent meal.

Billy moved quickly, but he knew if he ran, the dead would follow him. He made it back to the Starbucks and whispered through the grated front door.

"Let me in!"

He tried that and a few other ideas, but either there was nobody in the shop, or they didn't want to let him in. Billy made a face and moved to the side of the building. It was a few stories high, but the fire escape on the side was out of reach.

"Always with the fire escapes!" bemoaned the young man. He was able to semi-quietly drag a trash receptacle to the side of the building. When he balanced on it, he could just reach the iron ladder. It was difficult to pull himself up, but Billy was young and strong.

He used his elbow to break a window on the second floor and was soon standing in an insurance office. The plague hadn't reached this workplace. Everything was neat and orderly, with nothing overturned. No papers on the floor, no signs of struggle or the ever-present bloodstains he was used to seeing everywhere else. Billy searched until he found a set of stairs going down and used them to come to a small hallway. The hallway was for deliveries and ended in a roll-down door at one end. Marcom Insurance 201 was on the door he had passed through, with Starbucks 102 listed on the door across from him.

The entrance to the coffee shop was locked, but the interior lever-style door handle broke on the third try with the rifle butt. *I've wrecked more stuff with the wrong end of this gun than with the business end*, Billy thought to himself.

He slowly pushed the door all the way open and noticed a supply area with an ancient timecard machine and some plaques on the wall. Sundries and bags of stuff sat on shelves or the floor, while buckets and canisters of liquids resided against the far wall. All of it looked undisturbed except an open case of soda with several cans missing. The case of soda stuck out because it sat in the middle of the floor. Billy slowly pushed open a small divider door between the serving counter and the back room. The main area of the coffee shop was dark, with slivered beams of light streaming in through the mesh-covered windows at the front. His eyes roamed over the large room, searching for living occupants. He put his hands on the serving counter, his eyes flicking briefly over the multitude of coffee-making apparatuses. He could make out tables with chairs atop them, but not much else further in the room.

"So, is anybody here?" he asked in a hushed voice. "I'm the guy who just smoked all the rotten freaks that were about to smash in here and eat you."

He received no response, so he moved on into the main room. The dead rarely battered on doors or windows without provocation, so Billy was certain something alive had been spotted. He hoped it wasn't a rat. Billy *hated* rats. "It's not the tail," he muttered to himself, "it's not."

"Well, I haven't had a decent cup of coffee in months, so I think I'll just start up all this really loud machinery and grab myself a cappuccino…"

Billy waited expectantly, but nobody came forward. Retching off to his right clued him in to where the person was.

He smiled, moving past the serving counter and swinging around to the right. "You must have been terrible at hide and seek…" He cut off his own sentence with a quiet exclamation. "Oh."

A man, who would be tall if he were vertical, lay on the floor, a small handgun aimed in Billy's general direction. The man aimed the weapon with shaky hands. He guarded a boy and a girl, fifteen or younger, both of whom stared at Billy with terrified eyes. The girl cradled the man's feverish head in her lap. The boy held a bandage made of paper towels over a wound on the man's side. There wasn't a lot of blood, but Billy could see by the man's state that it wasn't the severity of the wound which was problematic, it was its nature.

Billy raised his hands in supplication. "Bitten?"

Nobody responded, but the kids looked even more scared, if it were possible.

"Okay, so you're freaking me out with that gun pointed at me while you're shaking like a Chihuahua with the flu." Billy kept his hands elevated, but pointed his index finger at the man. "You want me to look at it?"

The man kept his eyes on Billy as he turned his head to the left and spit. "Would it help?"

"Not if you're bitten and by the looks of it, they got you at least a few hours ago. You know what that means for them, right?" Billy indicated the kids.

The man narrowed his eyes. "I don't know you."

"I don't know you either, but of the two of us, I'm the one with the weapon pointed at him."

A slam from behind them made everybody jump. Billy put his hands all over himself for a second before he released a breath of terror.

The man looked at him oddly. "What are you doing?"

"Uhh…checking myself for holes. I thought you shot me!"

Another slam then several more made Billy look over his shoulder at the front of the store again. The dead had returned and were intent on getting in the shop.

Billy sighed. "Look, buddy, I realize that we just met and stuff, but I get people out of the city all the time. It's kind of my thing." He glanced at the kids then got on his haunches, looking the man in the eye. "I'll get them out."

The man began to cough, blood flecking his lips. He lost consciousness and the gun clattered to the tiled floor. Billy left it there as he moved in to check the man.

He put his hand on the boy's arm, nodding toward the man's injury. "Let me see, okay?"

The kid nodded and Billy pulled the paper towels away. The man had clearly been bitten. The wound was approximately three inches below and to the left of the man's left nipple and it stunk.

"What's your name?" Billy asked the boy as he put the back of his hand on the man's forehead. It was like caressing a furnace.

"Kyle," the kid said in a deep voice for one so young.

Billy looked at the young girl. "And yours?"

"Vanessa."

"Mine's Billy. Your dad... I mean, you guys know what happens, right? There's not a lot I can do."

"He's not our dad," Vanessa told him. "We're not even brother and sister. His name is Daniel and he's been watching over us."

"The three of us will watch over each other for a while." Billy looked back over his shoulder at the front windows. The grating wasn't giving way, but it was beginning to hit the glass. There were dozens of infected smacking their fists and palms against the metal now.

When Billy turned back around, Daniel was looking at him with one red eye. "Hurts."

"I know. I'm sorry. Can you move?"

"Not fast enough."

Billy nodded. "They'll be in here soon. How do you want to handle it? You or me?"

"I'll do it," Daniel told him through clenched teeth, "but not in front of the kids."

"Gotcha. Kids, say your good-byes." Billy stood. "We have to leave."

With tears in her eyes, Vanessa laid Daniel's head down on the cool floor.

"Take care of each other," he told the kids.

"Goodbye, Daniel. Thank you." Kyle stood and moved next to Billy.

The front window exploded from the repeated impact of the grate against it. Shards rained down on the floor at the front of the shop in a symphony of shattering glass. The mesh was spent and would hold the intruders at bay for only a few moments more.

"Good luck, Daniel," Billy said, reaching back to pick up the discarded weapon. Billy made sure the gun was loaded then pressed the revolver into the dying man's palm.

"Here, take this, too." Daniel tried to pass his backpack to Billy, but he lacked the strength. Kyle reached down and grabbed it, slinging it over one shoulder as he stood back up. Billy put his hand out and Vanessa took it immediately. They walked away from Daniel, each of the children picking up a small pack. Billy took Daniel's pack from Kyle and shouldered it. Vanessa looked back once and then Daniel was lost from sight.

Billy grabbed a six-pack of soda by one of the cans and broke off three. He passed one to each kid, popped the top of his, and guzzled half of it. A small burp later and he was telling the kids what was about to happen.

"Okay, so the street is thick with them out front. We can use the fire escapes and the roofs to get as far as we can then we hit the street all the way back to the school."

"School?" asked Kyle.

"Yeah. It's where I got all the other kids to."

Vanessa took a sharp breath. "There's other kids?

"Well, there were, but I already got them to—" A single shot from the front room made everyone go silent. It was extremely loud. Vanessa lowered her head and began to openly cry.

"I'm so sorry, Vanessa."

She nodded, still crying. Kyle put a hand on her shoulder and she sobbed. The grate came crashing into the room behind them, the sounds of feet on broken glass and the hissing hack of the dead filling the store.

Billy filed the kids into the hallway, closing the access behind them, but the handle was broken, so he couldn't lock it. He put his ear to the steel exterior door, shook his head, and decided to take the kids up through the insurance agency. The dead had made it into the back room of the Starbucks before Billy had closed and locked the delivery hall door. He and the kids climbed the narrow staircase up to the offices and Billy took them in.

He had a thought and he didn't like it. He hadn't truly cleared these offices when he had come through before.

"Let's catch our breath, okay?" He picked an office with a solid door, cleared the small room quickly, and ushered the kids in. "Here." He passed Kyle his knife, but the boy shook his head and drew a small pistol from a hidden holster on his right hip. The kid held the weapon with two hands, pointing down.

Billy raised his eyebrows. "Safety on?"

"Yes. Daniel was a stickler for that."

Billy turned to Vanessa. "And do you...?" She was already holding a large combat knife. *Well done, Daniel*, Billy thought.

"I'm going to check the other offices," Billy began, but the kids both took in a sharp breath.

Kyle narrowed his eyes. "Daniel said we always need to stay together. *Always*. What if you get bitten?"

Billy smiled. "I won't. This is one promise I can make for sure: They won't bite me."

Kyle was wary and Billy could see that he thought Billy's proclamation was dubious. "I still don't want to separate."

"Okay, but stay behind me. Vanessa, you stay in between us, and Kyle, you cover the rear?

"This is how we used to do it with Daniel," she told him.

They moved from the office, but before they could begin their sweep, they heard the delivery door crash open. They could hear the infected begin to swarm the stairs. Several thumps came crashing speedily up the steps and almost immediately, something began its furious hammering on the insurance office's upper door. There had been no inhuman scream, but the pace with which the thing had sprinted up the stairs and the pounding could only mean one thing: a Runner.

"Down here! Follow me!"

Billy raced through a few cubicles to the still-open window where he had gained entry to this floor from outside. He stuck his head out into the warm early-evening air to check the fire escape and it was clear.

"Go!" He started helping the kids through the window when the splintering crack of broken wood filled the air. Now the thing screamed as it tore through the offices, looking for the uninfected. Billy had Kyle almost all the way through the window when the creature tore around a corner, spying Billy over the chest-high partitions. It focused on him briefly, its eyes going wide, then it growled and came for him. Billy pushed the boy the rest of the way through the window, considered for a split second following him, but turned to face the oncoming threat. He was able to bring the rifle to bear and fire off one shot, striking the creature in the left side of its stomach, before it was on him.

The thing hit him full speed, the bullet not slowing it down. The rifle went sideways as they both smashed into the window frame, the back of Billy's head smacking against the bottom of the open window. He was stunned for half a second, but this thing was not. The creature had been an athletic young man and it was incredibly strong. It grabbed hold of Billy's right wrist while it slashed with its free hand. Billy felt the sting of fingernails carving furrows in his face and briefly wondered if he were now infected. He had battled these things and their dead cousins for a year and this was the first time one of them had broken his skin.

He shot his fist out, connecting with the thing's chin, forcing its head up. He punched it in the stomach wound and the thing screamed. The scream sounded like a normal Runner scream, not a bellow of pain. It stared at Billy, its eyes burning into him before it opened its mouth impossibly wide, saliva dripping.

Billy sucked in air to let out a yell.

"Hey, asshole!"

The young infected whipped its head up to glower out the window and received a shot to the forehead for its trouble. It collapsed and Billy shoved it off him quickly, extricating himself from the dead weight. He held his hand to his face and it came away bloody. He was still looking at his bloody palm when the dead rounded the corner and shuffled toward him. He climbed through the window and received a glare from Kyle.

"Won't bite you, my ass."

Billy scowled. "Rated G please." He gave a half nod toward Vanessa and slammed the window down, only to remember he had broken it on the way in.

He rolled his eyes. "Smooth."

Billy began to trek down the fire escape, the kids behind him. In a few seconds, the dead began to crawl through the window above them. Infected began to fill the iron catwalks and they filed down the steps after the humans. One toppled over the side and landed on the street below with the crunch of broken bones. Billy reached the ladder and climbed down, helping Vanessa after him, Kyle bringing up the rear. The undead that had fallen off the fire escape reached for them, but it was too badly damaged to move. Two more undead came around the corner into the street they were on, immediately heading in their direction. Billy began walking toward them.

"What...what are you doing?" demanded Kyle.

Billy pointed. "We need to go this way." He drew his knife, turned his back on the approaching dead, and folded his arms. Kyle and Vanessa, eyes wide, began to back up. When the dead were almost on Billy, Vanessa threw her face in her hands. Kyle pointed his weapon at them, but Billy held up a finger and nodded. The infected marched right past him, one of them looking at him briefly on its way to the kids. Billy destroyed both quickly and caught up to the children, looking smug.

"What do you think now?"

Kyle blinked. "I think you're crazy."

"Weerrp!" Billy said and touched his finger to his nose.

LINCOLN, NEBRASKA

Two scouts sat atop the roof of the abandoned Shuster's Meats meat-packing warehouse just off Route Six, northeast of Lincoln Nebraska. They had been playing five-card draw with a beat-up deck of playing cards for a day and a half. Their job was to guard this entry into the city of Lincoln. More to the point, they were to radio in to their base in Cornhusker Stadium if they saw anything. They would be relieved in twelve hours, just before eight PM. Barry had a low straight, and thought he would be taking Art's bet of four cigarettes, but they were interrupted. They stared at each other wide-eyed when they heard the strangest sound. The game forgotten, they dropped their cards. Barry picked up a huge pair of binoculars, Art a scoped Marlin hunting rifle. They peered cautiously down the road.

An ice cream truck drove slowly down Route Six, a tune blaring from it as loudly as possible.

"Oh my God, we're dead."

"Jesus…" Art breathed, "Jesus Christ! Call it in right now!"

Barry fumbled for his radio while Art tried to get a look at the driver. The front window of the good humor truck, as well as most of the vehicle, was armored. Art was unable to discern the driver through his rifle scope. The vehicle was perhaps a mile down the road, but the scouts were able to hear and see the truck because of the level terrain.

The truck was interesting, but what followed chilled both men to the bone. The driver towed infected behind him as far as the eye could see. Thousands, hundreds of thousands plodded along. A few hundred Runners were at the forefront of the mass, chasing the truck with woefully inadequate speed. They would catch the vehicle and it would speed up for a few hundred yards, then slow down again.

The truck was definitely leading the pack.

"Command," Barry blurted into the radio, "this is Northeast Six, come in!" He sounded terrified.

"We read you Six, what's on fire, over?"

"Command, we're looking at a swarm of infected! I've never seen anything like it. It looks like millions, over!"

A chuckle came over the radio. "Millions, huh? Barry, if you're drunk, it won't go well for you when you get back. The brass tends to frown on drinking on duty."

Art grabbed the radio. "Listen, Rocky, you little piss-ant fuck! Get someone who matters on the radio now or I swear to God I will kill you when I get back!"

"Uh, okay Art, hold on." The man on the other end of the radio, Rocky, knew that Art meant what he said. Several of the men in the Triumvirate forces were simply not to be screwed around with, and Art was one of them.

Less than a minute later, a new voice sounded through the radio. "This is Major Tower. Report, Six?"

"Major, I'm looking at the largest swarm of infected I've ever seen. There has to be more than half a million. They're being led by an ice cream truck."

"Copy that, Six. Hunker down and wait them out. We'll get you as soon as we can. Tower out."

"What?" demanded Barry. "What the fuck did he just say?"

Art clipped the radio to his belt and sighed. "He said he agrees with you; we're dead."

"Roger that," Major Tower said into a different radio. "Scramble two Warthogs and two Apaches, on my authority. Send them to the coordinates I've given you and tell them to engage.

"Sir," came the reply, *"Recht has given specific orders not to—"*

"I don't give a shit what Recht says!" Tower screamed. "That asshole isn't in charge of military operations, Bourne is! With Bourne and Brooks gone, military control starts and ends with me! Scramble the birds or I fucking shoot you! You have five minutes!"

As soon as Art had turned his radio off, the ice cream truck had stopped broadcasting its tune and had sped up. It flew by the meat-packing plant toward Lincoln. It disappeared into the city shortly after. The swarm continued to follow, and soon the cries and moans of the dead were so loud Barry put his hands over his ears and scrunched his eyes closed. Art glanced at his partner in disgust. If he didn't think he might need this asshole, he would kill him right now just for being a pussy.

The packing plant was sealed up tight with metal shutters, and even if the dead bastards gained entry, the stairs to the roof ended in a six-foot ladder to climb. They were safe.

Two A10 attack planes screamed overhead. They made a wide circle then they came back, their noses dipped slightly. They had begun a strafing run, one plane behind the other. A sound like a gigantic zipper being opened rent the air as 30mm rounds spewed from the Avenger Gatling cannon on the nose of the A10 Warthog. Both Art and Barry stood from their concealed positions to view the swarm after the first pass. The planes circled and returned for a second run.

Art smiled as the rounds impacted the horde. Burning pieces of the dead things were tossed into the air as the incendiary rounds tore into them. Barry cheered but Art pulled him back from the edge of the building. "Shut up!"

A huge swath of melted asphalt and disgusting pink goo interspersed with small fires made up what used to be Route Six next to Shuster's Meats. It had to be two hundred yards long. Art's smile vanished as the dead began to refill the opening in the street. He shook his head as he realized that the Warthogs would run out of ammo or fuel long before they put a dent in the amount of infected that made up the swarm.

The men could hear helicopters coming over the din of the dead. Barry pointed, smiling, but Art knew that these were attack birds, and couldn't pick them up from the roof. They were far off, and before they got on station, the A10s would get in at least one more run. The nose cannons opened up once more and Barry fist-pumped the air. Art recognized the two large canisters which released from the wings of the first plane, the tubes spinning end over end as they tumbled toward the infected. He also realized that he and Barry were way too close to where the canisters would hit.

"Motherfu—" he began as the napalm hit the ground with a spectacular explosion. Flames shot into the sky in a half mile long twenty-meter wide line. Any infected in the flame zone were instantly liquefied, and flaming individuals just outside the zone stumbled off and collapsed. Art and Barry caught the blast wave and were also killed almost instantly. Shuster's Meats was unrecognizable as a structure after the second A10 dropped her payload of high-explosive Rockeye cluster bombs.

The Apache helicopters arrived on station and began to fire their rockets and chain guns into the swarm. By the time they returned to base, more than sixty thousand undead had been destroyed.

Hardly a dent in the nine-hundred thousand strong horde on its way to Cornhusker Stadium.

The ice cream truck pulled off Route Six and into the open warehouse door of a landscape supply company. The driver had personally seen to the extermination of almost one hundred thousand infected in this area prior to his excursion to the east coast. On his return trip, he had brought almost ten times that number with him. He had known about the swarm moving west and had intercepted them when they had finished with Des Moines.

A Runner jumped up on the step of the truck, shrieking, and the driver slid open a gun port and shot it in the face. Couldn't have its cries bringing a bunch of infected in and bogging him down now; he was almost finished with this portion of his plan. He thought of his former comrades. Colonel Bourne was dead, but that damnable preacher was still very much alive. Alive and in the way.

"One down, one to go," Brooks said aloud.

He smiled at the thought of the aircraft raining second death down on the infected. If they had a hundred planes, they couldn't do shit. They would need a nuke or a couple of Hades bombs, and only he knew where the codes for the nukes were. He'd get the codes eventually, but in the meantime, he would watch the stadium get overrun. He smiled again.

There was no means of escape for Recht, the preacher. Nothing could save him now, not even his God.

Three infected stumbled into the warehouse. Brooks harrumphed and grabbed his MP5. He exited the vehicle, the dead stumbling toward him. He folded his arms and waited. The dead reached him, but lost interest and moved on. Brooks moved to the warehouse roll-down door and closed it. He dealt with the undead quickly then surveyed his surroundings.

"This will do," he said to himself. He smiled again. "Easy as pie."

UNKNOWN ROAD, MASSACHUSETTS

"Jesus…" Rick let the word hang as he passed a pair of binoculars to Dallas. Dallas used the glasses to peer at an elementary school with vast open fields next to it. Five white tents, perhaps forty feet long and ten feet tall at their centers, had been erected in one of the school's parking lots. The aluminum skeleton of a sixth tent sat partially constructed. The tents were surrounded by a chain-link fence, which in turn was encompassed by the parking lot full of abandoned vehicles. Desert-colored military vehicles sat next to civilian cars and trucks of all types. A Blackhawk helicopter, its side panel open to the elements, was positioned further off in the overgrown elementary school field. A gleaming red fire truck, which still reflected the sun brightly despite a year's lack of washing, blocked the entrance to the large lot full of cars.

Through the dingy windows of the school, Dallas could see figures moving about. Their numbers paled in comparison to the throng that shuffled back and forth between the cars and in and out of the tents. They stepped around, or stumbled over, the hundreds of white body bags neatly arranged in a row on one side of the small tent-town. Some of the bags moved, their occupants struggling to vacate their plastic prisons, but most remained stationary. More bags filled two dump trucks to capacity and a third was nearly three-quarters full.

From their vantage a few hundred feet away, Rick and his group could hear the horrible noises of the dead carried on the light breeze.

Seyfert lowered his own binoculars. "Looks like the remnants of a FEMA camp." He shook his head. "Look at them all. I'm not the least bit shocked it was overrun."

"Gotta be a thousand of them body bags," Dallas added. The big Texan looked from side to side, stretching his gaze as far as he could in both directions. To the left was the town center, which consisted of many buildings, including a supermarket and a large library. Other businesses were connected via a mini-mall type structure. To the right sat an abandoned fairground, a fire station, and several more businesses, which dotted the road. The focal point was the school.

"How're we gonna get around 'em?"

"I vote we put a plow on you, Hillbilly, and you just run through."

Seyfert looked behind them into the thick forest they had come through. He really didn't want to go back into those infested woods. It was miraculous that his group had successfully negotiated the trees with the amount of dead shuffling through them. Only a couple of times had they needed to battle undead and in both cases, the fight had been quick and quiet. He rubbed his side and made a face. He had survived eleven missions as a SEAL, torture at the hands of crazy militants, and crossing a United States beset by legions of undead, only to almost get cashed in by a rogue deer. He shook his head. "I don't know."

Anna, who was covering the rear and staring back into the trees, spoke up, "No chance we make it back through those woods without being bitten."

"Agreed, but look at that." Seyfert pointed at the host of former humans, shuffling through their existence, a few hundred feet away.

"I'm just as concerned with that," Rick said and pointed at a woman who was repeatedly punching and scratching one of the dead. She threw her head back and howled, every undead head in earshot turning to look at her. Dozens began to make their way toward the sound, only to realize that there was no food to be had. The infected thing began to tear at the walking dead man, slashing and biting him. He didn't seem to mind and kept trying to stand when she would knock him down. The thing picked another victim and did the same, focusing her efforts on this new challenge. One of the more industrious dead folk grabbed her by the back of the shirt and she whipped around, launching herself at it. They went down, her astride the dead thing and she ripped out its throat with her teeth while throwing haymakers and screaming. The noise brought more of the dead to her, but most ambled off when they realized she was tainted. Some stood around her, not comprehending why one of them could scream and move quickly, but they too eventually lumbered away.

"And that's the one we can see," Anna told them, staring back at the woods. "There might be another twenty of the speedy ones down there who aren't having a cow."

"Having a cow?" Seyfert repeated. All three men turned to look at her.

"Yeah, freaking out. I've seen the fast ones stand around, just like the dead ones until they see something that bothers them. Then they go ballistic."

The guys, silently agreeing with Anna, turned back around to survey the school and that which surrounded it.

Her sharp intake of breath caused them to spin their heads back to her again. She didn't say a word, so they followed her gaze.

Sitting on his haunches, his elbows resting on his knees, was a boy, maybe twelve, dressed in soiled shorts. He was barefoot with no shirt on, perhaps fifty feet from their position, with his head cocked to the right. He had scratches all over the front of him from running through the woods.

The team stared at the kid, the eyes staring back at them the deep crimson of ruptured capillaries. The lower portion of his young face was a different shade of red; the stains of blood, not wiped away.

"Contact..." Anna breathed almost silently, and the kid stood.

"Shoot it." When Anna did not fire, Seyfert repeated his command more urgently, "Shoot it, Anna!"

"Suppressor is burned out..."

"Shit!" Seyfert aimed his suppressed weapon at the boy, but before he could fire, the infected flexed his fingers into claws and he shrieked. Answering shrieks came from the woods, the camp, and through a broken school window. The rasps and cries from the dead amped up in volume as well.

The boy broke into an instant sprint, straight at Anna, and Seyfert double-tapped him in the chest. His little frame collapsed mid-run and the survivors could discern the infected child coughing his life-blood away over the din of the oncoming horde of dead.

"We're in it now," Dallas told them and stood. A dead woman stumbled out of the woods, followed by a second, then a dead man. Seyfert twisted and brought his rifle up, aiming back toward the school. The M4 barked once and he stood next to Dallas, Rick following.

"Fast one is down! Follow me!" Taking charge of the situation, the SEAL began to lope to the right, parallel to the forest, with the school and its bounty of death on their left. The dead commenced their plodding, tireless pursuit, angling to intercept the survivors. Infected started to step from the woods in larger numbers in front and behind the fleeing friends. Seyfert had to angle away from the trees and the sheer number of hostiles, but too much angle would put them into the oncoming crowd from the school. They would get pinched and overrun in a minute or two if he didn't do something fast.

A Runner burst from the trees. She sprinted straight at Rick, he being the closest to her. He fired, striking her in the right hip and knocking her down. He didn't wait to see if she was getting up and continued his sprint.

The businesses on the left crawled with monsters and the woods were just as infested. In front of them were the fire station and the fairgrounds. The brick fire station was two levels, but both garage doors were open. The SEAL didn't know if he could close the doors before the dead reached them, so it was the fair. He didn't say a word to his friends as he ran for the eight-foot chain-link boundary to the carnival. The infected were close enough now that he could see individual wounds on them. *We're not going to make it,* he thought as the frontline of the enemy began to close on them. The SEAL began to selectively fire into the crowd, dropping the closer ones. His friends followed suit, but they had to slow down to achieve any type of accuracy. The tactic seemed to work until the gap closed and the survivors were forced to go hand to hand.

Dallas fired his shotgun into the face of an emaciated woman who reached for him, her cranium ceasing to exist. Anna fired her pistol quickly, dispatching two but missing four more. Rick scored three headshots and his weapon clicked empty. He let it dangle on its single-point sling and drew his sidearm, dispatching two more infected before one grabbed his weapon hand and bit down on the suppressor. The thing's teeth shattered from the bite, making it easier for Rick to extricate the weapon and shoot point-blank into the creature's mouth. They had cleared a quick breach in the wall of death and the survivors surged forward.

A green and white sign on the fair-grounds fence read: *148th Annual Marshfield Fair! Join us for…* the rest of the sign had been torn away. The gate to the grounds was closed, but it was two hundred feet to the left and the dead were already between the gate and the living people.

Seyfert impacted the chain-link fence and began to climb immediately. He was up and over in no time, dropping to the other side and gasping from the pain which exploded in his left side. It was suddenly very hard to breathe. He ejected the magazine on his weapon and slammed another home. His three friends were scaling the fence, but Dallas was heavy and it was taking him a bit longer. It was Rick who had the most trouble though, as he was in a tug-of-war with a deceased man in the tattered remains of a hospital johnny. Both of them wanted Rick's right leg and they were struggling so much, Seyfert couldn't get a shot. He poked his rifle through one of the links in the fence, striking the creature in the throat. He fired and the thing's Adam's apple exploded, but it didn't let go. Rick kicked at the same time Seyfert adjusted his aim and fired again. Rick was finally free and climbed the rest of the fence. Anna and Dallas jumped down on the safe side of the barrier, Dallas taking a tumble. Dozens of infected impacted the chain-link before Rick could jump down and he lost his balance, falling on the twisted spikes at the top of the chain link. He grunted and tossed himself over, landing hard. Seyfert went to help him up, but a new level of agony lanced through his side and he knew his ribs were broken. He reached a hand down anyway, but Rick saw the rictus of anguish on his friend's face and declined the assistance, pushing himself up.

Dozens of dead were now just on the other side of the barrier pushing to get in, with hundreds more behind them. The ones in the front were being shredded between the ones behind them and the metal of the fence, chunks flaying off and dropping to the grass.

"We need to get out of sight!" Anna told them.

Rick was bleeding profusely from his abdomen and chest, but he helped Dallas up and Anna helped an ashen-faced Seyfert move.

"There!" The SEAL nodded and they raced as fast as they could up a hill to a green and white structure. A sliding wooden door barred their way and it was padlocked, but Dallas made short work of the hasp with the butt of his weapon and in seconds they were inside. Anna slid the heavy door closed, spinning back to clear the immediate area.

The survivors now stood in an open, two-story, hexagonal lobby area with framed old photos and paintings of the town they were in. Natural light filtered into the room through dusty windows, but that light seemed to be losing a struggle with dark shadows. Several rooms extended from the main lobby and an ancient set of wide wooden stairs rose to the second floor. The place was dusty with a musty smell instead of the reek of the dead.

"Anybody home?" Anna asked in a raised voice.

The quartet waited patiently for an influx of infected from the rooms or upstairs, but nothing came.

Seyfert evaluated their hideout quickly. "Can we shore up in here? That fence will be down in minutes. They didn't see us come in here, but that doesn't mean they won't come looking."

"I'll clear the rooms," Anna told them, "and check upstairs."

"Not alone," Seyfert said through clenched teeth. "Rick?"

Rick nodded, placing his ammo pack on the dusty wooden floor. He silently moved toward the lower rooms with Anna, who dropped her med pouch. Rick screwed a new suppressor onto his weapon. They pulled shades in two rooms and old wooden blinds in another to block the view from outside. Both looked up the stairs and then back at each other. The first step creaked incredibly loudly when Rick put pressure on it and he winced. The other steps weren't silent, but didn't compare to the sound of the first one. The top floor was identical in look to the bottom. They traded off who went in which room first, keeping their suppressed weapons at the ready, not that Anna's suppressor would function properly. The top floor was cleared very quickly. Each of the five rooms held nothing that would help them and more importantly, no infected. Anna leaned over the brown hexagonal wooden railing to see the SEAL and Dallas both sitting in chairs. Seyfert was leaning back, taking shallow breaths and Dallas was attempting to get his boot off.

"Clear up here," she told them.

"Not so much out there though," Rick said and pointed out the second-floor window. The dead were spread out much more than they had been at the abandoned FEMA camp down the street, but there were still hundreds of them. They meandered in and out of forgotten carnival rides, several stepping up on a carousel. Dozens more filtered into the wide-open green and white 4H barn and even more had made it to an overgrown horse track. A young woman sprinted past The Kiddie-Coaster, followed by two men and then a third. All four of them stopped together, frantically searching for something. *Us*, Rick thought.

One of the men screamed at another and they began to fight, tearing at each other and screaming until something made them whip their heads around. All four of them raced off out of sight to see what the something was.

"Shit, did we just trap ourselves in here?"

"Yeah," answered Anna, "but we weren't getting anywhere fast with Dallas's leg and the jarhead's ribs. I knew that deer kicked his ass. Must have cracked the bones and when he went over the fence, they broke."

"Must have," Rick agreed, as he felt his chest. He had said it with a pained voice and Anna caught on to it immediately. His hand came away bloody.

"Oh shit… Are you bitten?"

"No. No, it was the fence. Those little barbs on the top got me."

"Shirt off. Let me see."

He nodded and began to remove his tactical webbing and black camouflage T-shirt.

"Jesus…" Anna breathed when he had the shirt over his head.

Rick looked down at his chest. "Oh. Oh shit."

She had to concur. "Yeah, *oh shit* is right."

He had four separate lacerations, two across his left pectoral muscle that went under his nipple and two on his stomach that stretched from his left side, across his navel to his right hip. The two on his upper torso were slices and bled freely, whereas the two on his lower abdomen were where the chain link barbs had torn him open. The bottom two were vicious wounds and the purple of muscle could be seen under the lowest tear in the skin. Several other holes oozed blood where they dotted his chest and abdomen as well, but they didn't look as serious.

"We need to disinfect that right now."

"Shouldn't you look at Seyfert—?"

"*Right now!*" she reiterated. "The likelihood that either of those two numbskulls get an infection from galvanized chain-link is low. You, on the other hand…"

They moved back downstairs, Anna putting her sidearm on a small table and grabbing her medical kit. She glanced at Dallas, who was making faces at his ankle and Seyfert, who was still taking the labored breaths of someone with a rib injury.

"I know you're hurt, but we should probably think about getting upstairs and figuring out a way to prevent them from getting up there when they get in."

The SEAL took another torturous deep breath and stood. He nodded and moved to help Dallas.

"Don't be a dumbass!" Anna hissed and helped the SEAL to the stairs. She opened her bag and rooted around until she found a brown bottle of something and some gauze.

"What's that?" Rick asked nervously.

"Relax, it isn't the stingy stuff and it certainly isn't Kwik Clot." She glanced at him. "Pussy," she added. She dabbed a bit of the stuff on the gauze and motioned for Rick to lift his arm a bit.

Rick took an involuntary hiss of breath. "Jesus! You said it wasn't stingy!"

They both spun their heads toward the heavy sliding door as the farmer's porch on the building creaked loudly. The first sounds of the dead reached them as well and everyone went still and silent. Shadows moved across the outside of the shades in one of the rooms, some of which unceremoniously thudded into the exterior shingles. They weren't banging to get in, just smacking into the walls.

Seyfert snapped his fingers quietly and the group moved toward the steps. Dallas made to put his foot on the first step and Rick grabbed him, shaking his finger. They quietly climbed the stairs while the dead searched for them.

A scream from close by chilled Anna's blood. Two answering cries from further away increased her terror as she helped Seyfert over the last stair.

Her voice was the slightest whisper when she told Rick, "I need to finish cleaning you up." He nodded and she worked on him for a few minutes with the gauze and disinfectant.

He didn't like it. She winced when he winced and she put adhesive bandages over the smaller wounds. She used medical glue to seal the dual wounds on his chest and the top abdomen gash. In the waning light, she dug through her bag again, coming out with a suture kit.

Rick shook his head, *No!*

"Sorry, but the glue won't do it for that." She pointed at his stomach and a window broke downstairs. All four of the survivors stared at the open area between the floors. Nothing seemed to be trying to get in. The broken window was probably just from an accidental impact. Anna had a moment of panic where she frantically patted herself down then closed her eyes.

"I left my gun downstairs."

Before anyone could object, she moved silently down the old staircase. The three men watched through the hexagonal opening as Anna moved to retrieve her weapon. She had no sooner picked it up when a Runner's scream rent the air. The breaking of glass that followed sent tendrils of terror down her spine and through her stomach. She dropped down behind a display case with a large ship model in it. She scooched her back against the mahogany, momentarily closing her eyes and voicing a silent prayer. She held the weapon with two hands, knowing her suppressor was burnt out. Anna looked up at the rest of her friends. All three of them had their weapons trained on the doors near her, panning them around, looking for hostiles. Seyfert first put his hand on Dallas' shotgun then shook a silent *No* to Rick, who also lowered his weapon.

The SEAL pulled his combat knife and pointed at Anna. She understood and drew her own knife. Seyfert drew his finger across his throat and she swallowed hard, understanding what he meant.

Ragged breathing behind her made her almost soil herself. The thing was inside with her, not five feet away. She looked back up, noticing that only Seyfert remained visible. Barely. He was on one knee, his rifle aimed at the creature through the banister of the hexagonal railing. If he fired, she would be saved, but only briefly as the remainder of the things in the fairgrounds would storm their little haven and tear the survivors to pieces.

The creature began to make odd noises, like a cross between a cough and a bark, *Uh! Uh! Uh!* and she could feel it jerking and twitching on the floorboards. Then she heard something that terrified her more than anything else had since the onset of the plague. In a horrible, wet hack, the thing uttered, "*Wheeeeere?*"

A footstep sounded on her right and she directed her gaze that way. A shuddering shadow on the picture-framed wall told her the thing had stopped. Slow, deliberate scratching, fingernails on glass, commenced on the dusty case of the model ship above her. She considered that the thing might know she was in here someplace. Could it smell her? She looked up at Seyfert and he pushed his palm at her, indicating she should wait and not do anything.

Tap-tap. The creature rapped its knuckles on the glass. It gave a low growl and made another guttural noise. "*Booah. Uh! Uh! Booah...*"

Anna had never been so terrified. She glanced up at Seyfert again and he nodded his head almost imperceptibly. She felt the floorboards shift and whipped her head around to the right again. Seeing nothing, she dared a look to the left and saw the back-right leg of the thing. It was barefoot, wearing a pair of dirty blue jeans and a red T-shirt. It came fully into view and Anna almost shit herself. From the back, it looked like it had been a young man, but she knew that nothing about it, other than its shape, was even remotely human. The fingers on both hands constantly flexed into claws and the head jerked to the right while the body twitched all over. Its knees were in constant motion although the thing's feet were planted solidly.

This thing would eviscerate her and play hopscotch in her entrails and it was four feet away. Its head stopped twitching for a moment and it pushed its face forward, peering into one of the downstairs rooms. Anna put her left hand, which was still holding her sidearm, on the floor and pushed herself up silently. Even as quiet as she had been, the creature heard her and went into a half crouch. It jerked its head to the side looking for her, but didn't know she was behind it and looked the wrong way. She took one purposeful stride so that she was right behind it, reached her knife-wielding fist around to the front of it, and drew her blade across its throat as hard as she could.

Infected blood spurted the length of the room in front of the Runner and Anna in a great gout. The thing brought both hands to its throat, aware something had happened, but not sure what. It started to turn on Anna and she grabbed it by the hair and began repeatedly stabbing it in the back. As soon as she touched it, the creature went ape-shit and spun to face her, slashing with its fingernails. She had a handful of the thing's hair, but it was taller than her so when it turned she was jerked to the side. Anna fell and the infected dropped onto her, swiping at her midsection. She batted its attempts away, slapping and pushing at it. Dark fluids rained down on her chest from the throat wound and blood bubbled from its nose and spilled through its growling teeth over its lower lip.

Seyfert tightened his finger on the trigger of his weapon, but relaxed it a bit when he saw the creature losing strength. Anna could see it blinking rapidly and a large blood bubble formed on the wound she had created. She pushed it to the side and crab-crawled away from it, breathing hard. It looked up at her with sadness, not hate, on its face and it collapsed. A few more breaths and it was spent.

Rick was suddenly standing next to her and she began to cry. He reached down to help her up but she shrank away from him. "Don't touch me!"

Rick reeled back, horrified.

"No! No, no, no! I didn't mean it like that!" she said. "I'm covered in this shit and you have cuts. You stay away!"

She got up of her own volition and after Rick drove his blade into the newly dead thing's temple, they moved back upstairs together. She grabbed her bag and immediately began to cut her shirt off, right down the middle. She turned from the men and threw her shirt to the ground, slicing through her bra with the scissors. She used gauze to wipe herself off, discarding the infected medical supplies on the floor.

She was inspecting the front of herself for scratches when Dallas said, "Here," and passed her his button-down shirt.

"Do I have any scratches or cuts on my back?" Dallas and Rick both examined her, Dallas lifting her hair to check the back of her neck. She was breathing fast.

"Yer clean, kid," the Texan told her. "Also, remind me never to piss you off."

"What?" she asked, buttoning up the shirt, which was many sizes too large for her.

"Ya done kicked that thing's ass!"

She turned and saw Rick nodding. "You really did."

"I had to," she said and burst into tears. Dallas embraced her in a tender bear hug. She sobbed for only a moment. "I was so scared…"

Dallas let her go. "We all were." He made a face and she pushed gently away.

She furrowed her brow. "How's your ankle?"

"It's fine. Check…" They all looked at Seyfert. He was sitting on the floor, leaning against the wooden railing. The SEAL was breathing raggedly and each breath brought him pain.

"I think… I might need…a corpsman."

"Oh shit!" Anna moved quickly from Dallas and got on her knees by Seyfert. She unbuckled his tactical webbing, moved his weapon, and checked under his shirt.

He coughed, sending spasms of agony through him. "Tough…to breath."

"Jesus Christ!" exclaimed Anna, looking at the huge purple bruise with yellow edges on Seyfert's side. It extended from just under his armpit to just above his waist.

"Rick! My bag!" She felt gently where she thought the damage was and the SEAL hissed in pain. After the hiss, it was clear he could no longer breathe. He started to make odd sounds and Anna began to dig in her bag. "Where is it!" she demanded and upended the entire medical pouch onto the floor.

It was obvious that Seyfert was in a great deal of pain and nervousness showed on his face. Anna found a small blue pack with a zipper in the myriad of medical supplies now on the floor. She quickly unzipped it and removed a cylindrical, individually wrapped package. Tearing it open, she revealed it to be a large syringe, which she pulled the plunger out of and discarded. The needle had a twist handle as its cap. The medic tore open an alcohol swab, felt the SEAL's ribs again, and without ceremony, pushed the needle between two of them and twisted the handle.

The *PSSSSssssssssssss* of escaping air came from the needle and Seyfert could immediately breathe again. The look of pain he had was replaced with relief.

He nodded. "Better."

Anna also released a big breath. "Tension pneumothorax. That deer kicked your ass, Mr. SEAL."

Dallas also looked concerned. "Attention what-now?"

"One of his broken ribs must have nicked a lung. Air was escaping from the lung into the chest cavity, which then crushed and collapsed his lung."

"Is that bad?" drawled the Texan in a whisper.

"It would have killed him, eventually." She closed the twist-cap but left the needle in him. Seyfert made to pull it out, but she grabbed his hand, giving him a stern look. "Don't touch that." Using most of her medical tape, Anna secured the needle to his side with large loops that circled his chest. She wrapped his ribs with a compression bandage, careful to loop the brown dressing around the affixed syringe. "Anytime you feel pressure on your chest, or if it's hard to breathe, open the syringe and it will release the air. This won't fix your broken ribs though. They're going to hurt."

Seyfert nodded. "How long do I have to have this thing sticking in me?"

"I don't know. We'll take it out tomorrow and see if you're okay." She sat down next to him. "It spoke."

All three of them looked at her, but it was Rick who asked the question, "What?"

"That thing," she pointed at the body of the Runner, pathetically splayed out next to the ship model, a puddle of plague-infected blood surrounding it, "it talked. It asked *where*. It knew I was in here and it asked itself where I was."

"You're misremembering," Seyfert alleged, "it happens in situa—"

"No, I'm not. I heard it and I remember it clear as day. It spoke. That's why I was so scared. Well, that and I thought it was going to tear me to pieces."

"Well, ain't that a peach," grumbled the big Texan under his breath. "Maybe we can just ask them not to kill us now?"

SCOTT STREET, SAN FRANCISCO

Through the waning light, three people lying on their bellies looked down on an overgrown and trash-strewn Alta Plaza Park from behind a huge apartment window. The gorgeous flat had been unlocked and untouched and Billy had thought they were extremely lucky to find such a swanky place. The home took up both the second and third floors of the building and was extremely spacious, with an open floor plan and a giant fireplace below. A wide, winding, enclosed stairway led to four bedrooms and a bathroom in the loft above. Billy hated the black and white rug which sat under an ostentatious and no doubt extremely expensive coffee table. Other than that, the place was perfect. Especially the ratcheting metal front door complete with three deadbolts and a security bar which protruded down into a steel plate in the floor. All the windows were too high for infected to reach. If they drew the curtains and stayed upstairs, they might be able to ride out what the three survivors were staring at.

The boy still wasn't sure about Billy and he was constantly testing the waters. "We can make it."

"No, we can't. Look there," Billy pointed, "and there." Dozens of undead were milling about the street in front of them, but there were at least two Runners and they were game changers.

"Sorry, Kyle, but we'll have to stay here until it gets dark before we make a move. The fast ones will catch us, and those ones do want to eat me."

"I used to play there," said Vanessa as she stared longingly at the multi-colored, metal jungle gym. "We would stay here for hours, with Stephanie, my babysitter. I used to hate it when people would call her a babysitter. It made me feel like a baby." She absently put her hand in Billy's and he gave her a reassuring squeeze.

A dead man kept tripping over a curved, low stone wall built for use as a bench. The thing would trip over it, get up, take a few steps, and trip over it again going in the other direction. Another dead thing stood next to a blue and yellow teeter-totter with its hand resting on the metal. Two more were caught inside a blue and red geo-dome with yellow netting. The dome was too short to accommodate adult heights. Billy smiled at the thought of the two dead grownups bent over inside the child's plaything for eternity. His smile evaporated when he saw a child stumble across the concrete and repeatedly bump into a three-foot metal fence encircling the play area. The kid would forever be denied entry into the park and that made Billy sad.

Then he remembered that this thing was not a child anymore, but something wicked that had both murdered the boy then stolen his body. Billy didn't often get angry, but he felt his ire rising and had to will it back down. He looked at Vanessa and Kyle, two living kids that the dead one would gladly tear into and devour.

Billy sighed. "We wait until dark and then, if the street is more clear than that, we'll make a break for it." As if to accentuate his point, one of the sprinters took off at a lightning pace, tackled a dead woman, and began to punch and claw at it. The other Runner noticed and sprinted at the two infected who were battling. *Well*, thought Billy, *one is battling, the other is just minding her undead business.*

The second Runner, a male in tattered sweatpants, stopped short of the fight and screamed at the combatants. The first one, a female with extremely long dark hair, shot up and raked its nails across the male's cheek. Both screamed at each other then the man bolted forward, smashing itself into the female. They both went down screaming and slashing.

"Ohh!" Billy exclaimed. "I wish we had popcorn."

The two kids stared at him, aghast.

"What?" he asked when he figured out they were both looking at him. "Oh come on, I was kidding! Geez, so serious. Ten bucks on the dude, he's way bigger."

Kyle glanced at Billy before returning his gaze to the infected bout below on the street. "I don't have any money."

Billy reached down and grabbed his pack. He fished around in it for a moment before coming out with three neat stacks of cash. "Here's ten grand for each of you. Don't spend it all in one place."

The kids looked at each other and then at him. They both broke into ear-to-ear grins.

"I've... I've never seen so much money before!" Vanessa squealed.

Kyle sighed, hefting the banded bills. "I wish I could have had this when the video game store was still open. $100 on the woman. Guy might be bigger, but she is just nuts, look at her."

Billy gave him a sideways, knowing glance. "Done."

They never got to see a winner because something stole the attention of the infected in the area. The Runners both got up and ran off down the side of the park, screaming. They vaulted the small fence, sprinted across the park, and were lost to the invading evening shadows. Their dead cousins followed at a death-impeded pace.

Billy moved slowly into a crouch, thanking whatever it was that drew the monsters away. "Let's shut the curtains and do some planning. They all have their backs to us." He moved the heavy, dark drapes across the massive windows slowly until the three of them sat in partial darkness.

"I have to pee," Vanessa stated blankly and stood.

"There are two bathrooms, a big one down here and smaller one up there. Go for it." Billy pointed upstairs.

Vanessa didn't move. Billy was about to ask what was wrong, when Kyle interrupted, "Daniel told us we never went anywhere alone. Not ever."

"But I already cleared the place."

Both kids shook their heads no.

Billy shrugged. "Okay then. Upstairs or down?"

"Down."

The three of them moved from the living room across the white tiles of the kitchen to the bathroom. Billy moved in first, checking the small closet, looking in the claw-foot tub and even opening a large cabinet.

"Clear." He waved his hand, indicating the room was all hers. Delighted, she moved past him into the room. He made to close the door, but Kyle put his hand on it.

"We'll just turn around and let her go," the boy said. "We always stay in sight."

Billy smiled. "Daniel was a smart guy."

"We're alive because of him."

"Right. As of now, I adopt Daniel's *Always Stick Together* philosophy or whatever. I'm not watching anybody go to the bathroom though, that's icky. And weird," he added.

The girl finished up and the three of them grabbed their packs and moved upstairs. Billy had already cleared the rooms, but he did a once-over again, checking closets and large spaces. The place was clean for being deserted for so long, with a bit of dust here and there. The beds were made in all the bedrooms and Billy picked the room with the view of the park and portions of Pacific Heights. The room held a giant flat screen television, several chests of drawers, and two chairs with a small table and desk. Two tall, stainless steel lamps flanked the enormous king-size bed, which sat across from a set of mirrored closet doors. The bedroom door had a lock on it and Billy engaged it before he closed the vertical blinds to the window and drew the heavy drapes. He also took a hefty comforter from the decorative cedar chest at the foot of the bed and ran it across the curtain rod, wrapping it over the drapes. The room had become extremely dark when he covered the window.

He took a few steps back, putting his hands on his hips and admiring his handy work. He took a deep breath, taking in the scent of cedar.

"Should do it."

The kids had figured out what he was doing, having seen their former guardian do the same thing.

"We can have a light on now?" asked Vanessa.

"Yeah, why not? And guess what? I happen to have one." Billy began to dig in his pack, but Kyle beat him to it and popped on his flashlight. The kid covered the top of the beam so it would only shine into the backpack, helping in Billy's search. Billy came away with a wind-up lantern and immediately began to crank the handle. The item brightened instantly, throwing a moderate amount of light throughout the room. He stopped winding after about a minute then dug in his bag again. He produced a small bundle and unwrapped it.

"Prepare to get your butts kicked, young ones!"

He laid out a piece of multicolored cloth which turned out to be a representation of the board from the game *Sorry!* He also had three different colored pawns and a set of dice.

"Sorry has cards," Kyle told him.

"Sorry." Both kids looked at him. "No, I mean I'm sorry that *Sorry!* is supposed to use cards, but I have dice. A four or a ten moves you backward, everything else is the same. I've been playing this way for years. It works."

"Yeah, but—" began Kyle, but Vanessa cut him off.

"Shh! Do you hear that?"

All three of them cocked their heads and listened. The hacking rasp, mournful moans and terrifying hissing of agitated infected began to become audible. The dead hadn't moved off for very long and the noises were getting louder.

"Pack up," Billy quietly demanded of the kids. He switched the lantern off then moved to the drapes. He looked at the kids then moved the left side of the blanket he had added to the drapery. Dozens of infected were streaming through the park toward the building he and the kids were in. Some were already crossing the street between the park and the row of houses.

"They're coming," he told the kids and then a Runner screamed. The scream was outside, but close.

To their credit, the kids didn't look as frightened as he thought they should be. They finished packing and Billy pointed to the *Sorry!* game. "Don't forget that. Kyle, can you hold on to it for me?"

Kyle rolled up the cloth board as Billy checked his magazines. "I have fifty-one bullets. There are at least a hundred of them out there and more will come because of the racket these ones are making. If I shoot, every dead-head in the city will come looking. I'm going to have to go hand-to-hand." He hefted the combat dagger he had appropriated from the remains of the man who had tried to capture him. "I really wish I had my machete back," he added thoughtfully.

Although the apartment that he and the kids were holed up in occupied the second and third floors, there was a door which led to a hall. The hall led to the exterior door and there were already fists slamming against it. The living folks heard the shattering of glass on the lower level and in moments, the crashing around of infected who had gained access to the single-floor apartment below them. Billy had no doubt that they would gain access to the hall and then the short set of stairs to the apartment door.

The room was fairly dark, Billy's eyes slowly becoming adjusted. He still couldn't make out details and he wanted to search for an attic or roof access. He wound the lantern again and began to explore. He and the kids stuck together as they hunted for the access, but there was nothing in any of the upstairs bedrooms, even in the closets.

The sounds of the dead in the apartment two floors below were getting loud. Both the crashing and the vocal noises the dead made. "No wonder these people left. The floors are paper thin. Can you imagine trying to sleep with a big party going on down there? Sheesh."

The kids looked at each other, then at Billy. Fear was creeping into their eyes. He had been trying to make jokes because he couldn't think of a way out of this for the kids. There was no fire escape on this building and Billy thought that was ridiculous. What if there had been a fire? Or a plague of the living dead? How were these obviously wealthy people supposed to escape?

The door to the apartment below must have given way, because there was a large crash and then Billy could hear infected in the hall. He had a mental picture of the door coming open and the dead spilling onto the floor.

He just couldn't figure how they had known he and the kids were in here. He had been super cautious because of the kids. He sighed. It didn't matter. He had to get rid of the dead, so the kids would live. He looked at the dagger in his hand, shook his head, and made for the door.

"Where are you going?" Kyle demanded immediately.

"Um... So, there are a bunch of dead people down there. They want to be up here and we don't want that. I'm going to go kill the dead people. Re-kill?" He wrinkled his nose in thought. "Kill again? Execute? Slay? Um... Destroy! Yeah, I'm gonna go destroy them." He nodded in acceptance. "Destroy."

Kyle shook his head in the negative. "We stick together! Always!"

"Yeah, so, under normal circumstances, I would agree, but if you come with me, they'll eat you. They won't eat me, you've seen it, so this is a special situation. Capiche?"

"But Daniel—"

"Isn't here," Billy finished for Kyle. He folded his arms. "I'm open to suggestions, but you'd better hurry."

Fists started to smash against the door to their apartment. A couple of thumps at first, but then it sounded like the entire dead population of San Francisco was knocking.

"You two are going to have to hide up here. Lock and block the door and don't come out until I come back for you." He passed Kyle the rifle he had taken from his attempted captor. "Here's the safety. You eject the clip here, slap in another, pull this handle, and it's ready to go. Only fire if they get past me, then you're going to have to get as far from here as possible and quick."

Vanessa looked scared. "What about you?"

"If they get by me, I'm dead, so nobody will have to worry about me."

Kyle put the rifle on the bed. "How will we get past them?"

"Juke."

"Juke?"

"Juke. It means—"

"I know what it means!"

"Then what are you asking me for?" Billy moved to the door. "Lock this. Push everything in the room, even that," he pointed to a small black and white Teddy bear nestled between the pillows of the king-size bed, "against the door. And don't shoot unless you absolutely have to." He made to leave the room, but then rushed back in and gave each kid a hug. "If they get me, make your way to Alcatraz. Tell them I sent you." Billy nodded once and stepped through the door pulling it closed.

"Did he leave us?" Vanessa asked.

"No. He's the only one who can do what has to be done. We'll be fine." She swallowed hard and nodded her head in agreement. Without a word, the kids started the struggle of moving the big bed.

On the other side of the door, Billy cupped his chin in his hand and contemplated out loud. "Should I hope that they go away and leave the door closed? If they go away, we have a door between us at least. But if they don't go away, they'll break the door down. If I open it and let them in, we'll have a door, but I'll have to get them all before they figure out where the kids are. A conundrum wrapped in an enigma." He sighed. "Crud."

Billy moved down the carpeted steps and to the door. He placed his hand on the doorknob, glancing at the dust that was raining down from the ceiling above. He ripped his hand from the door and ran to the kitchen. In a big wooden block sat many heavy-duty knives and he appropriated a huge single piece stainless steel butcher's blade and a cleaver. He visually compared the new knife with the dagger he already had then shoved the dagger in his back jeans pocket in favor of the two new weapons.

With a gleaming stainless steel blade in each hand, he rushed to the door and opened it, backing up quickly. The hall teemed with the dead and the sudden opening of the door spilled the ones in the front to the floor. Their brothers fell on them as the ones in the back surged to fit through the door all at once. An enraged scream from the corridor made Billy jerk his head up. A Runner scratched and gouged its dead cousins as it fought its way toward Billy.

It got hung up in the doorway, frantically slashing at the dead around it and suddenly it was in front of him, glaring. It had been a young man once. Now it was just an evil husk of a human, deadly in its own right. He wanted to ask it why it wanted to hurt people. Why it thought killing was something it had to do, but in the end, he just brought the cleaver down on its forehead with all his might. The blade bit through the skull all the way to the bridge of its infected nose. There was a moment of surprise on its face before its eyes rolled back into its head and it fell to the floor.

Not seeing any other Runners, Billy began to stab and hack at the dead. The sheer number of them forced him back into the room and he killed as many as he could. They started to move around him into the apartment and he noticed they were getting bits of their nasty selves all over the horrible black and white carpet he hated. He could hear Kyle and Vanessa sliding furniture in front of the door upstairs and so could the dead. They didn't have the mental capacity to quickly realize how to get up to the sounds, but they would eventually stumble across the steps.

He no sooner thought that than a disgusting dead mail carrier, shiny black from putrescence, put its stinking, bare foot on the lowest step. He used the cleaver to end its existence, but the thing was so rotten, the blade bit all the way through the skull and lodged in its neck. It took him a moment to extricate the blade and when he turned back, he got a better understanding of how many dead had found them.

The large room was two-thirds full of the walking dead and more were coming. The hall to the outside was wall-to-wall as far as he could see. He stood in front of the entrance to the stairs, blades in each hand and waited. Several of the infected had been staring at the ceiling of the place. The noises from the sliding furniture had ceased. The doors to the loft bedrooms couldn't be seen from the bottom floor and Billy thought that would give him a little extra time. He moved forward a bit and crushed the skull of another creature with the cleaver. Anything that came near him was destroyed and soon there was a pile of rotten corpses at his feet. He had been keeping a tally at the beginning, but had lost count when the first thing had reached the stairs. He could sort out the numbers later.

He stabbed one of them in the eye with the butcher's knife, pulled it out, and jabbed the blade into the side of the head of another. They seemed to center on him and he realized they wanted to get upstairs. He stepped over his pile of bodies and into the crowd, stabbing and hacking. He was tired and covered in gore when the first one got past him, climbed the bodies, and began its slow trek up the stairs.

"No! Here!" he yelled and the dead looked differently at him. One put its hand on his shoulder and he pushed it off, cleaving its head for good measure. The tool stuck again and this time, he couldn't get it out. The thing on the stairs had looked briefly at him, but it turned back around and begun to plod upward. He switched the butcher blade to his right hand

and yanked the black dagger from his pocket. Vaulting the ever-growing pile of corpses, Billy caught up with the dead man on the stairs and drove his dagger through its left eye, catching it before it could fall.

More were coming up the steps now and Billy threw the corpse into them. They rolled and flopped back down, falling into the heap of decay. The things instantly tried to rise, but those behind them began to crawl over, pressing them down. There had to be fifty of them in the room now, not including the ones he had destroyed and they all seemed to want to come up the stairs.

Billy was exhausted. He had thought he was in good shape, but this was really taking a toll on him. He lashed out with his right foot, knocking the closest creature to him back down the stairs. Another three were in front of him in a moment, one pushing to get past him. He drove the dagger into its temple and it turned its dead, red eyes on him for a second before it collapsed, taking the dagger with it. He slashed the eyes of another with his last blade then drove the big knife into the forehead of yet another.

He realized this wasn't going to work when he heard the shriek of a fast one. It stormed into the room, noticed Billy on the steps, and began fighting its way to him. It was the woman from outside that he and Kyle had put a bet on. It began pushing and punching the dead in its way, the noise of it enough to turn the ones on the stairs toward it. This further impeded its progress, but not nearly enough. It made the stairs, fighting until it stood in front of Billy. Billy reached his hands out to both sides, grasped the railings, lifted his feet and gave a vicious two-footed kick to the creature's chest.

Surprise flooded its face as it flew backward into the arms of its cousins. The crack of its ribs was not lost on Billy, but the thing didn't seem to mind. It righted itself and came again, Billy repeating the two-footed kick. Once more, it soared backward, taking the few dead on the steps with it. This time, Billy followed it, rushing down the steps and driving his knife into its chest with two downward thrusts. He backed up quickly and the thing stood, its lifeblood coursing from its chest. The thing tried drawing in a breath to utter a shriek, but it began coughing and fell to one knee. Billy kicked the infected woman in the face and she fell back. She tried to stand, a look of hatred on her face, but one of the dead fell on her, pinning her. Two more tripped over them and she was lost beneath the pile

More undead began to file into the apartment. Billy began to retreat as they flowed up the stairs. How could they know that food was up there? The kids hadn't made a peep and the creatures couldn't possibly smell fresh meat through a door two stories up. He grabbed a dead man by his shirt and threw him down the stairs. He poked a dead thing in blue scrubs in the left eye, but it didn't drop, so he poked it in the right eye and kicked it in the chest. An emaciated creature wearing a green cocktail dress grabbed him and he lashed out with his forearm, snapping its wrist. It fell and took him down with it, three or four of the things getting past him. He grabbed the pant-leg of one of them, but it easily tore from his grasp. One stepped on his left hand and he felt a searing pain in his ring and pinky fingers. Another stepped on him and another.

Exhausted and with throbbing digits, he valiantly tried to stand. An errant step from one of the things connected with his jaw sending the back of his skull into the metal step. He saw stars and a green tunnel formed in front of him as his consciousness began to ebb. A dead child looked into his eyes briefly, then stumbled, pinning Billy's injured head to the stairs. He was in a panic, worried for the kids when everything went black.

ABANDONED FAIR GROUNDS, MARSHFIELD MASSACHUSETTS

Only one other infected had entered the building the survivors were in. It had been a dead one and the team had coerced it upstairs by making some noise and dispatched it when it arrived.

"Ugh," Anna grunted and held the back of her wrist to her nose. "This one is ripe."

The four of them glanced at the mottled, shiny black and gray skin of the thing splayed out on the dark wooden floorboards. It was truly disgusting, with maggots wriggling in a wide wound in its back. Dallas covered it with a framed diagram of a Ferris wheel. Rick and Seyfert studied another framed image. An old yellowed map of the fairgrounds sat between the doors to two offices, and Seyfert was pointing at the building they were in.

"It's at least three hundred yards to the road and there's got to be a fence over here someplace." He made to point to a spot on the map, but hissed an intake of breath and used the inside of his elbow to gingerly touch his wrapped ribs. He was careful not to touch the needle Anna had installed in his chest cavity. "Shit hurts."

"They're still out in force," Anna told them as she slowly closed the parted drapes in one of the offices.

The SEAL glanced at her as he sat in a rickety wooden chair. "How many?"

"At least a hundred. Probably more like two, but they keep moving so it's difficult to get a proper tally. There's at least one fast one, but I know I heard three of them scream before."

"Alright, the sun is almost down and when it's gone, we make a break for it and head for the eastern end of this place. We might have to cut through the fence, but if they're hot on our heels, we'll have to climb over again."

The Texan sighed. "Don't much wanna do that."

Seyfert took another labored breath. "Right there with you, Dallas."

"Seyfert."

The SEAL shifted his gaze to Anna. "You can't run," she told him. "Dallas is slow too with his leg, but you won't make fifty steps before you collapse. The pneumothorax alone could kill you and the broken ribs will stop you in your tracks."

He squinted in pain. "I'll be fine."

"I get it, you're tough, but you're not thinking it through. At best, you'll slow us down, at worst, you're dead before we make the fence. What's worse is that we'll stop to try to help you and then we're dead too."

"What are you suggesting?" Rick asked in an incredulous voice. "That we leave him?"

She nodded. "Yes." She looked at Dallas. "And not just the jarhead."

"I was in the damn Navy!" blurted the SEAL.

"Whatever. Rick, you and I will have to get a vehicle and come back for them. We can use some kind of sound diversion to draw the dead away and we'll pick them up and drive to the boat."

Dallas rubbed his leg. "We don't even know if there is a boat."

"There has to be," she said.

"Yeah? Why?"

"Because if there isn't, we're all dead."

"She's right," Rick told them. "Sorry, guys. We'll slip out in an hour and grab some wheels."

Seyfert gave a nod. "Ammo and supplies check."

There were seventy-seven rounds left for the handguns and three full mags for the rifles. Dallas had nine shells for his shotgun. Seyfert also had two hand grenades that he had appropriated from the PX at the bunker under the Vantel facility. The pistol magazines were reloaded, so each of the team had a full sidearm plus one full magazine and some loose spares.

"Shit's getting critical and we're not even halfway to the water." Seyfert glanced up at Rick. "You got this?"

Rick's eyebrows shot up. "You gotta ask?" Rick glanced at his rifle, picked it up, and ejected the magazine. He checked it again, returned the mag to the receiver, and held the gun out to Seyfert. "You might as well have two full rifles in case they get in here. Less reloading."

"Uh-uh. You'll need it. If you don't get us a vehicle, none of us make it."

"Yeah, but if we get back and you didn't have the ammo to fend off an attack, then we went for nothing."

Seyfert accepted the rifle and placed it next to his chair. "Good luck." He extended his hand to Rick who gently shook it.

"Don't need it." Rick thumbed at Anna. "I have her."

"This is textbook shit you are not supposed to pull in a horror movie," Anna breathed. "Splitting up."

Dallas produced a wry smile. "We been in a horror movie for a while now."

Anna hugged him and held Seyfert's hand for a moment before she and Rick made their way downstairs. The plan had been to slip out the same window the things had used to get in, but the shards of glass were coated with infected fluids. Rick began pulling books off a tall bookshelf as quietly as possible and handing them to Anna. She placed them on a desk until the shelves were clear, then the two of them slid the bookcase in front of the broken window. They put the books back and shifted the desk up against the shelves. It was a flimsy barrier, but better than a broken window.

Moving to a different room, Rick nodded to her then parted the wooden blinds to peek out the window. He couldn't see any dead on the porch, but he could see shapes moving through the gloom. He shrugged then they moved to the big wooden slider door where Dallas waited. Anna unlocked it, Rick slid it open two feet, and they slipped through into the darkness, closing it behind them. Dallas engaged the lock with a *snick!* and the two friends were immediately terrified.

Rick slunk down the porch steps with his knife in his fist and Anna on his heels. They didn't get twenty feet before an infected of the slower variety crossed in front of them. The thing hadn't seen them and kept going. They moved past abandoned vending and gaming trailers, the awnings of a few were still extended. The duo could hear the moans and hacks of the dead things in the night. The darkness concealed both the dead from the living and vice versa, but where the survivors were attempting stealth, the thing's which hadn't survived had no such need.

Stopping behind a red and yellow ticket booth, the pair surveyed the area. A tall structure, probably a Ferris wheel or other large ride, loomed behind them. The moonlight glinted off the metal of several other rides, but the darkness consumed most of the light, making the type of attraction indistinguishable. A Runner scream from far off rent the air. Even though the distance hadn't been close, it sent tendrils of terror through both Rick and Anna. Another scream answered, then another, then two more.

Several dead filed slowly past the ticket booth, all intent on searching for whatever had made the screams. Rick waited a full minute to make sure the things were out of earshot before he nodded to Anna and they darted around the booth...straight into the arms of a disgusting, rotten undead. Not making a sound, the thing latched onto Rick's shirt and arm. It leaned in to bite him, but he twisted, taking it to the ground. The creature began making a growling noise, but it was short-lived as Rick drove his blade into the side of the thing's cranium. The creature immediately let go of him and he fought not to throw up. It was as revolting as the one they had slain in the fair offices and teeming with insect larvae.

He stood, silently gagging. Anna put her hand on him and he whipped around, knife at the ready. She took a step back and he visibly calmed, nodding. He chin-wagged in the direction they needed to go and they moved off.

A large white barn with dark sliding doors barred their progress to the street, so they attempted to move around it. Rick stepped on something and it snapped under his foot. To the living, it sounded like a gunshot and they both froze, but nothing came for them. Not wanting to continue treading on sticks, Anna got down on one knee to check the situation. There were dozens of white sticks and rocks on the ground outside of the barn. So many that it would be impossible to negotiate the area without repeatedly stepping on them. She reached down and picked one up, curious. It was an animal bone. She stared at the sticks and stones, now realizing they were bones and skulls. The dead had eaten all the animals in the barn and deposited the bones here, or more likely, this is where the poor farm creatures had been overtaken.

They moved laterally to the right, coming up to an open-air pavilion. The same crunch of bones they had heard a moment before echoed to them and they both looked down. There were no bones on the ground. Another snap followed by more crunching and the two looked at each other. They hurried across the concrete floor of the pavilion, the moon showing them where picnic tables were situated, when Anna inadvertently kicked an empty glass bottle. The flask clattered across the cement, hitting something hard under one of the tables with an ear-splitting shatter.

Hissing and throaty gurgles followed the smashing of the glass, the sounds of the dead very close. Shadows moved off to the right, shuffling toward the pavilion. Something latched onto Rick's left ankle and he jerked away to the right, smacking his hip into one of the picnic tables. The table jostled a bit from the impact, the skidding of wood across cement as loud as the breaking glass. The thing that had grabbed Rick moaned. The pitiful sound was echoed by the creature's comrades and soon the noises of the dead were all around them and closing. A figure hurtled past them, running headlong through the night. Having heard the sounds, the Runner knew something might be around, but couldn't see Rick or Anna through the gloom.

The survivors moved forward, trying not to be seen. An infected shuffled into view just in front of them and they juked around its reaching arms. It caught a wisp of Anna's hair, but that was it. Several of the things materialized out of the evening murk in front of Rick, but this time there was no way to get past them. The suppressed shot was loud to Rick and Anna, but they both know the sound was confusing to anyone not very near to it, appearing to come from several directions at once. Rick dropped three of the things and the living burst through a gap in the dead line. They hurried past another structure and toward a wooded area. Another chain-link fence loomed in front of them and they hit it with a rattle. No words were necessary as both of them began to climb immediately. They were up and over in just a moment, dropping to the other side. Rick and Anna fled in the direction of the woods just as a few dozen undead thundered into the fence the living humans had just scaled.

They skidded to a stop on the moonlit grass before rushing headlong into the trees.

"Oh shit..." Anna let hang as many shadowy forms made their way toward them from the wooded side of the fence. They came in ones and twos, stepping from the foliage. The duo moved laterally to the right, keeping the fence to the right and the woods on their left. A fifty- foot gap resided between the chain-link and the wall of trees. They sprinted for all they were worth, but they soon began to tire. A few of the things were in front of them, but the vast majority trailed several yards behind.

Guttural grunts, unlike the sounds of the dead, but all too familiar also came from behind them and Rick dared a swift glance back. He stopped, spun, got into a firing stance and let two suppressed rounds fly before Anna realized she was alone. She looked back to see a Runner on its back, coughing its life out. Rick caught up to her and they continued their flight.

The forest ended on a road that traversed left to right. Across that road, the fire station they had seen before sat down a short hill, the inky blackness of the open garage doors both inviting and terrifying. The overrun FEMA camp was a quarter-mile behind and to the left of the fire station. The pursuing dead shuffled to the rear of Rick and Anna, but the way in front was unusually clear. Anna briefly thought that all the infected that had been in this area before must now be searching for the food they had chased into the fairgrounds. Houses perched on both sides of the street to their left sat abandoned.

Moving swiftly right, Rick pointed to a four-door ladder truck to the left side of the fire house. The long white ladder wasn't completely down, but that wouldn't deter them from appropriating this vehicle to save their friends. They hurried to it, stopping just outside the driver's door. Not wanting to lift himself up to the open window and have his face bitten off, Rick slapped his palm three times on the metal and was rewarded with nothing. He was about to boost himself up on the silver access step when Anna tapped him on the shoulder. He glanced at her and she was pointing behind the fire truck.

"Oh. Oh yeah," Rick said with approval.

A huge, six-wheel, yellow dump truck, parked immediately behind the fire truck, called out to Rick on a sensual level. The two raced to the vehicle, mounted the two folding steps, and climbed the five-rung ladder. The cockpit of the truck sat two and it was mercifully devoid of anything wishing to eat them. There would be plenty of room in back if it were also clear of infected and even if not, to the left of where they were standing would easily hold ten people under the ledge of the dumping bed. The railings had been removed though, so someone would have to hold on out there while they drove.

Rick entered the cab followed quickly by Anna. He looked at the myriad of dials and levers, but couldn't see much in the dark. Anna closed the door and Rick moved to the driver's seat. He flashed his tactical light on the dash of the big vehicle.

"Just like driving my Escalade, right?" He panned the light around, searching the cab for a moment, then reached up to the sun visor and yanked it down. Keys dropped and he caught them as they fell. He wasted no time in jamming the key into the keyhole, jamming his foot on the clutch, and turning the key. The effect was immediate. The huge vehicle screamed and protested at not having been started for a long time. It growled, obviously not happy someone had awoken it, and exploded to life on the second try. Rick glanced over at Anna with a slick smile and pumped his eyebrows up and down.

"If Dallas thinks he's stealing this truck, he can kiss my a—"

A weighty thud hit the outside of the truck below them and screaming started, followed by the savage pounding of fists on the steel. Rick fumbled for something and in a moment, the headlights came on, illuminating the horrors in front of them.

At least two hundred of the dead things shuffled and stumbled on their way to the yellow monstrosity that their late-night dinner sat in. Rows upon rows of shambling, rotting things made their way over the road, past the fire station, inexorably toward Rick and Anna.

Mimicking the last two words she had uttered, Anna breathed, "Oh shit."

SOMEPLACE WITH A CARPETED FLOOR AND LOTS OF SUN. PROBABLY SAN FRANCISCO

He woke to bright sunlight. A dull but strong pain behind his eyes woke with him. This was the kind of headache that wouldn't be debilitating, but would certainly linger. He raised his hand to place it in front of his face. The intent was to block the oppressive sun, but pain flared through his hand as well and he noticed his fingers were bandaged. He also noticed he was in a bedroom, painted white, with a large skylight. This was the source of the sunlight. He uttered a sound of discomfort before he realized he had momentarily forgotten his most important job.

He sat bolt upright and immediately wished he could take that action back. The throb in his head turned into a spear of white-hot agony, but it was mercifully brief. He searched for his weapons and pack, but they were nowhere to be found. He was in a bed in his underwear and he certainly didn't remember this being his last location. Jerking his head to the left, he noticed someone he didn't recognize sitting in a chair. The sitter was a larger guy, dark hair and a full but kempt beard with flecks of gray adorned his head and face. He was dressed in jeans and a San Francisco Forty Niners T-shirt. A military rifle sat across the lap of the stranger, who leaned back in his chair when he noticed Billy was awake.

"Took quite a whack to the noggin, sport."

"The kids?" Billy demanded.

"Fine. They're playing your board game a couple rooms over."

"Thank God."

The stranger leaned forward again. "Way I hear it, God had nothing to do with it."

"Huh?"

"You were on the stairs in that apartment, out cold, in a pile of the dead, with more of them all around you when we got there. Funny thing is, you don't have a bite on you, which is just plain not possible. The kids told us you were responsible for the fifty or so corpses we saw."

"Yeah, but they all deserved it. Who are you?

"Name's Tim. You okay to talk? Someone has questions for you."

"Wouldn't be a guy by the name of Cyrus, would it?"

Tim looked briefly confused. "Who? No. Guy by the name of Sergeant Martin. He runs our band of merry folk."

Billy smiled. "Like Robin Hood. Yeah, we're already talking, so sure, I'll shoot the breeze with whoever."

Tim appeared momentarily confused again and gave Billy an odd glance. He made to pick up his radio, but when Billy threw the sheet off him and swung his legs out of the bed, Tim stood with his rifle. His finger was on the trigger.

"Don't."

Billy blinked. "Don't what?"

"Get up. Don't get up."

"Uhh… I've got no pants on, Tim. I tend to like wearing pants when I meet the boss."

"Folded on a chair right there." Tim used the barrel of the rifle to indicate the chair. "Slowly. I still don't know you yet."

"Gotcha. Course, I don't know you either, but *you're* wearing pants."

"What?"

"Skip it," Billy told him and put his toes on the carpeted floor. He padded on his bare feet over to his clothes and began to awkwardly dress using his injured hand. His head also hurt and he noticed that his right sock had a hole in it where his big toe stuck through.

"Danny, he's up." Billy turned to see Tim using a small walkie-talkie.

The response was immediate, "Copy. Be right there."

Billy was just pulling his shirt down over his bandaged head when the door opened. Kyle and Vanessa entered the room, both smiling. Kyle put his hands on his hips, but Vanessa ran over and almost tackled Billy.

"Oof!" he said, returning her hug. "Like a rocket, this one."

She sat on the bed, still holding his hand, and he sat next to her. Billy gave Kyle a cross-eyed look, tapped his head with his palm, and his eyes righted. The boy shook his head, smiling harder.

Two other people had come into the smallish bedroom. The first was a woman with shoulder-length dark hair, five foot seven, maybe forty years old. She was not smiling and had a wicked-looking semi-automatic pistol pointed at the ground. The second to step through the door was clearly in charge. The man stood five foot ten maybe, with short-cropped mostly gray hair that had been dark when he was younger. Probably in his mid-fifties but very fit. A chrome revolver resided in a black holster on his left hip and an average size semi-auto pistol mirrored the revolver but on the right hip. Sunglasses adorned his head, but didn't cover his eyes. A large knife in a sheath on his belt and a tactical knife attached to his shoulder vest told Billy this might not be a guy to piss off. This man did smile. He took his military rifle off his shoulder and passed it to Tim. Two strides took him to the bed and he stuck his hand out for Billy to shake.

Billy looked at the offer for a moment, then looked to Vanessa, who shook her head yes. Billy looked to Kyle and Kyle also nodded in the positive. Billy stood and shook the man's hand.

"This is Charla," the man said, indicating the woman. Charla gave a curt nod. "I'm Sergeant Dan Martin, Paragould Arkansas. US Marine Corps retired. Well, retired until I find a unit to attach myself to."

Billy was thirsty, but he did his best to reply. "Billy. Uhh... San Francisco? Not retired, but willing to try. Second Dan I've met in two days." He looked around the room. "Where are we?"

"Still in San Francisco," Sergeant Martin answered him. "Two doors down from where you almost died. This building is infinitely more secure than the apartment you were in yesterday." Sergeant Martin looked concerned and Billy suddenly felt woozy. "Whoa," the newcomer said, "sit down before you fall down." He helped Billy to the bed.

Billy sat on the bed blinking. "Thanks for saving the kids," he said and let go of the sergeant's hand.

"They tell me you're going to Alcatraz. Are you sure that's the right play?"

"Yeah, Rick and Pittsburgh will take them in for sure. They love kids and there's a ton of them on Alcatraz."

"Pittsburgh?" Sergeant Martin looked confused. "Wait, you've been there? You've been to Alcatraz?"

"Yeah." Billy licked his lips. "Can I get a glass of water, or maybe an Orange Crush? None of that stinkin' root beer." He had pronounced root like you would soot, or foot.

Dan spoke into his radio, "Anders, can we get a bottle of water in here for our guest, please?"

The sergeant continued his questioning. "They're good people? Those on Alcatraz? We were thinking about going over there until we had a gun battle with another group of scavengers."

"Yeah, that was probably Cyrus and his group. Not great people. The folks on Alcatraz are great people. I got to the island with a few of them before I split. Rick was kind of the guy in charge and he had his dad and his daughter Sam with him. He picked up some more strays, including my friend Dallas and they got there safely. There's a whole bunch of people there now and then there's the sub."

"The sub?"

"Yeah. The sub. It's parked just offshore from Alcatraz. I'm guessing there's a bunch of sub dudes there now, too. You know, cuz of the sub?"

Danny was dumbfounded, but so was everybody else when they first met Billy. "Wait, you mean a *submarine*? A US Naval submarine?"

"I guess. I left before that showed up, but they must be good guys because I met Tony and Dave when they were out foraging and they didn't say anything about evil sub dudes. What do you call a sub dude? I mean, the real name?"

"A sailor."

"Right," Billy said a bit too loudly and winced. "Sailor. *Duh*."

A younger man, maybe twenty-five, entered the room with a bottle of water. "This is Anders; he's with us and there are two more on guard duty as well. You can meet them in a bit. Tell me more about the sub and her crew." Anders nodded and passed Billy the plastic bottle.

"It's big and black. I don't know anything about the sailors."

"Told you we should have checked out the Rock. We would have at least seen the submarine," Charla said.

The sergeant threw her a sideways glance and was about to retort when his radio came to life with a woman's voice, *"Danny, we've got breathers. Ten at least, maybe more. Two vehicles. They're going into the house we picked the kids up in."*

"Copy that, Joy. Is it them?"

"Definitely."

"We're on the way, out." He looked back to Billy. "We're going to have to move soon, will you be okay?"

Billy swallowed a big gulp of water, coughing once. "Right as rain." He put his hand to his head and made a face. He stood back up, glancing at Tim. "You're not going to shoot me, right?"

"Hope not," answered Tim and he winked.

Danny gave a chin-wag toward the bedroom door. "Follow us and stay low."

The group moved out the door and into a small hallway. Billy followed Danny and Charla, but Tim remained behind them. They emptied out into a large room, not unlike the living room of the house Billy had battled the undead in, except this room took up only one floor and had an eight-foot ceiling instead of the twenty footer in the other apartment.

Two women, both about forty, stood to the far-right, peeking through the blinds of a large window. The woman with the shoulder-length reddish hair wore a maroon T-shirt and shorts, the tattoo sleeve on her leg grabbing Billy's eye. He thought it odd that a gas mask dangled by its hose from her belt. The other woman sported dark hair that Billy could tell had fought her since she was a girl on whether to be straight or curly. Both ladies glanced briefly at the troupe coming into the living area.

"More like fifteen of them," the tattooed woman told them.

"Any heavy weapons?" Danny demanded.

Tattoos shook her head. "Nah, just pistols and clubs. One guy has a tricked out M4, but that was the only rifle I saw. Me and Tina are thinking they went in there looking to see what the dead were interested in."

"This is Joy," Danny pointed to tattoos. "And this is Tina."

Both women smiled and nodded. Tina strode forward and shook Billy's hand. "I think it's wonderful you've taken these children in."

"More like they attached themselves to me like a couple of ticks." Billy thumbed at Kyle. "Can't get rid of 'em. They're like...the plague."

Vanessa gave a quick giggle. "We sic'd the zombies on him, but he tastes like poop, so they wouldn't eat him."

Kyle smiled and shook his head.

"Yeah, we're going to have to visit that later," Danny said seriously.

"Oh shit!" Joy blurted. "They're coming out. One of them is holding his arm. He's been bitten!"

Danny's group jostled for window space, all peeking through the blinds. Tim remained behind. "Don't tip them off where we are. You're all attacking the window like a monkey shit-fight at the zoo."

Billy laughed out loud, covering his mouth at the auditory transgression, but Tim silently chuckled too.

Billy moved up. "Mind if I take a peek?"

Joy moved to her left, using a grand gesture with her hand for him to look through the blinds. Billy took a peek and noticed that he was now in a house across the park from where he and the kids had tried to hole up before.

"Yup, that's the New Society."

The entire room shifted its gaze toward Billy. "The who now?" asked Tina.

"They're a group of gangsters from L.A. who recruited a bunch of folks from all over. They moved into San Francisco at the start of the outbreak and set up shop someplace near the docks. Their leader is an old...*acquaintance* of mine named Cyrus. He's nuts. Like, certifiable, shock-treatment, booby-hatch crazy. Wicked smart though and for some reason, all these guys are afraid of him."

Joy pointed out the window. "Those are the dick-bags that have been shooting at us."

"Yeah," Billy stated, "they do that."

Tina, the only one still spying on the group across the playground, drew a sharp intake of breath which came at the same time as a gunshot from down the street. She backed away from the blinds.

"They just shot the guy who was bitten..."

"They also just brought any of those things that heard the gunshot," Tim added. "Hunker or move."

"Move," Danny replied immediately. "I don't know how, but the dead always seem to find us when we're hiding."

"Yeah, so, about that?" began Billy. "I can sort of walk around through them without getting bitten. As long as there are no fast ones!" he added quickly.

"Wait, what? Walk through who? The *infected*?" It was Danny who had asked the questions, but everybody was looking at Billy.

Kyle sat on a black reclining chair. He sighed. "It's true. I've seen him do it."

The entire room, with the exception of the kids and Billy, was dumbfounded.

"Bullshit," Charla said, but it was easy to tell she was on the fence about believing. "They kill and eat anything they can catch. Nothing can just walk past them."

"Except him," Vanessa pointed at Billy.

Billy's head was really starting to hurt from all the talking, the being vertical, and the sunlight. He visibly winced, but was determined to get the kids to safety.

"Look, they," he pointed to the kids, "are going to Alcatraz. There's nowhere safer around. You folks have taken my stuff, including my new gun, which I want back. I can get them to the island, but I need my stuff to do it. I'm sure you'd all be welcome there if you want to go. I want to have them there soon, so I can go back to my rescuing-people job. Technically, if you guys all go, then I can add you to my rescued people list. I mean, it was me who told you about it and it's me who's about to go out there and slay all the demons in a moment, so you're all on the list. You'll make..." he counted the folks in the room, "five, six...forty-four people. The bad guys are probably already in their trucks and driving away, but the creeps will be here soon. Gimme my stuff and I'll take care of them for you. Then we find a boat and I get you to the Rock."

Tim looked thoughtful then spoke up, "We did pull him out of a pile of corpses. He didn't have any bites. I know it's weird, but I think he's on the level."

The sound of vehicles driving past their hideout made everyone nervous for a moment. Tina and Joy both stole a quick glance outside. Joy sighed. "Breathers are gone, but the dead are on the way."

"Actually, they're here," interjected Tina. "Look."

"Shit, she's right."

Danny hustled back to the window, pulling a couple of blinds down with his index finger. "Okay, we move now. There're only a few and no fast ones. Back down Pierce, down Perine, and cut through the gas stations to the bank. Billy can go first and we'll see if he's telling the truth. Tim, give him his stuff back. If we get separated, the Chase Bank is on California Street next to Mollies. We have an ammo and food cache there and it's secure. Billy, you have a one-minute head start."

Tim passed Billy his pack, knife, and rifle. "Good luck, buddy."

Billy accepted the items and made for the door. He turned and walked back to Kyle, giving him a high-five. He got down and hugged Vanessa. "You two watch these guys. Keep them safe."

"We will," Kyle told him and Billy hurried out the door.

He moved down the hall, down the stairs, and out the front entrance. Six dead folks were ambling toward the building he had come out of. A huge smile split Billy's face as he regarded this new threat.

"No way…" he breathed. "Just no way!"

Two dead men and four dead women shuffled toward him. Five of the six were unimpressive; same old same old. The larger of the two men, formerly an Asian man, but now part of a different species altogether, possessed an interesting item. A katana sword stuck out of the man's chest. Billy rested his rifle against a street light.

He pointed at the skewered man. "I've seen you before! At a movie theater last year. You've been stumbling around with that stuck in you for this long?" He strode to the dead man, the other infected walking past him. "You mind?" he asked. He put a hand on its chest and yanked the weapon free. He hefted it for a moment, glancing back up to where his friends were undoubtedly watching his every move through the blinds. He flashed a wicked smile and fluttered his eyebrows. All six of the things stopped when he spoke, searching, but not being able to find anything to their liking, they moved on.

"Nope!" Billy said and they turned again. He strode to the heavy man he had removed the weapon from. Using two hands, he swung the sword in a sideways arc, hitting the dead man in the neck. To his utter disappointment, he was unable to decapitate the thing. It collapsed, the spinal column mostly severed, but the head remained attached to the body by some muscle. Billy extricated the blade as the creature fell and moved behind the next one. He brought the katana vertically down on the top of the skull of the first dead woman and the steel skipped off to the right, taking some scalp, plus her right ear and embedding in her collarbone.

"Crap!" he almost shouted. "This is harder than it looks on TV!"

The creatures once again rounded on him and he yanked the blade from the woman's shoulder. He slashed at the back of her neck and she collapsed. He opted for moving to the front of the small pack and poking the weapon through the eyes and faces of the remaining dead.

In short order, they were all on the ground, one of the infected women moving slightly, but unable to stand. The other five had been destroyed.

He practiced being a ninja for a few seconds by slashing the air with the weapon then remembered he was being watched.

"Oh, yeah."

He searched around for more infected in the area. There were sporadic infected down the streets and across the park, but none was close enough to cause trouble, although they were on the way. Billy made an exaggerated wave to the folks in the apartment, indicating they should come out.

He continued to slice and stab at imaginary opponents until the group of six adults and two kids met him.

"That…that was incredible!" Tina told him.

"*Arigato*," he said and bowed. He grabbed his rifle. "Danny, you all set?"

Sergeant Martin was looking oddly at Billy, but Billy was so used to this, he brushed it off. He used the sword to point behind them. "Anytime…"

The dead had gotten significantly closer, but were still a few hundred yards away.

"This way," Danny told him and they slunk down Pierce Street. There was little conversation as they moved, most of them choosing silence, but Danny and Billy began to talk.

"How do you do it?" Danny demanded in a hushed whisper.

"Well," Billy began, extremely loudly in the empty street, "I just—"

"Shhhh!" everyone said at the same time. Billy looked around, eyes wide.

He made the classic *Oops!* face. "Sorry," he whispered and they continued on, taking a left on Perine.

Danny strode next to Billy. "Quietly, how do you do it?"

"Dunno. They just seem to leave me alone. I've met a few others with the same…ability? Yeah, ability. It's kind of my superhero power. I didn't—"

A loud moan came from an open doorway to the right. A lone infected lumbered out of the open doorway to an apartment, heading toward them.

"Observe," Billy told them and made a grand gesture with his hand. He passed Anders his rifle and moved off to confront the dead thing.

He bowed to it as it stumbled toward the waist-high wrought-iron gate of the tiny front yard. He put his foot against the gate, stymieing the creature's exit. He was easily in reach of the thing, but it strived to get at the rest of the crowd of living people and ignored Billy completely

Doing his best impersonation of a samurai, he nodded once and said in a deep voice, "*Watashi no hobakurafuto wa unagi de ippai desu*," and slashed sideways as the thing pressed against the gate. This time, the infected's head leapt from its body and hit the concrete walkway with a meaty thud.

"*Yosh!*"

The group was flabbergasted.

"You speak Japanese?" Charla asked, her eyebrows impossibly high.

"Heck no. That phrase is in my favorite movie." He rolled his eyes. "Like I have time to learn Japanese with a plague of the living dead on us. Sheesh."

They began to move forward again, but dove for cover when gunfire erupted in front of them.

Charla was in the street, not moving. Her face contorted in pain, but her eyes moved to Danny, who was behind some overgrown shrubs and a blue mailbox. He used a hand gesture to tell her to stay still.

Tina and Joy were working on Tim, who had taken a round in his left hip. The gunfire continued but mercifully did not hit Charla again. Anders and Danny returned fire.

"Those jerks just shot at kids," Billy breathed in a non-believing voice. "Kids!" He stood, Danny grabbing for him but missing. Billy strode into the center of the street, between the gunmen and Charla and brandished his newly acquired katana. "Come on then!"

The gunfire stopped immediately.

"Jesus H Christ in a sixty-six Pontiac," Joy exclaimed. She looked at the children. "He's immune to bullets, too?

NEXT TO THE FIRE STATION MARSHFIELD, MASSACHUSETTS

"You know," Seyfert began through gritted teeth and short breaths, "when Boone and Pitt told me that there were going to be civvies on a suicide mission to rescue some scientists, I thought they were nuts. I thought you'd all be dead before we made landfall from Alcatraz. If we made it, I thought I would be babysitting you assholes the whole way and you'd get me killed." He looked at Dallas in the darkness. "I was wrong. You guys have more than pulled your weight."

"'Preciate that."

"This is coming from a SEAL, Dallas. I've seen some shit and been in it too. These are not words I would tell someone if they weren't true."

"You wanna kiss me, too?"

Seyfert smiled in the gloom, the smile quickly turning into a grimace of pain. "Not yet. If we don't make it out of here, I just wanted you to know."

"Don't make it? Son, do you know who that is out there? That's Rick n' Anna. They don't fail. Hell, I'll be surprised if they don't show up with a damn limousine."

Seyfert smiled again. The pressure in his chest was becoming very painful and he remembered his needle. He found it in the darkness and ushered a short hiss of pain when he bumped it with his hand. He twisted the small handle and a much louder hiss escaped through the contraption.

"Wassat?" Dallas demanded. "Did you hear that?"

"Relax, Hillbilly, it's just the thing Anna set up to let the air out of my chest."

"Oh. Does it hur—?" Dallas was interrupted by a loud and unmistakable beeping noise from nearby.

"I heard *that*," Seyfert told him. "Let's be ready."

"That's…that's a lot of dead people," Rick said aloud, looking at the sea of dead faces bearing down on the great dump truck he and Anna were in.

Anna glared at him, incredulity on her face. "No shit, Sherlock! Let's get out of here!"

Rick pulled the huge stick shift back and to the right. Immediately, an incredibly loud beeping noise ripped through the air. The backup alarm on the dump truck had kicked in. Rick slowly let his foot off the clutch and depressed the accelerator, but all the big rig did was stall. Anna glared at him, her eyes going wider.

"Uh... okay," Rick said to himself. He restarted the vehicle and disengaged the emergency brake. They began to roll backward, Rick using the side mirrors and backup lights to guide him in the darkness. He depressed the accelerator while letting off the clutch some and the massive vehicle shot backward. The wheel was cut to the left and the nose of the truck swung right until they were facing the fence which surrounded the fair.

Rick looked at Anna and she pointed to the fairgrounds. Rick smiled and nodded, throwing the transmission into first gear. He was in third gear when they hit the fence with a crash. The chain-link was an afterthought to the 300-ton behemoth and tore free from the ground in a sixty-foot swath. The galvanized steel wire made a tremendous clatter as it was dragged over the asphalt lanes of the fairgrounds. Rick tried to stay in the lane, but several gaming trailers and the steel barricade fence of a small children's ride were obliterated by the giant wheels of the yellow monstrosity. By the time they reached the offices where the SEAL and the Texan were holed up, the truck was dragging the fence and several pieces of smashed fair attractions. A few hundred hungry infected were also following the vehicle.

Anna got out of the cab, ducking under the massive overhang of the dump bed and switched on the tactical light on her rifle. She panned it around, firing twice to the right. The great green door to the building in front of them slid to the right, Dallas carry-dragging the injured Seyfert through it.

"Shit," the SEAL uttered when he realized he would have to climb the short ladder.

Dallas smiled when he looked at the big truck. "Thas' more like it. C'mon, buddy, let's get you to—" He was abruptly cut off when a streak from his right smashed into both he and the injured sailor. They went down in a heap, the tackler screaming and slashing with its fingernails. It raised its infected fists in the air to come down on Seyfert with dual crushing blows, but Dallas intercepted it, catching both hands in his. The big man effortlessly lifted the younger infected off its knees while it thrashed and screamed. He threw the thing against the door frame, the cracking of its ribs audible even over the engine of the yellow beast in front of them. The creature whipped its head up, red eyes glaring at the two men with hatred. It began to rise, but Seyfert shot it in the chest twice with his sidearm. It crawled weakly toward them before collapsing and gurgling infected blood onto the wooden deck. Dallas helped his friend to stand, but Seyfert was woozy.

Anna fired another round toward the growing crowd of shamblers en-route to their position. "Come ON!" she yelled. She moved to the edge of the front of the truck, looking down on her injured friends. She discharged two more rounds to cover them as Dallas helped Seyfert with the short climb. Anna shouldered her rifle, grabbing the SEAL by his outstretched hand. She pulled him gently, aware of his rib injuries, and he winced but accepted her assistance.

"Nope!" she heard Dallas yell and saw him kick free of two sets of hands that had grasped him when he began to climb. One of the attackers lost half of its rotten face to Dallas' boot, she shot the other.

When both men were safely out of the way, she turned to the cab. "Go, Rick!"

The backup alarm sounded again and the debris-laden chain-link fence let go of its death-grip on the front tires as the truck lumbered backward. Rick stopped the vehicle, shifting into first gear and stalled it out.

"You kiddin' me?" he heard Dallas ask.

Rick looked at his southern friend through the cab windows and shrugged. He started the truck back up and they jostled forward. They picked up speed as he shifted and soon were traveling at a comfortable fifteen miles per hour. Rick traversed the same lane he had used through the gaming and ride attractions before, the massive truck tires making short work of anything, including several stumbling infected, before it.

When he reached the gate, he could see a wave of rot coming toward him and he turned right. His friends didn't have anything to hold on to out on the steel of the truck and they slid into the side of the cab when he turned. Anna was able to reach the door handle and Rick slowed for her. She yanked the short door open and got Seyfert into the cab. She and Dallas held on to the cab door and each other as they sat under the bed overhang. Dallas drew his forearm across his forehead.

"I could use a beer."

"How about a vacation?" Anna countered. She stared out into the night as the truck thundered down the street.

Infected came from everywhere at the sound of the vehicle. They were passing down a street laden with businesses, none of which had been spared the walking corpses which were now commonplace. The big truck was too tall for the drooping suspended power lines. The first one struck the truck four feet above them and gave way with a mighty snap, the thick wire whipping off to the right.

Rick yelled to his friends, "Keep your heads down! I can't see the wires in the dark!" An island in the middle of the street loomed in the headlights. Seyfert winced as Rick drove over it. The SEAL made to release some of the built-up pressure in his chest with the needle contraption only to realize it was no longer there. He moved his hands up and down his chest using the cab lights to see if the needle was attached to him via some tape, but he came up empty.

"Uhh... Anna?"

She glanced at him while holding on to both the truck and Dallas. She cocked her head inquisitively.

"I uh... I lost the needle."

"I have anoth..." It was Anna's turn to run her hands up and down her body. She searched frantically for a moment, but the cab and the front of the truck weren't that big. "Shit! You guys didn't bring my med pouch?"

"Thought you... WHOA!" Dallas shouted as Rick took a slow turn. Dallas slid to the left, scraping his nails across the steel for purchase, but there was none to be had. Anna, holding onto the cab's open doorframe, grabbed for his beefy arm, but missed. The big Texan had one moment of panic on his face then disappeared over the side of the rig.

Rick slammed the truck to a halt, Anna crawling across the front of the truck to take a look down at her fallen friend. He was sitting up, rubbing the back of his neck. "He's okay! Get back up here you dumbass, or I won't have to kill you, they will!" She pointed down the road in front of them. The dead were coming, slow but steady.

"Yeah, yeah," he said to himself, "I'm comin'." He pushed himself up and pain shot up his leg from his ankle, but it wasn't horrible. *Prolly just a twist,* he thought to himself. He didn't get time for another thought as a dead woman crossed in front of the truck and lunged for him. He deftly caught her by the throat with his giant right hand and using his equally large left, slammed her head into the front of the truck. Her skull came apart like an over-ripe melon, showering the vehicle in a spray of fluids. Dallas didn't get a drop on him and so began his climb up the ladder. A stinging pain in his middle finger made him pause to check it out. He had bent the nail back when scrabbling not to fall off the vehicle.

"Crap."

Anna helped him when he reached the top of the ladder.

He looked her in the eye. "Ow."

She shook her head. "Are you okay? That was a long way down!"

"My daddy, I hated that sumbitch, always tole me the bigger they are, the harder they fall. He weren't lyin'. Gave m' ankle a bit of a twist and I could use a Band-Aid for my finger." He flashed her both his middle finger and a gigantic grin.

She looked at him cockeyed. "Bet you've been waiting since the start of the plague to do that. My bag is sitting back in that circa 1902 structure we just left though. I'll have to scavenge more stuff on the fly." She glanced at him apologetically. "Sorry." She had an epiphany and stuck her head in the cab as Rick let his foot off of the clutch. The truck began to move just as several thuds sounded on the left side of the vehicle. A blue first-aid kit was attached to the rear of the inside of the cab and she undid the Velcro to take it down. Rick switched on the cab light as Anna meticulously searched through the kit.

"Dammit," she muttered, "no needles." She passed Dallas two adhesive bandages and some antiseptic. "Sorry, John, but there's nothing I can use to painlessly poke you. I'll have to cut you to release the pressure when it comes back."

"Call me Seyfert. Only my mom calls me John. Do what you gotta d... HOLY SHIT!" He yelled and pointed to the front of the truck.

Scrabbling over the top of the ladder was an infected woman. She fell forward when she gained a foothold and shot toward Dallas. He whipped around and kicked her in the shoulder, but it was a glancing blow and she was on him in half a second. She scurried up him quickly, trying to get at his face, but he held her throat as he had with the dead infected, this time with both hands. Dallas' reach was so long that the Runner's hands couldn't reach his face or chest when she stretched out her claws at him. He looked in her blood-red eyes and all he could see was pure, unadulterated hate and fury.

She began snapping and Dallas had had enough. He drew a fist back to punch her, but Anna screamed at him not to.

"Hold her head off to the side!"

He put his other hand back on her throat and did as Anna had instructed, throttling the thing as an added bonus. A monumental feat since the creature was fighting and slashing at him the whole time. The thing's head snapped back and a loud report reverberated through the steel. Dallas, on his back, lifted his chin so he could look back at Anna. If it hadn't been dark, he would have been able to see the wisps of smoke from the business end of her sidearm.

"Thanks," he said and threw the corpse off the front of the truck. "Are we there yet?"

The big vehicle continued to rumble east through the small town. Rick slowed down when wires stretched across the road, but it was dark and the headlights didn't illuminate so high in the air. Three of them were in the cab now, but Dallas couldn't fit. He kept a constant death-grip on the cab's door frame to keep from sliding off the rig again.

Scores of dead things came to investigate the sound of the truck. They followed behind at a pathetic but unwavering pace. Several of the faster variety of infected also chased the yellow behemoth, but none could catch it.

All four survivors realized they were near the shore when the smell of rot was overpowered by the smell of the sea. Even Seyfert, with damaged ribs and a partially collapsed lung, took a deep pull of the salt air in. He let it out and noticed that the sky in front of them was brighter than it had been even ten minutes before.

"Sun's coming up," Rick said, mirroring Seyfert's thoughts.

The truck drove past row upon row of nautical-themed residential houses. Signs for Brant Rock greeted them and Rick drove further east. A lone infected was crushed under the huge tires, but the group could see there were shamblers in all directions. This must have been a very populated portion of town. A tall concrete structure jutted out of the earth and Dallas asked what it was.

"Submarine tower, built during World War Two," Seyfert told them. "I've seen them before. They're converted into housing or businesses usually." His eyes brightened. "Actually, it would be a great place to hole up if the front door is intact and there were adequate supplies."

Rick shook his head. "Not on our itinerary. But that is." He pointed to a large sign with *Marina* and an arrow pointing to the right on it.

"Kinda looks like where we came ashore the first time we got here," Dallas blurted.

Rick smiled. "Coastal New England, my hillbilly friend. Seabirds and dunes. We should get ready to disembark from this thing soon. Make sure to secure your seatbacks and tray-tables."

They came to the end of the road, a different street moving left to right. The Marina was left and Rick spun the wheel, but there was nowhere near the clearance he needed to make the turn. He turned a picturesque little water well into splinters and crushed a family of plastic pink flamingos on his way to the marina.

The road emptied into a large parking lot with two cut-stone jetties on the left, a channel between them. Beach and seemingly endless marsh stretched to the right, with several docks jutting out into the sea in front of the truck. A single red compact car sat undisturbed on the far-right side of the lot.

There wasn't a boat in sight.

PERINE PLACE, SAN FRANCISCO

Billy stood in the center of the street holding the katana in one hand, the blade resting on his shoulder. He stared at the four men coming toward him. They had various weapons aimed in his general direction. Two pistols, a rifle, and a shotgun. They stopped when they were about thirty feet away from him.

"This is him?" one of them asked the others.

The guy with the shotgun answered, "Yeah. Yeah, that's him. Billy, right?"

"You shot at children," Billy said calmly. "Kids." Billy looked past them to the truck that was parked on Steiner Street across the end of Perine Place. A man stood with a scoped rifle and he had it trained on Billy.

One of the pistol carriers strode forward and pointed his weapon at Charla. Billy stepped in his way, the barrel of the weapon almost touching his chest.

"Look, man, she's shot," the guy told Billy. "She ain't gonna make it. Might as well just let me end it. For her, I mean."

Billy shook his head. "For her. The her that you shot."

The man lowered his weapon. He pointed at Billy's face. "How'd you get that scar?"

Billy looked the smiling man in the eye. "By doing stuff like this." He brought the sword around sideways, the blade slicing through the front of the man's throat. Bright red blood sprayed from the man's wound and his gun went off, impacting the street. He dropped the weapon and grabbed at his throat. Two of the other men raised their weapons.

"Don't shoot him!" the shotgunner screamed. He took a bullet in the chest for his trouble, the other two men also being shot by Anders, Danny, Tina, and Joy. The men joined their comrade on the ground, two already dead, the man with the shotgun coughing. He tried to bring the twelve-gauge to bear, but Billy kicked it out of his hand. Danny began firing single shots at the truck down the street and the man with the rifle got in and left some rubber on the road in his haste to depart.

A growing puddle of crimson emerged from under the group of men and Billy stepped in it as he leaned down to the dying man who had held the shotgun. Billy stared hard at the man, the guy's ragged breath flecking some blood across his lips.

"Next time, don't shoot at kids."

The guy grabbed Billy's pant-leg but didn't say anything. Danny used his knife to destroy the other three men before they could turn. Kyle and Vanessa stood behind Billy. While Tina and Joy tended to Charla, Tim limped over, the right side of his jeans soaked in crimson. He held a bandage over his wound, but it didn't do much to staunch the flow of blood.

"She okay?" Danny asked about Charla. He kept his rifle trained on the bleeding man on the ground in front of them. "I said is she..." He looked at Joy and she was shaking her head.

"It's okay," Charla said weakly. "It's...alright. It's alright, Danny." She looked at Billy. "You get them...to Alcatraz."

Billy nodded, stooped down, and held her hand. "I promise."

Charla smiled and died on the warm asphalt of Perine Place.

"Two hundred feet from home," Tina said and started to cry.

Billy stood, shaking his head. "Which way to your safe place?"

Anders got down on one knee with a black dagger-style knife. He closed Charla's eyes and drove the knife into her temple. He began to pick her up and Danny asked if he needed help.

"I got her," was all Anders replied.

Billy looked confused. "What are—?" he began, but Joy cut him off.

"We're not leaving her here." She pointed to the growing number of forms shuffling toward them.

Danny led them down Perine to Steiner Street, but the dead were coming from all directions, particularly California Street, which was in the direction the living people needed to travel.

"Danny?" Joy asked in a nervous voice. She was helping a limping Tim, both covered in Tim's blood.

Danny nodded. "I see them. It must have been the gunfire. This is going to turn into a shit-show quick." He looked back over his shoulder. "We'll never make the Shell station. We fall back to the Chevron station and hide out in the auto repair garage. It's cleared and locked."

The group retraced their steps until they were halfway back down Perine Place. Two undead staggered out of an alley, but there were at least a hundred moving east toward them.

"We can make that alley if we run for it!" Tina whispered.

Tim stood tall. "I'm not running anywhere." He gently pushed Joy away. "I can barely move." He checked the load on his rifle quickly. "Take them Danny, I'll be fine. Anders, leave her with me." Danny nodded.

"We can't..." Tina began, but Joy had already given Tim a hug and grabbed Vanessa's hand. She trotted toward the alley with Danny, Kyle, and Vanessa in tow. Vanessa looked back at Billy, her eyes wide. Anders gently placed Charla's body on the ground, clasped forearms with Tim, and sprinted for the narrow path between the garage and a residence.

The bestial shriek of a Runner tore through the air, Billy and Tim turning to face it. Billy glanced over his shoulder to see Danny and Joy destroy the two shuffling monstrosities who barred entrance to the alley. Anders had to evade the outstretched, reaching claws of the half a dozen vanguard of the undead force streaming down the street behind them. Many of the things followed the living into the backstreet, but many more headed toward Tim and Billy.

Tim sighed. "Danny will take good care of the kids." He sighted the Runner and dropped it with a chest shot. He aimed at several other undead and put down six more with headshots. "It was nice to meet you," Tim told Billy and fired twice more.

"Meet me? It's almost like you think you're going somewhere. We're going to be besties after this." Billy strode to a black vehicle with the driver's side door open. He smiled and openly laughed out loud. "Epic." Looking back at Tim, he said the word again, "Epic, right?" Billy rushed to the back of the vehicle, opening the rear door. He checked the inside and it was empty except for a silver casket.

"In you go!"

Tim blinked, holding the bandage on his hip. "Really?"

Billy pointed behind Tim. "It's this or them."

Tim didn't even look and hobbled to the vehicle, climbing in the back. Billy closed the tinted window of the dusty hearse and spun to face the oncoming horde.

"Even the hurricane is afraid of the ninja," he blurted. He narrowed his eyes and strode forward, his new sword raised high.

A dead thing lurched into Danny's path from behind a blue dumpster and he cracked it in the face with his AR15. It dropped to the ground and he stomped its fragile skull, the contents erupting onto the newspaper-strewn asphalt. Danny brought the group to the door of the Chevron service station. The two tall, steel garage doors were down and locked closed, but the lock he had previously applied to the entry door himself was missing.

"Shit!" He glanced in front of him, and half a hundred of the things were now bearing down on them slowly from the short alley. He got the same view when he looked behind.

Anders showed up huffing and he pointed to the door with the lock removed. "Don't like that!"

"No choice," Danny said and pushed the door open. The rest of the group followed him through.

Several beams of sunlight streamed through the high garage-door windows slicing through the gloom of the garage bay. Dust was illuminated as it floated through the air. The sunlight glinted off some pre-apocalypse equipment. Silver toolbox handles, the rear window of a sedan up on a lift, the chrome of a forgotten wrench on the floor.

Danny flipped on a small tactical flashlight, panning it around the bays. "Joy, Anders, help me clear the garage. Tina, keep the kids with you and secure the door." He moved off with his friends to search the place for threats.

Tina was sweating profusely when she strode to a tall red toolbox. "Help me?" she asked Kyle and both kids moved to assist her with pushing the heavy box against the door. It was on wheels, but extremely heavy. They were able to get it against the door with some effort. The unit was taller than the dirty entrance window, not allowing an outside view into the garage. Tina pulled out two of the drawers on the box, yanked out some screwdrivers, and fell to her hands and knees. She drove the screwdrivers into the casters, effectively blocking them, making the heavy barrier more immobile. She stood and locked all four casters with her foot as well.

The cacophony of the undead hordes outside reached a crescendo as the two groups of infected met in front of the door. No thuds came and Tina thought that was weird. The dead must have seen the living run into this building. The creatures never gave up pursuit and should be attacking the door, but other than the sounds the things make, there was no indication they were trying to get in.

Tina tapped Kyle on the shoulder, indicating the kids should follow her. A small step ladder leaned against a wall and Tina unfolded it next to the four-door Crown Victoria police car up on the lift.

She nodded to Kyle. "Look inside the car. If there's nothing inside, we get in and wait it out up there." Kyle climbed the ladder, peered inside, and then opened the passenger door. Although dusty, the car was relatively new, but its door creaked like the vehicle had been sitting in a junk lot rusting for twenty years. The noises of the dead outside increased in volume and thumping began on the walls, garage doors, and the entry door. The toolbox barrier shuddered.

Danny, Anders, and Joy rushed back into the room, weapons raised and looking for danger.

Danny pointed at Kyle on the ladder. "Good idea!"

Kyle scrambled into the police car, hitting the button to open all the doors. A mesh grate separated the front and back seats. He climbed around the outside of the vehicle to get into the back just as Vanessa jumped into the front seat. Tina flew up the ladder, terror on her face, when the entry door gave way. The toolbox was nothing more than an afterthought and pushed sideways into the room.

The dead flooded into the room and Tina pushed herself into the car with a mighty shove for her small frame. Anders and Danny began to fire into the crowd from the garage floor as Joy scaled the ladder, mounted the hood of the car, and began shooting her lever-action rifle from her elevated position.

"Get up! Get up here!" Tina screamed.

Danny did some quick math and realized that there was no way both he and Anders would make the safety of the car before they were overwhelmed. Anders clicked empty and rushed forward, using his rifle as a club, trying to stem the tide of the dead entering the building.

"Go Danny!" he bellowed and crushed the skull of a dead little girl. One of the things grabbed Anders by the shirt and closed its teeth on his shoulder. He yelled and swung his rifle-club into the thing, the creature's lower jaw breaking loose and hanging to one side. Danny began to move forward as he fired, but he also clicked empty. Letting his rifle dangle and drawing his revolver, he fired six more times until that went empty too. A dead man in scrubs that were at one time blue grabbed Anders' rifle and the living man drew his knife, driving it into the eye socket of the dead nurse. He was being steadily pushed back

The garage continued to fill with dead. Danny wanted to save his friend, but also knew that the man was doomed with the shoulder bite. Sgt. Martin holstered his revolver and gripped his rifle tightly as he rushed up the ladder. He hadn't been fast enough. Two of the things had gotten behind Anders and had gone for Danny. He had his hands on the doorframe of the car, gripping the seatbelt with his left and the interior armrest with his right. He was heaving himself into the car when he felt an undead hand on his pant-leg. It slowed him enough that another thing was able to get two hands on his other leg. He felt the ladder go out from under him and he dangled in space, with the two dead things attached for a moment before Tina and Vanessa grabbed his arms and pulled.

Anders started screaming and so did Danny, who kicked and fought to pull away from his attackers. Two crazy-loud reports and he was free. He scuttled into the car, looking through the window at Joy, who shifted her aim to someplace behind him.

Danny looked back at Anders to see him on his back, punching and kicking the kneeling and reaching forms. Several of the things were ripping into him and Danny was able to see arterial spray before Joy put a bullet in Anders' forehead. She lay on her back on the hood of the police car, her rifle across her chest, breathing heavily.

"Don't look, honey," Danny told Vanessa and had her turn around in the front seat.

She squeezed his hand and looked up at him. "You shouldn't look either."

Danny smiled and squeezed back. "You remind me of my little girl."

Vanessa looked scared. "Is she…?"

"I don't know. She lives in Arkansas with her husband. I hope and pray every day that she's okay."

Vanessa clasped her hands together and began to silently mouth words.

"What are you doing?" Kyle asked from the back seat.

"Praying," Vanessa answered.

The first thing Tim noticed when he climbed into the back of the hearse was the heat. It was damn hot in there. It was pretty gloomy too. He looked out the dark tinted windows at the hordes of undead who streamed in his direction. A thump from the casket almost made him shit himself and he whipped his head around so fast he tweaked a nerve in his neck.

He sighed, rubbing this new injury. A couple more thumps emanated from the coffin and he sighed again.

"Perfect."

Tim drew his knife and felt around for the catch on the silver box. He found it and released it, the top part of the unit coming free. He smiled as it slowly rose and a hand sluggishly snaked out and rested on the side.

It looks exactly like every vampire movie ever made, he thought. *Except this undead wants more than just my blood.*

The occupant of the casket hadn't figured out that it could just push the lid with its hand and kept trying to sit up instead. It finally pushed the short lid up enough that it could turn its head. It looked the wrong way, at the lid itself, and Tim had to smile.

"Hey, dickwad," he said and it turned toward him.

It had been a younger man but was now a dried-out husk. Emaciated, it looked like a stiff breeze would completely destroy it. It opened its mouth and when it did, the left side of its top lip tore off and dangled as it reached for its food.

Tim thrust his blade into the thing's right eye and it ceased all movement. Outside, several of the creatures had reached his sanctuary and had begun to slap and smack at the exterior.

"Shit."

Tim began to pull the re-killed dead man out of the casket. The thing came out in pieces as each time Tim gave a yank, he pulled off another portion of the man. The window opposite him spider-webbed then caved in slightly and a decaying arm poked through the opening. The skin of the creature tore off on the exposed glass and black-purple muscle was all that was left.

Tim shimmied feet first into the coffin, doing his best to ignore the pain in his hip. He stared up at the shredded white linen of the coffin's interior and nodded. "Comfy. Pity nobody will ever use another one of these." The thing which had inhabited this place before him had scratched and torn the linen on the top lid almost completely away in its efforts to escape its erstwhile confinement.

He could hear Billy outside, pretending to be a samurai with his new sword. The window on the other side caved in and half a dozen hands reached through. Tim closed the top lid. The *snick!* of the locking mechanism was terrifying and all he could think was that he was being buried alive. Outside sound was immediately muted.

He reached across himself with his right hand, securing his radio.

"Danny? Danny, come in."

He heard nothing but static from the radio. He heard the sounds of the undead breaking into the hearse quite well, however.

He sighed a third time since entering the vehicle. "I hope they made it."

It had been hot when he climbed into the back of the hearse, but now he was shivering. He couldn't decide whether the shivers were from the dead surrounding him, or blood loss.

BURKE'S BEACH, MARSHFIELD

"Getting a bit difficult to breathe, Doc," Seyfert told Anna.

"Gonna be harder if they catch us," she answered, pointing to the growing crowd of dead coming from a quarter-mile back down the road. She began rummaging through the medical box she had found in the dump truck's cab. She came out with a gauze bandage and a bottle of rubbing alcohol.

Dallas and Rick climbed down from the truck and moved toward the closest jetty, Dallas favoring his newly injured ankle. A work raft, perhaps fifteen feet long and eight feet wide, sat tied by one line to a small dock. The boat had half a dozen or so milk crates on board full of rusty tools. Several yellow and orange buoys were tied to a post on the stern and two tires rested there as well. The boat had been hidden such that the survivors couldn't see it from the truck. It looked like it had been built in the nineteen fifties.

They heard Seyfert yelp, quickly followed by a short yell from Anna. "It's alright! I had to poke him to release some pressure in his chest!"

Rick looked both ways down the channel and across the marsh. No other boats were in the area. "Shit, Hillbilly."

Dallas thrust his large finger toward the outboard engine on the raft. Two orange fuel tanks sat in front of the motor. "Thas' a newer motor. If alls we need is to get on that and find a better boat, we get on that, right?"

"The only other option is to get back in the truck." Rick looked over his shoulder at the oncoming dead. "I think I like the truck better."

"Not enough fuel."

"No, and we're going to have to go over a huge bridge to get to the Cape. The bridge will be jam-packed full of abandoned vehicles. Shit! I'll get them out, you get that started."

Rick ran back to the truck as Dallas made his way on unsure feet down the jetty to the work raft.

Anna and Seyfert were climbing down the ladder, Seyfert grimacing when Rick showed up. "This train is leaving."

Anna helped Seyfert down the last few rungs and down the folding step-ladder. "There's a boat?"

"Kind of."

"Kind of?"

Rick chin-wagged back behind them. The vanguard of the undead horde was a hundred feet away and closing. "Yeah, come on."

The three of them rushed as fast as they could to the jetty. They heard the engine on the raft turn over a few times.

"You're shitting me, right?" Seyfert breathed when he saw their new ride. He looked over his shoulder at the truck and did the math on whether they could make it back to it before the dead reached it. They would just make it. He actually started to go, but Anna held him fast.

"This is our only shot!"

The SEAL was not happy. "Fuck!"

They made their way down the jetty to the raft. Seyfert sat on the deck, slapping his last magazine into his rifle while Rick cast off. Rick used an ancient oar to push away from the rocks. The engine simply would not start. Rick began to paddle, making anguished faces because of the lacerations on his chest and stomach.

"Anytime, Dallas!"

The Texan didn't reply as he took the cover off the outboard. He began to hand manipulate one of the engine parts and then began searching through the milk crates on board. He came up with a can of something and hurried back to the engine, but not before Seyfert fired a shot. Only he had seen the alabaster hand come over the starboard side of the boat. The hand was attached to a disgusting thing which tried to pull itself on board the vessel.

Dozens of dead crested the jetty and started down. Every one of them fell, some scraping rotten skin off on the rocks, others splashing into the salt water. A few got stuck in between the rocks as their brethren climbed over them and a few more snapped fragile bones when they stepped between the massive stones. There seemed to be no end to the dead as they continued to rain down. The things were walking the top of the jetty faster than Rick could paddle. Anna picked up another oar and began to help, but the wind was blowing the raft back toward the arms of the dead.

Two of the infected had fallen down the side of the jetty and were climbing aboard. Rick switched the oar from paddle to pole-arm and pushed one away. The other began to crawl toward him and he brought the heavy wooden instrument down on its head then pushed it over the side.

Seyfert began to select targets and dropped several of the closest attackers. Anna continued to paddle, but it wouldn't be enough. Two more undead climbed up on the starboard side and Rick used the oar to keep them at bay, but another was waist deep in the water and grabbed Rick by the leg. Seyfert shot it, but the damage was done and Rick fell to his side on the boat.

Dallas ran past Rick and stiff-armed both the things, pushing them back into the water on his way to the console. He tried the engine again and it caught on the second attempt. "Hold on!" he yelled and threw the throttle forward. The flat bow of the raft shot up and the vessel moved across the waves quickly, throwing Anna to the deck.

"Jesus Christ," Rick said blankly from his back, "Jesus Christ almighty."

Seyfert searched his pack and his tactical vest. "I'm out. We've gotten maybe five miles and I'm out of ammo." He stared at the open ocean in front of them. "Only about three thousand miles to go." He put the rifle on the deck next to him and stretched out.

Behind them, shrinking in the distance, were hundreds of undead on the jetty. Dozens were being pushed into the water by the ones behind them. The channel was filling up with weakly flailing bodies.

Rick stared at the wispy clouds overhead. "Head south, Dallas."

As they moved down the scenic coast, evidence of the plague became scarce. Other than the overgrown back lawns and one coastal house that was nothing but a charred skeleton, the view reminded Rick of when he had lived in Boston and had gone sailing with one of his police buddies.

Rick had been to Cape Cod on several occasions, but never by boat. He knew approximately where Otis Air Force Base was located and he could see it on the map, but he had never been there before. He spread a huge paper map, which he had appropriated from one of the cars at the Vantel facility, out on the deck of the raft.

"Wassat?" Dallas asked, pointing to a large structure up ahead.

Rick glanced at the structure then returned to his map. "That's the nuke plant. We would see steam, I think, if it were operational."

"Radiation gonna kill us all?"

Rick looked back at the plant. "Doesn't look damaged, but I'm not a nuclear engineer, so I don't know. All the same, I'm glad we're out on the water."

Seyfert and Anna moved to look at the map. Rick placed his index finger in the center of the widest part of the cape. "That's where the base is. We can land here and move south, but that's a lot of residential area. I think we should cut through the canal, head south, then west overland until we get to the base." He traced his finger to illustrate the journey.

"Agreed," said Seyfert. "I'm gonna take a nap." The SEAL made faces as he stretched his feet out on the deck.

"Rick, lookit that."

Dallas directed his gaze toward a pleasure boat anchored approximately a quarter-mile away from them. Dallas raised his eyes and Rick nodded.

"Yeah, let's check it out."

Dallas spun the wheel and they headed west. Seyfert felt the turn and tried to sit up. He gasped and put his head back down. "You guys can handle this one."

Dallas put the engine in neutral when the raft was forty feet out from the boat. The white vessel, a Wellcraft, looked to be about forty feet long with a cabin below. The blue Bimini top was torn and flapped in the light breeze. In blue on the stern, the name *Galapagos* bobbed just above the waves.

"Anybody home?" Anna called.

Dallas threw the engine in reverse for a moment to slow the forward momentum of the raft.

Anna called out again, "Hello?"

She, Rick, and Dallas gave conferring looks to each other. Dallas shrugged. "Thas better n' this. If we can git it started, I mean."

"I'll take Anna with me. You back off a few feet. If shit gets hairy, we'll jump over and swim to you."

The Texan nodded. "Roger that."

Anna reached out a hand and grabbed one of the chrome railings on the *Galapagos*. She pulled the pleasure craft closer and Rick climbed aboard, his sidearm trained on the cabin stairs. He stomped his foot three times, but nothing came up from below.

Bird droppings on the starboard seats and the torn Bimini top indicated that the *Galapagos* had been moored here a while, but that didn't mean there weren't half a dozen undead admiring the teak below. Rick took two steps down, undid the catch on the door, and stepped back.

The smell which greeted them was musty, not the obscene odor of the dead. "I'll go, you cover."

Anna nodded, having done this type of thing many times in the past. Both descended slowly into the cabin. It was a very attractive boat, with many features and amenities. What it lacked was people, undead or otherwise. No blood, no stains, nothing out of place except an abandoned bird's nest tucked under a false wooden beam. They cleared the head, two staterooms, a small storage area, and the engine compartment. Rick shrugged and Anna moved outside to signal Dallas.

Within fifteen minutes, all the gear and personnel had been transferred to the *Galapagos* with the work raft tied to the stern. Dallas was on deck with two toolboxes, one appropriated from the raft and one from the *Galapagos*. The big man was attempting to get the boat started. Rick moved the fuel tanks over from the raft as a backup supply. The boat had power, the indicators all in the green.

Seyfert was resting as comfortably as he could on one of the dusty beds.

Anna sat on a bench across a small table from Rick. "This is the first time I've felt safe since we left that bunker."

"Me too." He sighed. "I just wish Wilcox could be here."

"So do I." She smiled. "He was overzealous and jumped at shadows, but damn he was worth having around." The boat sputtered briefly, but didn't start. Anna looked up. "If anybody can get this thing started, it's Dallas."

"I miss my kid."

"You'll see her soon enough. She's cute as hell by the way, how did that happen?"

The short whine of an engine protesting a start filled the cabin followed by a coughing *Whoosh!* then the Galapagos was purring like a kitten.

A big grin split Anna's face. "See?"

A thirty-six-foot white and blue Wellcraft pleasure boat slowly rounded the southwestern tip of the Cape Cod Canal. The closer, northern shore held beautiful wind-swept dunes replete with sea grass and a sandy beach. A lone undead, dressed in a bright orange vest, splashed into the surf up to its knees before it stopped. It raised one hand toward the boat and began to plod through the water parallel to the vessel, unwilling, it seemed, to go further into the water. Another large structure on the southern shore sat on the edge of the canal, a large smokestack extending toward the sky. The boat made its way southwest through the canal from Cape Cod Bay toward Buzzards Bay, on the western side of the cape.

Three people stood on the deck of the Wellcraft staring up at the giant, arched Sagamore Bridge spanning the waterway. The gray steel structure was intact, with several dozen vehicles parked crossways across both lanes of traffic. Up to the roadblock, no other vehicles sat abandoned on the bridge. An obvious attempt had been made here to stem the tide of infected from the mainland to the separated cape. Meandering infected on both sides of the barricade 135 feet above the boat and on both sides of the canal, indicated the blockade had failed.

The sound of the *Galapagos* had attracted the attention of the infected and they showed up in force. The bridge seemed like a meeting place for the dead and dozens of them stretched diseased claws from the massive structure down to the vessel, far out of reach.

"Need to watch out for that," Dallas told Rick and Anna. He pointed to the northern side of the bridge where two of the more diligent infected had found a way over the bridge railing and plummeted into the canal more than a hundred feet below. "I don't reckon we'd be too happy iff'n one o' them hit us at a hunnert n' twenty feet per second. Might break my new boat." He patted the console. "She's pretty, ain't she?"

"She is," both of his friends agreed.

Dallas furrowed his brow in thought. "But what's a *Galapagos*?"

Both Rick and Anna were looking through two sets of binoculars at the bridge, the canal, and both shores. "Volcanic archipelago off the coast of South America on the Pacific side," Anna told Dallas. "Beautiful place to see some cool wildlife. There's another one!" she added and pointed to another undead jumper. The creature made no motions as it fell and impacted the water with a splash.

Rick lowered his binoculars. "Dallas, try going under the south side of the bridge. Looks to be less of them to rain on us when we pass." Dallas steered the boat a bit to starboard, angling toward a spot between the southern shore and the barricade on the bridge overhead. Rick glanced at Anna. "Will Seyfert be able to make the trip overland? He seems pretty busted up."

"He is. If it were anyone else, I would say no, but this is Seyfert." She smirked. "He gets through an entire country full of living dead and those Triumvirate assholes only to get his ass kicked by a deer." She glanced at Rick with a big smile. "That's never gonna get old."

"Yeah, but can he really make it?"

She shrugged. "He has to. Waiting a day will help and there's some provisions on board. If we park this thing offshore a bit and wait until nightfall to head in, we might be able to sneak past any of the damn zombies. I'm sure as shit not leaving him here."

"This *thing*?" Dallas asked. "You mean my beautiful new boat?" He patted the console again then squinted ahead of them. He put his hand out flat above his eyes to shield them from the sun. "Uhh...we got company." He pointed off the port bow. Both Rick and Anna raised their binoculars to see what was coming.

Rick was still looking when he sighed. "Shit."

Two boats were heading east through the canal, directly toward the *Galapagos*.

PERINE PLACE, SAN FRANCISCO

It didn't take long for the inside of the coffin to get unbearably stuffy. It wasn't hard to breathe yet, but Tim knew that time was almost upon him. *This coffin will have held two dead bodies if I don't get out of here soon*, he mused.

When he had closed the lid and that lock had engaged, he knew he was dead. This new guy would never be able to handle all the dead he had seen in the area. There were just too many and they had seen him climb into the back of the hearse. "At least it's peaceful in here," he said aloud, the sounds of the dead all but gone. The instant he said the words, he regretted them. Something was pulling on his refuge, the casket moving slowly backward. He was jostled a bit and he fought the enclosed space and the terrors thereof, to place his sidearm up by his head. He would get a couple of them before the rest tore him to pieces.

The wood and metal tube he was in shifted backward and slid down at an angle such that Tim's feet were lower than his head. Soon enough, the top portion of the coffin fell to the ground with a thud and he was horizontal again. He could hear muffled noises but couldn't tell what they were.

Thump! Something had hit the outside of his hideaway. *Thump! Thump! Thumpthumpthump!* Within seconds, dozens of fists were slapping and pounding on the wood. He didn't know how long the barrier would survive, but as soon as it was gone, he was dead. Infected would reach in and devour him before he could get out and run. Of course, he couldn't run anyway, with a hole in his hip.

Although resigned to death, he was still scared. The pain would be horrible, but it would be brief. He could always shoot himself as well. No. No, he wouldn't do that. He had six rounds in his revolver and if he could take out a few of the things before they tore into him, that was a few less in the world to kill someone else.

The pounding grew in intensity and eventually, bright sunlight assaulted his optic nerves through a thin crack right in front of his sweating face. Flashes of movement witnessed through the fracture threatened to drive his sanity from him, but he vowed to keep a rational grip if for nothing else than to destroy at least one of the bastards. Splinters rained down on his face, making him blink, then dead fingers poked through a widening chasm. The hands ripped and tore at the lid and suddenly they were gone. Tim could hear sounds a bit clearer now, but they were still distorted by the walls of his prison. After what seemed like an eternity, but in reality was only half a minute or so, he heard nothing at all. His eyes darted from the bottom to the top of the fissure in the coffin lid, but all he could see was the brightness of the day and a cloudless, blue sky.

He visibly jumped inside his tight confines when a knock came on the wood. *Shave and a haircut...*

He hesitated before meekly asking, "Billy?"

The catch on the now broken lid undid with another *Snick!* and the lid opened wide. Tim sat up fast, aiming his weapon in all directions. Billy was sitting on the street, his back against the casket breathing heavily. Tim surveyed the area. Dozens of infected littered the street. Billy had destroyed them all.

"Any room in there?" the young man asked. "I'm tired."

"Holy shit! You killed them all?"

"I did, yeah. They were going to eat you. I could go bring more if you like, but you'll have to kill them."

Tim began to extricate himself from his hideaway. "No thanks," he said with a big smile. "Let's get to the gas station and meet up with Danny and the others." Tim was reacquainted with the pain in his hip a moment later.

Billy sighed, nodding, and stood with some effort. He made to sit on the now empty casket, but suddenly stood stock-still. "Crap!"

Tim held his weapon up, panning it around. "What?"

"I didn't count! How could I forget to count?"

"Count? Count what?" Tim peered in every direction.

Billy began stabbing his right index finger at the re-killed corpses. "...seven, eight, nine..."

Tim looked at him sideways, understanding what was happening. "Uh...okay." He pulled his radio from a vest pocket and spoke into it. "Danny. Danny, you okay?"

The response was almost immediate.

"Tim! Tim, you made it! Don't come to the garage, it's full of the dead! Can you come up with some noise to draw them away? We're up on the garage lift in a cop car. There are a couple dozen in here anyway. They can't get to us but...well, you know how this works."

"Copy that, Danny. I'm with Bi..." Tim thought better of saying Billy's name over the radio, "...with our new friend. We'll think of something."

"Fifty-one!" Billy exclaimed. "That's...well, that's a lot! Gonna make a thousand before the end of the month I bet."

"Billy," Tim stated patiently, "Danny says—"

The younger man waved his hand impatiently. "Yeah, yeah. I heard him. There's a couple cars on Steiner that are buttoned-up pretty good. I'll set off some alarms. A lot more of them will come, but we should be all set by then. We can get our people out of the garage and into the bank, and then I can take a nap." Billy glanced at Tim. "But you can't come. You won't be able to run and if there are too many for me to handle, they'll get you."

Billy glanced around, his eyes settling on an apartment building to the north of them. It was taller than the rest.

Tim noticed his friend staring.

"Yeah, that's good. We cleared that one earlier in the year. Solid doors on the second floor. There are a few in the courtyard, but they can't get out." Tim grabbed Billy by the forearm, startling him. "Save my friends, yeah?"

Billy shrugged as he shook the man's hand. "It's what I do. Oh and I kill zombies too. Kinda." Billy pointed at Tim's crotch. "You're flying low. Made you look!" he added when Tim glanced down.

Yup, nuts, Tim thought as Billy moved off toward the gas station whistling. *But also damn handy.* Tim moved to the back door of the apartment building, opening it with a key that was in a broken mailbox.

Danny and Vanessa slowly turned their heads to stare at each other when they heard the car alarm a few streets over. Smiles spread slowly across their faces and Vanessa whipped her head around to see if Kyle was hearing the same sound. A huge grin split Kyle's face as well and he uttered one word: "Billy."

Joy peered over the side of the police car to spy on the dead. They shuffled across the stained concrete of the garage as would a flock of birds or a school of fish, filing out the door and moving toward the echoing clamor some few streets over. Some fought others for pieces of Anders which they carried away. Others callously kicked or stepped on the scattered remains of her friend and this filled her with an anger she hadn't felt in some time. She rested the back of her head on the hood of the vehicle and seethed.

"Should we get down?" Tina whispered.

Danny pushed down on the seat to raise himself up a little so he could look down into the garage. His hand came away sticky and he glanced at it as he answered Tina, "Let's wait a bit."

Vanessa uttered a quick intake of breath. "Are you hurt?" She pointed to his hand, smeared with blood.

"I don't think so," he answered, frowning.

"What's up?" Kyle demanded. "Who's hurt?"

Danny felt himself all over, glanced at Vanessa, then across her at Tina.

"Sorry, Danny." She was pressing her hand over her left side.

"Jesus! Are you bitten?"

She smiled. "No. I got hit when those people shot at us. It hurts, but I'll be ok."

"Why didn't—?"

Danny was interrupted by chatter from the garage floor, "Nobody said there were *two* gas stations! Ugh, what happened in here?"

The occupants of the car all rushed to the right side to stare down at a gore-covered man gripping a rifle in one hand and resting a Samurai sword on his shoulder. He searched the garage until he looked up and spied Joy staring at him from the hood of the cruiser.

Billy waved. "Heya!"

Danny opened the passenger side door, beholding Billy in all his slaughter-spattered splendor.

"Now where did you get a flying police car?" Billy narrowed his eyes then they went wide when he realized he was standing in smears of fresh blood and viscera. "Where are the kids?"

Vanessa poked her head over Danny's shoulder and Kyle rapped on the passenger window with his knuckles. Billy let loose with an audible sigh of relief, even though he knew he was probably standing in what used to be one of his new friends. The kids were safe.

"Can you grab us the ladder?" requested Danny. "They must have knocked it over when they were in here."

"That's a big no-can-do there, my new pal. There are still some just outside."

Something in a tattered brown UPS uniform shuffled into the garage after hearing the conversation.

Billy gave a larger-than-life hand flourish. "See?"

The creature sidled up next to the young man, looked him up and down, then noticed the juicy people in the car. It growled and lumbered forward, nudging past Billy with its shoulder. Billy's eyes went wide and he pointed at the thing in disbelief.

"Seriously?"

The dead parcel delivery woman crooked her head from side to side, probing for the speaker, but couldn't find anything it wanted.

He sighed. "Undesirable." Billy leaned his rifle against a tire-changing machine. He moved to the back of the creature who was now growling with arms extended upward toward the car and its contents. A swishing noise and the thing's head hit the concrete with the sound of a wet cantaloupe. The body collapsed and Billy immediately began to rub the right side of his neck and shoulder. He put his fingers to his lips in a shushing motion. He stepped back outside, looked both ways, and returned in short order.

"We're good," he told the car crew and righted the ladder so they could escape the vehicle.

"You coming?" Billy asked Kyle when the other four of the group were on solid ground. Kyle held up his hands in a helpless gesture.

161

"He's in the back of a cop car," Vanessa told them, giggling. "The back doors don't open from the inside.

Danny extricated the boy with the ladder while Joy stood watch, poking her head out the entry door and checking both directions. Kyle stood on the ladder three rungs up.

"How did you do it?" Danny demanded while checking Tina's bullet wound.

Billy pointed at himself. "Who me? I dunno. I guess I pulled it when I went on my zombie-cidal killing spree outside." He rubbed his neck again and made a face. "The real question is: How did all those ninjas and Samurais do it, like, all the time?"

"No," Danny added patiently. "I mean, why don't they attack you? I've never seen that before."

"Told you before, Chief; I have no idea. That's why Cyrus and his band of vicious nut jobs are after me." Billy shook his head. "They're crazy. And I know crazy!"

Joy looked back over her shoulder into the darkness of the garage. "We need to move."

"Where's Tim?" Danny asked suddenly, pausing in his ministrations.

"He's in a big house over on Perine. He said you guys cleared it already and there's dead folks in the courtyard or something."

"Yeah, I know where it—"

"Oh!" Billy exclaimed. "You should have seen him hiding in the coffin! It was epic!"

"Danny…" Joy questioned.

Billy continued, unperturbed. "He got into a hearse. Then the zombies—"

"Danny!"

Everyone looked at Joy.

"We have to move! *Now!*"

The living inside the garage were just starting to make out the sounds of the dead outside. Even with the car alarm still sounding, it seemed they were still hunting nearby for food.

"We go to the bank and wait it out. I'll call Tim when we get there. Everybody stay close."

They made to leave and Kyle jumped off the last few rungs of the ladder. He yelped and went down hard holding his ankle. He stood quickly.

"It's okay," he said through gritted teeth. "I just twisted it."

"I'll carry him," Danny told everyone.

Billy shook his head no. "*I'll* carry him. Piggyback time, Kyle."

They were out the door and moving left, Tina limping slightly and Kyle on Billy's back holding the sword. Even though he was in some pain, Kyle had a gigantic smile on his face. Billy had forgotten how exhausted he was and carrying Kyle while holding Vanessa's hand quickly became difficult. Danny, Joy, and Tina had outdistanced them by fifty feet or so when the trio of adults rounded the side of a large city bus. They were instantly set upon by a large group of infected that had been hidden behind the bus. One grabbed Tina, Danny shot it, and they ran. The entire herd of dead began to follow Danny's group.

Danny looked back to see Billy and the kids on the other side of Steiner Street with a few dozen infected between the two groups of three. "Get to the bank," he yelled. "We'll hole up there and go for Tim tonight!"

"We'll meet you at Alcatraz," Billy shouted back and to his horro, several of the dead reversed direction and came at him. "We'll meet you!"

He didn't know if Danny heard him or not, but waiting to find out was not an option. The dead behind them were a hundred yards back, but the ones in front were much closer. Billy plodded down Steiner Street, the dead in tow.

"I know a place, but it's three blocks. Darn it, you're heavy for a skinny kid."

Both kids were in no mood for talking, as they saw what was hot on their heels. They made it to St. Dominic's Church before a horrendous scream ripped through the air. Sprinting at them up Bush Street was an infected of the quicker variety. It was coming extremely fast.

"Gotta put you down, Squirt. Vanessa, help him walk, head up that way, I'm right behind you." The kids moved down the street slowly, Kyle a bit heavy for the younger girl.

Billy drew a bead on the Runner and fired off one quick shot with his M4. He hit the thing center mass and it stumbled, skidding on the pavement. Billy shot it again, but missed the head. The creature was crawling toward them, but it was done. The young man jogged up to the children and passed Vanessa the rifle.

"It's on safety," he told her. "Pass it to me when I ask."

She nodded and Kyle hopped up on Billy's back again. By the time they reached Fillmore Street, the dead had gotten a bit closer. Billy checked both ways before he crossed the westbound lane and entered a ditch between the east and westbound lanes. They moved up the ditch until they found a culvert with an iron gate.

"I used to live here for a while," he told the kids and produced a key for the locked gate.

In ten minutes, they were sitting on the second floor in a classroom with IKEA furniture, staring at a playground.

"We're just over a mile from the water. We'll move tonight and I'll get us to Alcatraz by morning."

The kids looked at each other and broke into huge grins.

BENEATH THE SAGAMORE BRIDGE, CAPE COD

"And you did this? With a hypodermic and some tape?" The doctor pointed to Seyfert's chest as he lay on the bed in the *Galapagos'* main stateroom.

"Yes. He was in rough shape," Anna answered.

The doctor stood and nodded. "Damn fine work. You saved his life."

Anna raised one eyebrow. "Hear that, Jarhead? I saved your ass."

"I'm a SEAL," Seyfert admonished one more time.

They let Seyfert rest and moved into the main cabin, where Rick, Dallas, and two more men sat talking at a round table. Dallas had his foot up on a chair; he had a high ankle sprain as diagnosed by the doctor. Rick had been properly bandaged as well, the doctor disinfecting his chest and abdominal lacerations.

When the two boats had come upon the *Galapagos*, they had appeared hostile at first. Weapons were aimed on both sides, but there had been nine people and consequently nine rifles between the two incoming vessels. When a man asked if anyone on board was injured and then had informed Rick's group that he was a doctor, Rick and Anna allowed him to come aboard alone and unarmed. His name was Richard Gormli.

The doctor had diagnosed Seyfert and Dallas quickly, but Anna told him they already knew the issues. He had smiled and repeatedly told Anna how well she had done. Two other men were allowed aboard and they began to discuss the best route overland with Rick and Dallas.

Simon, a tall man with a Scottish accent, and Chico, a smaller, portly man with a wicked scar extending from above his left eye, cutting through both lips and ending at his chin, pointed at a map of Cape Cod. Chico also sported a black eye patch, complete with skull and crossbones over his left eye. He caught Dallas staring and the Texan quickly looked away.

"I got caught by a horde. One of the dead scratched me," Chico said with a smile. "Bit me too, but I was wearing a leather jacket."

"You can make land here," Simon pointed, "in North Falmouth. But I wouldn't recommend heading inland at all." He drew a forearm across his forehead. "Damn dangerous in there. Might want to stay on this pretty boat." Simon's pronunciation of *boat* consisted of two syllables and *at all* had sounded like *a 'tall*.

"Yeah," echoed Chico. "It's bad in there. Especially near the Air Force base."

Dallas and Rick looked at each other. They had specifically left out their destination and were wondering how this man had known where they were headed.

"It's the only place anybody would want to go," Simon added. "But whatever you're looking for, it's probably not there. The place was overrun at the start of the plague, or so I heard." He put his finger on the map. "The base is here." The tall Scot glanced at Rick and Dallas. "But again, it's Hell in there."

"I would have thought," began Rick, "that the vehicles on the bridge would have provided some sort of barrier against the dead when they came east."

Chico and Simon appeared to fill with incredulity. "You've got it backward, pal." The shorter of the two said, "The bridges were blocked to keep the dead *on* the Cape, not *off* it. There were almost a million tourists on-Cape when the plague hit. They blew the Bourne Bridge up, but they never got to blow the Sagamore." He pointed up. "That's the Sagamore."

Dallas looked confused. "We thought you fellas was from the Cape."

"We're from…elsewhere," Doctor Gormli interjected, wiping his hands. "We don't set foot on the mainland." He glanced out one of the portholes to the port side of the *Galapagos*. "Because of that." The doctor pointed and everybody followed his finger. The beach to the Cape side of the channel had filled with milling bodies and more were streaming across the sand from inland. They had heard the sound of the boats.

There were hundreds of them. Some ankle-deep in the surf and others pushing for the front like teenagers at a rock concert.

"You're ten miles or so from North Falmouth," the doctor told them, "but the distance isn't the problem. What my friends told you is the truth. Cape Cod crawls with the dead. On top of that, your friend shouldn't be moving too much. His lung has come back pretty well from the trauma, but if he exercises too much, it could collapse again. The needle should be able to come out tomorrow," he added. "You could come back with us and rest for a day or so at our place, although he should wait at least a week before doing anything strenuous." Gormli indicated the resting Seyfert. "Then you could be on your way."

"We appreciate the offer, Doc, but we need to get where we're going pretty soon." Rick looked at his watch.

"I understand. You should understand, however, that you're going straight into Hell itself and your friend isn't going to make twenty steps before he collapses. Leave him or postpone your trip, but you can't bring him in there."

Anna closed the stateroom door. "He's right, Rick. Seyfert is as tough as nails, but he's hurt pretty badly."

There was some more discussion, but in the end, Seyfert weighed in with a raised voice through his room's door and said they would wait on the boat for a day then head overland to their destination.

"Good luck," Simon told Rick. "Use the codeword *Nachos* if you come across any of our people and they'll know you were the folks we met."

Rick had one more question, which he asked the doctor from his back in the bed, "Any hostile breathers around?"

"You mean living humans? We came across a group about four months ago. They weren't hostile and we absorbed them into our community. I know there were some holdouts at the nuke plant, but we haven't heard from them in a while." The doctor shook his head. "Everybody else is dead."

"Great intel, Doc, seriously." They shook hands and everyone filed out of the cabin and onto the deck.

Dallas gazed into the cloudless Cape Cod sky and breathed in the salt air deeply. He regretted it, as the stench of the hundreds of dead on the shore reached him. "They just gotta wreck every darn thing." He fanned his hand in front of his nose.

"Good luck," Chico encouraged and he stepped over the gunwale of the *Galapagos* onto his own boat. Nine folks waved a brisk goodbye, the two vessels continuing east on their original course.

Dallas got the *Galapagos* going again and she cut the waves to the southwest. The group was silent, anticipating what would happen when they made landfall.

Seyfert was out of bed that night at 10 PM. "Both the doc and you know your craft," he confessed. He raised his left arm and ran his fingers over the wrap the doctor had applied. "I feel worlds better."

Anna produced a stethoscope from the new set of supplies furnished by Doctor Gormli. He had given her some choice items from his medical bag. "I'll tell you how you feel, Jarhead."

Seyfert just shook his head at the misuse of the nickname. She listened to his breath sounds, nodding. "Sounds normal. Do they give you SEALs some kind of super-soldier drug in basic training or something?"

"Not Basic, BUD/S, and I wish. Still hurts."

"Ya done busted yerself up, kid. S'gonna hurt fer a bit."

Seyfert glared at Dallas. "I know."

They rested for a full day on the boat. Five in the morning saw some light mist, but it was easily discernible that the fog would burn off in an hour, at most. Seyfert was about to attempt some pushups and Anna told him she would shoot him if he tried. After a quick granola breakfast, Rick and Seyfert scanned the shore on the mainland to the south of Amrita Island in Falmouth. The thick tree line was only a few feet off the rocky beach and this is where they would go ashore. No infected seemed to be in the area, but that didn't mean there weren't thousands just ahead of them, unseen through the foliage.

Keeping the *Galapagos* at anchor, Anna found an emergency raft the four of them would use to get ashore. The auto-inflate capability of the raft had it inflated in seconds and the group had their feet in the wet sand in short order.

"Is it weird that I'm instantly terrified?" Rick asked.

Seyfert rubbed his injured ribs and made a face. "That's what's kept you alive through all of this."

"That and shit-tons of luck," Anna added.

"Alright, we need to keep it down," Seyfert chimed. "Only talk if we have to. Like Androwski used to say: constant contact, zero chatter. Hand signals only, I'll take point."

They crept up the beach soundlessly, their movements muffled because of the sand and surf. Anna pointed to something on the edge of the sand. The bleached bones of several partial skeletons greeted them. Not fifty feet into the trees they came across a small road running north to south. A small red car and a dirty white van sat abandoned, paint blistering in the heat. The doors were open on both vehicles, so appropriating one was out of the question.

They continued quickly across the road and into the greenery on the opposite side. Seyfert threw his fist up immediately upon stepping into the shade of the canopy. Not fifteen feet in front of them, a horrible specimen of the dead stood with its back to the survivors. Shirtless and wearing now black shorts, the creature was missing its left arm. It had no scalp and the remaining ribs on its left side protruded where skin and organs should be. The light in front of it shined through several holes in the thing.

Seyfert drew his knife, but Dallas put a hand on his shoulder and the SEAL nodded. The big Texan stole up behind the creature and ended it with a single swing of his rebar. They continued through the forest until it opened onto a destroyed Shell gas station and convenience store. A large propane fill tank off to the side of the building had exploded and burned two vehicles to charred husks along with most of the structure. More skeletons and assorted bones littered the area. Two more infected, both shiny black from rot, plodded away from them. A white sign on the road in front of the station listed 28A.

Hugging the tree line, Seyfert slunk west, crossed Route 28A and entered more forest, his friends following. This area appeared residential as well with houses down the street in both directions. Once again, they entered the trees and were relieved to get into the shade. A neighborhood which used to be quaint sat in a break in the foliage. A dozen or so houses in a cul-de-sac with more dwellings left and right on the street. An eerie silence, interrupted only by the faint sounds of the waves on the beach a thousand feet back, made Seyfert nervous. Where were the dead? Were there any Runners nearby?

The SEAL decided they would skirt the houses and keep to the trees. In a few hundred feet, they came across an overgrown swath of land which had been cleared at one time for high-tension electrical wires. Several undead squirmed as they hung by their necks on ropes from one of the transmission towers. A few more headless bodies littered the area, rot and gravity having separated the hanged from their nooses.

A few hundred feet further saw a four-lane highway split the land as far as the eye could see to the north and south. The highway was bisected by a fifty or so foot long median strip with trees and shrubs in the center. The asphalt steamed in the heat, as did the hundreds of dead stumbling and shuffling along the road in every direction.

"Well," Dallas whispered, "them folks from the boat weren't lyin' about this place."

"Why the hell are they on the road like this?" demanded Seyfert, shaking his head.

"Doesn't really matter, does it?" Rick asked. "We need to get across and we aren't doing it in the daylight unless we move laterally down the road and find a clean place to cross." Rick looked at his watch. "Not gonna get dark for another fourteen hours. We either wait here or backtrack and hole up in one of the abandoned houses, or we go back to the boat."

Anna wiped her brow, looked directly at Seyfert, and said in a whisper, "Abandoned houses have beds and chairs."

"They also have infected," Seyfert admonished. "Let's go clear one and wait until dark."

The house they chose did indeed have infected. Two dead women outside and one inside the small, sea-foam green split-level ranch greeted them. Rick and Dallas quickly dispatched the ones outside and Dallas was able to destroy the one locked in a bedroom in the back of the dwelling. The two friends cleared the rest of the building quickly while Anna tended to a fussy Seyfert, who was seated in a recliner in the living room.

Seyfert was growing impatient with her ministrations. "I'm fine."

"You are decidedly *not* fine. You have broken ribs and fucking tension pneumothorax, dumbass. I thought you Navy guys were smart?

"Finally," he said with a smile.

She shook her head. "We shouldn't even be here. We should have waited a week."

"Waited for what?" Dallas demanded as he and Rick re-entered the living room. He gingerly set his large frame on a brown sectional couch.

Rick pulled shades down over a massive picture window in the front of the house then closed blinds or shades on all the other windows he found.

"For this ninny to heal properly."

"Shh!" Rick said and snapped his fingers lightly. He peeked out of the right side of the shade and held his fist up.

Noises from infected entered the house, putting everyone on edge. A small crowd of dead shuffled through the yard and followed the street to the east. When the sounds drifted away, Rick rested his rifle on the arm of the couch and plopped down next to Dallas.

They talked in hushed tones about the mission and about how they needed to get back to Alcatraz in order to deliver mission-critical information. Rick talked about his daughter, Samantha. Dallas brought up their friend Chris Rawding, who they had left in Nebraska to help with an old missile silo and another friend named Mark Teems with his friendly biker gang.

"Yeah, we need to pick up that young fella. He was pretty handy."

"Agreed, Hillbilly," Rick said with a yawn. "If this big plane is still where it's supposed to be and we can fly it home, we might want to pick up Teems and his bikers as well."

Seyfert rubbed his side and grimaced. "They won't come. They're a nomadic group. The thought of settling down scares them."

The group talked quietly until nightfall. With no cloud cover, they would be able to see by moonlight, but also be seen. Rick looked at his watch: 9:26 PM. He stood and the others did as well.

Seyfert could see Anna's questioning gaze in the gloom. "I'm fine."

She pulled her stethoscope and listened to his breath sounds. "Actually, you sound great. If you need us to stop, tell us and we'll rest." She knew he would die first, but felt she should tell him anyway.

They slipped from the odd-colored house, making their way overland toward the Air Force base. The trees were thick, the canopy such that the moon was powerless to penetrate it. Hand signals were difficult to see, so when Rick threw his fist up, Dallas crashed right into him. The big man twisted his ankle and let out a hiss as he fell into the brush, thorns scratching his face. Hands seized him from the right and a different kind of hiss emanated from the darkness. The Texan was about to lash out when the hands let him go and everyone heard a body collapse onto the forest floor.

"It almost bit you, Dallas!" Seyfert whispered, wiping his knife on the grass.

Dallas hung his head for the briefest of moments. "Yeah, it sure 'nuff did." He sighed. "Thanks, Jersey."

Sounds of the dead came drifting through the evening, getting louder by the second. The collapsing infected had alerted its brothers to a meal with just a hiss and short rasp.

The bushes to the left of them rustled and two dead people emerged, looking in all directions. Focused on the two to the left, nobody saw the one behind until it came crashing through the fallen leaves and was in amongst them. Anna shoved her blade into its eye and it took a backward step before it did a half-turn and flopped to the ground.

The other two moved forward, both growling in anticipation of dinner. Dallas' rebar ended the shorter of the two with a meaty thud, but the second was grappling with Rick in an instant. It leaned in to bite him and he pushed its mouth as far from him as he could. The duo was spinning and lurching, making the dead man a difficult target for the humans to destroy. Rick gave a mighty shove and the creature stumbled. It turned its focus to Dallas and the Texan added another kill to his tally.

The sounds of a large group of infected behind and to the left was getting louder and the four friends ran through the brush as soundlessly as possible. They hadn't made a hundred feet when Seyfert began to wheeze.

Dozens of feet crashed through the foliage behind them, the things definitely chasing them now. The horrible noises the creatures make flooded the evening and reverberated through the trees. The friends ran.

Bursting through the brush into a clearing, Dallas and Rick saw that Seyfert was fading. They each grabbed an arm, all four of them pushing toward the far side of the small glade. They weren't halfway across before twenty creatures plowed into the clearing, falling over each other.

A structure loomed in front of Rick as he and Dallas dragged their injured buddy. It was a house, mostly burned. Several undead, also burned and trapped inside, began to growl and roar at Rick's group through a broken window as they passed. Crispy arms crackled as they reached through the shattered glass.

A guttural scream rent the night, followed by another. The hunting calls of Runners.

The team were suddenly on a small beach, a body of water in front of them. "We goin' in circles?" Dallas lamented.

"No, this is fresh water!" Rick huffed. "It must be a pond!"

Anna pointed. "I can see the other side," she stage yelled.

The dead erupted through the trees behind them hot on their heels. The moonlight, no longer stopped by the trees, illuminated more infected coming from both the left and the right.

"C'mon!" Rick started into the water, Dallas assisting in carrying Seyfert. Anna followed and soon they were shoulder-deep in the water. The dead had stopped at the bank of the pond, some splashing forward, but only ankle-deep.

Midway across the refreshing pool, Anna had to swim, but Dallas and Rick were still able to float their friend between them. The moonlight gleamed off the water behind them and showed the dead moving in both directions to circumvent the small body of water.

Anna made the far bank first, assisting her friend out of the water. With a little breathing room, the dripping group began to move as quickly as possible, using the moon as a guide to the east.

They crossed a small road, moved back into the trees, and back out again in a few hundred feet. A larger structure materialized in front of them and they made a run for it. Crossing a short parking lot, the group stormed up a short set of steps, the terrifying noises of a horde of dead crashing through the woods behind them.

Dallas pulled the handles on the front doors of the structure, but they were chained closed. A broken window, ten or so feet to the left of the doors and chest height from the ground, beckoned. Rick sprinted back down the stairs and over to the rectangular hole. Dallas followed him and gave him a ten-finger assist. Rick flashed his light inside then scuttled up the side of the building and into the room. Dallas heard Rick utter a quick "Jesus!" but in an instant, Rick was frantically waving his compatriots to the window.

"Room is secure!"

The other three made it to the window, Dallas boosting Seyfert using the same method he employed with Rick. Anna went next followed by Dallas and none too soon.

The throaty hacks and wheezes of several dozen undead were soon passing right outside the window. The survivors hunkered down, huddling together and listening to the mass of rot pass by not five feet from them. It took an hour for the things to move on, indicating there had been a few hundred, not just a few dozen.

Seyfert telescoped an inspection mirror and tried to see outside the building, but it was still too dark. The SEAL rested on his back. "Wake me if anything interesting happens," he whispered.

"Don't get freaked out by the skeleton," Rick whispered. "It's over there in the corner." He pointed, but his friends could barely see him.

Several hours passed, the group listening to Seyfert's even breathing as he slept. The first light of dawn peeked over the trees and the room began to brighten.

"I need to pee," announced Anna. She moved to one end of the room and did her business. "Jesus!" she exclaimed a bit loudly.

"Told you there was a skeleton," Rick chided when she returned to the group.

"Yeah, but you didn't say it was standing the fuck up! I almost had a heart attack!"

Seyfert was awake instantly, the three of them staring at her. Her eyes got big for a moment as she had some sort of epiphany. She used the improving light to examine their surroundings.

The skeleton was in a frame and stood in the corner. Charts and graphs were on the walls and several green file holders sat discarded on one of the desks. Anna began to breathe heavily and she opened one of the folders. She put it down slowly.

"No," she whispered. "No, no, nonono."

"What?" demanded the SEAL. "What is it?"

"This is a doctor's office!" she declared. Seeing the blank stares of her friends, she added to her comment, "We're in a damn hospital!"

"That's bad…" Seyfert let that hang.

The worst places to be during the initial outbreak of the plague were hospitals. Dozens, possibly hundreds of people, all having been attacked by infected and all seeking a doctor's help, flooded hospitals. The structures were quickly overcrowded and when the infected began to die and subsequently turn, the buildings were overrun in mere hours.

The group waited until morning, not wanting to go rummaging through a hospital in the dark. Dim light filtered in through the windows as Dallas gently opened the door to the office they were in. He looked both ways down a short hall then shrugged at his friends.

"Nuthin."

The four of them filed out of the room and made a left. The dim light of their surroundings was in contrast to a brightness at the end of the hall. Seyfert peeked around the corner with his inspection mirror, surprise all over his face.

"Huh." He moved around the corner, his friends following.

The entire front of the structure was gone. A plane had careened off the runway and taken off the northern wall. A small fire had destroyed a few of the offices, but most looked intact other than missing one wall. Anna looked up and could see into the offices of the two floors above her. No bodies or ambulatory dead seemed to be in the area.

Seyfert thumbed at a white door in the blue wall. A sign next to the door indicated it was a stairwell.

"We'll get better recon from an elevated position," the SEAL told them.

They cautiously entered the stairwell and followed the steps to the third floor. Another door led to the roof and Seyfert had to pick the lock for access. A few minutes later and the four of them were staring down at a sign across the parking lot which read, *Camp Edwards Medical Center*.

A lone zombie shambled down the street and was out of sight through the trees in a few seconds.

Rick pointed. "Look there," he said aloud.

The group saw he was indicating the end of a runway. At the other end, gleaming brightly in the morning sun, sat a gigantic plane nose toward the west.

"We made it. Now all we have to do is find a—"

"Look *there!*" Seyfert pointed as well. Hundreds, perhaps a thousand or more dark figures shuffled across the overgrown fields a few hundred meters to the west of the runway. They were moving away from the tarmac and consequently away from the living.

Dallas let loose with a big sigh. "The doc an' his guys weren't kiddin' when they said there was dead here."

Rick and Seyfert were looking through binoculars and Dallas had his palm over his eyes, shielding them from the sun as he squinted at the swarm.

All three of them turned when Anna uttered an "Uhhh..." She pointed to a shorter building about fifty yards to the north. On the roof of that building, a man reclined in a lawn chair. Wearing nothing but shorts, his legs splayed out in front of him, he held up a reflective fan high on his chest to catch the rays of the sun. The man tapped his foot and bobbed his chin as if an unseen band played for him alone.

Dallas blinked and continued to squint, "Is... Izzat guy alive?"

Rick, gazing at the man through binoculars, answered the question with a question. "Have you seen any infected who sunbathe? Oh shit..." If it were possible for Rick to look harder through the binoculars, he did.

"I see it too," Seyfert added.

Behind the sunbather, a figure appeared in the doorway to the roof. The figure was gray in color and possessed a single arm, the other ending in a yellow nub at the shoulder. It started toward the seated man.

"Jesus," Rick breathed, "he doesn't hear it!"

Seyfert was incredulous. "Because the idiot is wearing headphones!"

Rick let the binoculars dangle from the lanyard around his neck. He brought his rifle to his shoulder and aimed for the thing's head.

Seyfert glanced at the horde two hundred meters from their position. "You shoot that thing and we're all dead."

"I don't shoot and he's dead!"

"I like us better! Rick, don't shoot."

Rick wavered. He had been cop a lifetime ago in another world. It was his duty to protect this man. But if he pulled the trigger, he would never see Sam again. The end of his rifle dipped, but only for a moment. He brought it back up quickly. "Sorry."

The trigger on his rifle remained forward and he removed his finger from it. A light flickered across the man's closed eyes, cutting through the reflection of his tanning apparatus. Rick looked right, then left, and saw

Anna with a signal mirror. She caught the sunlight and wiggled the mirror, focusing the reflection on the man's eyes.

The guy blinked in discomfort, putting a palm over his eyes and searching for the source of flickering light through a squint. He shot upright when he saw four people leaning over the roof of the medical center frantically waving at him and pointing. He pulled earbuds from his ears and lackadaisically spun to face the threat crunching on the gravel rooftop behind him. He folded his arms and the thing shambled right past him, looking across at Rick's group, its one arm outstretched. It slogged to the edge of the building and toppled over the side.

Dallas pointed, "Did that—?"

"Yeah," Rick answered.

"And did he—?"

Rick cut in again, "Yeah."

The sun worshipper waved then held up his index finger indicating the group should hang on for a second. He put a shirt on, pointed at himself then at the group. Seyfert held up a radio and pointed to it, but the guy nodded in the negative, pointed at himself, then at Seyfert. The SEAL nodded and motioned the man over. The guy nodded and, leaving his tanning equipment behind, ran for the door.

"Rick, cover the building. Anna and Dallas, with me." Seyfert led them back down into the hospital and to the room they had initially entered.

Rick saw the man leave his building. He ran in a pair of sandals toward the medical center. Rick lost sight of the man when the guy ran under the overhang to the front doors, but then he backed out and looked up at Rick questioningly. The doors were chained. Rick pointed toward the side and the guy waved and started off in that direction. No one else came out on the roof or left the structure the man had been in. Rick scanned, but all the windows seemed devoid of people, living or dead, as well.

"Up here," Seyfert told the man as he ran right past the window. The guy searched for the voice, giving a gigantic smile when he saw the living people above him. He reached for a hand up, Dallas helping him into the building. The man, smelling of suntan lotion, stood in the room and smiled again. He raised his hands but kept his smile and completed a small circle so the three people in front of him could see he was unarmed. Anna and Seyfert had their rifles trained on him, but he didn't seem to mind.

"You are a very large specimen," the man said quite loudly, nodding toward Dallas.

"Keep your voice down!" The SEAL glanced over his shoulder at the frosted glass door.

"No worries, this building is cleared. I took care of it when I looted this place for food. Who are you guys?"

"Who are you?"

"Me? I'm John, but everybody calls me Jack. Or they did, before they all died. I used to be an Air National Guard pilot stationed at Camp Edwards, before. Can I put my hands down?"

"Not yet. Anna, search him."

She glanced sideways at her friend. "Do you want a full cavity search? He's in shorts and a tank top."

Ever so slowly, the man lowered his hands then pulled up his shirt, turning another circle. He began to unbutton his pants when Dallas stepped forward. "Whoa! Hang on there, pard." He patted the man down, but the only thing in the pockets of his shorts was a key ring.

Seyfert lowered his rifle and Anna followed suit. "What are you doing here, Jack?"

"Told you, I'm a pilot. My plane is at the end of runway 9/27. Kind of hard to miss. Big silver thing."

"No, why are you still here? Why haven't you left?"

"Where am I gonna go? I'm waiting for the other group from…from a secure facility north of here."

"That's us," Dallas told him.

"Uhh…while I appreciate you being not dead and let me tell you, you're the first uninfected I've seen in a long while, you don't look like the folks I'm supposed to transport. Annnd you're a tad late. What happened?"

Seyfert peeked out the window. "The zombie apocalypse."

"Yeah, but what about *after* the apocalypse."

"More apocalypse. Nobody else is coming from Vantel."

Jack raised his eyebrows then sighed. "Didn't think so." He squinted in confusion. "Then what are you doing here?"

"We need your plane."

"Okay."

Seyfert glared at the man. "Okay?"

"Yeah," Jack answered. "What am I supposed to do, say no? I ran out of ammo six months ago and you folks are covered in guns. The armory is empty. Besides, this place is boring as hell."

The door opened and Rick entered the room. "I don't know why, but that swarm is headed this way."

"Yeah, they do that." Jack stuck his hand out to Rick. "Jack."

Rick squinted at Seyfert, who nodded. Rick shook his hand. "Rick."

"What do you mean, *they do that*?" the SEAL questioned. "And why didn't the one on the roof attack you?"

"That herd of dead folks passes through here every few days. They'll move off in a bit. One of them probably saw a bird or something. I don't know why the slow ones don't try to eat me. But the fast ones…"

Rick sighed. "We've seen it before. What's the plan?"

Seyfert pointed. "Jack here is going to grab his stuff and we're getting on his plane."

"Stuff's already on the Galaxy," Jack told them. "We just need to get in and go. She's fueled and ready. Did a pre-flight check last night and every night before that since I realized the dead don't want me. The fuel has an additive that we got from Vantel before the plague. Should stay good for another couple of years. At least I hope so," he added. "Just one small problem."

"What?" asked Dallas.

Jack put a finger to his ear and everyone listened. The sounds of the dead reached them. The horde was loud as it came close to the building. Jack raised his eyebrows. "Wait it out or run for the plane?"

"We won't make it," Anna told them, listening to the noise. "Seyfert can't run."

"I can run fine." The SEAL was about to continue, but the din outside grew and the group could hear the shuffling trudge of the dead as they rounded the corner of the building. Four of them ducked down, but Jack remained standing, staring at his new friends. Anna motioned for him to duck down.

"Oh!" he whispered and sat cross-legged on the carpet of the doctor's office. He gave a big smile and a double-thumbs up.

Rick and Dallas stole a quick questioning glance.

"Remind you of anyone?" Dallas whispered.

Rick nodded. "Billy."

THE WOODROW WILSON ELEMENTARY SCHOOL, FILLMORE STREET, SAN FRANCISCO

"Billy."

The young girl tried to rouse her sleeping friend with another shake of his shoulder. "Billy!" She traced her finger in a line down the scar on his face. She shook him again and he opened his eyes. He smiled at her through the early evening gloom and she smiled back.

"What time is it?" he asked groggily.

She looked at her wrist then back at him. She had no watch. "Hair past a freckle?"

Billy broke into a second smile, a toothy thing that was as catching as the plague. "Vanessa, the fact that you can keep your sense of humor through all of this means that you and I can be best buddies." He looked around. "Where's Kyle?"

"He snuck out and went to the store on the corner."

Billy sat bolt upright, grabbing his rifle. Before he could do anything else, Vanessa covered her mouth and began to giggle. "Just kidding! He had to pee and went to the bathroom down the hall."

Billy's mouth was wide open in the shape of an O. He closed it with an audible pop, making Vanessa giggle more. He raged in mock anger, "Oh, you will pay for that one, young lady! How's his ankle?"

"It's better," a voice from the doorway told them. "I can put weight on it, but it hurts."

"Seriously, don't wander off, okay? Not everything is covered like these." Billy pointed to the windows in the classroom. They were blocked by multiple layers of shades and drapes. "If you walk around with that lantern at night, they'll see you. I've got all the entrances blocked, but I'm not here every day, and something might sneak in. We go everywhere together."

Kyle gave a curt nod. "Got it."

Billy pointed to the boy's ankle. "Can you run?"

"Nope! But I'm skinny. You can carry me."

Billy gave a sideways glance to Vanessa, who was still giggling. "You two! Should have left you out there. You would probably have eaten all the zombies!"

Kyle hobbled over to them. "I think I can run." He sat down on one of the bunk beds across from Billy. Vanessa sat on the edge of Billy's bed.

"Let me see it," Billy demanded.

Kyle stripped off his shoe and sock with a grimace. Billy checked the windows then snapped on a small battery-operated camping lantern. He moved to the edge of the bed next to Vanessa and motioned with his hand for Kyle to extend his foot for inspection. A purple bruise was evident on the outside of the boy's right foot. The injury was swollen, but not such that it interfered with him wearing a shoe. Billy held the foot by the heel and gently touched the ankle.

"Hurt?"

"Nah, it's not terrible."

"We're going to wait until tomorrow before we go. If the swelling goes down a bit more, it will be easier to walk."

"Awww...we wanted to go tonight," the girl pouted.

"Better to rest it. If we have to move quickly, it will be easier with another day's rest."

There were several board games on the big air conditioner/heater under the window and the kids picked *Clue*. It was full dark before Billy looked up from behind his cards and declared, "I have solved this murderous crime." Both kids looked at him expectantly and he raised one eyebrow. "It was Kyle in San Francisco, with the zombie!"

Kyle rolled his eyes but smiled. Vanessa looked from Kyle to Billy and back. Billy reached for the little envelope in the center of the board, but Vanessa put her hand on his. "You have to..."

A horrendous crash from the lower level of the school filled the three of them with dread. They grabbed their bags and weapons; Kyle now had the green-handled blade from a paper cutter and Vanessa wielded a broken wooden flagpole fashioned into a wicked spear. Billy stood and hurried to the window. "Douse the light," he told the kids. When the room was dark, he moved the shades aside and peeked into the night.

Hundreds of shadowy figures moved in the darkness below them. The moonlight revealed a steady stream of forms shuffling across the blacktop of the school playground.

"Oh."

"What is it?" Kyle demanded, fear spreading across his face.

"Rejoice, children! School's out!" He helped Kyle stand and both kids were already wearing their backpacks. "Nobody talks from here out, okay? Just follow me." They nodded and he held up one finger. "Two seconds," he whispered and stuck his head out the door. He looked both ways then indicated the kids should follow him. They filed out of the classroom and made for the stairs. They could hear the dead now, on the floor below them stumbling into desks and knocking things over. The noises they made also filtered up through the stairwell. Billy stole a furtive glimpse over the stairway railing then hurriedly told the kids to run with his hand.

They ran.

The classrooms whipped by as their sneakers slapped the tiles. A group of construction- paper dinosaurs, forever attached to a cork board in the hallway, flapped in the breeze they made as they ran past. They made the far stairway just as several dead made the top of the first set of stairs sixty feet back. Billy and the kids had made it onto the steps before the dead had seen them, but the lower floor was still crawling with the things. Hopefully, they hadn't made it to this stairwell yet.

Nine steps down and the group stood on the landing. Billy nodded and the three of them rushed down the last nine steps. He glanced back at the kids then yanked the windowless door open. A dead man stood immediately outside the door with his hand in place to push on it. Billy wasted no time in smashing the thing across the face with the butt of his rifle. The creature went down hard and he finished it off with two more thumps.

Two more were at this end of the hall, but the gloomy far end was jam-packed with dead faces. They all turned in the direction of the commotion and decided to give chase. Billy rammed the butt of his M4 into the face of another of the things, but the third growled and lunged for Vanessa. She sidestepped and the thing smashed into the door frame then fell to its hands and knees. Kyle brought his blade down on the thing's neck and it bit deeply into the spine. The creature started to shake in some type of convulsion, but Billy and the kids decided not to hang around to see if the job was finished.

Slapping feet behind them screamed a warning, Billy spinning to face this new threat. A barefoot woman sprinted at them, her eyes crimson orbs of hate. Billy brought his rifle up to double tap the Runner, but the weapon was empty after one round. The round took the thing in the left shoulder and it clutched at the wound with its right hand, letting out a small scream. It continued its dash toward the uninfected and before Billy could reload, it was on him, shrieking.

Billy jammed the rifle between him and the infected, pushing the upper receiver of the weapon into its face. The thing bit down on the plastic of the barrel shroud and Billy pushed for all he was worth. Two teeth flew, but the momentum of the woman carried both of them to the ground. Billy kept the weapon between them, the woman screeching and clawing at his face and stomach. So intent was the creature on ripping into a human being that it didn't consider trying to go around the rifle, but kept trying to go through it.

Kyle raised his paper-cutter blade, but Vanessa was faster with her spear. She thrust it into the side of the woman, who screamed in a different tone. The thing bucked to the side, away from the spear point, but the damage was done. The broken flagpole had penetrated deep into the side of the creature and when the thing turned its head toward Vanessa, the young girl growled at the Runner and shoved the spear deeper. Billy took that moment to swing the rifle into the thing's jaw, sending it sprawling to the left. Vanessa extricated the spear and the creature howled anew. On all fours, bleeding from its face and the gaping hole between its ribs, it still lunged for the girl. The ferocity of Vanessa stunned Billy when she thrust the spear into the Runner's eye. It collapsed and convulsed as had its dead cousin moments before. Vanessa pulled the spear out of the thing's face and pointed the spear down the hall.

Billy and Kyle noticed that the small horde had grown and the narrow school hallway was filled wall-to-wall with walking corpses. During the fight with the Runner, the dead had quartered the distance to the living.

"They're coming!" Kyle proclaimed.

Vanessa gripped her spear with both hands, the dripping end aimed toward the wall of undead. "Let them come."

Billy grabbed both kids by an arm and shot toward the infected. "That's a big no-can-do, kiddo."

"Why are we running at the things that want to eat us?" Kyle demanded in a tone full of terror and incredulity.

"We need to make that door before they do and they're almost there!" He chin-wagged at the door to the basement, but the kids didn't see it, they just ran with him.

The vanguard of the dead would reach the entrance at the same time the humans would. "Get downstairs and out through the car!"

"Then what?"

"Run!"

Billy let go of the kids, turned his rifle lengthwise across himself, and plowed into the front ranks of the horde. He moved in about four feet before the sheer mass of the bodies stopped him. Kyle yanked the door open, Vanessa scooting through and he following. They tried to pull the door closed, but two of the things had skirted Billy and gone for the kids. Rotten hands latched onto the door and pulled backward as Kyle pulled toward himself. He was pulled off balance for a moment and the door swung open to reveal the horror in the corridor. Kyle swung his blade and Vanessa stabbed forward with her spear. Kyle took off several fingers of a reaching hand. Vanessa missed her target and the spear penetrated the upper chest of a younger dead man with no nose or upper lip. The thing grabbed her weapon and she couldn't pull it back to her. Realizing the futility of the situation, she let the thing have the spear and grabbed Kyle by the wrist. They fled down the stairs, the dead following. The two of them passed a set of ancient boilers, stepped on a welcome mat, and were soon up against a rusty steel door. Vanessa turned the lock and the kids darted in, Vanessa slamming the door behind them.

They stopped to catch their breath for a moment, the safety of the door giving them brief peace of mind. A thud sounded on the steel, then several more. Soon, the pounding was so frequent it sounded like there were a hundred of the things on the other side of the door. Vanessa raised her eyes to view the dust that rained down inside the brick culvert they were in.

"They...they'll never get through that door," Kyle croaked breathlessly.

Vanessa grabbed him again and the two of them moved down the egg-shaped tunnel until they reached a floor-to-ceiling grate reminiscent of an ancient portcullis. She pushed on it but it wouldn't budge. She grabbed the bars and shook them. "Locked!"

Kyle grabbed the bars and soon both kids were shaking for all they were worth. A figure appeared through the grate at the far end of the tunnel. It ran toward them, both kids let go and took a step back. The figure impacted the barrier with a bone-jarring crash and began to shriek, reaching between the bars to claw at the kids. They backed up appropriately, out of the thing's reach. It had been a boy about their age. The creature wore naught but a pair of cut-off jeans, it's feet a bloody mess and missing several toenails. Deep furrows across its face and neck bled freely as it stretched and strained to rend and tear uninfected flesh. The beast howled its fury, banging its claws and fists against the steel. A tooth broke and fell to the brick floor when it bit one of the metal cross members of the grate.

Vanessa covered her mouth and nose with both hands and sobbed, staring at the infected boy. "I can't be one of them," she cried. "I can't!"

Kyle grabbed her and they held each other. "I won't let those things get my sister," he assured her through hot tears. "I'll take care of it."

She looked at him. "I'm not your sister."

"Yes, you are," he told her as the door to the boiler room broke open behind them.

OTIS AIR NATIONAL GUARD BASE, CAPE COD

A large gray aircraft sat undisturbed on a long runway, its nose facing west. A hundred yards behind the plane, lying flat on their stomachs in the high, untended grass, five people regarded the rear of the big jet.

"Holy crap, that's huge."

Jack glanced at Anna. "Yeah, I get that a lot." She glared at him and he tipped her an exaggerated wink. She rolled her eyes.

"Is that as big as a Hercules?" asked Dallas.

Jack harrumphed. "Take the wings off and you could stick C-130 *inside* my plane. That big bitch will hold six Greyhound buses two by two and side by side. She carries fifty thousand gallons of stabilized fuel and she's ready to go."

"It's right there." Dallas pointed at the massive C5 Galaxy transport plane. "It's three hunnert feet away. Let's just run for it."

Seyfert chin-wagged toward the west. The group of infected that had passed by them when they were hiding in the medical center had wandered off and were now meandering toward the center of the runway a thousand or so feet away. There were hundreds of them, all dead ones. They didn't seem to have any particular direction in mind, and just abled in several at once.

"Problem," Jack objected. "It takes some time to raise the ramp. Do you think they can get to the rear of the plane before that six minutes is up? Two yellow handles right inside the ramp. One of you will need to push a red button then pull the handle back. Don't push it forward, pull it back. I know, it's weird."

"Where are you going to be?" Rick demanded, brows furrowed.

"*Pilot?*" Jack reminded Rick. "I'm going to be in the cockpit getting that big, beautiful bitch started. Lucky I closed the nose on the fourth of July," he added to himself.

Seyfert swiveled his binoculars from the horde to the back of the plane. "Looks clear."

Jack shrugged. "It probably is. I leave the ramp open because they normally don't enter the plane." He shrugged again. "Nothing in there for them. Well, until now."

"So can we—?" began Anna, but Jack cut her off.

"But...as soon as you touch the ramp release buttons, a *really* loud alarm is going to sound. It's like, *really* loud. Any of you good at math? If you know how fast they are," he indicated the large crowd of dead, "then you can figure out how long it will take them to get to the ramp. If it's more than six minutes, then we're good. If it's less, then it's less good."

Seyfert rubbed his side. "We go now. The ramp will be partially closed before they can get to it. Anything that gains access gets a bullet."

Jack held up his right index finger. "Do not shoot my plane. I just washed it."

Seyfert and Dallas glanced at each other. The SEAL sighed and stood.

"Now," he commanded and motioned them forward. He led at a jog, the others with him. They made the ramp with no indications the dead had seen them, the noises the horde made unchanged. Jack and Seyfert rushed up the aluminum, Seyfert noticing an old, olive-drab army Jeep strapped to the far end of the plane near the front of the aircraft.

"It looks like a warehouse in here," Anna thought.

"This is Willy," Jack told them using a hand flourish toward the Jeep. "Willy is mine and we will discuss fares for rides later. You," he pointed toward Anna, "red button. When the alarm sounds, push the handle."

Anna's eyes grew wide. "You said to pull the handle before!"

"Oh yeah. Right. Ramp's coming up, pull the handle."

"Now?"

Jack shrugged at her yet again. "Whenever."

"On three?" Anna asked the Texan. He nodded and she counted down. She pushed the button and what sounded like a backup alarm on a huge truck sounded. Jack ran forward and through a small door up front.

The alarm *was* loud. Very loud.

Seyfert and Rick took firing stances at the pivot area of the ramp. True to Jack's word, the aluminum was painfully slow to rise.

"They're coming," came over a PA system into the cargo hold of the plane. Anna strained her neck forward to look to the right of the closing door. She could hear the sounds of the agitated dead over the alarm now, those sounds increasing in volume each second. Several dead people's heads came into view on the left side of the plane. Anna could see them through the ever decreasing, sideways V-shaped opening to her left. The ramp was two-thirds closed, no dead thing having the agility to gain access, but two of the creatures reached their arms in at Anna anyway. The dead arms were pushed out of the way by the closing ramp.

Another set of hands grasped the edge of the rising metal, but this time, a right leg swung up over and onto the ramp. The thing pulled itself up and glared at the people from all fours. It used to be a woman, and it stood on unsteady feet, snarling. The Runner glowered at Anna and received two bullets to the chest from Rick and Seyfert. The creature fell back then began to slide down the center of the ramp into the plane, leaving a streak of red behind it. The thing weakly lifted its chin to glare at Rick then began to crawl toward him. He finished it with two kicks from his boot then put his blade through its right eye. The ramp closed successfully, the group of friends giving a collected sigh of relief.

"*Please* tell me you didn't put holes in my plane!"

The four friends looked up at the ceiling of the cargo hold as if they could see Jack through the PA speakers.

The engines started, Rick thinking that they were a lot quieter than he would have believed. Rick and Dallas moved the dead Runner to the side, placing her hands on her chest.

"Where do we sit?" Anna asked. They all looked over the interior of the aircraft, but while it was huge inside, there were no seats of any kind. The only thing in the hold was the Jeep way up front. There weren't even any pallets or straps for cargo.

The group moved forward, following where Jack had disappeared. Anna parted a curtain and they were met with a door. It opened when she tried it, a steep and narrow set of stairs leading up concealed behind. The top of the stairs opened into a large compartment that reminded Dallas of one of the jet liners he used to service when he was younger, although there were no windows.

"Holy crap, this thing is big," Anna declared. "There's gotta be a hundred seats in here!"

"Seventy-five, actually," Jack said from behind them, "But you guys don't want to sit in here. There's a better set of seats, and two bunkrooms if you want to sleep while we fly. We also have two lavatories, one port," he pointed to the left, "and one starboard. If you want to use a bunk, follow me."

Anna had her eyes wide and her mouth agape. "Hells yes I want a bunk!"

"Follow me, milady." Jack used another exaggerated hand flourish and spun on his heel. The group trailed him into a small area where he slid a pocket door open. Three fold-down bunks, already made, greeted them, and Anna gave Jack a big smile. She put her pack down and climbed into the lower bunk on one side.

"I will have the filet and a bottle of your best champagne." She turned on her side, back to everyone. "Wake me when it's ready. Medium-rare."

"Three more bunks over here, fellas."

The men glanced at Jack, then the bunks. "Now this here? This is a good idea," Dallas told everyone and pointed to the lowest bunk. "I'm the biggest, I'll take the bottom."

"Don't get too comfortable," Jack interrupted. "You should be seated and strapped in when we take off."

Anna gave a loud and obviously artificial snore. "Can't hear you, I'm sleeping."

"Should we wait until the dead move off?" Seyfert asked Jack.

"They know we're in here," interjected Dallas. "They ain't never movin' off."

Jack shrugged. "Doesn't matter. When you got in the plane, we were kneeling. I'll rise us up and we won't even touch them much. The wheels will squish anything to pulp." He looked around at the confused faces. "Don't sweat the dead. They won't stop us or alter our taxi or takeoff in any way."

"Damn," Jack blurted in awe. "It really is all gone. I mean, I knew it was all gone, but to see it…" The pilot let that last part hang as he continued to stare out the window of the cockpit. He had brought the aircraft down from an altitude of forty thousand feet and was now looking at what was left of Cleveland, Ohio. The smoke had long since dissipated, several of the large structures obviously having burned. At two thousand feet, Jack turned on the belly-cam of the giant plane and zoomed in. The monitor showed that the dead shuffled the streets, but not many of them. It looked as if most of the city had moved on, leaving stragglers to search for any prey foolish enough to remain. Nothing else stirred.

"Can you land this thing on that skinny a runway?" Seyfert asked from the co-pilot's seat. A chart was spread out on the console between them. Jack tore his gaze from the monitor and regarded the map.

"We need both length and width," he answered. "The average pilot would need 10,000 feet of runway, but I'm good, so I probably only will use about 7,500." Jack traced his finger down the charted runway. He glanced at the SEAL. "That includes taxiing, chief." He nodded to himself a few times then looked back at the monitor. "The width will be fine. Yeah, fine. They upgraded this runway from 6500 feet to almost 14000 feet two years ago." He shook his head in awe again. "Man… Cleveland is just *gone*…"

"*Everything* is gone. That's why we crossed the country, to help some people get it back."

"Get what back?" Dallas asked with a yawn as he took a seat behind Seyfert.

"Everything," the SEAL responded. "Shouldn't you be sleeping?"

"Bad dreams," the Texan yawned. "Might as well tell ya now, Jersey: I'm takin' off when we land."

"Taking what off?"

"Me. I'm leavin'."

Seyfert was stunned. "What the hell are you talking about?"

Dallas yawned again. "Gonna go git Cap'n McInerney's wife. She's in Havre, Montana."

Seyfert blinked. "Are you fucking crazy?"

"Yup. Prolly why I'm goin'. Uhh… Jack? I was wonderin' if I could steal your Jeep?"

Jack turned in his seat and glared at Dallas. "You want to take Willy?"

"Yeah."

"Sure, he's all yours. I can fly great, but I can't drive for shit." Jack turned back around.

Dallas was a bit taken aback. "But I thought…"

"Skip it. Take Willy and be safe."

***

Less than three hours after they had left Cape Cod, Jack's voice came over an intercom in the bunk room. "Thank you for flying Jack's Awesome Airlines. If you would kindly ensure your seat backs and tray tables are in their upright positions, we can begin our descent to Harstedt Airfield."

Rick felt the plane bank a bit to the left and Dallas entered the room. The Texan collected Rick and Anna, the three of them moving to the VIP passenger area and taking some seats.

"Jack 'n Seyfert checked the runway as best they could. Nuthin' big to get in our way when we land."

"And you're really going to head to *Montana*?" Anna asked, putting emphasis on the state name.

Dallas smiled. "Yeah. Gonna find the cap'n's wife."

"I can't come with you. I can't protect you," Rick said as if he were embarrassed.

"I know that, Hoss. I wouldn't want ya to anyway. You get back ta Sam n' your pa. You tell them I said I'll see 'em soon. An' you," Dallas pointed at Anna, "you find that Chris fella. I like him."

"I will," she answered. Tears filled her eyes and she looked away.

***

"We'll check in every half hour and we'll be back in four hours," Seyfert told Jack. "It's a quick jaunt to the site, we pick up our friend, and we're back here. Button up if someone shows up with heavy weapons; make them blow this thing up before you open the door."

"Ramp," Jack corrected and swallowed hard. "Somebody might show up with heavy weapons?"

"No. Just don't let anybody in but us. Here." Seyfert threw Jack a deck of cards. "Four hours."

The cargo hold of the C5 was so massive, Dallas was able to complete a three-point-turn with the Jeep inside. Jack lowered the ramp for them and the team drove out of the plane.

"Nice day," Jack said aloud as he watched his four new friends drive away. He sighed as he closed up the back of the plane.

Towering stalks of corn sat a mere twenty feet off the road as they traveled in the Jeep. The fields stretched as far as the eye could see in every direction, the road in front and behind disappearing into the stalks in the distance. It was sunny but Dallas had no sunglasses. The Jeep's fold-down windscreen was extended, and the big Texan had to duck a bit as he drove to keep the wind out of his eyes. He squinted at a dead man as they passed him on the road. The thing immediately changed course to follow them. Several windmills stuck up from the fields, and Dallas took a side-road and headed toward them.

"Looks like the decay has slowed down," Anna thought out loud.

Seyfert stared uneasily into the corn, remembering the last time he had to run through a field, the tall stalks hiding countless undead. "What do you mean?"

"The ones we saw in Boston were rotten to the core," she answered, "but at that point, they should begin to come apart." She furrowed her brow. "I would think that all these dead things would be rotten to the point of disintegration by now."

Another creature stumbled out of the corn and began to plod after the Jeep.

Rick pointed at it as they drove past. "He didn't look all that disintegrated."

"That's what I mean. I..."

Dallas stopped the Jeep in front of the facility they had been heading to. It had been a decommissioned nuclear launch facility, complete with two silos and a hardened underground bunker. The structure on top of the bunker; a tractor and large machine repair facility, had been where Rick and his group had staved off an undead attack of sizeable proportions. They had also left one of their own, Chris Rawding, here to help in getting the facility running again for a group of friendly bikers that were going to try to survive in the bunker.

The building was gone. One partial wall remained, but the rest of the structure had been destroyed. Seyfert hopped out of the Jeep with his rifle at the ready. He peered almost casually at the surrounding eight-foot vegetation then made his way to where the entrance hatch to the launch facility had been. Explosives had made short work of the top hatch. He knew that if he were to climb down the ladder, a secondary door would greet him. He also knew that nothing would be able to get through that secondary vault door. He shined his flashlight into the chamber below but was unable to discern anything.

Shouldering his rifle, he made to climb down the ladder.

"No," Anna told him.

He glanced at her blankly.

"You still shouldn't be climbing ladders. I'll go."

"I don't think so," he began. "If I can't—"

She interrupted him, "You can't." She gently took his place and moved several steps down the ladder, but gasped and immediately shot back up. Two dead men appeared at the bottom of the shaft reaching up for the young medic.

She sat on the edge of the hole, staring back at them and shaking her head. "The door's wide open. I couldn't see anything else."

Seyfert turned to survey the corn. "No Abrams, no soldiers, no motorcycles…" He let that hang for a moment. "Whatever happened here, we missed it."

A dead man stepped from the stalks with a rasp. He was followed by two others, and more could be heard crashing through the fields. The four of them made to leave, Anna with tears in her eyes again, when they noticed a large rock that had no business being in a field in Nebraska. The rock was split in half, and a piece of plywood was wedged into the split, facing what was left of the building. Clearly printed in black spray paint on the wood were the words: *See you at Sam's place, Chris and Teems.*

The entire group smiled, and they quickly moved back to the Jeep. Chris would meet them at Alcatraz.

***

The wind felt good as they drove back to the runway. They radioed to Jack, and he had the ramp lowering as they pulled up to the plane. They had to dispatch a dozen or so undead before they could access the plane, and Jack smiled when he saw his friends.

His smile vanished when he noticed they didn't have a fifth person. "Where's your buddy?"

"He wasn't there," Rick told Jack. "Hopefully, he'll meet us in San Francisco."

Rick's group regarded Dallas. Anna was visibly shaken, and Rick was extremely unhappy. "Let the damn captain assemble another SEAL team to go get his wife. Dallas, this is *crazy*."

Dallas shook his head. "Kevin wouldn't send 'em. He'd go hisself an' prolly get killed doin' it."

"He's right about that," Seyfert agreed, pointing at the Texan. "McInerney wouldn't send a team for personal reasons. You should still come back with us then I'll come with you to find her." The SEAL put his hand on Dallas' shoulder. "You're alone if you go now."

"Been thinkin' about a long drive, kids. This is the perfect time. Besides, I'm already halfway there. We go to San Francisco, and I gots to come all this way again."

They discussed more on the dangers of the trip Dallas would take inside the plane, but in the end, the big Texan had made up his mind. He thanked Jack for all his help, including giving up the Jeep. Hugs and handshakes over, Dallas hopped in the Jeep and started it up. He waved once, stepped on the accelerator, and turned the vehicle northwest.

Rick wiped his right eye when the ramp began to close. He couldn't help but believe he was leaving another friend behind.

UNDER FILLMORE STREET, SAN FRANCISCO

Vanessa and Kyle held each other as the dead fought to get through the broken steel door. The rotten things jammed up in the partly open entry, getting stuck on each other, bits of them sloughing off on the doorframe. The shrieking of the Runner five feet away ended abruptly and both kids turned in its direction. The end of a katana disappeared back through the Runner's face and the thing slumped to the ground, truly lifeless.

"You comin'?" Billy asked, leaning his sword against the sloped brick wall. He produced a jingly key ring in lieu of a weapon and slammed a large key into the lock on the grate. He pushed and the bars swung toward the youngsters. His eyes went wide and both kids sprinted for the open gate. A mass of rasping dead things flooded the culvert from the boiler room, one swiping at Kyle as he juked past the steel bars and leapt over the dead boy. Billy charged forward with both hands extended, his palms impacting one of the dead things in the chest. It flew back into its brethren and the living man pulled the grate closed on the dead. They crashed against the bars, dozens of arms stretching through as the Runner had from the other side.

"They're...awful," lamented Vanessa, staring at the things.

Billy and Kyle also gaped at the dead things. "Yeah. Yeah, they are," the boy agreed.

"It isn't their fault," Billy told them. "But that doesn't mean we should hang out with them either. Let's try to get to the water."

The three of them turned in unison and made for the far end of the culvert. Vanessa glanced over her shoulder to regard the things one more time. Pity overwhelmed revulsion as she strode from the tunnel into the star-strewn evening.

"Does this run?" Kyle asked in a whisper when they came across the black Escalade doing its best to block access to the tunnel. "Can we drive to the water?"

"It might still run," Billy alleged back, "but the noise would call everything toward us and not just the dead."

They climbed through the vehicle and Billy noticed a shoe and what looked like blood in the starlight. The Runner kid had been able to shimmy under the vehicle but lost some skin in the process. He hoisted both kids over the stains on the gravel and they moved on. When they were across the street, Billy glanced back toward the school and sighed. "That was prime real estate for a while."

"How did they find us?" Kyle wondered aloud.

"Sometimes they just know. I have no idea how they do that. One minute they're…"

Billy stopped talking and the kids instinctively knew to keep quiet as well. They hugged the wall of the building they were next to just as the first of many undead shuffled out of the alley they were about to enter. The dead weren't silent, but most weren't making the rasps, wet hacks, or moans they usually did. They streamed past the living by the dozen, heading toward the school. The infected were unaware a meal was mere feet away. Vanessa gently took Billy's hand and nodded back behind them. The road behind was clear and the three slunk down the sidewalk hugging the storefronts. As they passed an abandoned 7-11, an arm shot through the broken front window and latched onto Vanessa's long tresses. She shrieked and stepped right, grabbing her own hair to protect it. Kyle used a double-handed swing and in a flash of metallic green, a severed hand dangled from the girl's hair. Billy stepped forward, punching the thing in the side of the head with his sapper gloves then stabbing it through the temple when it completed its stumble. Vanessa pulled the disembodied hand from her hair with a revolted whimper.

The horde renounced its silence. Hundreds of them flowed toward Vanessa's scream, their awful noises a herald. Dead things began to flood from the school as well, all toward Billy and the kids. Billy and Vanessa ran quickly with Kyle loping slightly behind. The girl noticed and she gave a slight pull to Billy's hand. They had two hundred feet on the dead, but Kyle was fading. He grimaced and reached down to touch his ankle then pulled his hand away quickly. He could see Billy looking at him inquisitively through the darkness.

"Hurts, but I can make it."

Billy nodded and they took off at a brisk pace again. A small group of infected lurched and stumbled from the road immediately to their front. Billy ran at them, bowling two of them over, but the other four instantly shuffled toward the kids. He gagged as he stood and tried to flick off the goo that now covered his chest and arms.

Kyle brought his paper-cutter blade down in an overhead swing and destroyed one of the things, but it twisted as it collapsed, pulling the boy down with it. Vanessa skirted around the reaching arms of three others. She ran up the road a bit and they followed her. Kyle was able to retrieve his weapon, but one of the things Billy had knocked down grabbed his ankle and he let out a quick shout of fear and pain. He chopped at the thing's hand, severing it enough that it lost its grip. Billy sprinted for Vanessa and she skirted back around the reaching arms toward Billy and Kyle. Billy used his blade to relieve two of the creatures of their heads and a big smile creased his face.

"This is getting *waaay* easier!"

He brought the edge down quickly and a rotten arm hit the pavement with a wet thud. "Take this!" he blurted, handing Vanessa his sword. "Get on!" He showed his back to Kyle, who had no idea what Billy meant.

"Piggyback! You're slowing us down!"

Kyle was tall but skinny. He crawled up onto Billy's back and they all ran down the road. The screeching of brakes behind them meant that either help or danger was close. Not waiting to find out which it was, the three of them ducked into the open door of a movie theater.

"Anybody home?" Billy called out. No sounds of the dead echoed through the lobby, and nothing came at them, so Billy put Kyle down then he and Vanessa pulled the heavy theater door closed. Compared to the starry night outside, the darkness was absolute in the theater. Billy dug in his pack for his crank lantern, but Kyle already had a large, black flashlight out. The beam cut the dark as he panned it around.

"You know, before this all happened, I hadn't caught a flick in about six years. Been to the theater twice now that there's no more world, and I *still* haven't seen a movie." He shook his head, "It's not fair. Can you walk?" he asked Kyle.

"Yeah, but it's really starting to hurt." The boy hobbled over to a small chair with a red seat and back, the beam of light bobbing as he took short steps.

"Trade?" Billy asked, cranking his lantern. "I want to clear this place so you guys don't end up a banquet."

Despite the pain in his ankle and the sounds of the noises outside, Kyle grinned and passed his flashlight over. They heard the vehicle speed away from the gigantic horde of infected.

Vanessa sat on the carpet next to Kyle. "Wonder who they were?" She wrinkled her nose. "Smells in here."

It did smell. Not the horrid smell of death and decay, but the lighter scent of mildew and an unkempt area. The door had been open for a year, the elements and probably countless infected invading the lobby of the theater. Billy used the flashlight to scan the immediate area. The whole front of the building was a solid wall with two sets of steel push-bar doors. No windows of any kind. The small lobby held a concession stand and a ticket booth. Two red velvet rope barriers on brass posts would have been used to funnel people to the snack bar. A third was knocked over and twisted. Billy flashed the light onto an old black and white photo of the front of the building. They were in the Clay Theater.

The white doors to the theater itself were open, and after checking the manager's office and two small storage rooms, he brought the kids into the theater proper. It was devoid of everything except some bird droppings which speckled the red and black carpet. The kids sat in the back row as Billy checked the two sets of fire doors near the screen and then behind the screen itself.

Passing the kids as he traversed the aisle, he made a quick stop. "Need to check the bathrooms." He swallowed and was immediately nervous. The kids picked up on it.

"What is it?" Vanessa demanded.

Billy shook his head. "There's *always* a zombie in the bathroom."

"Yeah, but they don't want to eat you!"

"If it's a fast one, there's not a lot of room to maneuver, know what I mean?"

Kyle stood, wincing. "We'll come with you then."

"Yeah, okay, just stay behind me."

They cleared both bathrooms in less than a minute. "Fine. So I guess there's *not* always a zombie in the bathroom." Billy shrugged. "Whatevs."

One last door just outside the theater doors needed to be checked. STAFF ONLY printed in red block letters adorned the top center of the white door. Billy pulled on the chrome handle slightly and was rewarded with an extremely loud creak. Stairs going up greeted him on the other side of the door.

They never got the chance to check what was upstairs. A single fist smacked against the front entrance and they all whipped their heads in that direction, fear welling up inside. Dozens more fists began to pound on the doors and soon the noise was very loud.

"Crud. Kyle, old buddy, we need to talk about putting you on a diet." Billy turned around and Kyle climbed up on his back again. "Fire doors it is then." They moved back into the theater as the cacophony of fists on steel got louder.

"Can we just run down the street that way?" Vanessa pointed to the east.

"Yeah, no. That's the medical center. Not going there. Over there is the park where we met Danny and his group." Billy pointed left. "We're going up to Broadway, and we're gonna take it all the way to the water." Billy opened the fire door a crack and peeked through. "Not exactly clear, but as good as we're gonna get."

They slipped through the doors and into the night, several staggering forms starting to pursue.

Two blocks later, Billy was getting tired. The boy he carried was getting heavy. They stopped under the torn blue awning of The Mayflower Market on the corner of Fillmore and Jackson. He put Kyle down to take a quick breather.

"You...you really gotta lay off...the snacks, fatty."

A dry rasp emanated from outside the church across the street and to the left. Two dead things were caught in the barred depression of the steps leading down next to the stone building. A dark streak shot out of the small grocery store across the road in front of Billy and the kids. It sprinted at the two dead things and leapt over the four-foot spiked fence, impacting one of the undead and taking it to the ground. The thing began beating the creature it had tackled, and started screaming in a high-pitched keen, "*No!*" It screamed in an inhuman cry, "*No! No! No!*" It moved to the other dead thing and began to smash its face into the bars and wail louder.

It was pissed.

"Did it talk?" Vanessa whispered, aghast.

Billy continued to stare. "Sure sounded like it."

"It really doesn't like the dead ones," Kyle said pointing. "It's beating the crap out of them."

"Disagree." It was Billy's turn to point. "Look! It *really* likes them!"

The light of the full moon revealed the fast one was taking bites out of the slower ones. The taller of the dead things reached through the black iron bars, stretching its claws toward a meal out of reach. Its eyes never left the group of three living people, even when the Runner bit into the side of its face. Rotten skin and muscle tore as the infected pulled its head back, a mouth full of its cousin. The sprinter chewed, swallowed, and went back for seconds. It was still chewing when it quickly turned toward the dead thing it had pushed down the stairs and leapt out of view. It was yelling and keening, but it sounded like its mouth was full.

"Climb back on there, Slugger." Kyle got on Billy's back again. "We're going all the way down Jackson until we hit Pier Three. I got a boat down there, and we can get to Alcatraz."

"Billy, that will take us under the 101," Kyle said, obvious fear in his voice.

"Yeah, we'll have to be careful."

The Runner moved in to attack the dead thing near the top of the steps again. It bit it on the shoulder but couldn't tear through the shirt it had between its teeth. It looked like a dog worrying a bone. In the process of eating, it noticed the warm meat moving away from it and it shrieked. The three living people turned to watch as the creature scrabbled up the short fence. It was a few steps down and the top of the fence was about face height to it, so it leapt up and began to pull itself over. It either slipped, or was caught by the ornate, gold-painted spikes on the top of the fence. Its hips and stomach ripped open when the iron penetrated its midsection, blood raining on the concrete. The creature upended forward, the barbs impaling it back toward its feet. The concrete was just out of reach of its hands and it screamed in frustration and pain as it rocked back and forth trying to get off the iron.

"Yuck," Billy muttered with a disgusted look on his face. They began a slow jog east down Jackson Street toward San Francisco Bay. The haunting screams of the dying Runner echoed through the streets behind them.

3000 feet above San Francisco International Airport

"Houston, we have a problem," Jack told his three friends as they circled the City by the Bay.

Seyfert immediately looked at the myriad of dials, switches, and lights on the console in front of him. He had no idea what a problem with any of them would look like.

Jack noticed his confusion and smiled. "The issue isn't with the plane, Navy. Look there."

Jack banked slightly left and pointed out the cockpit window. Anna, Rick, and Seyfert jostled to see what the pilot was referring to. On the main runway of the airport, smack in the center or the northeastern runway, sat a mostly destroyed passenger airliner. It had partially burned, and listed to the side on one wing. The other wing was a half-mile down the runway, glinting in the sun. The second runway, which sat parallel to the first but a bit to the south, had several vehicles dotting the asphalt, including a small private jet towards the center. The giant C5 Galaxy would not be able to set down here.

Rick sighed. "Shit."

Seyfert grabbed the radio. They had already been in contact with Alcatraz twice since they achieved radio range. "Rock, this is Wanderer Two, come in, over."

"Wanderer Two, Rock. We read you, over."

"Pull your team back, Rock. SFO is a no-go. Runways are FUBAR, over."

"Copy, Wanderer Two. Suggest using runway at Alameda approximately twelve miles to your north-northwest. Be advised, Wanderer Two, Alameda crawls, over."

"What else is new?" Anna huffed.

"Wanderer Two copies all. Will evac be waiting?"

"Roger that, Wanderer Two. Two teams will be ready for four friendlies to travel. Good luck and see you soon, Rock out."

Jack had already banked right and was heading for Alameda Island to the northwest. In just a few minutes, he sighed and shook his head. "This is gonna be tight."

"Say again?" asked Seyfert. "What's tight?"

"The runway. It looks a bit short."

The SEAL switched the chart a couple of pages. "Says here it's eight thousand feet. You said you only needed seven thousand."

"Yeah, to take off. Landing is different."

"How the hell is landing different?"

Jack rolled his eyes. "You keep to the sea and I'll keep to the air, okay Baron Von Richthofen. I've done this a couple times."

Anna looked nervous. "Can we do it or not?"

"We can," Jack said emphatically and nodded, "but it's gonna be tight. We might be going for a swim at the end."

Rick put his hand on Jack's shoulder. "Jack, my daughter is on Alcatraz. I didn't go all the way across the country and then back again to die within sight of her in a plane crash. You got this?"

"I got this. Buckle up."

Everyone got into a seat and applied the seat belts. Jack made a complete circuit of the island to check the runways, moved eight miles out, and came at the runway from the south-southeast on a heading of 310 degrees.

"I'd say hold on," Jack offered, "but there ain't shit to hold on to."

"Jesus, look at that," Anna said, pointing out the forward window. The streets were filled with the dead. They all moved toward the sound of the plane until it flew over them at about a thousand feet then they reversed direction.

Rick swallowed. "We're going to have to hurry when we land."

His statement was punctuated but the screech of immense tires impacting the tarmac. The C5 sped down the runway at more than one hundred and fifty miles per hour as Jack applied the brakes.

Seyfert pointed at the far end of the runway, it was coming up fast. "Uhh... Jack..."

"I know."

Sitting in the co-pilot's seat, Seyfert reached out to touch Jack on the shoulder, but he was too far away so the SEAL just waved his hand as the end of the asphalt loomed closer. "Can I help you with any of the controls?" he asked. "I could—"

"*Don't touch anything!*" the pilot shouted.

Seyfert pulled his hand back then placed both of them on his knees.

The plane had slowed substantially, but even at a thousand feet away, Seyfert could tell they were going to overshoot the end of the runway. He looked over at Anna, but she had her eyes clamped firmly shut.

"I thought SEALs were tough?" Jack asked through a smile as he turned to face Seyfert. The pilot flicked a switch and the plane's forward momentum jarred to a crawl. Had they been outside watching the landing, the passengers would have seen the nose of the vehicle slowly push over three warning hurdles at the terminus of the runway just as the plane stopped. The hurdles snapped like twigs from the weight of the aircraft and fell to the overgrown grass.

"Told you I was the best," Jack bragged. "Piece of pie."

Rick looked to Anna. "We're alive."

"For now," Seyfert interjected. "We need to move." He grabbed the radio, keying the mic, "Rock, Wanderer Two is safely on the ground." He looked at Jack. "We have a hell of a pilot." Jack beamed.

"*Copy, Wanderer Two. Teams en-route to your position now. They will be outside and covering you before you can exit the aircraft. Familiar faces will be there, over.*"

They were. Twelve men, armed with various weapons but all military stood or knelt in covering positions when the aluminum ramp touched the ground. The sound of a single shot tore through the air but that was all. The vanguard of the dead was a mile away at least on the asphalt of the runway.

Two men ran over to Rick, one throwing his arms around him.

"Hi, Pop. How's Sam?"

"You big shitburger!" Paul, Rick's father, yelled. He was emotional at his son's return. "She's fine, let's get you to her."

When Paul let go of Rick, a taller man shoved his hand in for a shake. He put his other hand on Rick's shoulder, shaking his head in disbelief.

"You must taste like absolute crap to make it all the way to Boston and back. Damn zombies wouldn't eat you, huh?"

"Mike. It's good to see you."

"Hundred and fifty meters!" one of the kneeling men called loudly.

Detective Captain Mike Meara, Rick's former boss and good friend, smiled through a sigh. "Let's get you all back to the Rock. Commander McInerney wants to debrief you."

Several of the soldiers and sailors that were covering the group simultaneously put hands to their right ears.

"Reaper one has two vehicles inbound from the mainland! They're already at the end of the—"

A hail of bullets ripped through the air from their left at the same time two of the military men bellowed, "Contact!"

Everyone dove for cover except Jack. He was staring at several new holes in the aluminum of his C5. "Sons of bitches!" Jack screamed and drew his sidearm. He began firing wildly at the hostiles who were approaching slowly from the north. A man next to Jack, who had begun to return fire, jerked slightly and dropped to the ground.

Two trucks sped west down the runway flying past the several hundred undead who were already on the way. The dead reached for them, but the vehicles were moving too quickly down the far-right side of the asphalt. Gunfire erupted from the trucks as well.

Rick and Seyfert brought their weapons to bear, aiming toward the trucks. Seyfert squeezed off one round, a hole blossoming in driver's side of the windshield on the red Ford. The truck immediately veered to the right and in two seconds slammed into the horde of dead approaching the plane. The vehicle briefly pitched up on two wheels, flipped on its side, and skidded further into the mass of rot with a screech of metal. Men flew from the back and into the greedy arms of the undead. Their screams went unheard over the gunfire and noise of the other truck.

A dozen men moved in from the north, firing as they came. One fell, then two more, but they kept coming.

"Fall back to the boats!" one of the soldiers ordered. Rick's group fired at the truck and the group of hostiles as they fled toward the water.

Jack had reloaded, and though reluctant to leave his aircraft, he moved with his friends. "They shot my damn plane! Those dicks!" He fired another shot and to his utter amazement, one of the aggressors grasped his shoulder and fell to the ground. "HA! Douche!"

Two men dragged the fallen soldier, firing as they did so, but one screamed, "He's gone!" and shot the unlucky man in the head. The entire group scrambled down the cut-stone embankment to the boats, both rigid inflatable operators already on their radios to Alcatraz.

"RHIB One to Rock, we have contact! Multiple hostiles and vehicles at target location! Request immediate assistance, over!"

"Get in the fucking boats, now!" the other boat pilot screamed. He covered the retreating groups but couldn't see very far over the high bank. When everyone was aboard, both boats began to speed across the bay toward Alcatraz Island. Twenty or so hostiles reached the edge of the hill and began to fire at the boats, the occupants returning fire. Two hostiles dropped, but one of the friendly sailors took a round to the head and toppled into the bay.

Rick reloaded and took aim at one of the men firing at him. The bounce of the rigid inflatable vessel skipping across the waves moved the barrel of his rifle all over the place. He squeezed the trigger once, missed, and was about to fire a second time when the large square stones the hostiles were standing on simply exploded. Men and parts of men flew skyward, raining down on the ground next to the runway, the embankment, and into the water. Rick followed a contrail until he found its source. A black, skinny aircraft with a wide wingspan continued its flight over Alameda Island, circling quickly. It fired another small missile at something out of sight and another explosion ripped through the air.

"Roger that, Rock. Reaper One has engaged and destroyed hostiles," the pilot of the vessel Rick was on spoke more into the radio, but Rick was focused on his father. Blood streamed from Paul's right arm as Anna checked him over.

"Through and through," she said to herself. The motors on the boats were extremely quiet, and Rick sighed in relief when Anna told Paul he would be fine.

"Welcome home," Meara said, clapping Rick on the back.

JACKSON STREET, SAN FRANCISCO

"This is my street." Vanessa pointed at a street sign with a smile. They had stopped to stare at Van Ness Avenue, more commonly known as the 101. The road was jam-packed with abandoned, or sort-of abandoned vehicles, as was this side of Jackson Street. Billy shook his head, envisioning what had happened here.

Most of the living population of San Francisco had waited too long to evacuate during the onset of the plague. When people decided to leave the city, they all had decided at the same time. The vehicles had come to a stand-still because of the traffic which was a perfect opportunity for waves of dead to attack the stuck vehicles. Even after a year, dozens of motorists still sat in their vehicles, buckled for safety. They would simulate driving their cars until they rotted away.

Billy looked left then right into the darkness. The metal tombs stretched endlessly in both directions. Grass had found its way into cracks in the asphalt and stood tall at about knee-level in some places. Several dead meandered between the vehicles, but they were unable to figure out how to escape the trap as the cars were bumper-to-bumper in most locations.

"We have to get across," Billy whispered to the kids. "How's your ankle?"

Kyle reached down to rub his foot. "Still hurts."

"Can we go around?" Vanessa asked.

"Nah, it's like this for miles." Billy nodded. "We're going to have to climb over."

"Over that?" She pointed to a dead woman reaching for them from the passenger-side window of a blue Subaru. Dozens of arms reached for them from dozens of broken windows. The noises were beginning to attract attention as well. A few infected had gathered behind the survivors and were shuffling in their direction. More were coming from crossroads and open doorways.

"Yeah, and we gotta go now."

Billy picked the spot with the least amount of reaching appendages and climbed up on the hood of a yellow car. He motioned for the kids to follow and helped Vanessa up. They climbed down and up, up and down over several vehicles. Billy used his sword to dismember or destroy four of the things that they couldn't go around. In just a few minutes, the three of them stood on the other side of the traffic jam.

"Easy-peasy," Billy chimed and a hand shot out from under the car next to him. It latched onto his ankle. "What?" he yelped in surprise. He pulled his foot away easily. The creature was stuck under the car and growling at them.

"That was freaky!" He smiled at the kids. They all looked up when they heard a gigantic plane roar over their heads not three hundred feet above. The plane shook the ground. Billy was still smiling when he returned his gaze to the kids. Both saw his smile vanish as he looked behind them. They spun and saw hundreds of dead coming for them on this side of the cars. They came from the front and the side. Billy swallowed. He hadn't seen so many in one place since the armored car heist he had pulled off earlier in the month. "Oh."

They moved to the east, with infected coming from three sides, driving them in that direction. They soon came across another traffic jam, also headed east. The followed that track, staying low and between the cars. They were mindful about any occupants of those vehicles, and Billy checked both inside and beneath the cars as they moved forward, but it slowed them down.

The dead had noticed them and were now converging on three sides. Billy looked up and suddenly he and the kids were between two massive concrete walls. Vanessa shook her head and pointed. Both Kyle and Billy followed her finger, now staring into the twin maws of a tunnel.

"San Francisco has a tunnel?" Billy asked.

"No," breathed Vanessa.

Billy looked momentarily confused. "Uh, yeah. I'm looking at it right there." It was his turn to point.

Vanessa shook her head, staring intently into the darkness. The sounds of dead things were clearly audible coming from inside the inky blackness. "No, we can't go in there."

"Have to," Billy told her, and grabbed her hand. She tried to fight him for a moment until the sounds of the dead behind her drowned out the noises from the tunnel. She dared a brief glance over her shoulder and felt a quick warmth grow in her crotch. A small bit of urine had escaped into her underwear. Thousands of dead were behind them, the closest less than hundred feet away.

"We're going to die in there..." Kyle let that hang.

"Maybe," agreed Billy, "but only for a little while. Besides, we'll definitely die out here." He put the boy on his back again, and the three of them moved between the abandoned vehicles into the tunnel, the darkness closing in behind them. Vanessa's ragged breathing was loud, and reverberated through the cars and concrete of the underpass. She heard it herself and willed herself to breathe easier.

Wordlessly, Billy boosted the kids up onto the concrete sidewalk used for stranded motorists and pedestrians. A metal railing was the only thing protecting them from the infected in the tunnel. He climbed up after them then took the lead.

He stuck his mouth next to Kyle's ear and whispered as quietly as possible, "Can you walk by yourself?"

"I can walk."

They inched down the walkway, their eyes unable to penetrate their dim surroundings more than a few feet. The darkness past that was absolute. It was odd, because fifty or so feet behind them, the opening of the tunnel allowed light to breach the gloom a few feet in. They could see out, but they hadn't been able to see more than a few feet past where the sun stopped. The dead would suffer the same problem. It didn't stop the infected from hunting though, and they poured into the entrance by the hundreds.

Hacks, rasps, and moans from the front alerted them to more undead in that direction. Vanessa started to breathe heavily again, obviously terrified. She put her hand into Billy's and wouldn't let go. The three of them hugged the damp tile wall with their backs, strung out in a line with Billy in the front and Kyle in the rear. They moved slowly with danger so close, but they didn't want to make any noise.

A shadow moved past them its chest at the level of their feet. More followed, traipsing on a collision course toward their brethren chasing dinner. Billy noticed the light at the far end of the concrete tube but was afraid to say anything to the kids. A simple gasp or a sigh and they were done for.

Dozens of shadows moved between the abandoned vehicles in the tunnel, their movements giving them away as what they were. Vanessa had been keeping her eyes closed, afraid she would compromise the stealth of the group should she let go with a scared shriek if she saw something awful. She opened her eyes when something growled in front of her and lunged through the railing. It couldn't reach them because of the height difference and the distance from the edge of the sidewalk to the ceramic wall of the subway. The thump of its head impacting the railing echoed through the small space, causing every dead eye to search the darkness with renewed vigor. Another thing reached through the railing, then another, all three growling and hissing at prey just out of reach. Kyle and Vanessa attempted to push further into the wall if that were possible.

Billy needed both hands to battle the beasts, but the terrified girl who had his left in her grasp simply would not let go. He had to rip it from her, and a second later, his blade flashed in a downward arc. Two severed hands plopped to the sidewalk and Billy smiled. He repeated the act, but two more creatures had heard the ruckus and were now stretching their infected claws toward the kids.

Most of the things lacked the capacity to figure out how to reach the meal that was so close, but one of them pushed itself up onto the pathway and stumbled after them. Billy moved back past the kids and slashed it across the face, destroying its right eye and flaying the rotting cheek off.

He used a forward stab and the blade stuck out a few inches from the back of the creature's head. For the second time in five minutes, something latched onto his ankle and he didn't even look as he swung the sword downward. He kicked off the severed hand and sped by the kids.

"We need to run!" he whispered. "Stay as close to the wall as you can and keep quiet!"

They ran.

As they moved quickly down the walkway, dead hands reached through the bars in the railing. The closest appendage was still two feet away, but a single misstep would put the living in the arms of the dead. The tunnel echoed with the noises the things made, further adding to the mounting terror.

A dead woman loomed in Billy's way and he cut her down with his sword. She fell backward, Billy and the kids vaulting over her easily. Kyle let go with a hiss of pain when he landed, but he kept up with the others. Vanessa dared a look back and could barely see the walkway behind them. It was no longer empty, dark forms traipsing slowly after her.

The light at the far end of the tunnel beckoned to the survivors with a warmth the gloomy, dank tunnel couldn't fight. Abandoned vehicles extended out the end of this side of the concrete tube as well. Billy noticed a large tanker truck, which would have been forbidden to enter the tunnel under normal circumstances, sticking part way out into the sunlight. Panic must have induced the driver into the tunnel, the vehicle becoming mired in the traffic like all the others.

The dead behind them continued to make their horrible noises as the trio burst back into the daylight. This side of the tunnel was devoid of the dead and Billy called a halt.

"What? What are you doing?" demanded Kyle breathlessly through pain-clenched teeth.

"Surprise!" Billy smiled. "I'm going to give them a surprise!"

The young man searched the rear of the tanker truck but couldn't figure out how to open anything. "Fine!" he yelled and spun. He and the kids weaved through the vehicles. "Let's get way back!"

They got another fifty yards back, and Billy stopped. "Watch this!" he bragged, putting his rifle to his shoulder. He fired twice, two holes blossoming in the rear of the tanker truck. Liquid spewed from the holes and hit the ground, the majority of which flowed down the slight incline into the tunnel.

Billy's eyes were wide. He rounded on the kids. "Crap! It didn't blow up! Why didn't it blow up? It blows up in every movie ever made! Crap!"

Kyle rummaged in his pack and held something out to Billy, who smiled a wicked smile, took the item, and ran back toward the tunnel. The dead were just starting to stream out into the sunlight.

Billy unscrewed the top of the skinny cylinder, rubbed the two pieces together, and was rewarded with a bright flame. He threw the road flare as hard as he could, the red stick tumbling end over end as it arced toward the truck. He turned and fled, not waiting to see if his ploy would work. He grabbed the kids on the way by and they hurried through the vehicles and onto a side street.

"Huh," Billy groused when they stopped to catch a breath. "I guess it didn't—"

A gigantic explosion ripped through the air. Flaming liquid shot in all directions, covering the abandoned vehicles and setting them ablaze in turn. Billy and the kids watched as the tunnel filled with fire. A dozen or so infected stumbled through the conflagration, but none took more than a few steps before collapsing. One of the vehicles near the mouth of the tunnel emitted a deep *WHUMP!* and the back of it jumped into the air a bit.

"That's our cue to skidoo, children." Both kids stared at him blankly and he rolled his eyes. "How's the hoof?" He pointed at Kyle's foot.

"Hurts. I'll be okay." The boy nodded.

"Looks as if we have a bit of a break from the dead." He put his sword away in the makeshift sheath he had fashioned out of a towel and a length of rope. It hung on his right side. "Hop on, kid."

Kyle climbed up. "Who do you think was in that plane?" the boy asked.

Billy shrugged. "Dunno. Big plane though."

The three of them could smell the salt air as they moved north.

ALCATRAZ ISLAND, SAN FRANCISCO

The most difficult thing Rick had done in the five weeks he'd been back in San Francisco was explain to his daughter why her mother hadn't come back from Boston with him. The second was to explain why her friends Chris and Dallas had remained behind with strangers. Little Sam hadn't taken either explanation well and had been sullen and angry for a month. The only thing that made her smile was her cat, Pickles.

The cat adored her, and she him. He was a calico, which was extremely rare for a male cat. She stared at him, lounging on his back on a cinder block window sill in the sun. She wiped her eyes and sniffled. She had been crying again because her mom hadn't come back to be with her. Sam knew what her mother was doing was important, but it was her mother. She should have returned with her father! Sam sighed.

"C'mere, ya big rodent," she demanded of the cat. The animal turned its head to regard her. She smiled because he sprawled on his back with his paws in the air. As most cats are wont to do, he made no move other than to stare back at her.

She raised an eyebrow and put her hands on her hips. "Oh yeah?" She moved over to him and nuzzled his nose with her own. He clawed at the air as she rubbed his belly. She sat in an ancient metal chair and sighed again. Pickles suddenly put his head in the air and stared no place in particular. He jerked his head to stare intently at the door at which point Sam heard movement on the stairs below her. She hoped it wasn't her dad. Her father would kill her if he knew she was in here. This was the Sally Port, and it was condemned. She wasn't really sure what condemned was, but she thought it meant dangerous. Sam had been so angry at and hurt by her mother for not making the return journey that she had come here on several occasions in the past month with her cat to get away from everyone. In addition to not being allowed in the Sally Port (which had a girl's name and was therefore cool), nobody was to go anywhere alone. Ever. She had gotten into trouble several times in the past month, and that was unlike her, but what could anybody do? How could they punish her?

The cat jumped down from the sill, cautiously moving to the door and peeking first left then right. Sam moved to the door and hid behind a low wall. She heard a voice.

"It's me. Yes. Yes. There are over two hundred people now. No, they're not newcomers. It's that asshole from Texas. Yes, he called in on the radio. The imbeciles in charge are very excited for his return."

"*Dallas,*" the young girl thought. "*It had to be Dallas!*" Sam shifted her position so she could hear a bit better.

"No, I wouldn't recommend that. Not yet. There are many soldiers here, plus the police, and even some Navy SEALs. There's... Wait a minute, I thought I heard something."

Sam heard someone coming slowly up the rickety steps. "Shit!" She heard someone shout under their breath and Pickles scrabbled out of the room and down the stairs.

"No, it's fine. It was that stupid cat."

There's a cat? Sam could now hear that the man outside the door was on a radio.

"Yes, one of the cops has a kid and she came in with it at the beginning. So, the rotational guard schedule is as follows..."

The owner of the voice, who Sam thought she knew but couldn't exactly place, began to walk back down the stairs talking. She didn't know why, but she was terrified. Not that she would be caught in the Sally Port, but that this man was a bad man and he was close.

Sam waited what she considered a long time then made her way down the stairs and out into the sunny, salty air. She searched for Pickles, but the animal had made his escape. Sam decided she would go speak to her dad and hang out with him for the afternoon. She saw a pair of roving guards and ducked behind a concrete support pillar. The men stopped right next to her and began to talk.

"Dude, next time you take off for ten minutes, I'm gonna tell Meara, I shit you not."

"Oh, relax. I had to pinch one off. I didn't need you watching me."

"Nobody alone. Ever. *Ever.* I don't care what happens, next time your ass belongs to Meara. He's itching to bust you anyway. Why do you have to challenge everything? They saved you. They saved all of us."

The second man laughed contemptuously. "Saved us. Sure. I had a good life before and now...now I just do what I'm told for crappy soup and a moldy mattress."

"You'd be dead any other way. When you figure that out, maybe you'll thank these people. I think our rotation is done. Let's get back," the first man said in disgust.

The men strode off in silence. Sam peeked out from her hiding place but couldn't tell who one of the men was. The other man was the guy who was always complaining and telling folks how to do things. She couldn't remember his name.

Her cat darted across the path behind her. He disappeared into the high grass without so much as a glance at her. Sam moved back toward the cell blocks smiling. She knew she wouldn't be able to find Pickles. Entering the large, white structure, she found her father speaking to his friend Mike. Mike was one of the bosses around here.

They rounded on her as she entered the walkway. Her father smiled. "Where you been, peanut?"

"Playin' with Pickles."

"Dallas is coming in on a boat right now," Rick told her. "Wanna come with Anna and I to pick him up?"

"Yeah," she smiled, "I want to."

A few hours later, Alcatraz was a happy place. Dallas had returned, and he had brought some people with him. Captain McInerney squeezed a woman in a bear hug and they both cried. A few seconds later, the captain threw himself at Dallas and began to hug him too. True to his word, Dallas had escorted Captain McInerney's wife Clara to Alcatraz. The reunited pair stood together on the dock with three new soldiers, a young woman, and giant bloodhound named Clyde.

The corpsman from the *Florida* interrupted the revelry. "Sorry, folks, but everybody returning from the mainland has to undergo mandatory two-day quarantine. The quicker we get you in, the quicker you can leave."

Rick, Captain McInerney, and a few others elected to stay with the quarantined folks during their brief internment. They couldn't be in the individual cells, but the captain and his wife spoke through the bars and Rick played cards with Dallas. The three soldiers were from an enclave of survivors in Montana. They also disseminated information to Captain McInerney and within a few hours, there were short-wave radio calls from California to Massachusetts to Montana.

Dallas had spoken of a pair of men who had literally pulled him from the teeth of a horde of infected. These men had also accompanied him, Clara, and Clara's friend Eleanor to a group of mix-matched military who had in turn escorted the three civilians back to Alcatraz. The men were headed to an oil rig in the Gulf of Mexico called Atlantis. McInerney tried to contact Atlantis, but the rig had been either unwilling or unable to answer the radio.

"Maybe they can't pick up our signal?" Dallas queried. "Any fours?"

Rick looked thoughtful as he said, "Go fish. Maybe." He squinted his eyes further in thought. "We can reach the east coast and Montana, but not the Gulf? Doesn't sound right."

"Naw. It don't at all."

The groups talked all day, with people coming to visit Dallas well into the evening. Sam sat with Anna and Rick the four of them playing cards together through the bars of Dallas' quarantine cell. Suddenly, a middle-aged man with glasses was standing next to Rick. Pickles, who had been curled up next to, of all creatures, the bloodhound Clyde, jumped up and slunk away. The dog stared after his new friend as the cat trotted down the cell block. Clara reached through the bars and scratched the pooch's head as she spoke with her husband.

"Welcome back, Mr. Dallas," the newcomer said. Sam gasped and suddenly needed to pee.

"Well, thank you, but it's just Dallas, please. How've you been, Mr. Martingale?"

"Very thankful that I have a safe place to stay. Your trip must have been terrifying. The other members of your group have been regaling us with your exploits."

Dallas glanced at Rick. "They have, huh? It was a team effort."

The man laughed a bit. "Of course. Welcome back either way." He strode off.

Sam stared at the man as he walked away. "What is it, honey?" Rick asked noticing.

"I don't like him," she said immediately.

"Me neither," Dallas agreed under his breath and winked at the girl. She smiled at him then continued to stare at Martingale's back until he started down the stairs.

The following morning, the Navy corpsman who had admitted the new arrivals to quarantine stood in front of Dallas' cell with Meara and McInerney.

"Dallas," McInerney said with an odd look on his face, "you have a phone call."

"Guy says he knows you," Meara added. "Says he met you in Montana."

"Normally, I wouldn't allow this," the corpsman told the group, "but none of you are sick, and you'll be coming right back into quarantine when you get back anyway, so you can go." He produced a key and opened the lock on the chains threaded through the bars.

Dallas looked bewildered. "Go where?"

McInerney answered, "To meet your friend. You can take the other men who came in with you if you like."

"I would. Thank you, Cap'n."

BEACH STREET, SAN FRANCISCO

Vanessa stood on the roof of the Maritime Museum. Kyle and Billy were sitting a bit away from her in lawn chairs talking and taking in some sun, but she stood, gazing at the beach and the bay beyond. Alcatraz sat high in the water, a little more than a mile away. They had made the museum home for almost five weeks now. Although she had no idea what day it was, she had been counting the mornings since they'd first arrived.

The museum had been under construction when the plague had struck. Caution tape blocked off several of the exhibits, which were boats and ships. Construction equipment and supplies were there for the taking, so Billy and the kids used some of the stuff to block the main entrance. They got in and out using a construction scaffold and a roof access, although Billy rarely left, and the kids hadn't been outside other than the roof for more than a month.

Someone had been using one of the large storage areas as a hidey-hole, but that person either bugged out when Billy and the kids showed up, or they had left before then. Several weeks-worth of rations and some camping equipment awaited them to their utter surprise. A short-barreled sawed-off shotgun also awaited them, and Billy appropriated it for himself, wearing it constantly strapped to his back.

The young girl was itching for a shower. She hadn't had one in weeks and felt dirty. She ran her fingers through her dark hair while she watched some seagulls out on the hooked jetty. A large black vehicle moved through the air to her right. It was coming in for a landing at Alameda to her southeast.

"Billy," she called. He and Kyle were sitting in beach chairs, catching the sun on their faces. Billy looked at her and she pointed. The three of them stared at a plane as it descended out of sight presumably onto one of the runways on the island.

"You'd think," began Billy, "what with the end of the world and all, there would be less trips scheduled. This is, what? The second plane in a month? I guess they don't cancel flights for a little thing like the apocalypse." He stood, clapping his hands on his thighs. "Well, kids, I think it's time we got to Alcatraz. I also think those folks might need some help." He pointed to the plane.

"Is the boat ready?" Kyle asked a bit nervously. He never doubted that they would eventually have to leave this new place, but he had become accustomed to the safety it afforded. They would have to traipse a full two hundred yards down the dock to Billy's boat. Two hundred yards was a long way to go in San Francisco nowadays.

"Yup! Put the finishing touches on it last night." Billy furrowed his brow in thought. "Couldn't find a pirate flag though. And thinking about it, maybe that isn't a good idea considering where we're about to go?"

Vanessa looked over her shoulder at the boys. "Alcatraz?"

"Yup!" Billy said a bit too loudly.

"It's a fishing boat, right?" Kyle inquired. "Do you think we can go fishing?"

Billy stuck out his lower lip and nodded a couple times before smiling. "Yup!"

"We have to get to it first," Vanessa said and pointed. A baker's dozen infected had shown up at the dock when they heard the plane. They milled about the planks, moving to the chain railing and shuffling in several directions.

The young man pointed at Kyle's foot. "How's the ankle?"

"Fantastic," the boy said and moved his bare foot in a circle. "Doesn't hurt at all.

Billy glanced at both kids, then to the infected on the pier, then back at the kids. He nodded. "Let's do it."

They had moved all the items blocking the rear entrance. The sturdy doors were now all that separated them from the infected on the dock to the left. The museum had its own dock, but Billy hadn't been able to figure out how to get the big boat into the small concrete channel outside the museum. He'd had to anchor the forty-foot fishing vessel further down the pier a bit.

He stared intently at Kyle and sighed. "Here." He passed the boy his katana. "It's longer than this." Billy hefted a wooden baseball bat he had appropriated from the cache of stuff they had found in the museum. Vanessa had the spear she had fashioned out of a broomstick.

"Me, first, then you guys. Don't shoot unless you have to." Billy pointed to Kyle's small pistol. "We go fast. Get by them if you can, I'll clear a path. Ready?"

Both kids nodded. Kyle drew the sword from the makeshift sheath. Billy pushed the door open and peeked out, looking both ways. He was out the door and holding it for the kids in a moment and soon the safety of walls and doors was gone.

They hurried down the concrete walkway next to the water and stepped onto the dock. One of the things began its trek toward them, but the others hadn't noticed yet. The creature let loose with a rasp, and the others turned and headed toward the survivors like a flock of birds.

Billy strode forward and swung the bat in a sideways arc into the head of a dead fireman. The thing crumpled, and the living man brought his weapon overhead, smashing it down on the top of a dead woman's cranium. Her head split like a rotten melon, fluids spraying.

"Ugh!" Billy shouted and continued his mayhem. They made it to the boat without incident. Neither of the kids had to use their weapons. Kyle and Billy cast off the lines and Billy started the boat.

"Dave taught me how to do this!" he shouted.

"Who's Dave?" Vanessa asked.

Kyle shrugged. "No idea."

The boat pulled away from San Francisco, making its way to Alameda Island in a short time. Billy showed both kids how to start, stop, steer, and throttle the boat. "This is neutral. Neutral is your friend." He killed power to the engines and chucked an anchor overboard when they were about eight feet from the cut-stone embankment of Alameda. He brought out a gangplank he had made from two 2x12 pieces of wood nailed together at intervals with 2x4s. It was heavy, but he and the kids were able to get it to the land from the boat.

"Stay here," he told the kids, pointing at them. "Pull the board back when I'm over. If I'm not back in a couple of hours, or if anybody else comes in a boat, you get to Alcatraz. If they start shooting at you, just keep your heads down, point the boat at Alcatraz, and push this all the way forward." He indicated the throttle.

"We're supposed to stick together," Vanessa told him.

He smiled. "I know. Those folks might need my help, and you have each other. Get out of here fast if anybody comes. The water is too deep here for anything to climb aboard, but if anything tries, don't let it."

Vanessa appeared frightened, but Kyle had a look on him that said he wouldn't fail.

He hugged them both. "They grow up so fast," Billy mock-cried as he put his boots on the island. He waved as the kids pulled the gangplank back.

They watched their protector make his way across the giant parking lot and disappear into the structures on the island. Two huge planes sat abandoned on the old runway to the far northwest.

Billy ran across a huge southern runway noting the two vacant airplanes to the north-west. He hadn't made it ten steps into the industrial/residential area of the island when the keening scream of a Runner echoed through the abandoned structures. The noise was immediately followed by several gunshots

"Uh oh."

He hurried toward a group of the things. They were seemingly intent on heading into an alley. Billy figured out why quickly. A tallish man was trapped halfway down the alley. A living man, with dead on both sides, converging on him. The man had nowhere to go but rather than panic and start screaming, he did something that made Billy smile.

"Come on then," the man said loudly. "Come on!" The guy fired into the crowd with a suppressed pistol. Billy's eyes went wide he thought that was so cool.

"I want a silencer..." he said thoughtfully, then yelled, "Howdy, partners!" The dead did what they always did when confronted with Billy; they turned to glare at him for a moment then resumed their relentless pursuit of something they thought they could eat. He waded into the ones in front of him, sounding off his count as he smashed them with his bat. He had left his sword with Kyle. "Fifteen! Woo-hoo!"

He tired quickly, and soon was huffing. "Nine...nineteen." Two of the things had reached the guy and Billy smashed one as it grabbed the man. The poor guy was using his knife, and he stumbled when a large undead fell on him snapping. Billy brought the bat around into the side of the creature's head, the crunch of the impact quite satisfying.

The man struggled to extricate himself from the two re-killed infected, but the ones from the far end of the alley had reached them. Billy drew his shotgun and fired point blank into the face of a dead thing. The number 11 on the creature's Utah Jazz basketball jersey was all but obscured by brown stains.

Billy fired again, jacking a fresh shell into the chamber. The man rolled toward his savior and Billy helped him up. The man made for the clear end of the lane. "Come on!" he shouted.

"Be right there!" Billy joyfully shouted back. He had holstered the shotgun and returned to his bat. He destroyed a few more of the undead before he realized there were too many. He pushed his way through the rest of them and caught up with the man, disbelief all over the newcomer's face.

The man was cradling his arm, a fact that didn't go unnoticed to Billy. "Hurt it earlier in the week," the man told him when Billy pointed at it and asked.

Weapons fire came from in front of them and two men rounded the corner of one of the buildings. Billy didn't know if these men were part of the group of killers from the city and was prepared for a fight, when more people, including a couple of kids, followed the initial two around the corner. One of the men was the biggest human being Billy had ever seen.

"Who's he?" one of the men demanded. Billy raised his eyebrows and pointed at himself questioningly. "Me?" He told them his name and that there were hundreds of infected on the way. "I got a boat," he added and after a moment, the folks agreed to come with him. They followed Billy and soon were standing on a cut-stone embankment, the fishing boat fifty or so feet away.

"Mickey! This is Bugs! Come get us!" Billy turned, checking the status of the Alameda infected. He pointed back the way they had come. The group followed his finger, noticing a thousand or more infected coming toward them. The infected were a few hundred yards away when one of the fast ones fought its way to the front and began to scream.

A handmade gangway was pushed with some difficulty toward the shore, and the group boarded the boat. Kyle applied the throttle and the vessel made its way into the bay.

"Where would you like to go?" Billy asked.

"Alcatraz," replied the first man Billy had helped. Apparently, the man had run across Dallas in the past, the Texan extending an invitation to join the Alcatraz Island community.

They spoke about Dallas and Alcatraz for a few minutes before Billy began to speak to Richy and Chloe, the two new kids, about cartoons. Kyle and Vanessa also sat with them, and the five of them chatted until a radio call needed to be made. Billy didn't know how to work the radio, so one of the newcomers showed him. In short order, two boats from Alcatraz were on their way to escort the group back to the island.

Billy pulled his new friend aside. "You have to take my kids to Alcatraz too."

The man looked confused. "You're not coming?"

Billy didn't want to get into why he couldn't come. He certainly didn't relish the thought of being incarcerated in a hundred-year-old prison, especially when he was one of the good guys. He thought about seeing Sam again, but then thought that she would have to talk to him through the bars of a cell if they let her. Then again, they might just kill him. Billy smiled when he thought of the ruckus that would cause. A few of the people there would go nuts. He smiled broader at the nuts thought. Just like me!

In the end, he hugged his kids and the new kids too. He took a small dinghy to one of the docks on the eastern side of San Francisco. The dock was teeming with infected, but Billy rowed right up to it and climbed the short ladder. Several of the dead things splashed into the water when Billy pushed them, a wicked smile on his face. He waved enthusiastically to the boat then disappeared into the throng.

SAN FRANCISCO BAY

A grin appropriate to his size enveloped Dallas' face. The man he was looking at across forty feet of inky black bay water had saved his life a few times after Dallas had split from Rick to find Captain McInerney's wife. Literally pulled him out of the arms of the dead at great personal risk. More than that, this man had skulked into the teeth of thousands of undead to procure medical supplies for sick kids. That alone had been very telling for Dallas. This man could be trusted. The newcomer would still have to be vetted through action before he would be completely trusted by Dallas' friends, especially Meara and McInerney, but Texan's word held a lot of sway, especially to the rest of Rick's core group and the captain of the USS *Florida*.

One of the soldiers that had helped Dallas, McInerney's wife Clara, and her friend Eleanor travel from Montana to California, spoke to one of the men on the other boat, and tensions relaxed on both sides when everyone realized that some of the folks on each side knew each other.

The boat Dallas was on tied up to the fishing boat. A third vessel that had come from Alcatraz sat off a bit and the men aboard looked in all directions with binoculars. Dallas boarded the fishing boat and enveloped his friend in a great Dallas bear hug. Ali had also come with Dallas. She immediately asked for Billy.

Ali was distraught when she heard that Billy had gone back into the city. She stared at the infected falling into the water a few hundred yards away and shook her head. She looked at the kids and smiled. They smiled back.

Within the hour, the three vessels had returned to Alcatraz and the new folks were on their way to quarantine. The following day, all the new residents of Alcatraz were let out of confinement to begin their assimilation.

Four of the newcomers were being debriefed by McInerney, Pitt, Seyfert, and Meara in the command center. Rick and Dallas were present as well. Dallas had vetted them, and they had had their weapons returned. One of the strangers was the largest man McInerney had ever seen. Until this man had shown up, Dallas had been the largest person on Alcatraz. The top of Dallas' head barely made it above the shoulder of the new giant, and he had to weigh four hundred pounds, all muscle. The huge man hadn't uttered a single word since he and his friends had been brought to the island. Two of the four were military; one soldier and one marine. Their mission had been to establish contact between Atlantis, an oil rig in the Gulf of Mexico, and an enclave of survivors in Montana.

Unfortunately, Atlantis had come under attack by a paramilitary group. The entire rig had been destroyed. The man whom Dallas had befriended, a taller man with brownish hair, possibly in his early thirties, introduced himself then his friends. "This is Alvarez, he's Army. This is Remo, he's retired MARSOC." Both Pitt and Seyfert looked impressed. The man reached his hand up to put it on the giant's shoulder. "This is Ship. He doesn't speak. He is a genius. He is also my comfort animal." The man smiled a wry smile as Ship looked down on him and shook his head like the new guy was the problem child.

"Out of curiosity," McInerney began, "did you notice any identifying marks on the uniforms of the group who attacked Atlantis?"

Ship wrote in a notebook and passed it to one of his compatriots. "Ship says he noticed a set of Roman numerals on the black BDUs of several of the douches who blew up my house. The numbers were here." The man touched his left breast with his index finger.

Seyfert looked sideways at McInerney, both Rick and Dallas mimicking the act and glancing at each other. "Triumvirate," all four men said in unison.

"Yeah, one of them said something about him *not* being Triumvirate," the new guy told them.

"Wait, not Triumvirate?" Seyfert asked.

"Yeah. I had just stuck my knife in his stomach. He was bleeding out and said they had conscripted him."

Meara looked at the new man oddly. "You...you killed him?"

"Nope. I stabbed him and let the dead kill him. The same dead who had been my friends before they were made dead by that asshole and his buddies. Triumvirate or not, that dickweed had to go."

Seyfert snorted, obviously agreeing with the stranger's actions. McInerney glared at the SEAL, and Seyfert stared at the ground.

McInerney sighed. "So, Atlantis is lost?"

"Yeah, it's toast. Those pricks blew it up. There were some survivors who escaped in boats to the other rigs and ships in the Gulf. There's a couple dozen big ships and several rigs out there." The man pulled a green spiral notebook out of his tactical vest and flipped open to the last page. A list of many coordinates and radio frequencies along with the names of some vessels adorned the back of the book. "You can check them out if you want. Give 'em a call, I mean."

McInerney accepted the book with thanks.

The man looked at Dallas and sighed. "Did you tell them?"

Dallas shook his head. "Tell 'em what?"

"About this?" The man pointed to a horrible scar on his arm. It looked barely healed. Both the Navy corpsman and Doctor Lefkovitz had checked each person during their quarantine. The bandage on the man's arm was clearly a bite wound, but as it was healing, and the man wasn't sick, both doctors cleared him of infection. The new guy said he had been bitten by a living man during a fight a few months ago.

Dallas looked around at his friends before replying. "Uhh...no. Thought you should do that." The big Texan pointed at the wound. "Another one?"

The man smiled. "Thanks, my large Texan friend. I need to ask you another question. Normally, I wouldn't do it in front of all these people, but if I'm going to live here, I gotta know: do you trust everyone in this room?"

"No," Dallas said immediately. "I dunno these three guys." He pointed at the man's friends, including the giant, "but if they're with you and you trust 'em, they're good enough for me, cuz I trust you."

The guy continued, "Right." It was Ship's turn to put his hand on his friend's shoulder. Ship shook his head, *No*. "Got to, buddy." He turned to speak to McInerney. "Captain, there are some things you need to know about me. Number one: I am a shit magnet. Bad things follow me around like a lost puppy. Number two: There are people hunting me. Not just people, what's left of the US government. Some of them are good people, and some are in league with the son of a bitch that tried to kill Dallas and your men in Massachusetts." All the men in the room looked at Dallas, who tried to make himself small. An impossible task for a man of his size.

"You divulged mission specifics to a...stranger?" Pitt demanded.

Dallas looked a bit sheepish. "Listen to what else he's got to say."

"I was hunted and captured by a man named Lynch," the new guy said and Rick's blood went cold.

"Holy shit," blurted Seyfert.

"Yup, except he was not the same Lynch as yours. Government douche, yeah, but my guy was torn apart by infected and Dallas killed yours. Unless he died twice, it wasn't the same dude."

Pitt looked concerned. "Why is the government hunting you?"

The guy looked at the giant, then at the Army guy, then at the marine. "Because of this." He raised his arm, the bite mark evident. Everyone knew it was a bite, but they also knew it was from a living human, as nobody would be alive after a day-long quarantine after being bitten by an infected.

The man looked down for a moment, put his hands on the table, then looked back at the group. "The guy who bit me was a little...less alive than I may have let on."

"What?" asked McInerney, a bit confused. Meara, Rick, and Pitt had their hands on their weapons quickly, but so did all the newcomer's friends.

"Relax," Dallas said and put his hand on Rick's arm.

"Dallas, he's bitten!" Pitt almost shouted.

Even with the tension in the room and hands on weapons, the guy smiled. "It was almost four months ago that I was bitten." He put his foot on the table and pulled his pant leg up. Another wound, clearly a healed bite mark, was present on his calf. "This was almost two years ago."

This revelation sparked a more intense conversation which lasted into the early evening. When the group broke for a meal, Dallas, Rick, the new guy, and his friends Ship and Remo stayed behind to talk for a few minutes. Anna Hargis showed up with some wild raspberries she had picked earlier in the day.

"They grow behind the water tower," she told the group. She had wanted to meet the new folks and had shown up at the end of the meeting to do so. She was introduced to the group and shook hands. She stared at Ship for a moment, but he smiled at her and she liked him instantly.

They stared out at the bay as they spoke, talking about different times while the sun sunk into the ocean. Lights came on throughout the island, and some could be seen in the city as well.

Rick pointed at the lights across the water. "Those would be the bad guys," he told the group. "They're the only ones with the stones enough to have lights burning."

"Bad guys?" the marine, Remo, asked.

Rick sighed. "Yeah. They've attacked us on several occasions during forays. They call themselves The New Society. Gangers from LA and their conscripts."

Remo and his friend looked at each other, Remo shaking his head. "We've dealt with their kind before. We'll help with them if you'd like."

Dallas smiled, and Rick was about to speak when a giant explosion ripped through the evening. Most of the people who had been conversing were now on the floor with their hands covering their heads. Dallas stood tall, looking out the dirty window toward the northwest.

"What the hell was that?" demanded Rick.

Dallas glanced back at his friend. "That was the sub…"

SAN FRANCISCO BAY

A small craft made its way from San Francisco toward Alcatraz. One man surveyed the area with binoculars, the other piloted the small boat using a fishing motor.

"No, I told you," whispered the man driving, "it ain't gonna sink. It'll be fucked up though. Enough that she won't be able to move."

"I never seen this much explosives before," said the man who had asked about sinking the *Florida*. He looked at the large bundles on the deck in front of him. He tried to stand in the small rigid inflatable boat he was in, but the other guy grabbed him and pulled him back down.

"If you stand up, they can fuckin see us on radar, idiot!"

"Yeah, but…"

The first man drew his sidearm and pointed it at the face of the second. "They can hear us too!" he whispered. "That thing can hear a mouse fart a half a mile away! Shut the fuck up!"

The second guy raised his hands slightly and nodded. The first holstered his weapon and put his finger across his lips. He didn't know if his stupid colleague could see his finger in the darkness, but he had seen the gun, so maybe.

A black shadow sat between the two men and the island of Alcatraz. They couldn't see the sub, but they knew where it was as it blocked the light from the island. The man cut the motor when they were a hundred yards out. He passed an oar to the other man. "Stay low," he whispered. "Paddle light but strong and don't make any bubbles. If they see any type of wake, we're dead."

Seaman Lillie pulled the binoculars from his eyes and sighed. "This sucks. I can't see shit because there's nothing to see."

"You can't see shit because it's dark," Petty Officer Second Class Guimaraes responded. "Keep looking."

The two had drawn deck watch this evening and stood on the aft deck of the Florida. They scanned the city and occasionally glanced at the bay if they saw any whitecaps.

"Dude, you gotta be kidding me. What the fuck is gonna attack a nuclear submarine? Those dead fucks can't get to us and the hostiles don't have the equipment to do anything."

"You forgetting about the TOW they fired at us? If they had hit us, we would have been fucked. Just follow orders and we can get some chow in a few hours. I'm going forward to take a look at the bay." Guimaraes moved off to scan for possible aggressors, even though he knew there would be none. This was his forty-sixth time on deck watch, and he had never seen anything other than some birds and a couple of seals. Not that he could even see those at night.

Guimaraes had stashed a fishing rod on the foredeck of the *Florida*. He and several other sailors used it when they were on deck watch. Captain McInerney knew about it and had told Pitt to inform the sailors on watch that as long as they kept a weather eye, they could make a few casts here and there. McInerney also loved fresh striped bass, so anyone catching a good one got a wink from the captain, and he got a filet from the fisherman.

The Petty Officer Second Class opened the communal bait-box left on the foredeck. Whenever someone caught something too small or inedible, it went in the box and was used for bait. Guimaraes baited his hook and made a great cast. Within ten minutes, he felt a nibble and a few seconds later he had a fish on. After a considerable battle, he held his prize in front of him: a beautiful striper, forty-five inches at least. He would eat well tonight.

Guimaraes moved back toward the aft deck, where he had left his watch mate. "Check this out!" he told the seaman. Lillie began to move toward Guimaraes and his fish. The petty officer smiled and put the striper on the deck, trying to extract the hook. He held the fish up by the gills just as Lillie reached him.

"Who's the man?" Guimaraes asked through a smug smile. He noticed too late something sticking out of Lillie's neck. Lillie grabbed him and sunk his teeth into his friend's throat, pulling back with a mouthful of flesh. The petty officer struggled briefly, but the initial damage to his neck had been substantial, and he weakened quickly, bleeding out. When he collapsed, they both went over the side with a small splash, sinking below the surface of the inky water.

"Good shot," the man with the grease-paint blackened face said to his colleague. The quiet sound of a crossbow being cocked and a bolt sliding into the firing mechanism wouldn't give them away. The two men watched as they rowed to the rear of the sub. The sailor who had been hit with the bolt began to rise before they reached the steel hull of the submarine. The man raised the crossbow again and took aim, but the first man told him to wait. They watched as one sailor killed the other, both toppling into the sea. The first man spit into a diver's mask and rinsed it with bay water. He slid over the side of the small boat, the second man passing him a large bundle. A light came on under the water shortly after the diver swam toward the aft-most portion of the sub's hull. The man in the boat smiled, but the smile turned to a frown when a light from the conning tower swept the area and quickly found him. He raised his rifle, but was immediately cut down by submachine gun fire from the sub. He slumped back, both he and the inflatable boat riddled with holes.

"Clear!" a black-clad sailor shouted. Several other shouts of *Clear!* echoed the first. The searchlight continued to pan around the sub, but nothing was revealed. One of the sailors jumped in the water and made his way to the small boat. The occupant had taken two hits to the head and wouldn't rise. There was nothing else in the small boat that the sailor could see.

"Boat is clear!" he shouted.

"I want divers in the water now!" the officer in charge shouted from the conning tower. The sailor in the destroyed boat did not get a chance to reply before a huge explosion rocked the rear of the submarine.

ALCATRAZ

Captain McInerney fumed. "What the hell happened, Commander?"

"Sir," Pitt began, "they were going for the prop or the rear dive planes. Either would have crippled us, but had they blown a few ballast vents, the *Florida* would have been on the bottom of the bay. They knew what to target, but didn't get a chance to get to it, or we'd be dead. As it is, not much was damaged."

"How bad is it?" McInerney demanded.

"We'll need some body work and a paint job, sir."

"Casualties?"

"We lost Lopes, Guimaraes, and Lillie, sir."

McInerney turned to stare at the lights in San Francisco. He gritted his teeth as he told Pitt, "This happy horseshit stops today. We're taking this to them." It was clear he meant the aggressors from the city. "Assemble two teams."

"Aye, sir!" Pitt exclaimed and turned to leave, but McInerney forestalled him.

"Commander?"

"Aye, sir?"

"Are you comfortable with allowing the MARSOC and Army assets that showed up yesterday on the mission?"

Pitt let loose with a sigh. "I heard their debriefing and they seem capable. Also, Dallas has vetted them, sir. That alone would have been enough for me. But," he took a deep breath then let it out quickly, "we are running low on capable men. In addition, one of them risked his life to save Dallas and help Dallas bring Clara to you. I would allow them on any mission, Navy or not. Yes, sir. I think it's a good idea to bring them along." Pitt dropped his gaze. "I only wish they could have been around to get Kim." Kim, commander Pitt's wife, had been in Austin Texas when the plague struck. Pitt hadn't heard from her.

"Me, too," McInerney said, nodding. "Commander, is there any way we can fake the sinking of our boat?"

"Sir?"

"I want the hostiles to think we've sunk and that the *Florida* is no longer a viable threat."

A wicked smile crossed Pitt's face. The commander didn't smile much. "Yes, sir. We can do that."

MARINA BLVD, SAN FRANCISCO

Several shadows were silhouetted against the top floor windows of the Festival Pavilion warehouse on Pier 1. A smile creased the face of Malik Phillips, AKA Doc Murda. He shifted his gaze to his father, Cyrus, whose face held a similar grin.

"Well played," Cyrus told him.

Doc Murda accepted his praise with uncharacteristic glee. "Thanks! Hopefully, our surprise was enough to sink the submarine, or at least disable it. This is going to be a good day!" He glanced over his left shoulder at his captain, Masta G, and his bodyguard and enforcer, Pee Wee. Both were impassive as ever. "Live a little, fellas. We have the world at our fingertips. If we were able to kill any of the soldiers or sailors, I call this a win."

Masta G and Pee Wee glanced quickly at each other, but neither said a word. It would take considerable resources to mount a successful attack on Alcatraz with the sub and her crew protecting the island. Dozens of civilians, all potential soldiers or slaves, had escaped the clutches of the New Society and made it to Alcatraz as well. All of the escapees would fight to the death to protect their sanctuary. The New Society had the numbers, but the military on Alcatraz had both the tools and the training to keep attacks at bay.

"We'll ensure the sub is damaged then launch an offensive." Murda cast a sideways glance at his father. "This time, we'll send two hundred men and attack under cover of darkness."

Cyrus nodded his approval. He reached his hand out to accept a large pair of binoculars, but he really couldn't see much in the darkness. The bay looked placid.

A figure with its arms crossed leaned against an unlit streetlight immediately below Doc Murda's crew. He watched them watch the bay. An undead UPS worker shuffled by and he nodded to it. Had the thing looked up, it may have seen the men in the warehouse window above it. Oblivious, it continued on its way.

The figure shook its head, knowing that the explosion in the bay had been the work of the men above him. "Can't we all just get along?" Billy asked himself under his breath.

He had appropriated a few rounds for his shotgun from the folks he had gotten to Alcatraz, and he loaded them into his weapon. He could get two of the gangers, maybe three before they got him. They were armed to the teeth, and he needed to make sure he got the leader, and hopefully Cyrus.

Plus, he didn't want to die.

A smile split his face as a contingent of twenty or so dead wandered down the pier.

He glanced up at the guys then back at the dead, who seemed to be milling about at the far end of the sidewalk.

"I *could* bring friends to this party."

Billy whistled, the dead turning instantly to come toward the sound. The men in the warehouse hadn't heard the whistle. When the dead reached him, they began to mill about again. Billy strode to an access door located one floor directly below the aggressors. The door was unlocked, and the cocky young man stepped inside and called under his breath to the dead. The creatures shuffled through the door and into the warehouse.

He counted twenty-four shamblers as they entered the building single-file. Smiling, Billy stepped back out the door as the last of the undead procession faded into the darkness of the warehouse. He returned to his light post and saw the men above talking and gesturing toward the bay. Billy aimed his shotgun at the second floor and fired.

ALCATRAZ

Dusk saw a group of eight warriors, fully outfitted with the weapons of their choice and other tactical gear, standing adjacent to the southeast dock. They checked themselves and each other over, making sure nothing had been forgotten. Their mission was simple: destroy the New Society.

Rick shook Seyfert's hand. "You sure? Your leg okay now?" Rick pointed at the SEAL's bullet wound from many weeks ago.

"Yeah, it's good. I'm more concerned with the folks I don't know," he said so only Rick could hear him. Seyfert looked over his shoulder at the four new guys who would be watching his back on this mission.

"Dallas and McInerney swear they're good," Rick told his friend. "But Pitt agrees, and that should sell them."

Seyfert nodded. "We'll see. MARSOC, Army, and two civvies." The SEAL shook his head and gave Rick a sideways glance. "A couple years ago, I wouldn't have even considered taking civilians with me. Some dumbass convinced me otherwise."

Both men smiled.

Seyfert squinted at Rick's father and daughter, who had shown up with a group of others. Sam went to talk to the new kids, who were hugging the giant, Ship, and his friends.

"What are you doing here, Pop?" Rick asked his dad.

"Making sure your dumb ass doesn't get on any boats," Paul answered, and folded his arms. All three men smiled again.

Sam looked up at the new people. She spoke to the one who didn't have a short haircut, "You're the one who helped Dallas, right?"

The man smiled and shook his head. "We helped each other. Dallas is good people."

Sam didn't smile. She glared across the bay at the shadow of San Francisco, dread filling her. When she turned her gaze back to the man, he was still smiling. "Please be careful. A lot of people don't come back when they go in there." She nodded toward the city. She didn't know why, but suddenly she was hugging the new guy.

"Are you kidding?" he asked. "Have you seen this guy?" It was his turn to nod and he threw a glance at his huge friend. "Zombies are afraid of him." He cupped one hand next to his mouth and said in a loud whisper, "So am I." He winked at her, and she did smile. "We'll be careful, I promise."

"It's time," Pitt announced.

More handshakes, some hugs, and not a few kisses were transferred as the eight men boarded a fishing boat.

Both sides waved as the vessel pulled away.

Sam put her hand in her father's. "Thanks for not going this time."

"Hey, I promised I would come back from Boston, didn't I?"

"Yeah, you did."

The orange glow from the west winked out as the sun settled beneath the waves.

"I always keep my promises, kid."

"Do they?" she asked and pointed to the departing boat.

EPI-PROLOGUE

There are four common definitions of a virus. The first definition is probably what most English speakers envision when they hear the word: An ultramicroscopic, metabolically inert, infectious agent that replicates only within the cells of living hosts, composed of an RNA or DNA core, a protein coat and, in more complex types, a surrounding envelope.

A disease. That's the second, informal definition.

The third meaning is: a corrupting influence on morals or the intellect; poison.

The fourth and final listing in Webster's is: a segment of self-replicating code planted illegally in a computer program or system, often to damage or shutdown a system or network.

Near the end of the twentieth century, a group of computer geniuses working for a private military company created a computer worm. It was a virus that was specifically designed to attack programmable logic controllers; the software that controls the automation of electromechanical processes. Stuxnet was the name given to the virus.

Another group of geniuses took Stuxnet and mutated it. They re-wrote some code such that Stuxnet would do worse things than bother the processes of an assembly line computer, or the software that turns streetlights red. Why couldn't the virus disrupt the spin cycles of centrifuges used to enrich uranium in Iran? Or shut down the power grid for the southeastern portion of Pakistan? Why couldn't it make the fuel rods in a nuclear submarine stop cooling?

Several iterations of the worm came and went as did the names of the worm itself. The destruction mounted, especially with the different uses for the virus. No matter the variances of the weapon, or what it was used to destroy, one thing was always the same: the delivery system. There was only one way to infect a closed system with the worm. Someone had to use some type of storage media; a flash drive, a compact disc, a memory card, to upload the virus into a system not connected to the internet. Someone not friendly to whatever system needed to be corrupted. A spy.

The problem with spies is that, inevitably, they get caught.

The last group of geniuses to play with the virus, which had evolved far beyond the original Stuxnet, worked solely on the delivery system. They needed to find a way to infect a closed system with the worm from afar. Initially, they tried radio waves and microwaves, both of which were successful, but both of which were easily detected and thwarted. There was an attempt at using photons, but that never panned out. A biochemist came up with an idea at an impromptu meeting of the minds in a burger joint at two in the morning: what if brainwaves could be used? What if a person's brainwaves could be infected with the worm and they could unknowingly carry the virus into whatever installation was on the target menu?

So, the smart folks worked. And worked and worked. It was challenging and it was fun. Furthering the efforts of those that had come before them, they figured out how to attach the viral payload to a human subject using virtually any electronic device. Furthermore, the subject could infect any electronic device merely by standing in close proximity to it. Once infected, the subject suffered no ill effects and was completely unaware they were carrying the virus. Using human brainwaves as a carrier, the subject could and did infect anything that was targeted. Because the delivery system worked using beta wave bursts, the upload was almost instantaneous. The scientists stopped calling the transition of the virus an upload and began referring to it as The Graft.

The final iteration of the virus was called Abaddon. It was the pinnacle of virus technology. The ultimate code. It could shutdown anything and it did.

What happens when someone creates the best of something? A new shampoo, a new toy, a new car? Someone else must make a better one. In the case of a computer virus, someone must create an antivirus.

The National Security Agency Cyber Division decided to quit screwing around when closed government and military computer systems began displaying symptoms of infection. The NSA recruited a new army of computer geniuses from the Massachusetts Institute of Technology and a small, private software company and put them to work. In months, they had a working prototype of an antivirus, with the same beta wave delivery system that Abaddon used. In a twist of karmic genius, the name given to the antivirus program was Rama.

Trials began in a small town in Massachusetts. Some infected technology was uninfected and things looked good. The idea was to kill the virus with the antivirus. If Abaddon struck, Rama struck back. Theoretically, if your car won't start? Abaddon had infected it. Car stars now? Rama fixed it. Early-warning missile detection system infected? Rama to the rescue. Where Abaddon was designed to shut things down, Rama was developed to either prevent the initial attack, or start an infected system back up again.

It worked.

When the infected system was jump-started, the antivirus would then seek out resources to repair the damaged system, appropriating any extra power or code needed to wipe out any traces of Abaddon.

A meeting was called about the fate of Rama at Vantel, the research company which had been employed to help sort out an antivirus. Vantel had the resources from private sector contacts that a university, no matter how prestigious, didn't. Several of the high-level staff that had been working tirelessly perfecting the antivirus were to present their product prototype to their clients: the NSA and the US Army. Twelve people sat around a beautiful mahogany table in very expensive wheeled chairs. Drs. Crisp, Copper, and Childs represented the Vantel Corporation. Nauls, Bennings, Palmer, Clark, and Fuchs from the NSA were present, as were Major Gary and Colonels MacReady and Windows from the US Army. The last of the twelve sat at the far end of the gorgeously polished table, keeping to himself. He had arrived with the clients, but hadn't been introduced.

One of the scientists who had initially worked on the source code for Rama, Dr. Donald Copper, had also stepped in to perfect the delivery system. The doctor voiced some trepidations at the client meeting about hijacking unsuspecting people's beta waves and using their brains as vectors for an antivirus. He stated that once an individual was infected with Rama, they couldn't be uninfected. There was no way to remove the antivirus from a host. The military and three-letter alphabet agencies involved countered with the fact that infection of a human didn't matter. There were no side effects. Moreover, should a person carrying Rama move near any type of vulnerable system, they would immediately transfer the code to that system, inadvertently protecting the system from Abaddon.

Copper countered by theorizing that the Rama infected person would not only infect any machines with a programmable logic controller, but all machines with any type of computer code. In addition, any infected human being that approached another human being would immediately infect them and so on and so forth. With Rama also being able to be transmitted via microwaves, radio, cellular service and television signals, the scientist told his superiors and his clients that should Rama escape into the general populace, the entire population of the planet would be infected in a matter of days, maybe hours.

Former Colonel Nauls, (U.S. Army ret.) now of the NSA, glanced at Dr. Copper after Copper had informed the board of his hypothesis and asked, "But that's good, right?"

Bennings and Norris agreed, stating once Rama was everywhere, Abaddon would be extinct. Drs. Childs and Crisp, two more of the computer scientists, spoke out against Copper, a man they had worked with for years. They said that Rama was a good thing. A necessary evil to combat a worse evil. "Plus," Crisp added, "there are no side effects. Relax, Donald, this will work."

"I *know* it works, that's what scares me!"

"Donald, please," began Childs, "there's no need to—"

227

The man at the corner end of the table sat up in his chair, interrupting Childs by moving. Everyone looked at him and suddenly the room was very quiet. "I would like to hear what the good doctor has to say."

"I'm sorry, who are you?"

"You may call me Brooks."

Colonel MacReady cleared his throat and spoke to Copper, "Don't worry about him, just continue."

"Mr. Brooks, gentlemen, I think Rama is dangerous. We don't have enough data to release this program. Yes, it does what it's designed to do, but do we really want to *infect* machines and people with this?" Copper had used the word "infect" like it was something dirty. "We should acquire some volunteer test subjects and perform as many tests as we can think of."

"While Abaddon runs amok?" Norris asked, incredulous. He continued as if he were speaking to a child, "I think not, Dr. Copper. Tomorrow could see us vulnerable to a missile attack from any number of hostile nations, or one of our power grids could shut down, or maybe a jetliner will crash into the White House. No, Doctor, we need this as soon as possible."

"Rama is ready for trials now," Crisp volunteered. "We just need something to try it on other than what we have here."

Copper noticed Brooks make an almost imperceptible nod to MacReady. MacReady stood up, immediately followed by Colonel Windows and Major Gary. "Doctors, the United States Government thanks you for your hard work and the service you've done for your country. We no longer have need of your services. Your staff will be moved from this facility back to MIT within the hour. You have the rest of the day to clear out your desks. No electronic media will be allowed out of the facility and personal media will be confiscated and replaced by week's end. Your security clearances will be revoked at the end of the day, so don't dally."

"What?" Childs and Copper stood. "That's ridiculous! We've dedicated half a year to this project!"

"And you will kindly notice quite a large sum in your bank accounts that wasn't there previously," MacReady stated. "This is in addition to the funds paid to Vantel. Your staff has also been compensated according to their level of contribution. Again, thank you, gentlemen."

Macready stuck his hand out to Crisp, who stood and shook it. Childs was beginning to get irate, but Copper looked scared. Childs began to raise his voice and put his hand on Crisp's shoulder. Childs felt a hand on *his* shoulder and spun to see who had touched him.

"Doc, it's done," Brooks informed him, turned, and strode from the office. The NSA men followed him out without another word. The military men began to shake hands with each other and Crisp. Crisp looked at Childs. "Was there something else, Alan?"

Childs, defeated, answered softly, "No."

The Vantel and MIT staff were escorted from the building at 4:48 PM the day of the meeting. Except for Crisp, he was nowhere to be seen and when the staff asked their soldier escorts where he was, they would only say that he would meet them at MIT. Every single staff member was incensed. They were pulled, some quite literally, from their labs and put on a bus. They were not allowed to take cell phones, tablets, MP3 players, or any other type of media storage device, even if it had been personal property.

Doctor Copper feigned anger, but in actuality, he was terrified. Doctor Copper was scared because he was a thief. He had stolen one thing in his entire life and the pilfering had happened a half an hour before the client meeting and before he was forcibly put on the bus back to MIT. The purloined item was a hard drive the likes of which this computer expert had never seen. A crystal-based storage system that he wasn't even supposed to know about. The drive had an immense capacity, but only one item was stored on it.

The bus arrived at the Cambridge campus just before seven in the evening (traffic). The staff and scientists scattered, all moving into various buildings. Copper made a break for it with his prize. He had no idea what to do with his small, lead-lined box, he just knew he couldn't get caught with it. He walked briskly toward the Kendall Square T subway station. He reached the station at 7:18. It was a Friday, so the place was packed with people looking to move about the city or travel home to the suburbs.

Copper moved toward the restroom through the throng of folks waiting for the train. It took him a moment to get there. Pushing open the door, he strode across the blue floor, shouldered the backpack he had been carrying, and stood in front of a urinal to relieve himself. He put his hand against the cool yellow tiles as he urinated a day's worth of terror onto the porcelain. Feeling better, he zipped up and heard the door to one of the stalls open. Thinking nothing of it, he moved to wash his hands. The automatic faucet turned on when his hands moved in front of the small green sensor. The water was cooler than the tile and he had a moment to wonder if the faucet could be infected by Abaddon and Rama before he looked in the mirror.

Brooks was standing behind him. The man shook his head in disgust. "Dumb, Doc. Just dumb."

Copper, wide-eyed, spun to face the newcomer and felt something punch him in the stomach. At the same time, he heard an odd sound and pain flooded his abdomen. He fell against the sinks and put his hand to his middle. It came away bloody and he looked up at Brooks, who was holding a small pistol with an extremely long barrel.

"Suppressor." Brooks raised his eyebrows and smiled. "Pretty cool, huh?"

Copper threw his backpack at the assassin, who deftly caught it and fired twice more at the now fleeing man, missing both shots. The doctor made it to the door and out, but there was no place to go. A train was pulling away, but the station was still overcrowded with people. Copper limped to the left and jumped down on the tracks, running as fast as his damaged body would carry him. Hot, sticky blood streamed from the wound onto his crotch and leg. The pain had subsided a bit, but it still hurt like hell.

The tunnel lights threw an eerie white glow, but it was enough that he could see by. Lungs burning, he ducked into a pitch-black alcove and tried to catch his failing breath. He pressed his left hand to his wound, which was about an inch to the left of his belly button. It didn't feel as bad to him as he thought a gunshot wound should. He reached into his pocket, pulling out the small box and clutching it hard.

"It wasn't in the backpack, Doc, where is it?"

Copper froze, terrified, his mind frantically seeking avenues of escape. "Give me that and I'll let you go," Brooks promised, pointing toward the hand holding the box. Not that Copper could see him pointing, in the darkness. The white lights from the tunnel illuminated the killer with an outline that looked like a full-body halo. His head looked all wrong. "You've got a .22 slug in you, but it isn't as bad as you think. Give me the box and I'll get you to the hospital, we can work this out."

"How…how can you see me in here?"

He tapped his head twice with his index finger. "Night vision. The box?"

Copper passed the box to Brooks but dropped it and it opened. The man with the gun bent down, keeping his eyes on Copper, closed the box, and picked it up. A train was approaching down the tracks. Brooks had to raise his voice over the sound of the oncoming train. "We use .22s 'cause they really don't make a lot of noise when suppressed. Thanks for this, Doc." He held up the small case, shaking it. Then he held up his pistol.

The train riders noticed no muzzle flashes as they thundered down the tracks. The suppressor took care of those. Even if the massive vehicle wasn't as loud as it was, no one would have heard the five suppressed rounds leaving the barrel of the weapon unless they were very close and even then, your average citizen wouldn't have realized what the sounds were.

Brooks looked at Copper's body and shook his head. On any other hit, he would have checked for a pulse to confirm death, but quite frankly, he didn't care if this guy lived or died. The assassin turned to leave but the train was passing the alcove, so he had to wait until it was all the way by. He stepped into the tunnel as the last car rumbled past, pulling his phone from a clip on his belt. "Lynch? Yeah, I got it. Pick me up at the Kendall Square Station, right outside the stairs. I know, right? It sounds like you're right next to me. Who would have thought reception would be so good in a subway tunnel? No, you need to stay at MIT for the foreseeable future. Yeah, I want to see how this plays out and you can keep tabs. Hey, I'm thinking Thai food for later." Brooks pressed the end call button and replaced the phone on his belt. He hummed *Sad But True* by Metallica as he walked the tracks back to the platform.

The delivery system the good doctor had helped create for Rama had gone to work the moment the lid on the small case opened, when it had impacted the ground in the tunnel at his feet. The program contained on the quantum europium embedded crystal hard drive enclosed in the case locked on to the beta waves of Copper and Brooks. Rama's quantum information, which had been written onto the nuclear spin of the europium using a spread-focused laser at Vantel, was then uploaded (Grafted) via the beta waves of both men in its entirety and stored in the hippocampus of their brains as memory. The procedure had taken approximately three-hundredths of a nanosecond. While both men were now armed with Rama, neither of them had the ability to manually access the code stored in the hippocampus, but both began broadcasting immediately.

Brooks, uninfected with Abaddon, suffered no ill effects of the antivirus and went on his merry way, albeit broadcasting Rama to every human being and machine capable of absorbing the code. Doctor Copper, also uninfected with Abaddon, but infected with six .22 caliber bullets, was not so fortunate. Nor were the people he would soon meet.

Doctor Donald Copper passed away at 8:08 PM on Friday, the fourth of June. Whatever thing that made Donald Copper Donald Copper fled or was forced from his body and he was, quite simply, dead. Rama, designed to remain dormant until Abaddon was detected, or a machine shut down, now had a task. As the doctor's biological systems began a cascading failure, Rama kicked in to turn those systems back on.

The near instantaneous assessment of the body's crucial structures yielded important information to Rama. The skeletal and muscular systems, similar to the housing and moving parts of a machine, were not badly damaged. The cardiovascular, endocrine, respiratory and lymphatic systems, much like fluid transfer or hydraulic lines, intake, exhaust, and self-diagnostics were put on the back-burner in lieu of more important issues. The nervous system, with its billions of components, was where the program began. The digestive system would be second on the list.

Rama began by creating imbalances in the positively charged atomic structure of the doctor's cells, thereby causing electrons to flow from one atom to another. This generated copious amounts of bio-electricity and caused the doctor's body some slight spasms. The re-routed residual and newly produced electro-chemicals were then stored in the neurons of each cell until enough charge was built up for a jump start of the entire system.

The thing that had been Doctor Copper ceased being dead at 8:23 PM on Friday, the fourth of June. It opened its eyes and sat up. A monumental task, considering it had not been alive an instant prior.

The antivirus now needed more resources than the former doctor's body could provide, so signals were sent out to the rest of the new creature's brain from the stored code in the hippocampus. More bio-electricity and fuel to sustain the reactions would need to be acquired. Driven by a singular need, the thing stood, listening for the first time. Auditory signals coming from the right compelled the creature to investigate and it moved toward the sounds, looking to fuel itself for further functionality. It stumbled and jerked, the motion not fluid as the neurotransmitters fired less efficiently through the synapses now. It reached the platform and surveyed the fuel sources in front of it, choosing the one that was in closest proximity.

Don Trapp, a Harvard frat-boy and a bit in his cups already for so early in the evening, noticed the doctor attempting to climb out of the tunnel, the smile on his inebriated face evaporated. He pointed toward the newest species on earth and stood up. "Hey, that guy fell off the platform!" Don, his two college buddies, and two subway patrons, rushed to help the former doctor out of the tunnel before a train could run him down or he stepped on the third rail.

The first to reach the hapless tunnel rat was Carl Willis, a sausage vendor who usually worked outside of Fenway Park, but was off today because he was on his way to his daughter's wedding. He grabbed the shirt and arm of what used to be Dr. Copper and Don's friend Matt Samuels, a good-looking undergraduate law student and defenseman for the Harvard Crimson hockey team, grabbed the other arm. They dragged him onto the platform, where Matt immediately received a bite on the hand. It was more of a nip really, the skin had barely been broken, but he still ripped his injured hand away yelling, "He friggin' bit me!" Carl, upon hearing what had happened, looked up in fear and rightly so. Strong hands fastened onto the jacket portion of the three-piece suit he was wearing for the wedding. The guy he had just rescued both pulled Carl in and leaned toward him. Carl felt pain explode in the lower portion of the right side of his neck just above his collarbone and a significant portion of his expensive jacket was torn away along with a moderate chunk of his trapezius muscle.

Carl yelled. Everyone else except former Doctor Copper backed up to assess the situation. During the assessment, the dead man leaned in and tore a strip of Carl's cheek away, exposing his molars and bicuspids beneath.

Carl screamed. Several people figured the time for assessing was over and jumped in to help. Don and another subway patron pulled the assailant off the bleeding man. The patron received a bite on the arm, not terribly deep, but there was blood in the semicircular wound. Don punched the man in the face as hard as he could. Growing up in rural Michigan, Don had never punched anyone before and was completely unprepared for the pain involved in performing the act incorrectly. He shook out his hand but was pleased as punch to see that he had knocked the assailant down, even if he had cut two knuckles on a tooth.

The man appeared to be chewing as he stood back up. He was chewing on the folks he had just bitten. Eating them. Many of the folks on the platform decided that this was enough, and they fled, some slowly, some in full sprint.

Two transit police fought through the crowd and seeing six people push one around, they naturally assumed that the one was the victim. Rushing in to protect the man, one of the cops began yelling at the attackers. The victim, now on the ground, grabbed his leg and bit into his calf. The leg must have been particularly tasty, as this time no amount of pulling or kicking would free the policeman from his attacker's grasp. Cop number two drew his baton and thumped what he thought was a man on the back of his skull. Stunned, the thing let its meal go and cop two put his knee on the thing's back and cuffed it.

Naturally, the thing was unresponsive to commands, so the policemen both whacked the thing again and put a zip tie around its ankles when it wouldn't stop trying to bite anyone within reach. More police and some emergency medical personnel arrived, took everyone's statement, (except the dead guy's) and then took Carl and cop one to the hospital.

Matt and the helpful patron were treated at the scene and told that human bites could be very serious, and they shouldn't wait to go to the hospital, as the bites could get infected quite quickly.

Don and Matt continued to further their inebriated states until the wee hours, when Matt began to feel ill. His arm looked infected and something smelled nasty, but his friends were drunk, too and passed it off as somebody didn't *pit-up*. Don had stumbled home a half an hour previous, not feeling well.

Dr. Omar Vencedees, a prominent reconstructive surgeon, showed up at six o'clock the following morning at Mass General Hospital to look at Carl Willis' lacerated face. Carl was quite ill. Being bitten in the face by another person will do that. When Dr. Vencedees removed the bandage from Carl's face to look at the wound, the smell made him gag. It was not possible for gangrene to have set in overnight, but this is exactly what appeared to have happened. Carl was prepped for emergency surgery, the doctor planning to remove the infected tissue before it could consume the poor man's entire face.

Carl never made it to surgery and expired in his room during the prep stage. He was pronounced dead by the floor-resident at 7:14 Saturday morning. He was un-pronounced when he sat up to survey his surroundings at 7:17. The resident actually held his stethoscope up to visually inspect it. The room nurse looked at Carl and knew something was amiss. "Doctor... Doctor, look at his eyes!" Carl's eyes were a deep red and a single tear of blood rolled down his cheek. The resident looked at his patient, the patient returning the stare.

The resident rushed to Carl's aid, donning his stethoscope on the way. Dr. Vencedees picked that moment to open the door and storm in, demanding to know how his patient had died from a bite on the cheek. What used to be Carl picked *that* moment to grab the resident, pull him toward the bed, and sink his teeth into the unfortunate doctor's neck. Arterial spray painted the white curtain, wall, and blood pressure machine. The nurse bolted in to help and the sausage vendor bit off her pinky and ring fingers at the second knuckles.

When security showed up, Dr. Vencedees was battling Mr. Willis using his clipboard and not faring well. Two security men and the doctor received bites for their trouble.

One floor down, Officer Tabor, the cop bitten on the leg, attacked the doctor and two nurses that had rushed from the nurse's station to check on him when they noticed his vitals monitor had flat-lined. All three were bitten before the officer could be restrained, one of the nurses quite badly.

Across town, Don expired at exactly ten in the morning on Saturday. His corpse stood in his dorm room, looking at its surroundings until it heard a noise in the corridor. It began banging on the door until someone asked if he was *alright in there*. Then he began banging and moaning. Quite a crowd had accumulated before the resident assistant showed up fresh from the shower, in a towel. He used his key to open the door and the thing that had been Don stumbled out and bit four people before the kids were able to hold him down long enough to tie him up with a fire hose.

The patron who had gotten a bite for his trouble in the subway died at six past ten on Saturday and murdered his wife as she slept next to him. They were sleeping in for the first time in quite a while. They both killed their teenaged son.

The next-door neighbor's black lab Brutus began barking at just before eleven in the morning and the neighbors investigated only to hear breaking furniture and odd sounds coming from the house. The police were called and both cops were attacked, one fatally, when they responded. The live cop shot the teenager and his mother twice each, none of the four bullets doing much. The dead cop stood and attacked the live cop. The patron, his wife, and son completing the job.

By noon that Saturday, there were sixty cases of folks being attacked by their friends or neighbors. By three o'clock, two hospitals in Boston were overcrowded with patients who had been bitten. By 9 PM, both of those hospitals were overrun with the living dead. Midnight arrived with more than seventy thousand infected either dead or alive. Two days later, Boston belonged to the dead.

The rest of the world would follow.

END

ACKNOWLEDGMENTS

Each time I complete a book, I am amazed at how many helpful people I know. As a general rule, people are horrible, so I am fortunate in my family and friendships.

Firstly, thanks to all of my family who humor me and tell me I'm funny. Donna, Danielle, Richy, Chloe, Mom, and Pops. You're why I keep doing this, and you've been my inspiration for several characters, anecdotes, and unique phrases in my work. My mom and dad made me, my wife and kids made me better.

In 2010 or so, I began reading zombie stories on a website. That site is Homepageofthedead.com, and it changed me a bit. I decided that I wanted to write, so I pumped out a couple of short stories which I uploaded to HPoTD and was rewarded with my first reviews. They were overwhelmingly positive, and that is what drove me to publish. I would like to thank all of the readers on HPoTD for telling me to get my ass in gear and write a book. Thank you, Neil, for such a great site as well.

While I was reading some fantastic stuff on HPoTD, I trolled the internet to find fellow lovers of zombie fiction, and was again rewarded with some new friends. This is where I first met Joy, James, and FF, three fantastic online friends who share similar interests. Several iterations of websites later, and Zombiefiend.com was born. It is the premiere living dead aficionado site on the internet. If you liked this book, or even if you hated it and like other zombie books, I highly recommend you head over to Zombiefiend and check it out. Jump into the chatroom and you can talk to some of the authors you have already read as well.

Speaking of authors, I would like to thank some of my fellow writers who have created unbelievable worlds full of horror, terror, great characters, and settings:

Thanks Dave Evans, Christopher Artinian, Jonathan Maberry, Craig DiLouie, David Simpson, James Jackson, James Schannep, Chris Philbrook, William Todd Rose, S.P. Durnin, Ricky Fleet, Bowie Ibarra, Shawn Chesser, and John O'Brian. There are dozens more, but these are the folks I've read in just the past few months, and they inspire me. They also piss me off because they think of things I should have thought of first.

Thanks to the folks who have made my stuff better by telling me I have no idea how to use a comma, where to put quotation marks, and that a banana cannot, in fact, be used to bludgeon someone. Tanya Saunders, Shelley Loring, Tamra Crow, and Dawn Trapp. You all have helped me so much. God help planet Earth should you ever form some type of cabal.

One final acknowledgement: Thank you George Romero. You are the creator of the modern zombie. You started an entire ethos, that quite literally, will never die.

CHECK OUT OTHER GREAT ZOMBIE NOVELS

DEAD PULSE RISING
by K. Michael Gibson

Slavering hordes of the walking dead rule the streets of Baltimore, their decaying forms shambling across the ruined city, voracious and unstoppable. The remaining survivors hide desperately, for all hope seems lost... until an armored fortress on wheels plows through the ghouls, crushing bones and decayed flesh. The vehicle stops and two men emerge from its doors, armed to the teeth and ready to cancel the apocalypse.

TOWER OF THE DEAD
by J.V. Roberts

Markus is a hardworking man that just wants a better life for his family. But when a virus sweeps through the halls of his high-rise apartment complex, those plans are put on hold. Trapped on the sixteenth floor with no hope of rescue, Markus must fight his way down to safety with his wife and young daughter in tow.

Floor by bloody floor they must battle through hordes of the hungry dead on a terrifying mission to survive the TOWER OF THE DEAD.

CHECK OUT OTHER GREAT ZOMBIE NOVELS

Z BURBIA
by Jake Bible

Whispering Pines is a classic, quiet, private American subdivision on the edge of Asheville, NC, set in the pristine Blue Ridge Mountains. Which is good since the zombie apocalypse has come to Western North Carolina and really put suburban living to the test!

Surrounded by a sea of the undead, the residents of Whispering Pines have adapted their bucolic life of block parties to scavenging parties, common area groundskeeping to immediate area warfare, neighborhood beautification to neighborhood fortification.

But, even in the best of times, suburban living has its ups and downs what with nosy neighbors, a strict Home Owners' Association, and a property management company that believes the words "strict interpretation" are holy words when applied to the HOA covenants. Now with the zombie apocalypse upon them even those innocuous, daily irritations quickly become dramatic struggles for personal identity, family security, and straight up survival.

ZOMBIE RULES
by David Achord

Zach Gunderson's life sucked and then the zombie apocalypse began.

Rick, an aging Vietnam veteran, alcoholic, and prepper, convinces Zach that the apocalypse is on the horizon. The two of them take refuge at a remote farm. As the zombie plague rages, they face a terrifying fight for survival.

They soon learn however that the walking dead are not the only monsters.